S0-BKR-052

Dear Reader:

The novels you've enjoyed over the past ten years by such authors as Kathleen E. Woodiwiss, Rosemary Rogers, Johanna Lindsey and Laurie McBain are accountable to one thing above all others: Avon has never tried to force authors into any particular mold. Rather, Avon is a publisher which encourages individual talent and is always on the lookout for new writers who will deliver *real* books, not packaged formulas.

In 1982, we started a program to help readers select new authors of exceptional promise. Called "The Avon Romance," the books were distinguished by a ribbon motif in the upper left-hand corner of the cover. Although every title was by a *new* author, and the settings could be either historical or contemporary, they were quickly discovered and became known as "the ribbon books."

In 1984, "The Avon Romance" will be a special feature on the Avon list. Each month, you will find novels with many different settings, each one by an author who is being introduced to the field. You will not find predictable characters, predictable plots, and predictable endings. The only predictable thing about "The Avon Romance" will be the superior quality that Avon has always delivered in the field of romance!

Sincerely,

WALTER MEADE
President & Publisher

ONYX FLAME

JAN MOSS

AVON
PUBLISHERS OF BARD, CAMELOT, DISCUS AND FLARE BOOKS

ONYX FLAME is an original publication of Avon Books. This
work has never before appeared in book form. This work is a
novel. Any similarity to actual persons or events is purely coincidental.

AVON BOOKS
A division of
The Hearst Corporation
1790 Broadway
New York, New York 10019

Copyright © 1984 by Jan Moss
Published by arrangement with the author
Library of Congress Catalog Card Number: 84-91104
ISBN: 0-380-87627-2

First Avon Printing, September, 1984

AVON TRADEMARK REG. U. S. PAT. OFF. AND IN
OTHER COUNTRIES, MARCA REGISTRADA, HECHO EN
U. S. A.

Printed in the U. S. A.

WFH 10 9 8 7 6 5 4 3 2 1

DEDICATION

To Ernie, of course

ONYX FLAME

1

Megan McBride had once been kept waiting over an hour to see her chronically late dentist. At precisely the sixty-minute mark, she left his office. Then the dentist mailed her a bill for thirty-five dollars, citing "Failure to keep an appointment." Megan responded cheerfully by billing *him* for thirty-five dollars, which was a carefully calculated undervaluation of the worth of her time, based on actual earnings. The dentist continued mailing his bill, Megan continued mailing hers. He turned her over to a collection agency, she turned him over to one. Then she filed suit in small claims court and collected her thirty-five dollars, plus court costs, plus interest.

Some people laughed about such "Meganisms" and referred to the red-haired, green-eyed Megan's Irishness, to a naturally endowed lack of patience. But those who knew her really well denied this; they claimed that Megan McBride was far too disciplined to become unduly impatient; they insisted she just refused to be victimized. They were right.

At three minutes before six o'clock on a mid-September evening, Megan found herself thinking about the dentist and wondering if her appointment today had been overlooked. This time the circumstances were different. Fifty-seven minutes earlier, neatly dressed in a navy suit and lightly printed silk blouse, she had entered the plush waiting room of a large im-

port firm, where a cheerful, chubby receptionist had
warned her there would be a delay in Megan's scheduled job interview. "Today was a disaster for the president," the receptionist had said. "One emergency after
another—and his secretary's out sick."

Megan had told the woman she understood, then had
forced her attention to a complicated financial feature
in *Business Week* magazine. At five-thirty, the receptionist had departed after apologizing to Megan: "I'd
stay late, you know, but my baby has a sitter . . ." Once
again, Megan had nodded her understanding, but now
she wasn't so sure. Since five-thirty, she had not seen
another human being. The president of the company
might have forgotten about her and left the building
from a back entrance. Megan fluctuated between puzzlement and anger. Finally she decided to make a mental calculation of the pros and cons relative to the sales
position for which she was applying.

The biggest pro was that this firm offered a sensational line of imported lamps and accessories. The line
practically sold itself. On the other hand . . .

"Miss McBride?"

Megan gave a startled little leap, then swiveled to
stare up at the man who had entered the reception area
with such stealth. He had pale ash hair, amazingly
light blue eyes, and a slightly crooked, almost boyish
mouth, which held an expression of constrained amusement. Megan had met a lot of attractive men in her life,
but this was the first time she had ever been actually
disturbed by someone's appearance; it was hard to concentrate.

"I startled you," he said. "I'm sorry." The provocative lips quirked slightly at the corners, and Megan
wondered if he were all that sorry. "My name's Michael
Richardson."

"The president of Ling and Son?" Michael Richardson was something of a legend in the import industry.
He was generally credited with the recent astronomical

success of this once minor-league company, and Megan had pictured an older man.

"That's me," he said with that peculiar half grin that seemed to be poking light fun at something. Whatever it was, she wanted very much to be let in on it. And *that* really surprised her; it was one thing to be fascinated by the man's physical aura and quite another to want him to reveal his every thought. Of all her reactions thus far, this was the one she found most disturbing; what she was experiencing was far more than mere curiosity—Megan wanted to know everything about what made Michael Richardson tick. Megan looked closely at his expression, then decided it was possible she had *never* seen a man display greater evidence of self-confidence.

". . . and the firm's actually run by Mr. George Ling, the son of the founding father. I'm just a highly paid enlisted man with a fancy office."

That wasn't what Megan had heard . . .

"I owe you an apology for this ridiculous amount of time you've been kept waiting."

Her lips parted slightly, then closed. Nothing came out. Although Megan was quite accustomed to speaking up, it was obvious Richardson simply wasn't the type one spoke up *to*. But why? she asked herself. He did appear to be the type of man who would welcome candor; something about the straight lines of that tall, lean frame suggested he would throw a yes-man bodily from the building rather than hire him. Whatever the reason, Megan was aware that she felt uncomfortable. Richardson had an indefinable aura of authority and power, and suddenly she was disturbed by her reaction to him.

Megan realized with a start that she was reacting to Michael Richardson as a man, not a potential employer. Well, that was nothing to be ashamed of; Lord knew she wasn't the first person in the world to go through something like this. But what a mess! And Richardson was standing before her, appearing totally unaffected, while she felt both awkward and defensive. She certainly didn't care to be in a position like that, not a bit. But there wasn't much to be done about it.

He was saying, "If you'll come back to my office, I'll try to explain."

She followed, telling herself she shouldn't pay attention to the broad sweep of his muscular shoulders or the narrow taper of his hips. When she almost stumbled she forced her eyes to lock on his deeply tanned neck, wondered briefly if he played tennis, then matched his long, unhurried strides as they navigated a maze of carpeted corridors before coming to an area of executive office suites. After they had passed through the deserted secretarial room, Richardson pushed open a paneled door bearing a brass plaque engraved with his name, then waited for Megan to precede him inside.

She liked the office. In fact, it sparked thoughts of her own ambitions; one day, when she had enough money and experience to start her own business, she would enjoy working in a room like this. It was a room you could relax and concentrate in. She wondered how much it told about its occupant. Since Richardson had asked her to wait a moment while he located her résumé, she settled into an upholstered wing chair, enjoying the opportunity for closer inspection of both office and occupant.

The room wasn't impressively large; if anything, one might describe it as cozy, intimate. But perhaps her eyes were fooling her, Megan thought at second glance, for Richardson's teak desk was certainly big enough. And her chair, matched by an identical one on the other side of a glass-topped lamp table, wasn't one of those that had been scaled down for office use. She looked down at the upholstery pattern; it was a salmon and brown floral print, bold and masculine but also warm in feeling. The office walls were painted in lighter but matching shades of salmon; accessories were scattered here and there—some, but not all, Ling and Son products, Megan decided after searching her memory of the company catalog. And the most outstanding single feature of the office was the lighting. This was hardly surprising; it was the firm's exceptional lamp collection that had attracted Megan to Ling and Son in the first place.

Her attention turned to the man whose name was on the door. How tall was he? Let's see, Megan thought, trying to calculate from her own height . . . I'm five-feet-seven, which makes him at least six feet, judging from the difference when we're both standing; maybe six-one. She wondered how old he was, then searched for clues and found a college diploma; counting upward from age twenty-one, she figured Richardson would be thirty-seven. Seven years older than I am, she thought, and then asked herself what difference that made. What bothered her was the answer her mind kicked back: it wasn't his age but the fact that he could become her boss that made the difference!

When he stopped rummaging among his papers, evidently locating Megan's résumé, he took a seat in the matching wing chair, ignoring a desk piled high with what looked to Megan like sales reports. She said, "Mr. Richardson, your office is lovely."

"Thanks. How do you like my choice of lamps?"

She responded with a wry smile. "They're exquisite. I admire your line tremendously. If I didn't, I wouldn't have applied to become the Ling and Son Southern California representative. I have several years of experience dealing with quality buyers, and there's no question about the quality of your product."

Richardson chuckled. "You come right to the point, don't you? Most people in sales are equipped with a repertoire of constantly polite chatter. Something tells me you aren't the normal sales pro, though; you don't even look like one."

Megan tried to mask her reaction, but, in fact, his statement had confused her at the precise point when

she thought she finally had her bearings. Had her in-
terviewer suddenly revealed himself as the type of man
given to leering preoccupation with women's looks?
Suddenly it occurred to her that wasn't the case at all.
Richardson had simply taken the first available opportunity to seize total control. She could almost read his
mind: he was thinking she wasn't going to get the job
just because she knew how to make flattering noises.
Immediately she was on the defensive again. She
clasped her hands, making tiny crinkles in the pleated
fabric at her lap.

Her entire thought process had taken only a couple of
seconds, but Megan became aware of her failure to respond. What had he said last? Something about her professional appearance . . . Oh, yes, that's what had
started the mental tangent; he had said . . . what exactly *had* he said? That she didn't look like a pro? Her
jade eyes widened. Surely he hadn't said that! After all,
she was wearing a two-piece business suit; what could
possibly be more appropriate?

Now she began to notice that Richardson appeared
unperturbed by the silence. Only people with the most
extraordinary self-confidence could resist the temptation to fill awkward conversational gaps. Megan took a
deep mental breath and forced a smile, noticing a slight
tremor of her lower lip. Finally she spoke. "I'm sorry.
It's late and my mind's wandering. At any rate, I'm not
as alert as I should be. Did you say I don't look professional?"

He grinned. "No, but I like your honesty. And you're
right: it *is* late. Which reminds me that I want to explain why you were kept waiting." He glanced quickly
at his watch. For the first time, Megan noticed that the
man was desperately tired; without appearing to realize he was doing it, he trailed the back of one hand over
his forehead. "What I'm getting ready to say," he went
on, "will also help you understand this business. You're
aware all the Ling merchandise is made overseas,

mostly in the Orient, to our specifications? Good. Two more questions then: have you ever handled imports, and do you know what a shipping container is?"

Megan answered no to the first, then told him she believed *container* was the word used to describe a standard-sized cargo box designed to be lifted from the ship by crane, then dropped directly onto a specially designed truck bed for overland delivery.

He nodded. "Our overseas agents collect and consolidate lamp bases, statues, and various other accessories we've ordered from individual artisans. When there's enough to fill a container, they ship. I think you'll see from this example that selling imports is a good deal different from selling domestics—good old made-in-U.S.A. products. Especially if you have any idea of the sheer size of a container: remember, it really *does* take a crane to get it off that ship and onto the truck."

"It sounds efficient, though," she said. "Saves the extra cost of unloading and reloading."

"Exactly. But yesterday we received one that won't save us anything. It was filled with lamp bases, but not a single one is correct. I don't know how it happened; what I do know is that the problem created an emergency. You see, our Ohio sales rep broke a cardinal rule. He sold a retail chain on cataloging an item we had on back order. As soon as the poor Ohio retailer got his catalog into the mail and to the customers, orders started pouring in for our lamp. But we couldn't supply it because our shipment from Japan was late. Then the container finally arrived and, sure enough, every single one of the porcelains is wrong—wrong shape, wrong color, wrong pattern." Richardson sighed. "The customer *is* always right; in this case, it certainly isn't the retailer's fault his catalog orders can't be filled. Now if there's any way possible I've got to track down the right porcelains and airfreight them over here so we can assemble the lamps and truck them to Ohio. Just as you arrived for this interview, the call came in from Japan. If my secretary had been here—"

"You would have sent her out to explain," Megan finished dully, wishing she hadn't added to the man's problems by mentioning the lateness of the hour. Megan had plenty enough experience to understand that, no matter what else demanded attention, the needs of the customer got priority handling. She stared into space for a moment, considering Richardson's dilemma. Then suddenly it occurred to her that he had mentioned having the porcelains airshipped from Japan. The businesswoman in her reacted. "Good grief! If you airship that order, the cost will eat up the profit!"

"Doesn't matter. Nothing matters but straightening out the mess we made for our customer," Richardson said bluntly. "It's something you should understand about Ling and Son; I believe in keeping promises."

Megan took careful note of his wording. He had talked about Ling and Son but then he had said *I* believe in keeping promises, not *we* believe in keeping promises. For years, she had heard that one of this company's chief problems was low morale; since Richardson had taken the helm there had apparently been a positive surge. Perhaps there was friction between him and the owners; perhaps not—that little glitch in the wording might not have meant a thing—but Megan nonetheless filed away the question.

Megan shook her head slowly, thoughtfully. "I must admit I really hadn't considered the import factors; my sales technique will have to be adjusted considerably." She finally felt she had made an intelligent statement. Despite the fact she continued to feel like a schoolgirl with a crush on her high school principal, her confidence was at least somewhat restored.

Actually, Megan had hit on precisely the right analogy. If there had been time to think it through, she might have remembered that first adolescent infatuation and applied it to her current disturbance; it had oc-

curred shortly after her seventeenth birthday, and the
object had indeed been the high school principal. The
man had just replaced a retiring headmaster; on the
day Megan was called to his office to report her plans as
editor of the school newspaper, she was seeing him for
the first time. Unfortunately, it wasn't to be the last,
for during much of that senior year she had lived in
dreadful fear that Mr. Comstock—who must have been
all of thirty years old but who seemed to her like the
epitome of the desirable "mature" American male—
would see through her carefully poised facade into a
thousand feminine fantasies. He took a special interest
in the newspaper; whenever he wandered in to ask
Megan to explain policy or show him the week's copy,
she immediately felt inferior—it was a matter of his su-
periority versus her helplessness. By the end of the
year, when her perfectly oval face, clear complexion,
and green eyes won her the "Most Beautiful" title, the
fantasies had been replaced by a very real whirlwind of
dating. But the experience might have accounted for
some of her discomfort with Michael Richardson; even
without the big age difference he still seemed superior.
Megan's business dealings with men had long ago accustomed her to dealing with them on an equal basis.
Now, at the age of thirty and sitting across from a potential employer, she failed to realize that she wasn't
actually helpless, nor was this the type of man who
would want to make anyone feel that way. Megan was
merely disoriented; later, when she finally did have
time to reconsider the situation, she would realize that
this man's charisma—or whatever the appropriate
term might be for an unusually potent combination of
good looks, casual charm, and sheer power—would
place most women, and many men, at an accidental dis-
advantage. Right now, all she knew was that she didn't
want to give him the opportunity to see right through
her.

Richardson was saying, "With domestic products you

can promise your customer a stock order on a reasonable delivery schedule. Even if you know he's planning a full page ad at the end of the month, you also know that all you have to do is pressure your factory to hurry up and fire the kilns. When you're dealing overseas, it just doesn't work that way. So you protect the customer; don't let him get in a tough situation."

She started to say something but hesitated—and he caught it. "Question, Miss McBride?"

Still unprepared, her next words rolled out tentatively: "Not really . . ." Megan's lips curved and then spread into an undisguised smile. She knew quite well that her eyes were affected also, and that the expression was inappropriate, but this wasn't something she could control. Her father had called it "the mood." How often he had said, "Oh, Meggie, me lass—how I do love it when you get the mood! Brings out the Irish diamonds in those big eyes. When you're a-lookin' that way, then I'm a-thinkin' that me daughter's just the prettiest elfin girl in the whole bloomin' world."

If he had been struck by lightning on a sunny day, Michael Richardson couldn't have appeared more startled. And as soon as Megan saw his surprise, a rosy bloom crept into her cheeks. Oh, me! she thought to herself, I really am blowing this interview—and it *must* be a case of schoolgirl nerves; only even as a kid I never acted quite this silly. For some reason, her mood had altered; although she was still disturbed by the very presence of the man, she had actually started to enjoy the feeling; it was an energizing type of disturbance. Michael Richardson had turned Megan once again into a seventeen-year-old, when the world was new and when fresh exciting people made life worth living. And he is *so* exciting . . . The blush deepened.

Now he was grinning broadly. "I would literally give a month's profit sharing to know what you're thinking!"

She managed to respond, at the same time trying to

suppress a nervous giggle. "Well, you'll never understand. But you've been talking so much about protecting the customer, and it suddenly popped into my mind . . . you're the first person who's failed to give me that old lecture; you know—the one that goes like this—" Megan paused to rearrange her features into a mask of mock seriousness, imitating the average executive conducting a job interview. When she continued, it was in a caricatured baritone. "Miss McBride, are you prepared to give your all to God and company? We expect you to do anything for a sale!"

The minute Megan had played out her little drama, she regretted the choice of words. She hadn't meant *that*, not the implication that anyone had ever told her to do *anything* for a sale! Oh, Lord, she thought. Why can't being a woman be just a little easier? When there are so few men who make me feel totally feminine, why does this one have to be a prospective employer? She also wanted to run and hide, so embarrassed was she by the suggestive choice of words—and by the fact that she was throwing away her opportunity to get this job.

But Richardson was laughing. It was a wonderful sound, full and resonant and . . . and *fun*, she thought. There wasn't the vaguest sign that his mind had made any association with sexual innuendo. Megan expelled a deep breath of purest relief. She was thinking how much she had begun to like Richardson.

With laughter still in his voice, he said, "I hate to tell you this, but I'm not all that different. Get the sale; that is the name of this game." Then, more seriously, he added, "Just make sure it works to the benefit of the customer."

Megan grew very still. She was confused; the man was talking as though he had already hired her. Although she knew he hadn't even interviewed her yet, she began to hope against hope that she hadn't blown it, after all.

Richardson cleared his throat. "By the way, what I

said a few minutes ago is that you don't look like a *normal* sales pro. I'm accustomed to dealing with exceptional professionals and you're obviously one of them: way above average. And I like a sense of humor, Miss McBride. This place could sure use a bit of that."

So he *had* missed the sexual connotation! "Thanks," she said with more sincerity than he could have realized, "but, still, I shouldn't have sidetracked. You must be anxious to get home. I'm ready to concentrate if you are."

For reasons she couldn't yet understand, her words had an immediate and visible effect. Richardson relaxed. As tension drained from his shoulders, he also unfolded his long legs, stretching comfortably in the chair. Megan took uneasy note of the fact that he wore light gray wool trousers which accented rather than concealed firm musculature. Unconsciously, she bit her lower lip and waited.

Finally he said, "To be fair, I've decided there's not much point to the interview. That is, considering your résumé and your reputation and what I've learned of your personality today, you'll sell a hell of a lot of lamps for us. And we need a female rep—badly." He smiled, displaying brilliant white teeth along with that boyish quality Megan had found so disconcerting. "Actually, Miss McBride, the sensible thing for us to do at this point is to go out and get some dinner."

"No!" She cursed herself for the abruptness of the response. Where on earth was her normal poise? But Megan knew the answer to that one: she was afraid of this man; Richardson was far too perceptive to miss all these telltale clues of infatuation and he was now her employer as well. On the off-chance that Richardson might suggest a romance, Megan wondered about her ability to resist it. Lost was the elation of having been hired; her mind was a jumble of messy contradictions.

"Oops, sorry," he said, obviously amused at her reaction. "Talking business at a restaurant is a fairly acceptable practice, you know, even when the people doing it happen to be male and female. I hardly think you need feel insulted."

Megan knew she'd just received her first official reprimand. "You didn't," she stammered, feeling the deep flush creep along the curve of her cheek. "I mean, I'm not insulted."

His expression told Megan she'd failed to convince him. Half rising from the chair, he asked if she'd care to join him in a snack. "There's a refrigerator behind those panels," he explained, gesturing toward a wall behind his desk, "and I'm fairly certain we'll find milk and yogurt."

"You really *are* hungry," she said, amazed.

He cocked an eyebrow, and commented, "It's seven o'clock."

Megan smiled weakly; her earlier reaction had indeed been silly. All she said, however, was: "Then perhaps we should find a restaurant, after all. I won't be responsible for having a new employer die of starvation."

As Michael Richardson stretched his long arms into his suit jacket, Megan McBride wondered if she might not live to regret this particular dinner date, if that were the proper description. In truth, she was in an almost unprecedented state of happy excitement, both at having gotten the job and at the prospect of spending the next hour or so with the man who had given it to her. That wasn't a combination too likely to help her behave with her normal businesslike composure, the composure she hadn't thus far been able to maintain. And, once again, her new employer was unwittingly reminding her of the exact reason she was so far off stride.

Some people could make the simple act of pulling on a jacket seem provocative; Richardson was doing just that, although Megan couldn't possibly have identified the precise physical movement that caused her to tremble slightly, then look away. A slight wriggle of the hips, perhaps . . . All of a sudden it occurred to her that she had better start taking the situation more seriously . . . stop asking herself questions with no answers and begin a determined, concentrated effort to get whatever-it-was in perspective and totally out of her system. This is no joke, she thought soberly. Michael Richardson really is my boss.

The little Italian restaurant was within walking distance but the neighborhood wasn't the best in Los Angeles; they took Richardson's car. On the way, he noticed Megan's wedding ring. "I guess I should be calling you Mrs. McBride. Do your husband and children, if any, object to all the travel these jobs demand?"

"I was married less than a year," she said, "and I have no children."

"Why the ring, then?"

"Because it's an appropriate gesture for a widow and because it saves me a lot of trouble on the road."

"Smart move," he said admiringly. She in turn silently thanked him for skipping the expressions of sympathy she was accustomed to hearing from those who learned she was widowed.

He swung into the parking lot. Impulsively, Megan asked, "And you—are you married?"

"Also widowed. But I've got a fourteen-year-old son. Actually, there's a nineteen-year-old in the house, too, a niece on my wife's side. When Tara came from Oregon to attend UCLA, she asked if she could live with us so she could keep Jeffie company."

Megan was about to question him about his son when the owner of the restaurant greeted Michael like royalty. They both ordered fettucine Alfredo, then agreed to switch to first names. When he excused himself, explaining he wanted to call home, Megan sat with both hands folded on the table, trying not to think of him. It was an exercise in futility. Men as outstanding as Michael Richardson weren't that easily banished, either from memory or from sensory perceptions, and her senses were working overtime; his existence had speeded the pace of her reactions. Colors were more vivid, smells more tantalizing, and sounds more resonant. As for sight and touch, her mind was like a screen filled with the portrait of him, her body felt the fantasy of his fingertips against her skin. She commanded a return to reality and brought the subject back around to the new job.

Megan was thrilled about getting it—there must have been fifty well-qualified applicants for the position—but she now questioned the excitement. It would be more than a week before she could begin selling for Ling and Son, and she was frankly wondering if it would be tolerable to go that long without seeing Michael Richardson; under those circumstances, Megan could hardly pretend her enthusiasm was entirely professional. But it *is* a marvelous career opportunity, she reminded herself; she had certainly worked long enough and hard enough to earn a job with a high-end firm; there was no reason, not even this misbegotten attraction to her new boss, that she shouldn't take pleasure in it.

She never told him what was on her mind, of course. Instead, when he returned from the telephone, Megan made a polite comment about the fact that raising a son was a pretty big job for a single man. With a mischievous grin he told her she'd just made a flagrantly sexist statement. "Think about it, Megan. Wouldn't raising a son also be a big job for a single woman?"

She grinned and raised her wineglass. "Touché."

After the toast, Richardson told her that he considered raising children, alone or otherwise, to be an enormous privilege.

She nodded her agreement. "I absolutely adore kids. My idea of relaxation is a group of tiny Japanese-Americans who meet once a week at the downtown YMCA. I tutor them. Michael, they're fantastic!"

"I saw that mentioned on your résumé. It sounds interesting. What subject do you tutor?"

"English. Most of the kids are first- or second-
generation Americans who haven't had the opportunity to learn fluent English from their folks."

He was confused. "But do you speak Japanese?"

Megan nodded. "Yes. Not the everyday thing to do, is
it? But I grew up in Japan. We're a ridiculously international family. Dad speaks with a brogue thicker than
Irish stew—he graduated from the University of Dublin
College of Architectural Engineers and then came over
here for his first job. He married an American, my
mother, and became a citizen sometime just before I
was born. Then, about the time I started walking, his
company transferred him to their branch in Tokyo; we
didn't move back to the States until after my thirteenth
birthday . . ."

She continued in that vein for two or three minutes;
and somewhere along the line she realized how far she'd
deviated from her vow to keep things businesslike. But
still she rambled on. It was a happy story and she was
happy telling it; he kept a rapt expression, as though
he actually *cared* about the thirty years preceding
their meeting tonight—and she wondered what he
was really thinking. At the end, Megan said, "So I
got into the tutoring program as a way of keeping up
with the language; that's how I discovered my love of
kids."

Michael's laughter signaled his approval of her story.

For Megan, whose concentration had been malfunc-
tioning ever since her first sight of this extraordinary
man, his laughter served to jar her back to her senses;
Michael Richardson had better things to do than listen
to frothy feminine chatter. She felt her cheeks coloring
again; this was getting ridiculous. Megan renewed her
former vows: starting now, she would concentrate,
really concentrate, on sticking strictly to business.
While she searched for a topic, she kept staring at the

tabletop, almost as though she expected to find answers written on the checkered cloth. At length her eyes came to rest on the center arrangement, a tiny vase nestled between two matching scaled-down candleholders—perfect.

She said, "That grouping . . . it's lovely, Michael. I think it's porcelain. Does Ling have anything like it?"

"Let's see . . ." Carefully, to avoid disturbing the tiny flickering flame, he raised one of the candleholders. Megan was intrigued by the pinpoint light suddenly reflected in his eyes. Fire and ice, she thought, and then: I wonder if there's passion beneath that calm exterior?

Her mind refused to let go of the thought. As Michael peered at the delicate floral pattern dancing under the candle flame, she tried to picture her new employer in a personal scene. If this were a real date, she thought, if he were attracted to me, how would he be likely to show it? How, exactly, would he behave, alone with a woman he cared about? She wanted desperately to know. And she wanted to believe that Michael Richardson was a man given to sudden bursts of wild impulsive energy, a man capable of grabbing her in the middle of a crowd and pulling her into his arms without caring about anything but the joy of the moment.

She sat a bit straighter in her chair, realizing with a surprise approaching sheer awe that she had converted natural curiosity about an unusually attractive man into a very personal fantasy. I'm in more trouble than I thought, Megan told herself.

"It's porcelain," he confirmed, oblivious to her deeply personal thoughts as he replaced the little piece next to the vase containing fresh sprigs of pink bougainvillea.

"From Japan, do you think?" Megan said, struggling to keep her tone even.

He shook his head. "I doubt it. Look at the squared-off shape. So far the Oriental artisans have refused to produce anything but their traditional round shapes."

He lapsed into preoccupied silence. Megan suspected he was thinking of the botched shipment of porcelain lamp bases. Richardson had leaned back in his chair, allowing his eyes to wander toward the ceiling; it was a problem-solving posture. When he started running two fingers slowly up and down his chilled water goblet, making clear streams in the icy mist, Megan grew tense. There was something provocative in the languid motion, and she unwillingly projected his fingers onto her body, as though Michael were caressing her instead of the glass. Her lower body was flooded with a warm fluid pressure.

"I'm sorry," he said at last. "Can't keep my mind off business."

Too bad, Megan thought wryly.

"Tell me about that red hair."

"What?" Megan was startled by the change of subject, not to mention the unexpectedly energetic tone of voice.

"Your hair," he laughed, flashing one of his lopsided grins. "Does everyone in your family look like a walking torch?"

Before Megan was tempted to describe each individual on the Irish side of her family, the waiter arrived with two plates of fettucine. For the next few minutes, they gave undivided attention to the food. When Michael did speak again, the subject was safe enough. "Ever consider becoming an interpreter, Megan? There couldn't be too many Americans capable of fluent Japanese."

Since she could imagine the language problems he must have encountered in his Oriental business dealings, she knew he was aware of his understatement. She answered by saying, "Sales is the only field I've ever found compelling. It makes me feel good to put someone together with the right merchandise. Besides, this is one area in which the sky's the literal limit, especially for women. Which reminds me: what did you mean earlier, when you said you need to hire a female rep?"

"Well, one of these days I'm going to get my comeuppance from the Equal Opportunity people. Before you, I've purposely kept an all-male team."

"How come?"

He hesitated, placing his fork on the side of the plate. "I feel strongly about women traveling alone, Megan. Very strongly, in fact. Nowadays especially, the roads aren't safe." He threw her a brief, troubled smile. "Maybe I should have requested photos along with the résumés. Now I feel doubly threatened. How're you going to be able to guarantee your personal safety?"

Very gently, but with emphasis, Megan said, "Must I guarantee safety, Michael? As you said, sales is the name of the game."

For a moment Megan wondered if this were some sort of test. It would hardly do for her new boss to think she was the type who'd be afraid to drive alone at night to a showroom.

"My niece claims I have a hang-up on this," he countered dryly, "but I'm damned if I can see what's fun about worrying about someone's safety."

"Then why worry at all?" Her tone made it obvious she was trying to tease away the entire topic. Michael ignored the attempt.

He leaned forward, far forward. With both elbows on the table, he appeared to be settling in for a spell of research; Megan was the subject. Nor did he make any attempt to disguise his analysis: the light blue eyes were piercingly reflective, slightly narrowed in concentration as he looked deeply into her eyes. For the first time, Megan realized that his eyes were more than merely provocative; they were incredible. She was captivated by the thick fringe of dark brown lashes and the unusual light hue of his eyes; to reproduce it, Megan supposed, one would have to experiment with sky blue drops of color on frozen water. No, she decided, Michael's eyes could never be simulated: the look she was getting wasn't icy; it was warm and interested and . . .

When he spoke, it was to ask something totally unexpected: "Megan, how would you react if I said I'd hate for anything to happen to you before we get a chance to know each other better? Would you consider it an insult?"

"Um . . ." She was speechless; was he speaking personally or merely using her as an example to illustrate a point? There didn't seem to be a safe response, anyway.

"Come on," he prompted. "It was a simple enough question. If it'll help, I'll put it another way: why would anyone object to someone else being concerned about her?"

That answered it; Megan was the example, not the point itself. She felt miserably let down; for a moment, she had been so certain she was seeing evidence that he was, after all, feeling the same runaway attraction for her that she felt for him. And that moment had been enough to let her know she would forfeit the job for the personal relationship without thinking twice. Now, as on so many other occasions that evening, she felt ridiculous.

"I didn't say I'd object," she answered, relieved to have thought of anything at all at that point.

"But you would. Well, wouldn't you?"

"Oh, dear," she murmured. "You really want an answer, don't you?"

"If you're going on the road for me, then we'd better go into it right now."

Megan didn't like the sound of that. She checked her temper; perhaps he was thinking of the several thousands of dollars' worth of merchandise she would be carrying in her car; if so, then her new employer had every right to his line of questioning. She sighed.

"Speaking personally, I'm extremely careful when I travel. My car doors are locked at all times and there's also an alarm system. I have a CB radio so I can call for help. And that's in addition to several strange little protective devices I carry in my purses; want me to describe them for you?" She looked purposefully mischievous and he laughed.

She breathed a sigh of relief. The ordeal was over.

Not quite. He said, "You started that little speech by saying, 'Speaking personally . . .' What's your opinion in general? Why would anyone object to someone else's concern?"

Megan's doubts about the nature of the conversation dissolved. If he had been testing her, he certainly wasn't now. Michael Richardson was flirting all around some issue of considerable importance to him; although she was intensely curious, she was also worried about responding. She supposed it would be impossibly rude for her to refuse to answer, but she knew he wasn't going to like it if her opinion differed with his; whatever they were talking about, he was touchy on the subject. One quick glance at his face was confirmation: for the first time, Megan saw a hint of vulnerability, just a tiny crack in the flawless armor. She felt a sudden flood of buried feminine instincts overflowing the surface.

"I asked a question," he reminded her; she was pleased to hear a remnant of the previous laughter.

"So you did, boss. Okay. The best I can do is this—it depends on the *degree* of the concern. If it creates a restriction of someone else's freedom . . . well, then it seems excessive. I gather that you've deprived several women of rep jobs these past years."

The fine lines surrounding his incredible eyes changed to a network of pain. Megan had the feeling that, if she asked, he would reveal the reason, and she was pretty sure that, whatever was troubling Michael Richardson, it was very deep, very real, and very personal. She was momentarily paralyzed with indecision. What Megan actually wanted to do was reach across the table and take his hand. For at least the tenth time

that strange evening she asked herself if it were wise to
take this job. The fact that Richardson seemed to need
her—a need she very much feared might exist only in
her overactive imagination—served to heighten her desire.

While Megan struggled with her thoughts, Michael
managed to rearrange his, or so it seemed, judging from
the gradual return of his normally confident and controlled demeanor. Suddenly he was the bright and
cheerful executive, perhaps a trifle more fatigued than
before, but definitely in control. Megan mourned the
lost opportunity. Then she was struck by a seemingly
unrelated thought: tonight was the first time she could
ever recall feeling immediately close to a man. She took
another bite of fettucine and looked across the table at
the man responsible for her unprecedented feelings.

The eyes were unquestionably just as impressive as
Megan had judged them to be earlier, perched underneath brows forming an almost perfectly straight line.
As for the rest of the face, Michael had a flawless complexion still tanned from summer. His nose and mouth
saved the face from being mannequin-perfect, for one
wasn't quite classically straight while the other comprised those tantalizingly crooked lips which had
seemed to mock her during the early moments of their
meeting. She lowered her eyes and contracted her ab-
dominal muscles. There was no doubt about it: the degree of her desire for Richardson was intense enough to
create a definite physiological response.

Once again she tried reasoning with herself. Forcing
a last appraisal, she concluded the man had a decidedly
sexy appearance, the way some box-office attractions
have "star quality."

"How's the fettucine?" he asked.

Megan smiled, feeling totally confident for the first
time since their meeting. "Fine," she answered. "But
I'm eating more than I should. Perhaps you should order me to stop."

His smile was fantastic. "I can't do that. It wouldn't be fair for me to display excessive concern for your figure. That's your business."

"In that case, perhaps I'd better just put down the fork. Now what, boss?"

He scowled, pretending to think. "Well, I guess the next step is to call for the check."

There was one final disturbing note to the evening. While they waited for the waiter, Michael's brow furrowed and he leaned across the checkered tablecloth. "Megan?"

"Hmmm?"

"Megan, what's your opinion regarding our relationship? Should it remain strictly business?"

Now it was her turn to react as though struck by lightning. Her mouth literally fell open; as a cover-up she quickly dabbed at her lips with the checkered napkin. And she regained her composure quickly, for common sense prevailed. No doubt the question had simply been an unusually polite way of testing her ethics— good employees *always* frowned on inner-company romances.

Smoothly enough, she answered, "That's one unwritten law with which I perfectly agree. Business and romance definitely do not mix." It had been a good response, Megan knew. But she wondered what her employer would say if he could know her thoughts . . . If you were as interested in me as I am in you, you wouldn't have bothered asking that question.

He looked beyond her, narrowing his eyes in concentration. And then, finally, he nodded his head very slowly, still staring at some speck on the far wall. He was biting his lower lip. Megan had no idea of the meaning of these gestures. Either he was unusually tired or he *was* attracted to her, after all. Megan blinked, then shook her head to clear it. Maybe it was she who was unusually tired.

She had no idea what to make of the situation.

2

The knocking on her door wouldn't stop. Megan finally gave up trying to cover her head with the pillow and climbed out of bed; as she struggled with her robe, she was hoping for the newspaper boy's sake that he wasn't trying to collect at this atrocious hour. Once she had made a tiny crack in the door, though, she changed her tune. Her three Saturday-morning tennis buddies were standing on the stoop looking puzzled. During the next few days, she would have to concentrate on keeping better track of weekdays versus weekends; she had a whole nine days before the start of the Ling and Son job, and Megan was unaccustomed to calendars without definite job punctuations.

Her friends forgave her, although later she took quite a bit of good-natured ribbing to the effect that she had played a Monday-morning game. It was true and she knew it; her mind seemed permanently stuck on the previous evening and, in particular, on the man she'd spent it with. Megan's entire week would be like that. Fortunately, there would be plenty of times when she was so busy that thoughts of her new employer receded to a subliminal level. Saturday morning just didn't happen to be one of them. And neither was Saturday night, when she went to a dinner-dance with an old industry friend who had been asking her out for quite some time; Megan felt sorry for him—and ashamed of herself— when she kept stepping on his toes during a perfectly simple two-step; it was obvious to them both that her mind was elsewhere.

By Tuesday, she was calmer; only those who knew her best could have picked up signs of preoccupation—which was just as well, since that was the day Megan had chosen to spend with the sales manager of the company she had just left. It was a day demanding full attention, for she had promised to bring him current with information regarding Southern California customers and the status of each account. While she was doing it, she was surprised to find herself still depressed about leaving this particular firm. Not even the thrill of obtaining a place with the prestigious Ling and Son could change the fact that an important era in Megan's life was ending.

She had graduated from UCLA with a degree in business administration, then dutifully enrolled for her master's; the day before classes started, however, she suddenly thought, To hell with it—why not get out and live it instead of just learning about it? Her first offer in the field of sales had come from a furniture manufacturer and she'd been in it ever since. In the beginning, it hadn't been easy; in fact, it had taken every bit of pride and courage she had to turn down her parents' continuous offers of financial aid. After a year, despite the fact she had been forced to start representing several different lines at once—including one for a low-end lamp and accessory company that would teach her how *not* to produce the merchandise she decided she wanted to specialize in—she knew the scary part was behind her and that she had been right to choose professional sales as a career. She had a growing regular customer list and if she wasn't wealthy, at least she was able to set aside a little money each month. Her two roommates—a beautician who would later move to Idaho and a UCLA med student who would remain Megan's closest friend for life—teased her about her spending habits: "Megan, it's supposed to be the Scotch, not the Irish, who can't let go of a dime!"

They were exaggerating, of course: Megan was far too generous and far too fond of life actually to pinch pennies. On the other hand, she had one dream she was determined to fulfill. Although California real estate was zooming skyward, she was determined to own a house.

Before the savings account would permit such a thing, she met a handsome young naval lieutenant, junior grade; they were married two months later. And eleven months after that, he was gone, erased by two words that Megan had already learned, from other young widows, weren't as innocent as they sounded: "mechanical failure." On the day she dried her tears beside the new grave, she realized she and her young man had never even had time to get to know each other.

For the next year, she took refuge in her mother's and father's West Los Angeles home. Her former in-laws lived in Montana; staying in touch with Megan seemed to trigger so much grief that she finally took her mother's advice to let the relationship drop altogether; it was a step that speeded her recovery as much as it helped her husband's bereaved family. Little by little she began to adapt normally to new situations and new friends; at the end of that year of adjustment she was once again doing well at sales and she moved back in with Sharon, the med student—now a resident in psychiatry. By the time Sharon lost her head over a surgeon named Ed, there was enough money for the down payment on Megan's dream plus a sufficiently successful track record to qualify for the mortgage loan.

She found a house in Westwood and purchased it more for location than structure. The place was a wreck; but it was her wreck and she loved it. After six months of accepting offers of help from anyone who knew how to hold a hammer or swing a paintbrush, Megan looked around and realized that both her new home and her new life were together, totally together.

Soon she was coming home from work to a precious little California bungalow on a lot with plenty of room for the two antique brick patios she would someday build among the scattered fruit trees. There were many evenings when she chose *not* to return directly from work, and then she had the world's most devoted friends to play with.

Before the refurbishing was completed, her dad had decided to take early retirement and return to Japan on a two-year consulting contract. When Megan saw her parents off at the airport, she couldn't help noticing they were as vibrant and excited as newlyweds. She felt a pang of guilt for all she had put them through, a year they had given with no apparent thoughts of themselves.

Four and a half months later, Megan briefly dated an assistant district attorney but that ended almost at the moment it started. If her relationship with the D.A. hadn't turned out well, at least it had resulted in Megan obtaining an extremely fine new lamp line. Someone in the prosecutor's office knew someone who knew someone else who introduced her to the owner of a reputable high-end manufacturing firm. The owner recommended to the sales manager that Megan be hired and—voilà!—she had the prestige accessory line she had always wanted. Her income doubled, and little by little she thinned her other lines until, at last, she was representing just the one company and still making more than when she had carried several lines. Life was less complicated and more fun all at the same time.

Except for the fact that Megan McBride was lonely during periods when, before, she had cherished her privacy. And she occasionally felt left out. Of the original group that had helped her with her house—Megan McBride's Home Beautiful Association—she and Sharon, now divorced from surgeon Ed, were the only unmarried members. Megan wasn't ready for marriage, but she wouldn't have minded finding a satisfactory replacement, and she refused to accept the possibility that there might not be such a thing.

There's one *convenient* replacement for marriage: the office family. Just as she had been with her house decorating crowd, now Megan was fortunate with the quality of ownership and staff at her new lamp and accessory place; more often, she found herself calling the office to see if Joan's mother needed more chicken soup for her chest cold or if Mr. Carrington's son had been accepted at Harvard Law School. Since she had always underestimated the power of her personality and organizing skills, she was surprised when her two social groups, the old and the new, blended quickly into one. Now a Mammoth Mountain ski trip included a caravan of ten cars, not five, and Ticketron agents shuddered when Megan appeared at the window to arrange seats for special events.

Her escorts for the special events were chosen from the group. Megan did occasionally date so-called new men; rarely did she accept twice from the same one, though. Sharon tried to question her about it but she shrugged and insisted she just hadn't met anyone interesting enough. That wasn't strictly true. Megan had found two of the men quite attractive, but when she considered that all she had to look forward to was inevitable pressure leading to the bedroom, the attraction disappeared.

When the accessory firm was sold, it had come as a real blow. Megan's old boss, a man with good business sense and a reputation for fairness, settled into retirement, often inviting his former employees for barbecues or a rerun of home movies. Everyone began to believe that nothing much would change, after all. But the new owner cut back warehouse wages, and the ensuing walkout brought the firm to its knees. Within a few weeks, a starkly worded memo went out to the reps informing them of an official reduction in commission scales; when the third such memo arrived in Megan's mailbox, she took a look at her declining investment account balance and reluctantly dialed her sales manager to tell him to find someone else for Southern California. A couple of days later, feverishly scanning the trade publications, she ran across the Ling and Son ad.

The sad day with her old sales manager finally ended; all the tears were shed, all the good luck wishes exchanged. Megan drove home with a feeling of irreplaceable loss. Fortunately, she knew her spirits would revive as soon as she changed into jeans, ate a sandwich, and started over to the YMCA for her weekly tutoring session; she determined to get out of the house as quickly as possible.

But she had trouble getting *into* the house. With the same absentmindedness she had been experiencing ever since that strange evening with Michael Richardson, she had locked her keys in the car and had to trudge back to the garage and search for the spare set. She was ready to call a locksmith—thinking, naturally, that any thief probably could have found the damned things!—when they turned up on the lid of a discarded trash can, and then, from the house, she heard the telephone. What next? Megan asked herself.

It was on its fourth ring when she answered. And it was her new employer. Megan froze.

The voice was the same as she remembered, and Lord knew she had heard it often enough in her mind since their parting a few nights ago. And although she hated to admit it, even to herself, a call from Michael was something she'd been hoping for.

Stop it, Megan! she told herself. You're no adolescent dreamer anymore! And besides, what makes you think an affair with this man is what you want?

"Have you been running?" he asked. "You sound slightly breathless."

He was right; she *was* breathless. Her dash from the garage wasn't entirely responsible for the condition, either; on the other hand, it certainly provided a reasonable excuse. She explained she had just gotten home, and he apologized for calling at a bad time.

"That's all right," she said, grateful to hear her voice sounding more normal.

At the other end there was a split second's hesitation. "I'm just double-checking," he said. "Do you still plan to start working next week?"

"Monday," she confirmed, then added, "If that's okay, I mean."

"We could sure use you earlier. Megan, are you there?"

"Oh! Yes, sorry," she said, "I was thinking . . . You know, I just don't believe it's possible to get all the loose ends tied up before next week, Michael. Isn't the old rep doing anything at all?"

"No, thank heavens," he answered dryly. "I didn't tell you what the situation was there, did I? Our former rep was hired before I was; nice man, but way out of his element; I tried to put him back on the right track but it didn't work out."

"Customers complaining?" Judging from what he'd just said, it was a question Megan needn't have asked. But she wanted to prolong the conversation. Only a few minutes earlier, she had been despondent and irritable; now, hearing his voice, she thought life seemed wonderfully worth living.

"Yes; it could be worse, though. And . . ." he paused for effect, then continued in a lighter, almost teasing tone. "I'm sure you'll be good for whatever's ailing the customers, Megan; you'd be good for whatever ails *anyone.*"

She was inordinately pleased. There was literally no one on earth from whom she would rather have heard a compliment than Michael Richardson. Of course, she had no idea what he meant by ". . . good for whatever ails *anyone.*" Her reaction was another example of running with an imaginary ball to an imaginary goal line. Megan sighed.

"You're tired, aren't you?"

The question startled her; obviously the sigh had been audible.

"No. Of course not."

"Sorry I asked." He sounded amused.

Megan was embarrassed. The man had expressed polite concern, and she might just as well have told him to mind his own business. She struggled: what on earth could be said in such a situation? Suddenly it occurred to her to simply give up and tell the truth—at least a harmless portion of it. She said, "I don't know why it is, but when you and I talk, things don't always come out of my mouth sounding the way I intended them to."

"Why do you think that is, Megan?" His voice held a new quality, more intensity.

She reminded herself to stick to a version of the truth. "Nerves?"

"Why would you be nervous?"

No answer.

"Want me to take a guess?" he prodded.

Megan's hesitation was caused by his tone, not his questions. Once again, as in those few brief seconds at the Italian restaurant, her new employer was sending distinctly unbusinesslike signals. At least that's what she was receiving.

"Megan?" he said softly.

Although she didn't trust her voice, she tried a small sound: "Hmmm?"

"Do you think maybe you should come over to the office where we can talk this over privately?"

All of a sudden she started babbling. "Um, Michael, I'm not dressed. I mean, I'm dressed but I've got to *get* dressed! Again. I've got to go downtown. To teach. You remember the little Japanese kids I told you about?

Well, tonight's the night I help them with their English. So, you see, I really—"

"Am afraid to come over here," he finished for her.

"Oh, no! That's not it at all!"

More gently than she had ever heard him speak, he said, "Megan, give it up. Right now, you don't know *what* you want. But tell me something: are you still determined to take this job?"

She told herself to wake up . . . Snap out of it or you're going to find yourself sleeping on the streets! With forced sobriety, she said, "You're wrong, Mr. Richardson." Her next sentence came out in an erratic pattern, probably because she wasn't entirely sure she meant what she was saying: "I . . . *want* . . . to go . . . to . . . work . . . for you. That much I do . . . know."

It was his turn to sigh. "All right. I can't claim this has been the most satisfying conversation of my life, but at least we're setting the record perfectly straight. By the way, because of the situation with our old rep, I'm going to take Monday and personally introduce you to some of the customers. If you change your mind about the job between now and then, please, Megan, call me right away."

Before hanging up, Megan assured him she wouldn't change her mind. When the phone was safely back on the cradle, she collapsed against a wall and thought, I don't blame him for doubting me—I don't sound bright enough to make my own decisions!

Wednesday started out quietly. Megan had planned to revise her bookkeeping method to accommodate the Ling and Son pricing system, but she couldn't make herself do it. Instead, she wrote a short letter to her parents and then went out to lunch and shopping with Sharon. Although Michael Richardson's name came frequently to mind, she never thought of a subtle way to work it into the conversation; since she was beginning to feel increasingly in need of guidance, this bothered her.

On Thursday, the first call of the morning created problems. It was one of Megan's "just once" dates. He was a newly elected state senator, and Megan suspected it was his profession that accounted for his persistence. And this time he really *wouldn't* take no for an answer. The next night, he had to be in Los Angeles to give a campaign speech for someone or other's brother; if Megan refused to go out with him, he promised to camp on her doorstep. She sighed and gave up, then asked where they were going. When he suggested they attend the final session of the summer concerts and told her Barry Manilow was at the Greek Theater, she brightened considerably. Not only were those tickets nearly impossible to obtain but an evening in the lovely outdoor amphitheater couldn't be too bad. One last note soured it for her, though: after she had become irrevocably obligated, the arrogant young senator said, "You don't mind dressing formally, do you?"

"The Greek's not really for ballgowns," she reminded him.

"Well, I know," he said brightly, "and I didn't mean *that* formally. But I've got that speech to give to the Bankers' Association. Unless you come along, we won't make the concert in time. And, by the way, a few people from the bankers' group will be with us."

When Megan hung up, she thought, Great! Here's one I'll have trouble with on both ends! He wants me to play hostess with him before the date and heaven only knows what he'll want me to play afterward. She wasn't being entirely fair and she knew it. The politician was glib, yes, and he knew how to bring people to his point of view, yes, but he was a *gentlemanly* smooth-talking manipulator! She decided to wear a pretty dress and make the best of the evening. The man was good-looking and famous, the evening would more than likely be balmy, and it could provide a few hours' res-

pite from thoughts of Michael Richardson. With that in
mind, Megan put the whole thing out of her head. As
her time between jobs drew near the end, she wasn't
going to let anyone spoil it for her. Not her new employer and—especially—not a politician. She finished
putting on her clothes and then hurried out to the garage for her fishing gear; she and one of the former sec-
retaries for the old lamp and accessories firm were
going to San Diego for a day on one of the tuna boats.

By Friday evening, when it was time to start dressing
for the Bankers' Association, whatever that was,
Megan was so tired she didn't think she'd make it. Although she wasn't the type to cancel dates, she would
have made an exception this time, only she couldn't call
the senator; she hadn't asked where he was staying.

For comfort, Megan pinned her long auburn hair up
and secured it with tiny pearl barrettes; when several
thick strands insisted on escaping to fall in waves on
her face and neck, she looked in the mirror and said,
"To heck with it—the carefree, windblown look!" To
draw attention from the unruly coiffure, she gave a
little extra attention to eye makeup, and when she saw
the effect she decided that, for an impulsive experiment, it wasn't half bad; her sea green eyes sparkled
and looked larger than usual, more dramatic, but not
overdone. She skipped foundation and blusher; yesterday's hours of hanging over the side of a fishing boat in
a bright sun glare had taken care of that. Lip gloss was
the only finishing touch she would need.

Choosing a dress would be more complicated. Since
Megan was already tanned, it wasn't as apparent as it
would have been in early June, but she had definitely
gotten an overdose of sun; the only thing she craved
against her hot skin was a tub of cool water. Her eyes
came to rest on a white chiffon dress with an extremely
low-cut back; the front was much higher—square cut
and straight across the collarbones—but Megan figured, Oh well, you can't have everything, at least the

chiffon's soft! She put on a necklace of beaded jade the
exact green of her eyes and a pair of matching jade ear-
drops, then looked at her watch, knowing she had just
made it. If the honorable senator planned to be on time
for his speech, he would have to ring her doorbell
within five minutes; as it turned out, it was only three
and a half.

The bankers turned out to be a lively crowd. The only
one who seemed to be thinking about money, in fact,
was Megan's date, Senator Matthew Taylor Maxwell
the Third. Between salad and dessert, he pitched pretty
heavily for whoever's brother was running.

While Megan wondered if he'd hired his speech-
writers from among Johnny Carson's rejects, she also
noticed Matt wasn't having any trouble holding his
audience; she decided her mood was unnecessarily
cynical and went back to picking at the vegetables;
after she finally managed to skewer a sodden brussels
sprout, she accidentally caught the eyes of a couple of
women who were staring at her with frank envy.
Megan had a feeling it wasn't the brussels sprout they
wanted: it was Matthew Taylor Maxwell the Third;
she was highly amused, for, although the man was an
imposing figure, most of his appeal could be stripped
away as easily as flash normally disappears when the
spotlights go off. On their one and only previous date,
Megan had found that his conversational repertoire
was strictly limited to political double-talk. Never
mind, she told herself; she didn't have to marry him,
she only had to survive the evening. Sudden visions
of Michael appeared in her head: she had a feeling
that if he were a politician, he'd enthrall listeners
with speeches that actually *said* something. Megan
popped the brussels sprout into her mouth and looked
down to conceal a naughty expression: if women were
intrigued with this handsome but vacuous young
state senator, they would never survive Michael
Richardson as a politician!

Fatigue plus continued preoccupation with thoughts of her employer combined to make Megan miss the fact that many more men than women were sneaking glances at her. Still she must not look quite as bad as she had assumed, she thought, as the rented Rolls-Royce limousines delivered the party to the Greek Theater.

In one important respect, her instincts had been more than correct; at eight-thirty on that particular September evening, the air was still summery, turning slightly cooler, of course, as it always did in Southern California; there was even a scent of night-blooming jasmine wafting in and out and around on a gently playful breeze. Matthew Taylor Maxwell the Third had made sure that his potential contributors got the best seats in the house, of course, and in addition to that, the group was well ahead of the crowd; it was the only time Megan had ever been to the Greek that her toes had survived intact.

Until Barry Manilow took the stage, she sat and made easy small talk with Matt and the bankers, mostly just reveling in the pleasures of the setting; she wasn't even distracted when the latecomers in the next row back took their seats right in the middle of the singer's first number, "Copacabana."

Manilow was making a real hit with the capacity crowd, and Megan closed her eyes, now feeling more relaxed than exhausted. Occasionally someone to her right or left would whisper a comment about the performance, but, generally, she was left alone to float with the mood; up until the time the air turned chilly enough to make her regret the decision not to bring a coat, she would have judged the experience an unblemished delight. And it wasn't until Manilow went into the last song before intermission that she started shivering; he was crooning "I Write the Songs That Make the Whole World Sing," and Megan was wishing he made the coats that made the whole world warm. When she felt a man's coat slipped over her shoulders, she was immensely grateful and turned to thank her date.

But Matthew Taylor Maxwell was still wearing his coat. He was also looking toward the row behind them, evidently trying to figure out where the wrap had come from. Puzzled, Megan followed his gaze until her eyes were locked onto the amused expression on Michael Richardson's face.

Since it was hardly the time or place for exclamations, Megan just stared numbly at her unexpected benefactor; if she could have seen her own wide green eyes, she would have had no trouble at all understanding the look in his. Meanwhile, Barry Manilow went right on making the whole world sing.

During intermission, she performed the introductions stiffly but accurately: "Matt, I'd like you to meet my new employer. Mr. Richardson, this is Senator Matthew Maxwell. And our friends, Mr. and Mrs. Sanders." For his part, Michael was much more casual; he introduced the raven-haired beauty at his side as, simply, "Jeannette," and also stuck strictly to first names with the remainder of his party.

She insisted on returning the coat, of course. It was Jeannette who expressed concern for Megan's comfort; Richardson chose to stay out of the debate, but when Jeannette turned out the loser, he gracefully took the coat and put it back on. Then he turned expectantly toward Matthew Taylor Maxwell the Third, who obviously had no idea what this stranger was waiting for. After a moment's awkward silence, one of the bankers' wives, a lady brought up in the deep south, said, "Senatuh, may-bee you wanna give Miss McBride *yoah* jacket. It *is* kinda cool out heah."

The senator was hardly the type to stand around in shirt-sleeves while everyone else remained formally dressed. While Megan went about the task of extricating him from the no-win situation—she told him she wouldn't wear the coat if he *did* take it off—she also

wondered if Michael Richardson might not have been
making a purposeful attempt to make her date appear
foolish. Judging from a barely perceptible quirk of the
provocative lips, plus a mischievous gleam in the light
blue eyes, it seemed a distinct possibility.

But why would he do such a thing? she asked herself.

Manilow's closing song was "I Can't Smile Without
You," and long before that, Michael had slipped the
coat back over her shoulders. Megan's eyes glistened
with unshed tears. She was afraid the lyrics of that
haunting melody might have special meaning for her.
And the only person who could have sparked a smile
was sitting near enough to touch. With another woman.

3

Now there was no choice. Having found one excuse after another to avoid setting up the new bookkeeping system, Megan was running out of time, and this particular deskwork was literally the last thing on earth she wanted to do. The anguish she had experienced last night was like nothing she had ever known; by nothing more dramatic than being in the same place with her new employer, she had learned what an impersonal relationship with him would cost. And the price was too high. Sitting near Michael Richardson, yet aware that only a woman in Jeannette's position—never a mere employee—could be genuinely close to him . . . it was too much for Megan to ask of herself.

She tried to think of a way out. There was none. For one thing, she had to work; no one was handing out free groceries or mortgage money this month. For another, even supposing she had another job lined up, she had promised to call him with plenty of notice if she changed her mind about Ling and Son. That was only fair, and less than forty-eight hours wasn't reasonable. Perhaps she should mail her résumé to a few more companies today, then, after a month or so, take the first offer that came along; it wouldn't be as good as Ling, nor would it be the most up-front plan Megan had ever undertaken, but it was worth considering. Besides, how good a job could she do for a man whose presence was a reminder of the one thing in life she felt she couldn't live without yet could never hope to live *with?*

She made herself go to the desk. It was at the far end of the spot Megan considered to be her home's biggest asset. On the advice of the friend with the most decorating savvy, she had knocked out the dividers between living room, dining room, and a large hallway storage closet; the result, after enlarging the windows looking on to the backyard, was a cheerful area comprising more than half the square footage in her little house. Dividing techniques had been chosen according to individual function; for instance, Megan's "office" was punctuated by a literal wall-jungle of exotic plants, some potted, some hanging, which provided sound insulation whenever she had houseguests and needed to work. The orchids and ferns and cymbidiums also provided a fitting environment for her roommate, who lived in a magnificent antique brass birdcage Megan had spent months renovating. Her father's old overstuffed "think chair" stood in a corner, reupholstered in bold lemon and white checks that picked up other yellow accents throughout the office.

She got up and walked to the cage, opened the door, and offered her finger. Evidently the little parrot was as anxious for diversion as she was; he wasted no time climbing aboard.

"Hello, Sinbad."

"Hello!"

"No wonder I've neglected you this week! You never have anything intelligent to say!" She put the bird on her shoulder and, reluctantly, took the desk chair again. But she went at the task halfheartedly, paying more attention to Sinbad's excited squawks and chatter than to the books.

From a neighbor's yard came the sudden rumble of a lawn mower starting up.

"Phone! Phone! Phone!" Sinbad screeched.

Without batting an eye, Megan reached for the silent

phone—it was symbolic, a Cinderella facsimile given to her at the completion of the Home Beautiful project, and she treasured it—and put the glass slipper to her ear. Then she moved it close enough for Sinbad to hear the dial tone; after two or three seconds of cocking his little head first this way, then that, he finally shook himself and said, "Hello! Hello! Hello!" When he heard another loud rev of the lawn mower engine he showed only a moment's uncertainty before announcing, once again, "Phone!"

Megan couldn't help herself; she laughed. "Well," she said at last, "you're making as much sense as Matt's silly speech last night—and he was squawking at three hundred bankers!"

She tried to get back to work. After only fifteen minutes, though, she accidentally punched the wrong line of figures into her pocket calculator, then sighed. Chucking the delighted bird under his chin, she said, "Damn, Sinbad!"

And he said, "Damn!"

"Uh-oh . . . I say it that much, do I? Listen, bird, I'd do anything to get out of this nonsense. Look outside—it's a beautiful morning: Saturday! Why don't you make the phone *ring*, Sinbad, instead of just talking about it? I want someone to give me an excuse to stop working—why, I'd even talk to Senator Matthew Taylor Maxwell the Third if he called!"

When, at that precise moment, part of her wish came true, Megan jumped almost clear out of her chair. As she reached to answer the phone, Sinbad said, "Door!"

"Hello," she said.

"Hi, this is—"

Megan said to Sinbad, "Hush, silly! I'm not talking to you!"

"Then who *are* you talking to?"

She made no attempt whatsoever to disguise the frustrated groan. Naturally, the caller was Michael Richardson; with whom else would she choose to begin a conversation so childishly?

"It's early," he said, sounding unsure of himself for the first time, at least in her experience. "Maybe I shouldn't have called so soon. Did I wake you up?"

Megan bristled. If he thought she was talking to another person, and if he suspected she might have been asleep . . . Just who did he *think* was with her? Of course—the senator! As unjust as she felt his presumption was—if in fact she hadn't imagined it—she decided she would feel even worse if she dignified it with a comment. And she could afford to hold her temper, anyway; the mere sound of his voice had provided the lifeline formerly missing from her erratic morning. Sunshine suddenly came through the wide windows in great generous splashes of sparkling yellow. Megan smiled broadly and wondered how to keep this reaction to herself. So far, consistent with the way she'd behaved the last time he had telephoned, she was doing a good job: saying nothing was an efficient enough way of disguising her feelings!

Despite the contradictions in her thoughts, her spoken words were chosen with extreme care. "I'm sorry, Michael. You caught me in the middle of paperwork and my mind doesn't seem to be making the transition." Good, Megan thought, at least he'll know I wasn't in bed, alone or otherwise! Simultaneously it occurred to her that within her own house, her whereabouts and company were none of his business, boss or no boss, and she decided to confuse the issue a bit. Later she would admit to herself that pain from the night before, when she had had no choice other than to sit near Michael and his girl, had influenced most of her actions that day. She said, "Maybe I *was* asleep, after all."

"Then welcome to the world," he said, apparently unaffected either by her games or by her refusal to identify her companion. "It's a beautiful day. What's on your calendar? Not much more of the paperwork, I hope."

Megan didn't want to tell him how dull her day appeared. As ridiculous as it seemed, even to her, she wished he had asked that particular polite question at a more normal time, when she could have announced that she was on her way out. Well, she suddenly thought, my personal plans are also none of his business; I can be as vague as I choose to be.

"Oh," she said, trying to sound casual, "there's always more to do on a Saturday than sit at the desk. I've got plans." Which wasn't entirely untrue, Megan thought, since she doubted she could stand being cooped up all day; if she had to spend part of tomorrow on the books, then so be it.

"In that case," he said smoothly, "I can probably accomplish my simple task without throwing you off stride. You evidently haven't noticed that we forgot to go into the office and get the catalog and other material you'll need; I'm talking about the night we had dinner. Anyway, I've got the stuff, and if the address on the résumé is still good, we both live in Westwood. Just give me the directions and I'll drop it off."

"That's nice of you," she mumbled, then supplied the route.

"What time are you leaving?" he asked.

"Oh, in about forty-five minutes," she said, thinking fast and talking even faster. "Do you want to leave the stuff by the front door? There's a wrought-iron chair that might hold it."

"That should be okay. I don't think anyone will be tempted to steal this kind of thing." He sounded casual, totally unconcerned, and Megan couldn't help but wish it were otherwise; she would have given anything to hear in his voice some of the tension she herself was feeling. Although she had known several days ago that she was feeling things for Michael Richardson she had never before felt in her life, it seemed there was one extra dimension after another yet to be discovered; she imagined her emotions as some crazy cake; each new layer clashed with the flavor of the one underneath.

"I appreciate the trouble you're taking," she said evenly, pleased with herself.

"No trouble at all. I'm sorry I'll miss seeing you. Have a nice weekend, Megan." After the good-byes, Megan sat and held the phone at arm's length, staring with her mouth open wide. She was astonished by what had just happened. When she had finally replaced the receiver, she took Sinbad from her shoulder, shaking her head. "Sorry, little bird," she said sincerely. "I guess my hand's unsteady, huh? But surely you can't blame me; I just got myself into a situation where I have to run away from my own house!" She moved toward the cage and, just before placing Sinbad inside, she said, "I guess you think I'm nuts, don't you? I'll bet if you had your eye on some fancy lady parrot, you wouldn't fly the coop just before she came to visit!"

And then Megan went tearing into her bedroom to change into tennis clothes; she was planning to unleash some pretty violent energy on the municipal park backboards.

There was a dangerously weak seam in her ball bag, and she decided it wouldn't hold. So she withdrew two air-vac cylinders and, balancing these plus her racket and purse, barely managed to get the front door open without dropping the whole lot. Michael Richardson was standing on the other side, just poised to ring the doorbell.

For a moment, Megan just stared at him, torn between anger and embarrassment. He had certainly given no indication that he planned to deliver the material immediately. As she struggled to compose herself, one of the slender ball cylinders shifted from its resting place in the V of her elbow. With a barely audible *pop!* the lid fell away and a pair of yellow tennis balls slithered out to bounce along the brick walkway. Richardson's arms were filled with a three-inch stack of office paraphernalia, but he reached instinctively for the balls; a collection of books and papers slid to the ground. Megan bent down to prevent the loose papers from escaping in the slight breeze; she dropped her racket and the second ball cylinder. She and Richardson straightened; they exchanged totally bewildered glances.

The tension was too great. Something had to give and, as usual, it was Megan's composure—she burst out laughing. After one quick indication of surprise, Michael Richardson joined in. By the time they recovered, the fenced courtyard was littered with balls and papers.

She went to the left, after the tennis stuff, while he collected the business material. Then, with their arms once again overfull, they stared at each other self-consciously. It was Michael who broke the silence: "We're right back where we started. There must be a safe way to get this into *your* hands."

She nodded. "We're just going to make another mess, aren't we?"

Something about her question appeared to click in Richardson's mind; there was a look of instantaneous comprehension—as though an important point had been scored—and then he seemed to make a decision. His eyes narrowed. With unexpected severity, he said, "Megan, put down those balls."

He might as well have commanded the nearby tree to drop its apples. For Megan, the tension had begun to re-build at a dangerous clip. The man whose presence had the ability to inflict simultaneous pleasure and pain stood within three feet of her and, as always, he had taken total charge. Inappropriately, she found herself wondering why he was wearing business clothes; somewhere along the way he had stripped away his suit jacket, but the crisply tailored dress shirt and obviously expensive tie still didn't go with a Saturday morning. In comparison, Megan's tennis outfit, white shorts and a kelly green halter top, felt skimpy; her mind formed a vague question about the reason for this attraction to someone who made her feel inferior. All the thinking provoked a defensive posture; instead of following his mandate to put down the tennis balls, she clutched them tightly to her breasts.

Michael appeared to be accepting her reaction; just as clearly, he was determined to get his way. He set his mouth in a tight line; this Megan noticed just as she saw something slightly frightening in his eyes. Whatever his mission, he expected her full cooperation to accomplish it. When he placed his own books and papers on the ground at his feet, she just waited.

"Megan, come here," he commanded.

She stepped forward, but not too far; in her eyes was a look of vulnerable pain, like a child fearing reprimand for some unknown misdeed.

"Now," he said, much more softly. "Put . . . the . . . balls . . . down, Megan."

No use; she only tightened her grasp.

He smiled weakly, then shook his head and said, as though talking to himself, "You're more confused than I realized." After a split second's thought, he added, this time in a stronger tone, "Are you listening to me at all?"

Megan nodded.

"Then pay attention to this and see if you don't agree . . ." The voice was deadly serious, she followed it with unconcealed fascination. Very deliberately, Michael said, "Megan, we're not going about this at *all* the right way. At this rate, we're likely to make a bigger mess than you can even imagine."

She said nothing, afraid to believe her interpretation of the words. Her eyes searched his; without uttering a sound, she seemed to be pleading. As if in consent, Michael's expression softened; the eyes held liquid warmth and fiery promise. Standing in full daylight, separated by stacks of trivia, the two looked as helpless as lovesick teenagers.

"Megan? Honey?"

She *couldn't* talk. Perhaps he knew it; he waited, apparently with patience. The next move was up to her. And Megan had heard him use a word employers just don't use with mere underlings. *Now* she understood.

The tension of Megan's morning evaporated to be replaced by another type: a literal volcano of pent-up sexual pressure. Without conscious thought, she reacted in a totally uncharacteristic manner. Never taking her eyes off Michael, she slowly and deliberately opened her arms and released the tennis balls. Then she took two steps forward, and when he locked her into an embrace, the violence of his movements was met not with fear, but with a passion Megan had never before displayed.

"Oh, God!" she heard him say. "This is what I've wanted since we met. Last night, I knew I couldn't wait any longer for you."

He pinned her more tightly against him. Megan rose on her tiptoes; she slid her arms around his neck and buried her face in his shoulder. They were breathing raggedly, both of them.

He kissed her eyelids, her hair, her neck; when his lips brushed near her earlobe she trembled.

"You *do* want me," he said simply. "Thank God! I couldn't stand to see you with another man again."

"Yes," she whispered, "I want you." To herself, she was thinking there wasn't a woman on earth who wouldn't want Michael Richardson; he even felt like a fantasy: perfect, totally male, like his appearance. The flawless skin was cool and subtly fragrant with the remnants of after-shave; she wondered at the ability of textures so smooth and soothing to ignite such heat. Megan's body was undergoing a series of small explosions; the fires started at the top, wherever his lips touched sensitive skin, and sparked a larger, even more exquisite passion at the precise spot where her hips met the tensed muscles of his thighs. She started to say

something but was interrupted by the almost bruising
pressure of his lips on hers; after that, all thought was
lost; her body moved toward him, moved with him, in a
frenzied rhythm of its own.

He took a long shuddering breath and moved his lips
to her hair. As if by command, his hips became still.
Then he tightened the arms enfolding her and stood
that way until his breathing was steadier. Although
Megan tried to match her own retreat to his, her body
wasn't ready; she wanted more; if he had stepped away
at that moment, she would very likely have fainted. Michael sensed it; he began stroking her hair: very slowly,
deliberately. "Shh, baby," he said. "Calm down now."

And she asked herself, Why? I've waited all my life to
reach a moment like this. But when she instinctively
tried to press closer, Michael stiffened and drew back.
Staring down at her dilated pupils, he said, "When I
first laid eyes on you last night, I was sure I would
never see anything more beautiful. But today you are.
It's the eyes, honey. At the concert, they were cool, like
the jade necklace you were wearing; now they're hot,
like emeralds in the sun." His voice grew hoarse again,
then dropped almost to a whisper: "I want even more
than that—I want to see what happens to your eyes
when we *touch* the flame, Megan."

The suggestion, and the voice with which he made it,
created an urgency even more demanding than the desire she had felt against the pressure of his body; with
those words, "when we touch the flame," Megan had no
doubt what Michael was referring to. She moaned; he
had chosen a confusing time to hint at erotic future sce-
narios; although his hands still gripped her shoulders,
the touch was now light, with no remaining traces of
their former probing passion.

He said, "Honey, in about two minutes, I'm going to
have to turn around and walk away. It'll be the hardest
thing I've ever done, but there's no choice; I've got to
catch a flight to San Francisco."

"Oh, Michael, no!" she thought, then realized the words had been spoken aloud.

He grinned. For the first time Megan failed to appreciate the irresistible expression; she had to accept the fact that he had changed moods: Michael was once again the boss, now dealing humorously with an employee failing to grasp some significant point. It triggered a harsh and thoroughly unwelcome reminder—Megan simply didn't feel capable of handling the quick-switch requirements her new job would require, from Michael's equal to his employee.

As though reading her mind, he said, "It's not that bad. I'll be back late tomorrow night and then, Monday after work, we can pick up where we left off." His voice suddenly turned serious again. "But, Megan, I want you to stop worrying about the employment factor; I agree it would have been better if we hadn't let things get to this point—working together's a challenge we could have done without—but it's also not *that* complicated, you know. We aren't the only people who've gotten caught in this situation; if others can solve the problems, then so can we."

She nodded, not exactly knowing why, and he dropped his hands from her shoulders and stepped back. With an elaborate sigh, he asked if she'd be okay until he returned, and Megan said yes. And then Michael hesitated before turning, as though he were waiting for her to stop him. Finally, he strode slowly but resolutely from the yard.

When she started moving, it was in slow motion. She made two trips into the house, piling books, papers, and tennis equipment unceremoniously on the kitchen table. Then she walked like a robot into the office and plopped onto the think chair; with her legs thrown over the footstool and her head angled so far back she was staring at the ceiling, Megan tried to force herself into a logical, rational thought process.

How did this happen? she asked herself, and the an-

swer was that no one understands the reason for so-
called fatal attractions between men and women. In her
case, she had found a potential employer irresistible
from the moment of first meeting and later, after she
had been hired, nothing she had done or thought had altered her feelings; in fact, they had grown stronger.

She asked herself what she might have done differently. That was simple: knowing how she felt about Michael Richardson, she should never have *accepted* the
job. So what? The mistake had been made, and it was
definitely too late to undo it, both for her sake and for
his.

How could I possibly have missed the signs that he
felt the same way? she questioned. It was ludicrous, especially considering how desperately she had wished
for it. Megan sighed, thinking the answer was probably
uncomplicated; from the beginning, she had assumed
that no man as attractive as Richardson could possibly
want *her*.

One question she didn't bother with was: how do I
really feel about this? To know she was having her first
taste of euphoria, Megan hardly needed to talk to herself. All the sappy romantic poetry was true: until Michael's return, when she would feel his arms around
her again, minutes really *would* pass like hours.

4

When Megan awakened Monday morning, she was drenched in perspiration and totally exhausted. She skipped coffee, reluctant to mix caffeine with taut nerves, and went directly to the shower, where she cut the warm water by gradual degrees until she was standing under a cascade of icy needles. Finally feeling both awake and alert, she measured out a normal luke-warm flow and shampooed her shoulder-length hair, a thick mass of auburn so deep that, in dim lighting, it appeared to be a rich burnished mink. When she started the normal soaping, Megan stepped impul-sively from the shower and padded over to a nearby cabinet, where she unwrapped a cake of perfumed soap—Opium—which had been lying neglected since Christmas. At that point, Megan's morning ritual veered toward her subconscious images to become a viv-idly erotic daydream.

Beginning with her feet, Megan soaped upward along the slender legs which accounted for much of her five-feet-seven-inches. And she found herself wondering . . . Now that she knew, from Saturday, the exquisite sen-sation when Michael's fingers touched her skin, how would she feel if he were the one guiding the Opium, very slowly, along her bare thighs? And then, when the soap dropped from his hands . . .

Megan's hips, tapering to a small waistline, were softly rounded but not as abundant as she would have liked; her tummy was perfectly flat. When he looked at her, would he approve? When he touched her there, would she be able to stand it?

Her breasts were small but firm. When she imagined Michael's fingers feathering against the soft pink nipples, converting them to fiery tips of pleasure, she moaned.

Megan leaned back against the shower wall. The spell was broken but she was breathing hard and irregularly. For the first time in her life, she stood alone and blushed.

Now she was in a hurry. Fortunately, a minimum amount of makeup would do; the red from Thursday's fishing excursion had calmed to an even tan, and the weekend tennis had polished her cheeks a faint coral. She applied a touch of foundation to blend the smattering of Irish freckles across the bridge of her nose, then a dab of coral lip gloss. As she reached for mascara, she stared briefly at the large almond-shaped green eyes in the mirror and said aloud, "Megan, what world are you living in today?"

From the closet, she took a classically tailored two-piece beige business suit and then, looking at the no-nonsense white shirt she normally wore with it, shook her head. Her eyes surveyed the wardrobe and came to rest on a silk azure creation that scooped gracefully in front and then fell in wide soft ruffles narrowing to the waistline.

Just before locking up, she dropped her briefcase by the front door and ran back to the bathroom. Standing right next to the spot vacated by the Opium soap was a small container of perfume, part of the same Christmas gift. Megan opened the elegant bottle and applied Opium in all the prescribed places.

During the drive from Westwood to East Los Angeles, Megan would have given a week's commissions to rid herself of the Opium. It had the desired effect on her psyche—she certainly felt feminine—but she wondered if she might not be broadcasting a message intended for Michael alone.

The receptionist greeted her like a long-lost friend, then said, "Mr. Richardson wants you to go right on back." When Megan reached the office, Michael was on the phone; he gestured a warm signal to be seated, then returned to a discussion about the porcelains that had been causing problems last week. During the approximately five minutes that passed before he replaced the receiver, Megan relaxed about her perfume. If she were broadcasting a provocative message, then so was Michael. His suit was an extremely well-cut designer label, deep marine blue with subtle flecks of burgundy, and he wore a solid burgundy tie; when Megan realized it was pure silk, she reacted with something akin to relief, thinking of the ridiculous amount of time she had spent choosing a blouse. Michael also smelled of something that was definitely not drugstore after-shave. What a terrific feeling! Megan thought. Whatever they were doing to each other might not be headed anywhere, but at the moment it wasn't harming them, either. She felt more alive than at any other time in her life.

Michael hung up the phone and swiveled to face her. "I'll say one thing," he commented after a thorough appraisal. "When I introduce you, the buyers are going to be more impressed than ever with the good taste of this company." There was nothing wolfish about the remark; Megan smiled her appreciation, reminding herself at the same time to follow his example. Her employer—for that's definitely what he would be for the duration of the business day—had struck a carefully poised balance between his executive responsibilities and his personal feelings; although the scales had ended up tipped in favor of the business situation, Michael had nonetheless managed to let Megan know she was special to him. For herself, Megan decided against trying to send personal signals; that might be an em-

ployer's prerogative but it certainly wasn't one for an
underling. Since she and Michael were locked into this
tenuous aspect of their association, she intended to concentrate on nothing more than getting the job done.
Megan was also aware that she wanted very much to
erase any false impressions lingering from the giddy
behavior that had characterized their brief phone conversations. If there was ever a time in her life she
wanted to establish a positive image, it was now; she
was determined for him to see her as a thoroughly com-
petent sales pro.

Looking now at her boss—casually seated, hands
folded loosely on the desk, apparently comfortable with
the silence—Megan couldn't help wondering what he
was thinking. Despite the cool facade, was it possible
he, too, worried about how to make the transition each
day, when the evening bell rang down the business period? At the moment, the man she was studying seemed
almost formidable: secure in his authority to direct
Megan and twenty others in her position. There was
suddenly no way to imagine herself having nerve
enough to slip her hand into his, say, or wrap her arms
around him as she had on Saturday. In fact, Saturday
was now heartbreakingly remote, an occurrence from
another time in another world, a vacation place bearing
no resemblance to this awkward limbo in which they
seemed permanently trapped.

She refocused, back on business, and asked politely
for an update on the missing Japanese porcelains. Michael reported they had just arrived via Pan Am and
his entire warehouse crew was primed to get them
wired and shaded, then immediately on a flight to Ohio.

"My customs broker guaranteed they'd clear before
noon," he said, "but that's not what's on my mind. Today, Megan, my only concern is you. Here's a list of the
buyers you'll be meeting. Actually, in addition to regular clients, we'll make a detour: out to LAX. There's a
Welcome Hotel contract agent flying in to discuss the

lamps for a new place going up in the Valley; I thought you'd want to be in on it from the beginning."

"We're not being considered for the entire hotel contract, are we?"

"No. Just the suites. We don't have anything low-end enough for the regular rooms. And the public areas haven't been mentioned yet; I trust you'll maneuver onto that subject."

"Naturally," Megan said, grinning. Then she reached for Michael's list of buyers, which included some of the most prestigious names on the American retail scene. "Good grief—I *am* impressed! Are we currently doing business with all of them?"

Michael shook his head. "Negative. After three years of steady orders from Hendrick's, they dropped us a few months back."

Megan didn't ask why. She recalled he had told her that the former rep hadn't been quite up to the job; as a result, there would undoubtedly be several customers with legitimate complaints. Michael pushed his chair back and stood up. "Ready to hit the road?" he asked.

The first visit was easy. Megan learned she would be dealing directly with the proprietor of an ultra-exclusive decorator's outlet; the owner, Mrs. Klein, turned out to be as modest as her store was pretentious. But there was a problem: it seemed she had Ling and Son on an arrangement calling for the rep to keep regular tabs on inventory, then automatically restock sold merchandise. Now, in a soft shy voice, she said, "Really, Mr. Richardson, our sales haven't tallied with the bills for months now." To Megan this was clear enough warning: the account was in serious jeopardy. She asked Mrs. Klein about her inventory, explaining that she wanted to know if the owner thought she had actually *received* all the merchandise listed on the Ling invoice.

Instead of answering yes or no, the woman said, with no small amount of amazement, "How did you know?"

"I didn't," Megan admitted, "not for sure. But when
you handed me the invoice I noticed a charge for some
small bronze statues, a matched set of three wise men.
One set is on the floor—gathering dust, I might add—
and then, according to this bill, you received another
set two weeks later. There's no reason to restock pieces
that aren't selling. It's either a computer or a delivery
error. But the point is, you shouldn't have to worry
about it." She paused for a moment to give the client a
chance to comment. Mrs. Klein's head bobbed enthusi-
astically up and down, so Megan continued. "I'd better
check our invoice against your entire Ling inventory.
While I'm at it, I'd like to make some changes; those
statues aren't right for you; at the moment, your
displays need large important accessories, and you
could also use more color. Let me come in on Saturday.
I'll move all the dead wood back to the warehouse and
wipe it entirely off your bill. Okay?"

"Mr. Richardson," said Mrs. Klein emphatically,
"this is a *big* improvement. Before I met Megan, I was
thinking our arrangement with Ling wasn't going to
work out."

Later, as they maneuvered onto the freeway, Megan
sat back comfortably. She was delighted; not only had
the account been saved but Mrs. Klein's complimentary
remark about the service had provided a well-timed
morale boost. Now she was anxious to hear from Michael, but he was quiet during the ten-minute drive. He
kept his eyes straight ahead and, in fact, was so obviously preoccupied—judging from a certain "executive
expression" Megan had seen often enough—that she
herself was afraid to speak. By the time they drew near
their next destination, not a single word had passed between them; to say that Megan resented it would have
been absurd understatement. More correctly, she was
furious. It wasn't often a chief executive had the chance
to witness his new-hire salvaging accounts manhandled
by the predecessor; the least he could have offered was,

"Well done," or "Thank you." Megan translated total silence as an insult, just as if he were saying, "That wasn't worth talking about; maybe you'll do better next time."

During the last mile of the drive, her practiced professional discipline kicked into high gear. Michael or no Michael, she wasn't about to let personal frustration interfere with her chances to straighten out whatever kinks existed in the Hendrick's line; it was high-quality, successful chains like this one in California that kept firms like Ling and Son in business. And their purchasing agents were necessarily demanding; reps who failed to concentrate on the stores' needs wouldn't be given a second chance.

The Hendrick's buyer was a big, friendly looking man who shook Michael's hand with sincere enthusiasm. Then he told them he was sorry, but he had switched to another lamp line. "God, Michael," he said, shaking his head, "whatever firm you've been associated with has always managed to produce the best merchandise; I've been carrying your products for as long as I can remember; that last rep, though . . . well, we just couldn't work it out. And now that we've made the change, I just don't see any point in rehashing what went wrong."

Megan hesitated only a fraction of a second. She glanced at Michael; when he gave a tiny gesture granting the go-ahead, she turned to face the buyer.

"I agree with you," she said boldly. "If the new line's working, there's no point in discussing this any further." The big Hendrick's man looked astonished. Megan continued. "But you've still got four of our lamps on the floor. All of them have problems. I'd like to straighten that out for you."

The buyer, still appearing stunned, said, "Why don't you take me out and show me?"

"First of all," Megan said, once they were on the floor and staring at a group of hand-painted porcelains

marked for retail in the four-hundred-dollar range,
"this metal gadget the shade's sitting on is called a
harp, and all these harps are the wrong size. If it's okay
with you, I'll bring the right ones in tomorrow morning
and replace them. You aren't likely to move a piece this
expensive when the shade isn't sitting correctly. Next,
this Kutani needs rewiring. I can bring a tool in and do
it before the store opens." Megan jiggled the lamp and
the bulb flickered. "You see? And there's nothing
wrong with the bulb; while we were waiting to see you,
I tested it. By the way, you've got several lamps from
other companies that need a little of this, that, or the
other. If you want, I'll see to those tomorrow also."

"You're joking! You're going to come in here with a
tool kit?"

"Yes, sir. If it's all right with you."

"Would that be part of your normal servicing?"

"Of course. Don't you usually get that from your
reps?"

"Ms. McBride, I've never seen a male rep with a tool
kit. I still think you're putting me on."

Megan's eyes twinkled; her point had clearly been
won. "No, I'm most assuredly not putting you on. Every
customer should be able to depend on the rep to replace
a harp or fix the wiring. It's not going to do me much
good to sell you lamps if they don't look good or if they
aren't functioning well enough for you to move them off
the floor. And speaking of selling you lamps, I'd be
happy to."

There was only a moment's hesitation while Megan
continued to gaze directly into the buyer's eyes. "I don't
think there's any way on earth I could pass up the opportunity to find out whether you mean what you're
saying," he said. "I'll leave word that you're to be admitted tomorrow morning through the employee entrance. After you've finished working on the lamps, call
for me and I'll take a look at what you've got to offer.
No! On second thought, call me *before* you finish. I've

just gotta see what you look like with a tool in your hand!''

When the session ended, Megan stole a glance at her watch. Ten-fifty-five. She calculated backwards: five minutes from car to purchasing offices, five minutes surveying the showroom floor, five minutes waiting for the buyer to emerge, another fifteen minutes to regain the account. If *that* didn't please Michael, nothing would!

The train of thought disturbed her. She wasn't supposed to be working for compliments, just for results, nor had she ever before dropped into such a trap. Naturally, it was a bonus to receive a pat on the back from an employer; on the other hand, reps who assumed ego strokes automatically went with their territories had no one but themselves to blame for the inevitable fall. If nothing else, time alone made it impossible; anyway, the paycheck was supposed to be the reward.

A familiar little bell sounded, the elevator doors rumbled open, and they squeezed in with morning shoppers for a white sale. Megan found herself wedged securely between two women overloaded with purchases. Each time one of them adjusted a package, she and Michael were thrown closer together. Before the doors even completed their ponderous roll-and-connect, imprisoning the passengers, the soft silk ruffles of her azure blouse were being crushed against the rougher fabric of Michael's suit coat.

It was necessary to appear unaffected. She pinned her eyes to an imaginary point over his left shoulder; instinctively, she also tried holding her breath, as though the maneuver could create nonexistent space. His cologne floated on the same airwaves that carried the Muzak. Of all things, the tune playing was a version of the one Manilow had closed with, "I Can't Smile Without You"; for some reason, this heightened Megan's sense of helpless embarrassment. When she felt it coming on—"the Irish plague," her father had teased during those preteen years when it had struck with such excruciating frequency—there was nothing to do except pray he wasn't looking at her; the blush spread, then deepened like a rose in the exciting flush of first bloom.

The door slid open on the third floor; Megan sucked in to make room for departures. She was thinking that, thank God, she too would be able to move; incredibly, however, for each person who got *off,* one and a half got *on.* The final sardine into the can threw her totally off balance. Michael's arm was suddenly around her waist, steadying her. Her spontaneous reaction was a quick, grateful look upward—if it were possible to laugh without actually making a sound, she saw immediately that Michael was doing just that! One side of his mouth tilted into a dimple she knew would disappear in a serious mood; the eyes were surrounded by deep crinkles and bright with suppressed laughter. Also in his expression was an element of tenderness, almost as though Michael were saying, "If I could, I'd get you out of this. Since I can't, we might as well make the most of it."

Megan was fascinated; she could no more have removed her eyes from his than she could have made the elevator stop, and whatever he read into her gaze, it had the effect of altering his. By the time they reached the second floor, the couple had inadvertently managed to capture the attention of everyone in the car; the tension between them spread like invisible sparks in an electrical storm: this was no ordinary attraction.

Neither of them noticed their audience, of course. For Megan, the intensity of his nearness blocked outside stimuli; energy was consumed by desire. His hand, now resting lightly on her waist, was a mysterious, potent sensory conductor; from the spot of contact, with nothing but thin silk protecting her bare skin, warm, pulsing rushes of passion flowed down, finally creating dangerous weakness in the long slender legs; she swayed once, his hand tightened and she felt the slight tremor in his fingers: the torture increased. The situation was one Megan could not have borne much longer; she didn't have to, for the elevator finally ground to a halt on the first floor. Just before the crowd began pushing from behind, he bent to whisper in her ear, "Will you be all right?"

Megan managed a wide-eyed nod, her head still upturned, eyes still locked onto his.

Michael said, "I'm glad. I really *can't* smile without you, you know."

As she tried to walk a straight line through the store and to the car, a tremulous little inner voice kept saying, There's no way. I can't work with him. I just can't do it.

The remainder of the day went quickly. Following their meeting with the Welcome Hotel contract agent, when Megan and Michael headed for his silver Porsche in the airport parking lot, she was surprised to see her watch showing five o'clock. A moment of panic took hold. This was it: bewitching hour. The problem was, Megan was so confused she had forgotten whether it was time for her to turn into a coach or a pumpkin. Inwardly, she smiled, relieved to realize she hadn't lost her sense of humor along with the rest of her wits. As Michael held open the passenger door, she stole a sidelong glance at him; one thing wasn't in doubt—the prince hadn't turned into a frog.

"I think we should have a glass of wine," he said. "Perhaps champagne would be better. To celebrate."

After he slid behind the wheel, she said, "Celebrate? Just what are we going to celebrate? I didn't write any million-dollar orders."

"Yes, you did. In your head, you wrote several. Now, how about that drink?"

"Okay, boss." She wondered if mention of a celebration drink was Michael's way of paying a compliment. The tiresome theme had played in her head off and on during the entire day; one moment she was telling herself not to be silly, that her relationship with her employer didn't entitle her to special praise, the next minute she would find herself once again indignant about his silence. Whether or not this was unreasonable, Megan wanted desperately to know what was going on in Michael's mind: did he approve of her sales technique and, if so, what would have been the harm in saying so? Vaguely, she suspected she had fallen somehow short of gaining complete professional approval; not only did this create anxiety, but she couldn't pinpoint an area in which she might be faulted; the day had gone remarkably well.

Michael concentrated on traffic. He was as poised behind the wheel as he was in his business dealings, exerting pressure only when absolutely necessary to negotiate a clean path through the chaotic rush-hour patterns. Megan noticed that every time he shifted, she could discern the slight ripple of muscles straining against the thin fabric of his shirt sleeve. It was the first time that day she had seen him without the suit jacket; before she knew it, her mind had returned to Saturday morning, to the feel of those arms around her, the hardness of muscles gripped in passion. Had it not been for the dramatic few minutes aboard the elevator, she might have doubted her employer even remembered the events in her yard. She continued looking at his arms. They were slender, like the rest of him, but there was also evidence of strength. Or is it power? Megan asked herself.

With the limitations of the business day behind her, Megan released her mind to wander freely. Michael's cologne, now faint, and her perfume wafted into the clean leathery sports-car smells, he shifted into second and made a left turn, and thoughts of where he was headed became secondary to where *they* were going, together.

Megan no longer had any doubts: no matter what direction he might take next, she wanted to be included.

Michael Richardson wasn't the type of man one could expect to meet twice in one lifetime; even if he wanted her along for only a few short turns of the calendar page, it would undoubtedly be worth the trip. It wasn't just his physical magnetism that created this desire, either; no, she realized that her respect for him was total, absolute. Perhaps this had been the ingredient missing from other might-have-been relationships, for Megan had always been a singularly nonjudgmental person, quick to like someone for what he was rather than what she wanted him to be, quick to translate faults into lovable little eccentricities; respect, however, wasn't easily earned or bestowed.

He switched on the car stereo. As Megan watched him adjust the settings, once again she became intrigued with the slender arms, the clear sensory memory of the time she had been folded within them. A sudden fantasy took hold: it had to do with all of Michael, not just the powerful arms, and Megan wanted to look to her left but dared not. Unwillingly, she had caught a glimpse of an occasion not yet enacted between them: not the vacation scene in her yard, with its built-in safety factors—no time, no privacy—and not today's limbo, either. Megan had conjured up a new and totally different world, one that was in many ways the most realistic. There were no clocks ticking, no planes to catch, no possibility of intrusion. In this scenario, Megan wasn't dressed in tennis shorts and Michael wasn't wearing business clothes. He advanced toward her . . . Slowly, she lifted her arms in willing submission . . .

A molten bolt of desire caught her unaware; she shivered. By the time Michael swung onto a quaint waterfront complex in Marina del Rey, Megan's frenzied mind had flashed portraits of passion she actually found frightening. Along with it, her intellect had also started flashing messages. Troublesome messages. One was in the form of a question: Could Megan lie alongside this man? Or would she be caught beneath him, trapped under the awesome power?

He parked directly in front of a grocery store, then left the engine running while he opened his door. Megan looked over quizzically.

"I'll be just a minute," he said. She gathered he had a plan, but by the time she could ask, he was halfway into the store; when he emerged he was carrying a nondescript brown sack that he placed in the back of the Porsche without a word. As he slid the little sports car smoothly in with the traffic on an adjacent street, Megan thought wryly that Michael Richardson wasn't a man who offered explanations; with that firm sense of confidence that sometimes appeared on his face as downright arrogance, he simply made up his mind, then, zip, he accomplished the task. She asked herself why this trait, in Michael, was attractive, when it revealed other men as shallow, one-dimensional, and boringly selfish. Finally, she sighed, wondering why she was making such a big deal of a grocery sack; he had probably been asked to pick up a loaf of bread for his home, or something equally mundane. A few minutes later she would recall the thought with the realization that *nothing* Michael Richardson did could be described as mundane.

About three minutes later, after a few zigs and zags down side streets leading to the ocean, he parked again, this time in a beachfront lot. Three weeks after Labor Day, it was sparsely populated; a few summer diehards—high school kids who inevitably hit the beach at the end of each day's classes—trudged toward their cars, surfboards in hand. As usual, Megan thought it was a shame the schools had to reopen in September. During her own student years, the month, traditionally California's loveliest, had been symbolic: like life, it teased and excited while it also demanded a renewal of allegiance to duty. On this particular day fading into evening, it was at its elegant best. Crystal-clear warm air magnified the sun and settled onto both sand and surf in countless infinitesimal specks of diamond dust; sea gulls circled innocently, then, with unerring accuracy, zeroed in on invisible prey.

Michael had swiveled to face her. One arm was draped casually over his seatback. "Feel like taking a walk?"

Instinctively, she looked down at her high-heeled shoes. It was a reaction he had apparently anticipated. He said, "We can follow the sidewalk and then stick to the pier; I think it'll be okay as long as you don't get into sand."

He didn't wait for an answer; before Megan knew it, her door popped open and Michael extended a hand to help her out; with the other, he gripped the grocery sack.

5

As it turned out, Michael had stocked up for an impromptu picnic. With the waves lapping below them, trying as always to loosen the pilings of the ancient historic pier, he covered the planking with a paper tablecloth—she noticed it was checkered, like the one that night at the Italian restaurant—and then pulled a chilled champagne bottle plus two perfect little plastic goblets from the brown bag. Just as she was certain all the rabbits were out of the hat, he dug to the bottom and came up with two slender tapered candles in an ingenious package containing disposable wax candlesticks.

"You know," she said softly, then waited for the hollow but familiar *Pop!* as Michael coaxed the cork free, "I . . . I really think this is wonderful."

He handed one of the little goblets across the checkered cloth, then raised his own. "To our new rep," he said simply. "May you have the success you deserve."

They sipped the bubbly drink in silence. Megan didn't know why, but it seemed right. The chatter from the gulls filled the space and the time; it was the transition she had needed.

"Refill?" he asked, raising slightly on his knees.

"I will," she said, still in an unusually gentle voice, "if you'll let me make the next toast." He nodded and stretched to pour the champagne. Before he settled back onto the planks, sitting with his feet crossed

Indian-style, he loosened his tie and unbuttoned the top of his shirt; with her glass raised in the toast she had planned, Megan stared with frank fascination at a tiny line of perspiration on the summer blond hair of his chest.

When Michael stopped fiddling with his shirt, he reached for his own newly filled champagne goblet. But then, looking at Megan, he changed his mind and released the glass, then began methodically restructuring his seating arrangement. By the time he finished, only his left leg remained in the Indian position. The other foot was flat against the pier, supporting his right leg in an inverted V. He propped an arm casually atop the raised knee and then, leaning back against the other arm, studied Megan with as much interest as she was studying him.

She finally put down her glass. "What are you thinking?" she ventured shyly.

"That there's something you need. Something I want to give you." In a second, he was up. In another second, he had crossed the distance and pulled her to her feet; he pinned her firmly within his arms and spent the next few beats of time gazing down into her glazed eyes. Then he kissed her, and Megan met his lips with exquisite hunger; her tongue probed for his with a need immeasurable by normal standards; she pressed her body forward, and when that wasn't enough she joined him in the writhing movements choreographed and understood only by lovers. For Megan, every square centimeter of skin was alive with nerve endings desperate for fulfillment. Her nipples were heated points of friction searching for the right contact. If she had been capable of conscious thought, she would have recognized a striking irony.

Megan was experiencing the most purely pleasurable sensations of her life. Through an unfortunate but common syndrome combining nerves and doubt into a form of self-induced mental paralysis, she had denied herself

these feelings until the inevitable time—now—they
would be forced to the surface by a man of Michael's
sensual power; in other words, someone who literally
could not be resisted. But the intensity of the pleasure
was building to a plateau creating unbearable need for
relief, and she was seeking it in the wrong way; by
twisting her body in cadence with his, she only increased both pleasure and need. Her instinctive pelvic
motion against the hardened throbbing center of Michael's identical need was a struggle in vain; layers of
clothing took care of that. He gasped and cried out her
name—or was it she who gasped and his name the one
that echoed across the pounding surf?

Terrific tension is a tight, fragile wire that can be easily snapped. For Megan and Michael the breaking point
came in the form of a sudden cacophony of cheers and
whistles and catcalls; if a great white shark had dived
onto the pier's planks, the reaction would have been the
same; they loosened their holds and stood stock, stone
still. Her heart continued racing, but for a different reason. And then Michael chuckled. "Guess what?" he
said. "We've been providing entertainment for the local
fishermen. Take a look down the pier."

Sure enough, about fifty feet distant, a group of five
old geezers wearing grimy overalls were huddled together, obviously enjoying the show. Megan groaned.

"Oh, come on, honey!" Michael teased. "Don't let it
get to you. There's no harm intended."

One of them broke away and started walking briskly
in their direction. By the time he drew near, Megan was
standing sedately at Michael's side, hands folded; she
was so busy fighting back "the Irish plague" that she
failed at first to notice what the weathered fisherman
was carrying, which turned out to be a string dangling
two newly caught halibut, each about a foot long. When
he thrust it toward her, she almost missed and ended up
with a silk halibut blouse.

"The fellas and me want you to have it," he said,

looking down and shuffling his feet. Then he mumbled, "I guess it's true the whole world loves a lover. Anyway, you folks capped off a pretty good fishin' day for us, so . . ."

Michael extended his hand and said, "Mighty nice of you, mister."

The fisherman's reaction made it clear that any further expression of gratitude would make him uncomfortable. Megan admired the way Michael chose to handle the situation. He gestured toward the checkered cloth and contents, including the half-filled champagne bottle. "If you'll pick this junk up for us," he said, "I'll take the lady here somewhere we can cook up that fish."

The old guy nodded, understanding, then bent and scooped up the champagne. Without another word, he headed back to his friends. Michael took the string of fish from Megan and reached down for his tie; when he had it in hand he said, "Get your purse, Ms. McBride. It's time for us to make a standard decision: your place or mine?"

Driving north toward Westwood, Megan was prepared to answer: "My place." Before she got a chance, though, Michael told her his question had not been serious; he wanted to check on his son, he explained, so their fish fry would take place at the Richardson house. He added that the housekeeper would have left his and Jeffie's dinner under the kitchen warming lights, as usual, then grinned and said, "We won't even have to share our catch. Jeffie hates fish." Megan decided not to tell him she hated fish, too. She sank into the cushy upholstery of the car seat, totally mellow. Come what may, she would be spending the evening with Michael; for that, she would gladly have eaten broiled gorilla toes.

They pulled into a circular driveway. Michael's home was a charming two-story English Tudor structure of old brick peeking from beneath overgrown ivy.

"Uh-oh," Michael said as he cut the engine. "There's a note on the front door. That usually means trouble."

Megan sat up straighter, watching him cover the short sidewalk with long, purposeful strides. He ripped the white paper from its fastening on a decorative brass knocker and scanned the sheet briefly, then returned with it to the car. She had rolled down her window and he leaned through it.

"My niece has taken Jeffie to the UCLA Medical Center, Megan. According to this," he rattled the paper, "he's got a bum ankle—from football practice—that keeps swelling. When Tara couldn't reach me, she assumed I'd want it X-rayed."

She nodded, noting his expression. Since Michael wasn't the type to overreact to a sports injury, it wasn't difficult to deduce he was going through the guilt all parents experience when they're not available to help a child.

"Mind driving over with me?" he asked. "It isn't exactly what we planned . . ."

"For heaven's sake!" she said, genuinely surprised. "This is no time to worry about *me.* Come on, let's go."

The UCLA Medical Center was only a few miles from Westwood; during the drive Megan tried to keep Michael occupied answering questions about his boy. She learned that Jeffie was a high school freshman taking his first serious crack at team sports. His father said he was an amazingly strong punter and that succeeding at football meant a great deal to him; it seemed that Jeffie was smaller than most ninth graders.

"It's a moot point now," he said. "You can't punt with a broken ankle."

"Don't jump to conclusions," she said gently. "Maybe it's just sprained. Look, there's the emergency entrance."

Michael was at the information desk longer than he should have been. Megan finally grew concerned; she put down the magazine and crossed the waiting room to

stand beside him. He told her there was no registration
for a Jeffrey Allen Richardson. "They're checking the
emergency room at pediatrics," he reported, looking
grim.

"Why don't you come over and sit down?" she suggested.

"I couldn't do that, Megan." His voice was stern; she
had a feeling, however, that Michael was reprimanding
himself. The tiny threads creasing his brow spelled a
distress pattern; the man was convinced he had com-
mitted a dreadful parental misdeed, as though being
absent when Jeffie was injured was the same as gross
neglect. She had seen this syndrome often enough with
friends to know better than to think she could relieve it.
A nurse appeared to report that she was sorry, they still
hadn't located his son. Now Michael appeared totally
anguished, haunted. Megan felt helpless; as much as
she wanted to help, she couldn't imagine what she
might do. Feeling silly, she asked him to tell her his
niece's last name.

"Montgomery," he answered. "Why?"

If Michael hadn't understood the reason for the question, the nurse had. She raised a panel and stepped to
the other side of the information desk, then sat down
and started pressing keys on a computer. After only a
few seconds, she looked up and smiled. "Mr. Richardson, it appears that one of our brilliant technicians
couldn't tell your son and your niece apart; we now
have a patient named Jeffrey Allen *Montgomery*. But if
you want to see him, you'll have to go back to the casting room; according to this, he's about to be fitted for
half a pair of white plaster trousers."

A male orderly took Michael through swinging doors
marked PRIVATE: NO ENTRY. Megan crossed the room
again; when she found that both her seat and her magazine were in use, she decided to remain standing. In less
than ten minutes, Michael was back. This time he was
wearing a rueful expression; it was an improvement

over the look of agonized guilt she had last seen. "Well, that's it for football," he said.

"I'm sorry, Michael." Megan touched his arm briefly with her fingertips. "How's he feeling?"

"Terrific," said the beleaguered father with a grin. "Somebody shot him full of Demerol. At the moment, Jeffie thinks the world is rosy, just rosy."

Megan grinned back. "Is it a bad break?"

"No, but it'll still keep him in a cast for six weeks, maybe longer."

"Where's your niece?"

Michael laughed. "Jeffie talked her into going with him to the casting room. He was singing the 'Star Spangled Banner' and insisting he needed a soprano for harmony."

Megan giggled. "So now what?"

"I told Tara we'd be in the coffee shop when the patient is ready to be transported. You and I can drive him back and get him settled, then we can—"

Megan reached out and touched Michael's hand with her fingertips. "This is a night for family," she said gently. "I'm going to call someone to pick me up."

His face fell.

"Awww . . ." Megan teased. "Don't look like that, boss! Tomorrow's a new day. And surely you agree your son needs all your attention tonight."

"But you can help, Megan. You know, fix hot chocolate, something like that. Then we can stoke up a big fire and—"

"Wait a minute," Megan laughed. "Who normally fixes the hot chocolate in your household?"

"Well, Tara, but she—"

"But she might not take kindly to finding herself replaced."

Michael was silent for a long moment, lost in thought. When he spoke, it was with firm deliberation. "Nope. What you're suggesting is possible, granted, but I think both my son and my niece are more secure than that. Anyway, I'm not prepared to be as cautious as you are, Megan. What do the psychologists have to say about grown-ups who need grown-ups?"

Megan was shaken. His point was inarguable. She said, "I'm willing to take the chance if you are. Come on, let's grab that cup of coffee before Jeffie gets out of the casting room. By now, they're probably singing the third stanza."

As it turned out, there was a hot and cold beverage machine in the waiting room, which was just as well; they would never have made it back from the cafeteria in time for the emergence of the patient; from the time she stirred milk into her coffee, the wait was probably no longer than a quarter hour. And then, just as soon as a nurse warned them to watch the swinging doors, Megan saw a small brunette girl bounce through, survey the waiting room and then wave to Michael; this, she figured, must be Tara, his niece.

Jeffrey Allen Richardson, with a new cast from the toes of his right leg to just above his knee, was a surprise. Megan hadn't been expecting the exact opposite of Michael, but the nurse wheeled in an elfin child who looked more like ten than fourteen; he had jet black hair, brown eyes, and a deep olive complexion. Jeffie gave the impression that, even without the Demerol, he was delightfully full of spirit and personality. When Michael introduced them, the teenager actually winked. Then he said—much to Tara's evident disapproval—"All riiiight! It's about time Dad got himself a pretty girlfriend! Hey, you wanta be the first one to sign my cast?"

"That's quite an honor," Megan replied with mock gravity. "How can you be sure I deserve such an accolade?"

"Hey, Dad!" Jeffie threw an excited look at his father. "Didja hear that? She used the word *accolade!* And she used it properly!"

Michael's eyes twinkled as he turned toward Megan.

"I can assure you that in my son's eyes you have just joined the ranks of the very deserving. Jeffie's what you might call a dictionary buff; and I think it's fair to say his pet peeve is abuse of the English language."

Megan said, "Is that so? Apropos of our signature ceremony, then, I shall guard my reputation against any and all malapropisms."

Her word play went unnoticed, at least by Jeffie. His head relaxed to one side, his eyelids drooped closed despite a single valiant attempt to keep them open, and he started snoring. The white-uniformed nurse hastened to assure the group there was nothing amiss. "He hasn't fainted. His body's just stopped pumping excess adrenaline. The Demerol, plus his own fatigue, have taken over. In all likelihood he'll sleep right through the night. In the morning he'll be mystified about how he got home."

She was right. With Tara following close behind, Michael and Megan pulled into the circular driveway. It took all three to maneuver the small slumped form through the front door, up a winding staircase, and into a bedroom cluttered with books and posters and gadgets, including an impressive-looking computer. While the other two supported Jeffie, Megan turned down the covers of the double bed, noting with sadness that the papers she removed were Xeroxed diagrams of complex football patterns.

Megan waited in the wide hallway while Michael and his niece coaxed the thwarted punter into pajamas. This portion of the large house was dominated by a family photo gallery which spanned much of one corridor wall from ceiling to floor. Megan wandered over to peer more closely at the literally hundreds of pictures. It was a historian's delight; there were sepia-toned portraits dating back to the early nineteenth century. She worked her way forward in time, finally coming across a photo that she thought, at first, was Jeffie. With a jolt that sent shivers along her spine, though, Megan soon realized she was looking at the boy's mother. There was the same dark complexion, identical brown eyes and thick black hair cropped short and framing an elfin face; nor could there be any doubt where Jeffie had inherited his small stature.

Megan liked the story unfolding along the picture wall. The Richardson clan had been a happy one; and the harmony hadn't stopped with Mrs. Richardson's death, either. Michael had kept the gallery updated with photos of various individual milestones plus father-son occasions: the normal things—snapshots of grade school graduation, a picture of Jeffie and Dad wearing leis and waving from the foot of an airline boarding ramp—and the impression was of a boy who had grown increasingly secure in his father's love and interest.

Her eye was caught by something a little out of the ordinary, a plaque arranged within a frame containing a newspaper clipping; she stepped closer to the wall, squinting to read the copy. The plaque had been received eight years previously by Ann Montgomery Richardson, University of Southern California, Department of Chemical Sciences: Instructor of the Year. When Megan reviewed the accompanying article, she realized Ann Richardson had never known about her award, though. According to the *Los Angeles Times,* Mrs. Richardson, an amateur downhill ski competitor, had been killed two days before the ceremony, struck by a fragment from a boulder disintegrating higher up the mountain.

Megan had become so immersed in her inspection of the gallery that she hadn't heard Michael's approach on the thick carpeting. Now, standing directly behind her, he said, "Ann wouldn't have complained, at least not about the way it happened. It was painless, instant, and it occurred when she was doing something she loved. Even Jeffie agrees with me."

She turned and offered a weak smile. No one was in a

better position than she to understand the factors involved in accepting the death of a young person; obviously Michael *had* accepted it.

She asked about Jeffie. "Still asleep?"

"Yes, and I've learned something. He may not weigh very much, but as a bundle to be carried up that particular staircase, it's plenty! Thanks for your help, Megan." Just then, Tara walked out; he asked if she knew what time it was.

"A little before ten."

"No wonder I'm hungry! Have you eaten?"

Tara shook her curly brown head.

"Then let's go downstairs and see if we can remedy the situation."

Tara said, "I can't, Uncle Michael; I've got an English lit quiz tomorrow. If I don't go over to the library and study Keats, I'll never—"

Her uncle interrupted with unexpected severity. "No. You're not driving alone to the library, not at this hour."

Megan steeled herself for the inevitable indignant response. The niece surprised her, however. She just looked fondly at her uncle and then said, teasingly, "The last time this happened, you asked me to remind you, *next* time, that I'm a big girl now."

"That has nothing to do with it," Michael snapped.

"Now you're going to give me the lecture about what kind of people are out driving around, and I'm going to say the campus is only five minutes away, then you'll—"

Michael raised a palm. "Okay," he said wearily, "I surrender. You're right about that." When he paused at that point, the piercing look he gave his niece was enough to make Megan squirm. There was something vaguely familiar about the scene but she couldn't recall what; as she searched her memory, Michael completed his argument to Tara with: "What you're wrong about, young lady, is almost everything else; since you know how I feel about you driving alone, though, we'll skip it for now. Go on and get your studying done."

Still smiling—which Megan thought exceedingly odd under the circumstances—Tara stood on tiptoes to peck her uncle on the cheek. With a wave to Megan, she scurried down the stairs and out of the house. About the time Megan heard the front door slam shut, her mind kicked in the strange conversation she and Michael had had at the Italian restaurant. He had been uncomfortably persistent during a discussion on the subject of physical safety; she also recalled her suspicions that something personal and painful was at the root of his probe. Evidently she had guessed correctly, although there was no way for her to discern, from the scant exchange between him and Tara, what had happened to create such concern. At the moment, she was less curious than she might otherwise have been; Megan's primary interest was the fact that she and Michael were alone again.

"How about you?" he asked. "Have you got to run to the library, too, or are you still hungry for fish?"

She wrinkled her nose. "Michael, we didn't take them out of the car—"

He snapped his fingers. "Damn! I doubt they're safe to eat now. Sorry, Megan."

"I'll live," she mumbled under her breath.

"What'd you say?"

"Oh, nothing," she said quickly. "What shall we eat, then?"

"Follow me," he said, heading downstairs. When they reached the bottom, he told her to circle around the staircase, down the hall, and take the first left. "I'll take care of our interrupted cocktail hour," he promised. "If there's no champagne, will Chablis do?"

By the time Michael joined her in the kitchen, a large modern expanse of white that would have appeared clinical had it not been for a virtual jungle of hanging greenery plus a central island of bright green Spanish tile, Megan had located a skillet and a pound of bacon.

"Breakfast okay with you?"

He was rummaging through a drawer. "Sounds fine. I put your wine on the counter by the stove and—oh good, I found it—here's an apron. Let's see if it makes you look domesticated." Megan slipped into the frilly smock and tied it quickly around her waist. Michael studied the effect, then shook his head. "Nope. I don't think there's any way you're ever going to fit the stereotyped image of a *Hausfrau.*"

"Good. Who waters all these plants?"

"I do. It's sort of a hobby. In fact, there's a greenhouse out back. I'll show it to you in the morning."

Megan's heart lurched. She tried to sound casual. "In the morning?"

"Sorry," he said. "That kind of slipped out. But I do want you to stay the night. We've got a tricky situation; your car's still in the office lot. If I drive you home, we'll be leaving Jeffie alone. So you can stay in the spare bedroom and—"

Her heart was racing. Even though she realized the issue was the same his niece had confronted, mention of spending the night in this house was playing all sorts of games with Megan's heart and head; she was assaulted by a combination of erotica and unwelcome fantasies in which she *belonged* here, cooking bacon and eggs, waking up beside Michael every morning . . .

Reality beckoned. "You don't need all those complications tonight," she said sympathetically. "If Tara's not back from the library in time, I'll just take a cab." When she saw the look on his face, she stopped talking. This was getting complicated! Unless Megan were very much mistaken, the man straddling a bar stool beside the center island was now very much an employer; he wore an expression of imperious dignity, as though he were trying to rise above his disgust with some flagrant display of stupidity. She turned quickly back to the stove, not wanting him to see her reaction. In this area, Megan didn't have the tools to cope; she lacked Tara's knowledge and experience. Furthermore, it was late, she was tired, and she hadn't eaten since noon; her temper was short and she didn't want that sort of spontaneous combustion to ignite between her and Michael. Taking a deep breath, she started a silent count to ten; by the time she turned around again she was calmer.

Michael was tired, too, that much she saw at once. His blond hair was tousled and a single thick lock waved over his forehead; the shirt collar, unbuttoned earlier that evening, fell into a loose V. Megan could see two distinctly contrasting elements: the man of authority whose decisions had the power to send shock waves through several corporations and hundreds of employees, and the man who felt pain just like everyone else, a man who could be comforted by a gentle caress.

Without intending to, Megan had just grasped a new concept. It was the first time she had ever thoroughly understood the relationship between men and women; without any real background, she had always overcomplicated it. And it was amazingly simple: if things were right, two people could stand for each other like a permanent barrier against the harshness of the world. Now, in place of the anger she had felt a moment ago, she wanted desperately to walk across and put her arms around Michael—what difference did it make that they disagreed about how she would get home that night? Her first priority was to make him feel better—but she didn't have the nerve.

Once again, she turned back to the bacon, trying frantically to think of a way to get Michael to relax. Suddenly it occurred to her—just change the subject, start his mind on a different track. Little did she know it then, but with all good intentions she was about to make a serious error in judgment. If Megan's timing had ever been off, it was now.

She chose a topic of mutual concern. Keeping her voice casual, she said, "I really appreciated your taking time to introduce me to the buyers today, Michael. But, you know, with all the excitement and the interruptions, we never had a chance for a wrap-up. Anything you want to say now?"

It took him so long to answer, she began to think he hadn't heard her. Then he said, with apparent resignation, "I'll have to say it sooner or later. For an experienced rep, Megan, you should know better than to take back merchandise we've already listed as sold. I'm talking about that stunt with the bronze statues at Mrs. Klein's store."

She whirled to face him, immeasurably stung. "You're joking!"

He leaned back on the stool and folded his arms across his chest. If the tilt of his provocative lips was any indication, he was amused by her indignation. "No," he said deliberately, almost mockingly, "it's hardly a joking matter, Megan. Who gave you the authority to do that?"

"You did!" she snapped. "The night you interviewed me, you made some pretty strong statements about making sure sales work to the benefit of the customer."

"We were discussing back orders, if you'll recall. Nothing else."

Megan's green eyes flashed and narrowed dangerously. If this man were trying to humiliate her—She opened her mouth, then bit back the words she had been about to speak. Wait a minute, she suddenly thought: this can't be treated as strictly business; Michael *isn't* just a new employer. Clearly they had just hit the first of the quirks she had known might damage the budding relationship. Unless she wanted it to happen, she would have to tone down, find a reaction acceptable in both areas, business and personal. And she resented it.

"I suppose you would have handled Mrs. Klein's

problem differently?" she asked. The question hadn't
come out quite right; she had intended merely to throw
the ball back, but somehow a note of sarcasm had crept
in. Like a shot Michael was off the bar stool and standing behind her. With hands placed firmly on her shoulders, she was forced to turn; once she faced him, looking
up at ice-cube eyes, Megan knew their troubled waters
had grown deeper. As she tried to keep from squirming
under the authoritarian gaze, she also realized, once
and for all, this wasn't a man to fool around with. All
Megan's previous years of practiced independence in
what was still, after all, a man's world couldn't alter
the fact that whatever Michael Richardson said, if he
were convinced he was right—*that was the way it was
going to be.* And now, with his fingers clenching her
shoulders, he was talking to her in a voice so unnaturally
calm and low, it was threatening for just that reason.
"You suppose wrong, Megan. I would have done exactly the same with Mrs. Klein. But I'm the president of
the company; when I hired you I expected you to know
enough to ask for my decisions, not to try making them
for me. As long as Ling and Son pays my salary, I have no
ethical right to let an employee—not even you—sidestep
policy. I'm paid to ensure Ling's profits."

What incredible arrogance! Megan thought. Now she
was far too angry to examine the issue beyond its facade. And yes, she admitted to herself, she was also
hurt. Only a couple of minutes ago, she had reminded
herself Michael was more than an employer. This was
the man who had stood with her on a pier and, just before sunset, raised her to heights previously unex-
plored; too quickly, she was learning that the same
mind and body could plunge her to frightening emotional depths. And for what—saving an account? The
frustration she had felt earlier, when he had failed to
comment about it, fused with her current resentment
and pain, culminated in an automatic power surge.

"Take your hands off me." The words were pronounced slowly. She started untying her apron. "If you wish to issue an official reprimand, Mr. President, you may do so during business hours. I'm on my own time now and I intend to go home to my own house."

He didn't release his grip; he tightened it. But when he spoke there was a new note, a weary suggestion of sympathy that belied the actual words. "Megan, stop acting like a prima donna. Please. This isn't the time or place, I agree, but you're the one who brought up business, not I."

When she tried to interrupt, he put two fingers gently to her lips, then quickly replaced his hands and used them as levers to pull her forward. Once she was pressed against Michael's tense, firm body, pinned by arms locked behind her back, he continued. Now his voice was extremely soft and unmistakably sympathetic. "Baby, listen to me . . . when you've heard the explanation you'll understand. What if Mrs. Klein were the type to call the office constantly, placing reorders before she'd checked her inventory? We've got a few of those, you know, and some of them are purposely trying to confuse the billing issue so they can delay payment. Until you're more acquainted with the client list, you'll *have* to check with me."

Megan went limp in his arms; it wasn't relaxation, it was a total cave-in. Unfortunately, his words had found their mark; he was absolutely right; she couldn't believe she had provoked such a scene. With a bit less emotion and a lot more logic, the whole thing could have been prevented, in the beginning, with a simple request for explanation.

Evidently Michael misinterpreted her reaction. As soon as he felt Megan's tension drain away, his own body also slackened. He brought his lips gently to hers. When she failed to respond, he looked down, puzzled.

All Megan could think of to say was, "Michael?"

"Yes?"

"The bacon's burning."

6

Tuesday morning, she awakened in her own bed. Michael's car was in the garage. Halfway through their late-night breakfast, while they were pretending to eat, Megan had remembered her commitment to repair the Hendrick's lamps before the opening of the store. It had turned into an easy point for compromise; without a trace of emotion, Michael had suggested she take the Porsche. He explained he wouldn't be leaving for the office until Jeffie was awake; after that, Tara or the housekeeper could give him a lift. "Whenever it's convenient," he added, "you can switch cars in the company lot."

She had barely made it through her front door before she heard Sinbad screech, "Door! Door!" Sure enough, the phone was ringing.

"Just wanted to make sure you're home, safe," Michael said, and then, "No, that's not true. There are two other things. First, I want to see you when you come by the office tomorrow. Second, I suggest you avoid thinking about what just happened, at least for tonight, Megan. You're exhausted. And besides, this is a matter the two of us need to communicate better; if we don't, all the thought in the world isn't going to help. Agreed?"

After mumbling her assent, too tired to have much of an idea what he was saying, really, she spent a few minutes with Sinbad and then dragged herself into the bed-

room. Just before she fell asleep it occurred to her that,
for the very first time, her bed wasn't the cozy refuge
she had always considered it. Her life could now be
sharply categorized: pre-Michael Richardson and
after-Michael Richardson. This realization frightened
her, for it seemed that recent events had probably
closed off all possibility of ever sharing a bed with him.
As Megan's eyelids drooped shut, she was thinking, I
wanted you tonight, Michael. Back there in your
kitchen, I should have put my arms around you. If I
had, would we be lying together now?

Surprisingly, she slept well. And her mind was on Michael before she ever opened her eyes. In the light of
day, when she once again reasonably rested, things appeared considerably less serious. She stretched, then
sank back under the covers to think. What she decided
was that *he* hadn't said anything to indicate he wanted
to end the relationship (almost before it got started!)—
she couldn't be certain of that, of course, for she seemed
to misunderstand so much of what he said—which
therefore left the issue to *her*. And she wasn't about to
give up; anyone who could make her feel that good, and
that bad, she admitted ruefully, was worth fighting for.

If she were going to make it to Hendrick's on time,
she would have to start the morning routine. Megan
swung her feet over the side of the bed and slipped into
little satin footlets. She went to her closet and, ignoring
the business clothes again, pulled out a pale gray,
clingy wool jersey dress; before she left the house, she
remembered to apply Opium.

By the time she turned into the office parking lot, it
was well after noon. She entered the reception area
with a brisk step, then forced herself to slow down and
greet the receptionist. As soon as she passed toward the
inner corridors, however, she picked up the pace again.
She was desperate to see Michael, to be reassured that
all was well.

There was a woman in the formerly empty anteroom, apparently the secretary who had been absent because of illness. She looked up curiously. "May I help you?"

"I'm Megan McBride, a new rep. He's expecting me."

"Oh! It's nice to meet you," the woman said. She was a pleasant-looking grandmotherly type; she was also very nervous, Megan thought. "I haven't been back long enough to catch up on all the news," she continued, "but Mr. Richardson said he'd hired someone fantastic for this area. Congratulations . . . we sure need a good rep."

"Thanks. Can I go in?"

"Not now, I'm afraid. He's with Mr. Ling." Apparently the secretary was distressed by this fact. Megan was intensely curious about George Ling, the son of the firm's original founder. The Ling family had fueled many a Southern California rumor for the past five decades. It seemed that each big bank had a Ling on the board of directors, each major university boasted either a Ling regent or a Ling building. Depending on whom you believed, the Lings were either a family of benevolent benefactors or descendants of Chinese mobsters.

"Shall I wait here?"

The secretary glanced anxiously at her watch. "Are you sure you want to? It might be quite a while."

Michael's door swung open and he stepped out. Just behind him and visible through the crack in the door, Megan glimpsed George Ling's blue-suited back. She turned her eyes toward Michael and smiled warmly. He answered with a brief nod. "You've met Adelle?"

Before she could answer, he had turned to the secretary, who was reaching for the papers he extended. "These are the Italian confirmations," he said. "Try reaching our agent at home. Before Friday, I want every foreign order confirmed, and I want you to do it personally; by phone, not Telex. And that memo to the showrooms is just as important. Can you get it typed and mailed this afternoon?"

Adelle nodded as though she had been expecting the orders. "Do you want me to put your personal stamp on the confirmation?"

"At this point, it's meaningless. Let's just do it this way and hope it flies." He turned to Megan, who had adjusted her expression to fit the serious business atmosphere.

"I haven't got time to talk. In fact, I've got to make a four o'clock flight to New York. Can you do me a favor?"

She nodded. "First, though, here are the car keys."

He pocketed the small silver ring with the Porsche keys, then extracted them again and pulled one loose. "This is the house key," he told Megan. "I'd like you to keep it and look in on Jeffie at least once while I'm gone. This trip wasn't exactly planned. I've talked to Mrs. Simmons and she's going to sleep at the house, but it would make me feel better if you'd go over and check, anyway. I wouldn't ask if you didn't live so close."

"Of course," Megan mumbled. She wanted to know how long he would be away but something prevented her from speaking.

"Thanks," Michael said before turning toward his office. Then he stopped and turned back. "Megan, some time in the next couple of days, I think you should stop back by here and take a look through the warehouse. They're too busy in the back now—everyone's wiring those porcelains for Ohio—but there were some new arrivals over the weekend. They haven't been photographed yet, but I don't see any reason you can't take Polaroids and sell them while I'm gone. Either Adelle or the warehouse manager can give you the prices and the quantities." He walked into the office and shut the door behind him. Two of Adelle's telephone lines started ringing.

Megan slipped unnoticed from the office. When she reached her car, she slid in and grabbed the steering wheel. She bent her forehead to touch the backs of her hands, then let out a prolonged ragged breath. "Oh God," she said to the empty car, "I was just saved from the worst mistake of my life. I don't even *know* that man in there." When she finally straightened up, she remembered to put Michael's house key on her chain. What an irony, Megan thought.

She forced herself to make two more sales calls. The results were encouraging, and Megan accepted a glass of wine when the owner of the second store closed his doors for the day. By the time she emerged, after six o'clock, she was in better spirits. With a new perspective following the miserable sojourn in Michael's office, Megan had decided that, once again, her reaction was silly. Her employer had been caught in both a time and a business bind; he had reacted exactly as she probably would have under the circumstances. What could he have done differently, she asked herself—thrown his arms around her and declared his intentions for the entire company to hear?

Actually, she was being too hard on herself. Somewhere in the back of her mind, Megan also knew that a scene like the one at Ling and Son would have been equally upsetting to Michael; there were *excellent* reasons for avoiding a romantic liaison with an employer. In fact, she was finding it nearly impossible to adjust to being treated in the efficient, impersonal manner required during business hours. And, Megan reminded herself, there would be many other times Michael would be forced to act as he had this afternoon. In order to survive the traumas, they would have to have the stamina, determination, and resilience of quick-change artists. Did they? She was almost grateful he was in New York; both of them needed time to think.

Standing on her doorstep at home she struggled, as usual, to balance her briefcase and get the door open when she suddenly stopped, staring in puzzlement at the keychain. Of course—in the intervening time, she had forgotten Michael's request that she look in on Jeffie. Anticipating a quiet night at home because her tutoring session had been rescheduled to Thursdays, she sighed, and headed back toward her car.

Tara answered the door. The minute she saw who it was, she said, "Oh, good! Uncle Michael said you'd stop by. And I think you're just what the doctor ordered. Come on in, Miss McBride."

Megan asked how she had done on the English lit quiz. Tara answered that if she hadn't made it over to the library she would never have passed. "And, by the way, Miss McBride," Tara said, "I'm sorry you got caught in that last night." All at once, she smiled broadly. "But then, I guess we're all used to it by now. One of these days Uncle Michael's bound to get over it, huh?"

Obviously Tara wasn't aware that Megan and her uncle had known each other such a short time. She was about to ask for an explanation when the niece bounded up the first steps of the circular staircase. Megan followed; she was thinking it was probably just as well they hadn't gotten sidetracked; although she was intensely curious, she hadn't forgotten the purpose of her visit.

Jeffie was lying on his bed with the casted leg propped on a pillow. To Megan's surprise, he remembered her from the night before; this elicited a grin. "I guess you thought I was too doped up, huh? Well, guess what? There's a red marking pen over there and I haven't even forgotten you promised to be first to sign my cast. Ready?" Tara brought the pen from Jeffie's desk and, after Megan's signature glowed against the spotless white plaster, added her own with a flourish; then she went downstairs to check the progress of dinner. Jeffie wrapped his arms dramatically around his midsection and rocked to and fro. "Ahhh . . . what I wouldn't give to be able to get to the kitchen! That roast beef smells sooo good—and I can't steal even one little bite!"

"You haven't been stuck up here all day, have you?" Megan asked.

He nodded. "You should have seen Dad struggling to get me downstairs; it was a riot. For a few minutes, I thought we'd both end up with broken bones. Anyway, after a few stairs, I asked him to bring me back."

When Megan recalled the difficulty three of them had experienced the night before, she had no trouble imagining the scene. "It must be kind of lonely up here," she said. "Are you going to get dinner on a tray?"

Jeffie wrinkled his nose. "Affirmative. And you're right about it being lonely. I should have let Dad take me down. Now I'm stuck here because the doctor told Dad this morning that the only way I could move any distance was to be carried. I'm not allowed to hop around on the leg, and I can't even start using crutches until this blasted thing's been X-rayed again." He thumped his cast and grimaced. "That's not for another week."

"What will you do up here?" Megan was worried. Michael had undoubtedly assumed he would be returning this evening. Now that he'd been forced to leave town, there appeared no safe way for Jeffie to maneuver between the floors of the house. And he needed an occasional change of surroundings to avoid depression. If nothing else, Megan thought he should be moved downstairs permanently; there, he could talk to people passing through the living areas. She remembered herself at Jeffie's age; several days' confinement to one room would have been intolerable. In fact, she thought, it wouldn't be much easier for an adult.

"I can slither over to my Apple, though," Jeffie was saying. His eyes went to the machine Megan had noticed the night before. "If I can't play football, at least I can fool around with the computer."

She asked how he felt about missing out on football.

"I blew it!" he said vehemently. "And I'll never make the team next year, not without actual game experience. Besides, the other guys will have grown and it'll be doubly impossible—why should Coach want a shrimp, anyway?" His next words were spoken with such sadness they broke Megan's heart. "I could've done it. Right now, at the beginning of the season, I was punting forty yards, even longer sometimes. I'm stronger than I look. Now there's not *anything* for me. I'm not fast enough for track, too short for basketball . . ."

"Jeffie, that leaves tennis and golf and any number of other things."

"But I want to be on a team!"

He might as well have cried, "I want the other guys to accept me."

She said, "Your dad brags about how smart you are. What about grades?"

He shrugged. "I do okay. What that means is that some of the kids call me 'eggroll' instead of 'shrimp.' "

The boy's already depressed, Megan realized. With forced energy she said, "Jeffie, we're going to move you downstairs. I'm going to find some enormous man and come by here in the morning. Is there a bedroom on the first floor?"

"No. They're all on this level."

"Well, there must be somewhere you can sleep down there."

"Dad's office sofa makes into a bed."

"How about moving in there until your father comes home, then? We can take your computer"—she looked around the room—"and whatever else you might want."

He brightened. "I'd like that. Would it be too much trouble to get someone to carry me down?"

Megan laughed. "Jeffie, trust me. At eight o'clock tomorrow morning I'll be here with someone who can get you down those stairs as easily as you and I can lift a feather."

She felt good when she left the house. Megan always felt good around children, and Michael's son and niece had been both pleasant and grateful. Mrs. Simmons, a roly-poly lady who looked too old to be working, had been elated. "Oh my, Miss McBride, you can't imagine what a relief it would be to have the boy down here! I've been trying to think of someone myself to call. It sure wouldn't be good for him to stay cooped up there until his father comes home. Not good at all . . ." She had invited Megan to dinner and, when Megan declined after explaining she wanted to get home in order to start rounding up a man to move Jeffie, Mrs. Simmons had stuffed a Tupperware bowl with enough roast for at least three meals.

The arrangements were as easy as one telephone call to the YMCA where Megan tutored. A beefy swim instructor named Chad agreed to meet Megan at the Richardson home. In addition, he suggested that a fourteen-year-old in the throes of depression should be taken out of the house once a day, a task he offered to perform after explaining that the Y pool was closing for repairs. Megan was astonished at Chad's generosity; when she mentioned it, he said, "Oh, Megan! You've been volunteering your services to this club for years without asking anything in return. How's it going to hurt me to make the next few days more pleasant for an orphaned fourteen-year-old?"

"Where will you take him?"

"Anywhere he wants to go. I'll put one of the club's wheelchairs in the car. Then Jeffie and I can decide on our destination after we've had a chance to talk."

For the rest of the evening, Megan worked on the new customer orders. When she tallied them, she was pleased to see that the day had been more successful than she had realized; Michael would have been especially happy about the order from the Hendrick's buyer. She imagined herself laughing with him about the affable man's reaction to the sight of her on hands and knees repairing lamp wiring; Barnum and Bailey could not have created much more consternation if they had paraded their elephants through the elegant lamp showroom.

As she recalled Michael's curt, impersonal response to her smile of delight upon first sight of him that afternoon, her current amusement faded. Frankly, Megan still found the memory chilling.

7

Chad was thirty minutes late after calling to explain that he was going to detour by the Y to pick up the wheelchair. Since Megan had made appointments in San Diego, she had very little time to spend at the Richardson home. However, she was present for what Jeffie referred to as "the body removal," and from that alone she concluded that Chad and Michael's son would get along famously. Chad had a way with children; he could pull a half-drowned toddler kicking and screaming from the pool and have her laughing and swimming again within seconds. Megan's departure was hardly noted above the happy sounds emanating from Michael's study-turned-bedroom. As she drove toward the San Diego freeway, she felt unusually warm and comfortable despite a drab day with drizzly rain. Being around Jeffie, playing an important role in his recovery, made her feel close to his father.

She wasn't exactly making her decisions easier. Megan was getting in deeper and deeper. She gunned the accelerator and forced her mind to business.

By five o'clock, half of Southern California was flooded, and many of the freeways were impassable. Megan called for a motel reservation and then accepted a dinner invitation from an old friend, a decorator, who was preparing to open his first retail store that weekend; he had taken one look at Megan's Ling photos and decided to switch his entire lamp display. While they

sat at Anthony's restaurant watching the phenomenal
rain pelt the Pacific Ocean, Carl asked the name of the
Ling designer.

"Those pieces are stunning," the decorator said.

Megan looked at him strangely. "It's funny . . . I've
never asked about the designer. As many compliments
as I've received the last few days, you'd think it would
have been one of my first questions. Michael Richardson heads the firm."

"Then that's your answer," Carl said matter-of-factly
as he took a bite of clam chowder. "Most of the outstanding lamps in this country come from Richardson.
Lord, if he got the same credit that artists get from, say,
oil paintings, his name would be a household word."

"You're joking!" Megan actually gasped.

Carl shook his head. "Uh-uh. The man's a national
treasure. One thing I wish he'd do, though—get the Oriental artisans to take a chance on some new shapes.
People are sick of the same old round things and just
another version of the temple jar."

After her years in the Orient, where her father had
fought a constant battle regarding production of con-
struction pieces unfamiliar to the Japanese, Megan
could have explained the artisans' reluctance to produce new shapes. But she didn't. She was preoccupied
with the shock of learning that Michael could design.
Megan was always impressed with talent; in this case
she was overwhelmed. Her respect for her employer
took a multiple leap. Where on earth did he find time to
design? Most of the pieces in the Ling lines were
exclusives—at least they were exclusive until another
manufacturer knocked them off—and the line changed
constantly. Buyers entering showrooms to be confronted with the same designs they had seen three months
previously would turn away; reps trying to sell an "old"
line would receive about the same attention as a store
offering nothing but yesterday's fads.

"Well, anyway," Carl continued, "Richardson's designs are fresher than everyone else's. It's a matter of color and detail. Even if he isn't getting anywhere with shapes, at least he's got his people doing, oh, something besides Chinese red; and themes, Megan—some of these are almost contemporary! I can sell a lot more Oriental products now that they have scenes different from Japanese gardens and birds. *Boooring!*"

"Oh, Carl," Megan teased, "you're so dramatic!" She changed tones, then said, "Tell me . . . what's Richardson's background?"

"I'm not the one to ask. All I know is that he started Light Years when he was in his mid-twenties and—"

"Light Years? The company that used to be such a power?"

Carl nodded. "Started it from scratch and built it into one of the most influential forces in the industry. And then sold it a few years back. Just like that." He snapped his fingers.

"Why?"

The decorator shook his head. "I'm trying to remember. There was something mysterious about it . . ." Carl paused, frowning, then scratched his dark curly head. "Well, if not mysterious, then at least very much out of the ordinary. But I can't remember the details. Anyway, he dropped out of sight and then emerged as president of some company or other; after he put them on their feet, he moved on to Ling. No wonder Ling's doing so well. My memory's terrible; if I'd known that's where Richardson was, I'd have bought from them before now. And if I were you, Megan, I'd always tell the buyers that Richardson's your designer; it's likely to swing quite a few sales."

Megan suddenly realized that Michael had stood near her on that day of her introduction to customers. He had heard a dazzling array of compliments regarding the designs, yet never acknowledged his part in it. Was it possible the man was modest in addition to everything else? She shook her head; when Carl asked the reason, she just smiled and told him he'd never understand.

By morning, the rain had slowed to another drizzle, and Megan had little trouble negotiating the freeway. She got an early start and pulled into the Ling and Son parking lot before nine. Adelle was looking considerably more relaxed than she had during Megan's previous visit.

"Where have you been? Mr. Richardson's been looking for you."

"Surely he's not back!"

"No such luck," the secretary said. "Anyway, he asked me to have you call him in New York if you came by the office. Why don't you go on in and use his office phone? Here's two numbers for you to try: the showroom and his hotel."

Megan's heart skipped a beat. When she talked to Adelle, she tried to sound calm. "While I'm in there, do you think you could ring the warehouse and see if the manager's got time to show me the new samples Michael wanted me to look at? Also, I've got a couple of days' worth of orders and I don't have the vaguest idea where the order department is." Adelle agreed to take care of both items, then got up to open Michael's office door. Megan was relieved when the secretary pulled it closed behind her; her hands were trembling and she knew she could manage the call much more easily in private.

She sat at Michael's desk chair and breathed in the familiar masculine smells; a faint remnant of cologne from their last day together clung to the soft leather of the chair. Megan drew a mental picture of him: tall, blond, tanned, lean and slender and hard. She pictured the light eyes that seemed capable of penetrating her soul, and the thick lashes that had swept her cheeks that afternoon at the Marina del Rey pier. And she *felt* him . . . a tensing of muscles, the contraction of his thighs against hers, arms rippling with strength yet struggling to hold her gently. A flood of paralyzing emotions swept Megan. And she asked herself, Is it possible I'm falling in love with this man?

At length she dialed the first number; he wasn't at the hotel. At the showroom the manager reported he'd just left and wasn't expected back until later that afternoon; she asked him to tell Michael she'd tried to return his call. When the receiver had been replaced, Megan was torn between bitter disappointment and a strange sort of relief. On the one hand, she wanted desperately to hear his voice; on the other, she dreaded the possibility it would be the same one, cold and impersonal, now so painfully seared into her memory. She emerged from Michael's office to find Adelle was no longer at her desk; by the time the secretary got back, Megan was once again the picture of cheerful composure.

"I got your orders started," Adelle told her. "But I'm not sure I understood the one for San Diego—you want to deliver it personally?"

Megan nodded. "It's for a store opening. Saturday night. After the customer saw our line, he canceled every single one of the lamps ordered from another firm. The least I can do is get the stuff to him by Saturday. Otherwise his showroom's going to be awfully dark for the opening night party!"

"That could present a problem," Adelle said uneasily. "If this is his first store, he won't have credit established under a business name."

"As a decorator, he's dealt with me for eight years," Megan said casually. "He was never so much as one day late with a payment. Besides, I put his credit application with the order; there shouldn't be any problem checking it. That gives the credit people almost two full days: today and tomorrow. I don't need to pick the lamps up until Friday afternoon late."

Adelle rolled her eyes. "You're right, of course. But these things have a way of getting fouled up when Mr. Richardson's away."

Megan frowned. "I don't understand."

"Well, I hope you won't find out," the secretary warned. "Just keep your fingers crossed. And I didn't have any luck on the warehouse thing, Miss McBride. It seems that Nikki—Frank Nichiroupoulos, the warehouse manager—missed a dental appointment the day we had that rush job for Ohio. He's there now, having wisdom teeth pulled. There's no one else who can show you the new samples; for security reasons, new shipments are placed under lock and key until they've become an official part of the inventory."

"It's okay. Maybe I can come in early enough tomorrow." Megan stayed to pass a reasonable amount of polite chatter and then headed for the car.

She returned to her house early. Thursday was now the evening she spent with the Japanese students and Megan wanted to drop by the Richardson house to check on Jeffie. She showered and changed into a favorite pair of jeans and a soft turquoise pullover, then pulled her hair back and tied it with a white scarf.

"Miss McBride? My law—you look about twelve years old!" Mrs. Simmons had opened the door, and Megan could see Tara approaching in the background. Michael's niece laughed and said, "For goodness sake, Mrs. Simmons, let the poor woman in!"

Jeffie was propped up on the sofa and talking like a speeded-up record. "Hey, slow down," she laughed. "I take it you're enthusiastic about our friend Chad?"

"Megan, he's fantastic!" the boy said excitedly. "Guess where we went today?"

"Um . . . to the seashore to pick seashells?"

Jeffie rolled his eyes. "Chad took me to the Dean Witter offices—you know, the big brokerage firm—and showed me around their computer room. You wouldn't believe all the information they hold in those computers. If that amount of data were kept in regular files, it would cover half a city block! The Dean Witter ma-

chines use Pascal and they have sixteen-bit micropro-
cessors."

"You're really into computers, aren't you?"

"It's the future," Jeffie said. "Why fight it? Tomorrow Chad's taking me to the UCLA film library, and
we're going to check out their files on computer ca-
reers." He looked at her shyly. "I've designed a couple
of programs. They're simple but they work okay."

Megan was impressed. She had an elementary knowledge of computer science from two electives at UCLA,
enough to appreciate the challenge of developing an
original program.

"What's the subject?"

"Vocabulary. They're both word games. What I'd like
to do is take the best elements of the two and put them
together into one package that's really good." He hesitated, then said, "I guess that's a silly thing for me to
say, huh? My games wouldn't sell."

"Jeffie! Who told you that?"

"No one would ever take a fourteen-year-old seriously."

"If the product is good enough, age doesn't matter,"
Megan said firmly. "Business is a reliable common de-
nominator, Jeffie. For instance, if your father received
lamp designs so outstanding that he could predict good
sales, do you think he'd refuse to buy them once he
learned they'd been done by a fourteen-year-old?"

"I see what you mean," he said slowly. Megan stayed
only a few more minutes. Her young friend's mind was
on a different plane, occupied with more important
things than polite conversation.

On her way to the Y, she stopped at McDonald's.
Halfway through the quarter-pounder, Megan realized
she was extremely tired, and the tiredness remained
through the tutoring session. She even let her students
go five minutes early. When she finally entered her
own house, she felt a literal craving for the comfort of

bed. Just before she switched out the bedside lamp, the phone rang.

"Miss McBride, this is George Ling of Ling and Son."

Megan sat straight up. "Yes, sir?"

"I'm sorry to call so late. Your line didn't answer earlier this evening." The voice was soft and well-modulated; it might have belonged to a college professor.

"That's perfectly all right, Mr. Ling. I was still awake. Is there something I can do for you?"

"Not exactly. But I thought you should know we won't be able to process the credit application in time for that new store opening in San Diego."

Megan tensed. "I don't understand, Mr. Ling. I've been selling to that man for eight years. His credit is excellent. Also, I supplied a credit report from every major firm he's done business with. Since I filled in his social security number, driver's license, everything that's necessary, why should it take more than forty-eight hours to process the application?"

George Ling cleared his throat. "Your customer's doing business under the name Surfside Interiors. He hasn't established credit under that name."

Megan ran a hand through her hair, not believing what she was hearing. "Mr. Ling," she said coolly, "his store hasn't even opened yet. Previously, as an independent designer, his credit history was kept in his personal name. It should be simple enough for our people to confirm his rating with the firms I listed."

"Well, we just can't do that, Miss McBride. You sales people have to understand—it's management that takes the risks. We'd be out of business if we let you decide to whom we should extend credit. I suggest you try this customer again when his new business has a good track record."

Megan's mind raced. She could just imagine poor Carl without a single lamp for his gala opening event.

She tried to keep her voice calm. "Mr. Ling, are you aware of my personal sales background?"

"No, Miss McBride, that sort of thing is hardly within my domain."

"If you were—sir—you would know that I don't jeopardize the firms I work for by taking on marginal credit customers. This man is *not* a risk. Besides, he canceled the lamps he had originally planned to open the store with; under the circumstances, don't you think we should be as accommodating as possible?"

Ling emitted a derisive chuckle. "Not for a man with no credit. Surely you know that. Look, Miss McBride, I'm getting very weary of this conversation. As I've explained to you, Ling and Son will not extend credit to your customer."

"Do you realize that you're getting ready to turn down a man whose interiors have been featured in both *Designers West* and *Architectural Digest*?" Megan asked sarcastically. She doubted that George Ling had ever heard of the all-powerful trade magazines. "It just might do Ling and Son some good to have our lamps associated with Carl Jurgen."

"Why don't you ask the man to pay up front?"

"In full?" Megan gasped. "No one asks an established designer for full advance payment!"

"I do, Miss McBride. Now that's my final word on the subject. I bid you good night."

Megan stared at the receiver and then flung it across the room. Before she trudged across to pick it up, her mind had flown like a whirlwind over the various options that might save Carl Jurgen from this idiotic indignity. Under better circumstances, Megan would have offered to guarantee her customer's credit against her own earnings; that approach had seemed useless when Ling had admitted no knowledge of her sales background—as yet, Megan had not received a commission check from Ling and Son.

She had finally replaced the receiver and was on her

way to the bar for a soothing glass of wine when the
telephone rang again. She hoped fervently it was
George Ling so she could give him her opinion of his
business policies. Snatching at the phone, she barked,
"Yes?"

It was Michael.

"Did I catch you at a bad time?"

Unfortunate, to say the least, Megan thought to herself. She doubted she was a good enough actress to coax
a social lilt into her voice; then too, it was possible that
Megan's business problem was a matter she was obligated to discuss with her boss. She played for time: "Actually, your timing could have been better. How are
you?"

"Fine. Shall I call back later?"

"Um . . . where are you now?"

"Still in New York."

From that distance there was nothing he could do.
And Megan knew that until she calmed down and figured a way to salvage Carl Jurgen's opening night
party, her voice would continue to reveal signs of tension. She said, "No, don't call later, Michael. Considering the time difference, it's best that you get some
sleep. Can we talk some other time?"

There was a pause, then: "I guess so. Is something
wrong, Megan?"

Megan was tempted, but there wasn't a single thing
to be gained from unloading the crisis on him. "I'm just
. . . well, involved in something right now."

"Oh." He sounded puzzled. After a moment he repeated the word more emphatically. *"Oh!* I'm sorry I
bothered you. Um, listen, I'll be back sometime Saturday and I was just . . . just calling to thank you for
everything you've done for Jeffie . . . nothing important. Good night, Megan." She heard a click and the
line went dead.

With the phone still dangling from her hand, Megan
dropped onto her bed and reviewed the words that had

passed between them. When she got to her statement, "I'm just . . . well, involved in something right now," it struck like a physical blow that she had inadvertently given the impression there was another man nearby. Frantically she searched her memory for the name of Michael's hotel; it would be better for him to know about Ling's phone call than to suffer that kind of letdown. But Adelle hadn't given her the hotel name, just the number. For fully five minutes she sat with her head in her hands, racking her brain to recall the greeting of the hotel switchboard operator: "Good afternoon, this is the . . ." Nothing. Evidently Megan hadn't been paying the least attention.

With a hard tight knot in her stomach, partly anxiety for what Michael might be going through and partly fear for what she might have done to the already tenuous relationship, Megan breathed deeply and commanded herself to accept the fact there was nothing she could do until morning. She threw on a robe and walked to her desk. Sinbad said, "Hello!" and Megan said, "No, bird. This is the time to say damn!" She withdrew her investment portfolio and checked the balance in her money market account; first thing in the morning she would liquidate fourteen hundred dollars to pay for Carl's order. She groaned. Oh God, that would mean hanging around until her bank opened at ten. She had made an appointment in Laguna Beach at ten-thirty, planning to visit with Jeffie for half an hour, and then to make a leisurely drive south. She could probably reschedule the appointment, but then when would she arrive back at the office? She had to avoid rush-hour traffic in order to allow time to pay Carl's bill, check the condition of his lamp order, and then load it into the back of her Toyota station wagon. If only the office were open on Saturday, she lamented. She was so tired.

Suddenly it dawned on her that she wasn't merely tired. She placed a hand on her forehead. She was coming down with the flu. Somehow, the realization was calming. Megan got sick so rarely that she could hardly rail against the fates. Then too, this was a problem she could understand and deal with; she wasn't about to let a slight illness keep her down. She took a couple of aspirins and settled back into bed with a half-read copy of *War and Remembrance*; her light was still burning and the book was lying open beside her when the alarm went off Friday morning.

8

Mrs. Simmons told her not to worry, that Jeffie had been exposed to the flu so often, once more wasn't going to matter; she also stressed that the boy had already set up the computer for their games. Megan dressed for warmth and comfort, dropped the bottle of aspirins into her purse, and headed out.

Very shyly but with evident pride, Jeffie taught her the mechanics and rules of his programs. She was amazed to see that he had also structured graphics. Essentially both games were the same. On the screen, there was a library background. The foreground flashed a definition: *a container, usually square or rectangular.* As soon as the player typed in the word *box,* a section of ladder would appear; for each correct answer, the ladder grew taller. The faster the player's reaction time, the greater the portion awarded; when definitions were missed, the ladder started disappearing. As the game progressed, definitions became more complex and the time allowance shorter. When an entire ladder had been constructed, symbolizing that the winning player had reached the Winner's Dictionary on the top library shelf, each player was awarded points commensurate with the time performance, plus a hundred-point bonus for the winner; that way, the game could be played continously, with a running score simply stored in the computer.

Megan lost the game by half a ladder. After that she

wasted no time telling Jeffie he could go to the head of the class. In fact, she was so excited, she canceled her Laguna Beach appointment and stayed to discuss the project. The other version of Wordteach, designed for preschoolers, was even more ingenious than the first. She was positive Jeffie could refine the package into something salable once he got help improving the crude graphics. When she realized she absolutely had to hit the road, she promised to return for dinner.

At the office, after she had gone to the bank, she had to wait for Adelle to get back from an errand. She got a Coke from the coin machine and tried to make herself comfortable, then gave in and took another two aspirins although it was twenty minutes short of the prescribed four-hour period. She was beginning to ache painfully, and her own voice rang in her ears like an echo.

Adelle gave her the New York numbers again. As usual, Michael was unreachable. Megan trudged back to the order department and paid Carl's bill, then asked the billing clerk to mail the customer a statement just as though nothing had gone wrong. It got complicated; the clerk couldn't figure out how to handle the computer entries. "Believe it or not," he said, "if I enter this as an advance payment in full, it's going to hurt your customer. He'll automatically be required to do the same thing next time. I mean, the computer will put him with all the other credit risks we require advance payment from."

"You have *got* to be joking!"

The man looked wounded. "No, it's true. And I don't think it's right to have him down that way when he's not even the one *making* the advance payment."

Megan wanted to scream; instead, she requested a conference with the Ling comptroller, whose secretary informed her that he was tied up in a meeting with a computer specialist. Megan turned again to the clerk. "You know, it's really not necessary to make an entry now. We can just wait until Mr. Jurgen's personal payment comes in and then we can—"

"But I have to file today's payment," the man protested. "And that brings up another problem—somewhere along the line, the computer's got to show that the account was paid twice. When that happens, the company will assume that Mr. Jurgen accidentally made the dual payment. They'll mail him a refund when it's your money we need to get returned."

Suddenly Megan felt too drained to continue tilting against this imaginary windmill. She asked the clerk if he had a small index card; he nodded. "Well, then," she said between gritted teeth, "why don't we forget the computer and do this thing the way a human being would do it?"

"How's that?" The man was incredulous. Megan stifled a giggle at his expression. What an irony that the company comptroller couldn't meet with her to solve a computer problem because he was in a meeting with a computer specialist! With a shudder at the implications, she told the clerk to get out the index card and a pen; then she told him to write: "On this date Megan McBride prepaid Invoice #6007–A and is due a full refund at the time of customer payment, when the account will be credited as paid in full." He dated and signed the statement, apparently satisfied, then pinned the card to his bulletin board. As Megan was leaving he gave her an exaggerated wink, as though the two of them had just pulled off some unthinkable con. Shaking her head in disbelief, Megan stuffed her carbon copy of the fourteen-hundred-dollar money order into her purse and walked away without looking back. Forty-five minutes later, she had completed checking and loading Carl's lamps and was on her way back to Westwood.

At home, she returned backlogged telephone calls left with her answering service. When she got up from the desk at six o'clock, she arched and tried to massage the ache in the small of her back. A clap of thunder sounded and she peered through parted draperies to see fresh rainfall. It occurred to her that she really wasn't feeling well enough to go out in that weather. But she had a literal craving to be with people. Megan was beginning to miss Michael in a way that she had never before missed another human being; passing the time with his son was enormously helpful. She took another two aspirins and changed into the most comfortable thing she could find: a lime-green velour jumpsuit. On the way to the Richardsons', she stopped at the drug store for cold capsules, then downed one with her first sip of wine at the house.

Mrs. Simmons had set the family room game table for dinner. "On a rainy night, it's best to eat in front of the fire, doncha think, dearie? And look—Tara's laid such a nice one!"

It *was* nice. Mrs. Simmons's table was set with a floor-length rust tablecloth, bone china with a tiny French floral design, crystal water goblets, and an autumn chrysanthemum centerpiece between two tapered candles. Tara's fire jumped and flickered and crackled, and the rainy night seemed far, far away. "Mr. Richardson likes things to be particularly homey for the children when he's away, doncha know?" the housekeeper said. Barry Manilow sang softly in the background, and just as the two teenagers and Megan sat down for fried chicken, mashed potatoes, and a gorgeous tossed green salad, she heard him chant, "I Can't Smile Without You." The words brought back a terrible pang of longing for Michael.

The trio interacted with total ease and spontaneity. With amazement, Megan recalled the various times she had told herself her life was complete as it was, that she wasn't one of those women who needed a family. Perhaps she wasn't, she now conceded, but there's still nothing better. Then she told herself to watch out—this particular tribe was on loan only until the chief returned. And considering her last conversation with the chief, she thought painfully, it was possible that the only way he'd let her stay in touch with Jeffie and Tara was by smoke signal.

She told them about the afternoon run-in with the company computer. Tara thought it was hysterical but Jeffie reacted with all sorts of warnings about poorly programmed and operated machines. When his cousin tried to tease him out of it, he started telling true horror tales: when someone's husband died, a government employee punched the "deceased" button twice, canceling her social security as well and causing the IRS to start dunning her children for estate taxes. "For eighteen months now," Jeffie said, "she's been trying to get the mess straightened out."

Dryly, Tara said, "That's impossible, of course, since she's dead."

"You've got it!" the boy confirmed. "Now let me tell you one that's even worse . . ."

As he related the woes of a brilliant college student whose transcript got switched with that of an ex-convict failing all his courses, Megan grew increasingly warm and wondered if perhaps she should trade places with Tara, who sat farther from the fire. She took a sip of water and waited for Jeffie to wind down his dramatic story. His voice grew distant. She reached again for her water goblet. Before she got it to her lips, though, it slipped gently to the table and Megan slumped, unconscious, in her chair.

Their next-door neighbor, a doctor, came over. He said there was no danger; Megan had a high fever and had probably stayed overlong in a warm room. Coming to, she told him about the drugstore medication, and he commented that cold capsules frequently cause dizziness for those unaccustomed to taking them. She was ordered to remain at the Richardsons' that night; she didn't argue. She still felt lightheaded and extremely warm; her only conscious thought was of the irony: four

days after refusing Michael's invitation she was to end
up as an uninvited houseguest.

She longed for him, often feeling more distressed by
the loneliness than by the fever. Mrs. Simmons had put
her in Michael's bedroom because of the convenience of
the connecting bath; Megan couldn't clearly make out
the shape or decor, but she was intensely aware that
Michael belonged in the big bed. From some place far
away, she heard his name being called; Tara placed a
cool cloth on her forehead and said, "He'll be home
soon, Megan. Try to sleep."

Around daybreak, she thought she saw him. "Please,"
she moaned, "please hold me." Although she knew she
was dreaming, she thought she felt the length of his
body against hers; she sighed happily and fell into a
long untroubled sleep.

9

A grandfather clock was chiming. Megan stirred, then lost track of the count and dozed again. Michael's arms were still around her . . . she even thought she heard his soft regular breathing; she wanted the dream to continue. For a few minutes she lost herself in the warm sensations.

After a while, the thought of his body entwined with hers triggered sexual responses. Megan's body arched forward, craving relief. Then the figure of her dreams moved . . . sensually, determinedly. She breathed his name. "Michael . . ." Involuntarily, her hips thrust forward. She heard her own name whispered in response. Cool lips touched her forehead.

She tensed momentarily, then relaxed. "This is no dream, is it? You're really here."

"I'm here, darling. I got home at five-thirty."

"This is . . . frightening." Megan was still whispering; as yet, she hadn't opened her eyes. "What am I wearing?"

"A blue shirt, one of mine. Mrs. Simmons said you went through three of them, sweating out the fever. Why are you frightened?"

She didn't know. It was an old fear but she couldn't quite remember its nature.

"Not because of me?" he asked.

"It couldn't be," she answered slowly, aware she wasn't making sense. "Michael . . . ? Michael, I need you. Don't leave me again."

He pulled her fiercely closer. A hot prong ignited her lower body, burning away the fear. "Listen to me, honey. I've got to get out of this bed."

"No! Why?"

"Jeffie and Tara. Supposedly I'm just sitting in here, watching over you. I've got to go get Mrs. Simmons, try to make everything look normal."

Megan jerked free. The children! She tried desperately to clear her mind. "What time is it?"

"Ten o'clock."

She swung her legs to the side of the bed. Her eyes darted furiously around the room, searching for her clothes.

He sat up, but pushed her gently back onto the mattress. "Shh . . . slow down, honey; you're still not thinking clearly. Where are you going? You're sick, you know."

"But, Michael, I'm not. Not anymore."

He finally laughed. "And to think I used to give you credit for common sense! Relax—and do as you're told! In a few minutes I'll be back with breakfast."

Megan realized he was right. She started to tell him so, but just at that moment he stood up. He was dressed only in blue bikini briefs that clung like a second skin; the undergarment might have been designed to accentuate the secrets of his body, not to conceal. She drew in her breath. Michael was indescribably beautiful: the lean powerful frame was bronzed from the summer sun and accented with sun-bleached hair. As he stretched for the clothes which lay folded over a nearby chair, Megan saw the contraction of his buttocks and a slight rippling along the upper back; in immediate response, her own thigh muscles tensed, then trembled.

Sitting on the chair, he paused in the act of coaxing on a sock. Regarding her with amusement, he asked, "Do you like what you see?"

She should have been embarrassed; for some reason, she had never felt more natural. Megan moved her head slowly up and down. "You're perfect," she whispered.

His eyes closed. "Oh, God," he groaned. "Do you know what happens to me when you use that tone of voice? Shall I show you?"

She said, "Show me," still too fascinated to feel the familiar inhibitions.

His eyes remained closed; he began to breathe through slightly parted lips. After a long moment the breathing became even and he finished pulling the sock up. Finally, the eyes opened again. He stared at Megan and said, "It's possible, just possible, that I've never wanted anything as much as I want you right now." There seemed a clear warning in the words: "Don't push me, Megan." She blushed, aware at last of the uncharacteristically brazen nature of her behavior. Or had it just been the final effects of the feverish night? Megan wondered.

Michael rose and headed for the door. When he disappeared into the hallway, Megan slid under the covers and emitted a deep, shuddering breath. It was a long time before Megan's body calmed.

"I've got to dress and go home . . . pack a suitcase for San Diego." They were sipping orange juice and eating buttered croissants from the silver tray Mrs. Simmons had prepared. Megan was propped on several pillows, Michael seated in the lounge chair. The bedroom door was open and they were both talking calmly, as though there was nothing unusual about the setup. Meanwhile, Megan's heartbeat quickened when Michael's light blue eyes probed her own.

"What are you raving about now?"

She sighed, ordered her heart to slow down, then explained about Carl Jurgen's store opening, the party, and the lamps in the back of her Toyota.

"I'll arrange for someone to deliver the lamps," Michael said firmly.

She shook her head. "No. The fever's gone; it was just

one of those freaky things, Michael. I'm a bit weak, I admit it, but definitely not enough to keep me from the party. I feel strongly about this particular obligation."

"Will it do any good for me to argue with you? This is insane, you know."

Megan smiled. "To you, it must seem that way. But I know how I'm feeling. Haven't you ever had a spell of illness that ended, just like that?" She snapped her fingers, then rushed on with: "Anyway, if I stayed home, it wouldn't be any less exerting than going to San Diego. At least I'll be sitting quietly in the car for a while."

He finally nodded, grimly. "Have you made reservations?"

"At the Del Coronado. Carl's store is on Coronado Island."

"Then I'll go with you."

"Oh, Michael! Could you? Carl Jurgen would be enthralled. To him, you're a living legend. But what about leaving Jeffie? After all, you just got home."

"Well, he'd never forgive me for not taking proper care of you," he said, smiling at last. "And if I can brighten your friend's opening night—God knows why —then I guess my attendance is mandatory."

She insisted she could dress without Mrs. Simmons's assistance; when Michael teasingly offered his, she feigned shocked indignation and threw a pillow at him. Megan was both surprised and delighted to discover this playful aspect of his personality. When she emerged from the bathroom, once again dressed in the green velour jumpsuit, she put her arms around him and confided that he made her feel like a teenager. He answered that, whatever age she felt, he must be at least a year younger. Looking into each other's eyes with expressions of awe, both of them agreed they had never felt better in their lives. A few minutes later, Michael pretended to pout after being told he wasn't needed as a chauffeur.

She indulged in a half-hour soak when she got home,

then washed her hair and soaped with the Opium. Another thirty minutes passed while she arranged her hair in a manner she seldom wore it. The coiffure was perfectly in keeping with her mood, both carefree and exotic; it was piled loosely atop her head; soft tendrils fell toward her face and onto her neck. The impression was totally natural and uncontrived.

Clothes were no problem. From the moment Megan had learned that Michael would accompany her, she had decided to take along a dress she had worn only once before, when the reaction of those who saw her in it convinced her it was too provocative. The bodice was imported handmade lace studded with hundreds of tiny seed pearls. Although it was a high-collar design with tight lace sleeves running right to her wrists, it was far more suggestive than most outfits with deeply plunging necklines; not only was it designed to be worn without a bra, so that patches of bare skin showed through the lace between strategically placed pearls, but the lace was a perfect contour of Megan's firm breasts. The skirt, a thin silk shaded the subtle pink of the pearls, fell in graceful lines, clinging to Megan's derriere and thighs. She would wear tiny heels with a seed pearl inlay, and small dangling pearl earrings.

Because of Carl's lamps, they took Megan's Toyota. Michael drove while Megan talked. And talked. And talked. She was amused at herself. Although she'd been aware of storing countless mundane details to pass along when he returned, she had not recognized that she actually *needed* to communicate with him. Megan was normally a careful, overly punctuated conversationalist who measured her speech in terms of the other person's response time. Since Michael made no attempt to interrupt her bubbly nonstop chatter, not the least of which was about Jeffie's computer programs, she assumed he was enjoying it. At the very least, she told herself wryly, he must be convinced of her renewed good health. She had trouble imagining she had been so

ill the previous night; she suspected it was Michael's
presence that accounted for the lightning-fast recovery.
In her current mood, time and space were matters to be
reckoned with as a means of savoring hundreds of millions of microshocks of pleasure, each one coming right
on top of the other. Realities like George Ling's telephone call didn't fit the electric pleasure syndrome and
were therefore easy for Megan to omit from conversation. At one point Michael asked her to tell him how she
had managed to get the lamp order processed so
quickly; Megan said that Nikki, the warehouse manager, had done a superb job, then she hurried on to another subject.

They dropped the lamps at Surfside Interiors. The
new store looked wonderful, decorated in varying
shades of gray with bold white accents; against that
background, each sale piece would show brilliantly.
Megan was disappointed that Carl wasn't there to see
Michael. Although she knew the two would meet in a
few hours, she found it difficult to suppress her antici-
pation; for the first time, people would be seeing them—
Michael Richardson and Megan McBride—as a couple.
Well, she thought, there *had* been others, actually . . .
the fishermen at Marina del Rey. Recalling the episode
at the pier, she felt her knees weaken. That had been
the height; since then her emotions had been a crazy
roller coaster—swooping to the bottom the night of
their ridiculous argument, cruising toward the top
again this morning—and it occurred to her to wonder if
tonight she might not actually reach the pinnacle. Or
would something else go wrong? She shook off the for-
bidding thought.

They entered the famous Hotel Del Coronado, a historic rambling pink castle which had provided backdrop for many a romantic film. At the reservations
desk, Michael confirmed the readiness of Megan's
room, then requested a suite for himself. She was startled. Although the subject of accommodations hadn't

come up during the drive, she had thought they would
just boldly check into the same room. Standing beside
Michael during the inevitable paper shuffle, she suddenly realized she had been assuming a great many
things. She felt awkward. When Michael summoned a
bellboy and told her to go on ahead to her room, then to
call him when she was ready for the party, she began to
feel downright nervous.

Megan sat on her bed to think. Considering her unprecedented chatter during the drive, she was unable to
assess Michael's mood. He could easily have been upset, or at least unusually subdued, and the symptoms
would have escaped her. It was also possible he was exhausted from the all-night flight from New York. She
shook her head; that wouldn't account for separate
rooms. With a wave of dread approaching nausea,
Megan switched on the television and lay back to wait.

When it was almost time to leave for the party, she
called his room from the cocktail lounge, needing the
safety of a public place to cover her raw emotions. By
the time he arrived, she had downed half a glass of Chablis and was swallowing back tears. Although Megan
wasn't aware of it, her super-sensitized condition, combined with a brave determination to conceal it, added
an extra dimension to the startlingly beautiful portrait
she presented. Her mouth was softer, more pliant and
feminine; her green eyes were wider and brighter. The
impression was one of irresistible vulnerability. Michael stood before her; Megan misunderstood his deep
intake of breath as a sign of tension. In turn, her own
psyche melted completely at the sight of him in a black
dinner jacket with an exquisite pinch-pleated white
shirt and perfectly tailored black dress trousers. Every
ash blond hair was in place, his eyes blazed with a light
Megan dared not try to identify, and his alluring lips
were slightly parted.

"Don't you want to sit down?" she asked shyly.

"With you? Yes." He never took his eyes from her.

While the waiter took his order for a martini, Megan decided not to attempt decoding the confusing signals. Politely, she inquired about his suite and about how he had passed the time.

"It's gorgeous, up to the hotel's standards. And I returned a phone call, took a nap. Nothing exciting." Megan sensed he was being evasive.

During the cocktail period, she became certain he was as uneasy with her as she was with him. Not that he was rude, or even particularly distant; he couldn't take his eyes off her and made no attempt to hide his admiration. But the rhythm of their exchange was off. If she had felt more secure with him, Megan would have simply asked what was wrong; as it was, she felt she had no right to request access to his private thoughts. Whatever it was, he had clearly chosen to keep it from her. Discouraged, upset, and hurt, she wondered what on earth could have gone wrong since their playful—but very serious—experience this morning in his bedroom. Surely he wasn't brooding about that ill-timed phone call from New York! Megan couldn't believe that. For a split second, she was tempted to bring up the subject anyway, just to make sure, but she discarded the notion when she decided it wouldn't be fair for Michael to have to deal with details of George Ling's idiocy just before a party.

She steered the conversation to her newly acquired knowledge of his design talent. He acknowledged designing the Ling line and told her he worked for an hour each day in a little studio on the second floor of the warehouse. The conversation wasn't very satisfying. Megan was too nervous to convey the actual depth of her enthusiasm, and Michael was evidently accustomed to handling compliments with extreme modesty. Or maybe, she thought to herself, he's really that unimpressed with his talent. She hoped not. For Michael's sake, she wanted him to be able to share totally in the pleasure of his incredible creativity, if only with her. With a painful pang of longing, she realized once again that she cared deeply for this man.

Carl Jurgen created a powerful diversion when they entered his shop. He literally dragged Michael to each guest, raving in no uncertain terms about his talent and accomplishments. Many of the guests had already met him, and in those cases Megan was struck by the warmth of their greetings; he was enormously well-liked. In many instances, someone would turn to Megan with a tale of how Michael had helped him or her get started in the industry. Megan's feelings for him expanded to an even greater extent. He was, in fact, an industry celebrity. She also noticed the way women looked at him, the brightness in their eyes when he addressed them, the way they touched his arm and stared after him when he walked away.

She was also well-known to the group. At least three of the men had tried at various times to get her to accept dates, and she had worked with many of the women, some of whom were decorators and some of whom were buyers. It was a colorful assemblage of individuals Megan respected and enjoyed. Nonetheless, she was strangely ill at ease, for her association with Michael was creating precisely the effect she had looked forward to earlier that evening. People were reacting not to her, but to *them.* Instead of being liked by the women, she was being idolized. And men who normally engaged in harmless after-hours flirtations became wary: "Careful now, this is Michael Richardson's woman." For Megan, the problem was that she was engaged in a full-fledged mental battle to regain her autonomy; since she needed to deal with the subject of Michael in some realistic perspective, then she also needed others to deal with her in some realistic perspective. The assumption that she and Michael belonged exclusively to each other wasn't necessarily correct, as Megan alone knew.

He sought her company often. Megan would take the

first polite opportunity to break away, usually when someone approached to engage Michael in conversation. She laughed just a little too frequently and talked just a little too loudly. When a small combo started playing and she saw him approaching, she quickly accepted another invitation to dance. It was a rock number and she threw herself into the rhythm with a vengeance. At the end, Michael walked briskly to her side and grasped her forearm. After a light interchange with her dance partner, he led her to a dark corner of the showroom, his eyes blazing.

"What do you think you're doing?"

"I don't understand," she said truthfully, "and you're hurting my arm."

He dropped it, appearing startled. "I'm sorry. I just—" He closed his eyes, as if seeking extraordinary patience. "Megan, have you forgotten how sick you were? It's been less than twenty-four hours. And I'm sorry about your arm. I guess I was afraid you'd try to escape again."

She dropped her eyes, sorry to hear that her maneuverings had been obvious. She was trying to protect herself from further pain, not to inflict it on Michael. "I'm sorry, too," she said softly. "In fact, I *did* forget about the fever. I shouldn't have been dancing like that."

He nodded. "The last thing we need is for you to end up in an unconscious heap on the floor. I'll say one thing, though: you certainly are the life of the party. Are you really enjoying yourself so much?"

She opened her mouth, intending to lie, then dropped her eyes again and shook her head.

"Then why the act, Megan?" His tone was angry, demanding.

Megan raised her chin defiantly. If he felt he had a right to question her behavior, then she had a right to question his. "I'm not acting, Michael; I'm reacting. There's a difference. Ever since we checked into the hotel, something's been wrong between us. Since you've chosen to keep the reason a deep, dark secret, then maybe it hasn't occurred to you that I'm acting in the only manner I know how. And that's all the explanation you're going to get."

A look of pain crossed his face; but it was also mixed with an angry expression Megan recognized as pure defensiveness. She took a step backward. "Michael, I'm going back to the party now. I'll be there if you want to discuss this. Just don't start one of those I-don't-know-what-you're-talking-about routines. I'd rather have you say nothing at all than that. Remember, I woke up in your arms this morning. Since then we've become almost total strangers." She turned on her heel and left, surprised she'd had the courage to speak her mind.

Twenty minutes passed. Megan had been talking—quite calmly, for her outburst at Michael had taken the edge off her nervous energy—to a trade magazine editor bemoaning the effects of the recession on the furniture industry. Michael approached and asked if he could borrow her for a moment. The editor agreed, laughingly insistent that the least Michael could do in exchange was give his advertising manager the appointment she'd been trying to get for months. When Michael nodded, Megan could tell he hadn't even heard the request; he was looking at her pointedly, and it wasn't advertising that was on his mind. When she didn't resist, he led her to the dance floor.

"This is appropriate, don't you think?" They were moving stiffly to the music.

"What is?" She could smell his cologne and feel the texture of his muscles beneath the dinner jacket.

"The tune: 'Strangers in the Night.' Our song."

She didn't answer. Her mind was working along the same sarcastic lines as his.

He took a deep breath. "Megan, I don't want us to be strangers," he said fiercely, suddenly pulling her close. She literally melted against him, powerless to do otherwise. After a long moment, he said, "Oh, God," and she felt the quickening of desire as his breath ruffled her hair and caressed her ear. Then: "I don't think, before you came along, that I even understood the nature of passion."

She couldn't talk. The way they were dancing, combined with the pulsating tone of his words, was almost public lovemaking. Megan's breathing was uneven and her arm had crept to stroke the hair on his neck. From time to time he kissed her very softly: on her hair, on her neck, on her cheek, on her ear. His fingers moved against the palm resting in his hand. Megan closed her eyes. Her lips parted slightly and she stood on tiptoes, pressing her thighs more closely to him. Her passion was reflected in the recognizable hardness of his loins. Megan shuddered violently.

"For God's sake, let's get out of here," he breathed.

She nodded, and at length they were able to break the embrace. For a long moment before walking away to seek their host, they stood together on the dance floor, just gazing into each other's eyes.

Carl wanted Michael to look at the placement of a particular porcelain lamp. He led them to the back of the showroom, where the piece was positioned near a large silk floral arrangement. "Your design, Michael," Carl said rather shyly, "is magnificent. That floral could have been picked fresh out of a country garden, it's so well-detailed. Anyway, the minute I saw it, I knew it should be beside this silk arrangement. Look at the similarity of the colors!"

Before Michael could complete his sincere expression of approval, Carl's assistant interrupted to tell the host he was wanted by another guest. Their farewells finished, Michael and Megan were left standing alone before the lamp. The interlude of spellbinding sensuality had passed; although he continued to hold her hand, Megan could tell by the way Michael studied the porcelain lamp that his mind had wandered to another quarter.

Finally he said, "Megan, I asked you earlier, during the drive, if you had any trouble getting hold of these lamps on such short notice. You said Nikki had helped—I could tell that from the way they were packed into your Toyota. But there must be more to the story than that. Getting the company to release merchandise to new reps is usually impossible when I'm out of town."

She hesitated for a moment, then decided he had given her no choice in the matter. "It wasn't easy. I ended up paying in advance. Please don't mention that to Carl, by the way. The whole thing was . . . well, unpleasant, to say the least."

He turned to face her, then took her other hand in his. His eyes betrayed an attitude of total sympathy. "You've been purposely keeping this from me, I think." He released one of Megan's hands and then ran a forefinger softly along her cheek.

She smiled sadly. "You're right. It wasn't something I was anxious to unload on you."

Michael was quiet for a moment. Then he shook his head; the way he did it, she could tell what he was thinking: "People do the damndest things!" With a sigh of resignation, he said, "Megan, I think we're even, but, God, this is a painful way to learn a lesson! Where business is concerned we just won't be able to protect each other. Let's go back to the hotel. I'll explain."

At the Del Coronado, he steered through the lobby and to the cocktail lounge; just inside the entrance, he said, "No, stay here. Don't bother coming in any farther. I'll be right back." Since nothing Michael did surprised her anymore, Megan simply folded her hands and watched him negotiate something with the bartender; it didn't take long.

"What was that all about?" she asked as they wound

through the lobby again; Michael directed the route with one hand placed gently on her back.

"I ordered a bottle of champagne—we never finished our first one, if you recall—and said I wanted it by the pool. It's too pretty a night to be cooped up in a cocktail lounge."

The idea appealed to her. She wondered about all the unconventional little intrigues he cooked up, the snappy way he organized to put them into effect. Life around Michael wasn't going to be boring! As they walked through the rear doors leading to the pool area, Megan remembered that she had once fantasized about how he would be with a woman he cared for. With evident instinct, he chose the most sensual elements available in any given set of circumstances; and if he didn't possess all the tools to make the scene perfect, the force of both his wit and personality was strong enough to enlist others to the cause. Suddenly it hit Megan with full impact *what* the cause was tonight; half of her had feared the occasion while one hundred percent of her had desperately desired it, which made at least as much sense as everything else she had experienced since falling for this man.

They were approaching one of the outside tables, complete with umbrella, when something else emerged from her memory files, a question: will I be able to lie alongside Michael or will I be caught beneath him, trapped under the awesome power? The thought made her nervous.

Megan couldn't imagine how, but the waiter had beaten them. He popped the champagne cork, filled their crystal goblets, then made a discreet retreat. As she watched, she also saw that at this hour, she and Michael were the only occupants of the pool area.

"This time, let's drink to problem-solving," Michael said, raising his glass. When she had dutifully performed her part of the ritual, he leaned across the table. "That's a contract, Megan. We *can* clear away the junk that's coming between us. Start at the beginning and, for God's sake, don't leave anything out."

It didn't take long. She related the whole story, including Ling's first telephone call and her futile attempt to reach Michael after realizing that when *he* had called, her abrupt reaction had probably made him think she was with another man. He said, "You were right. That seemed the logical explanation. But you can stop worrying. When I got home to find you in my bed—and to hear what you'd been doing for Jeffie—I knew there hadn't been time for anyone else. Okay? Ready to go to another subject?"

She hesitated. "Just out of curiosity, Michael, was there another time you telephoned, one day early, when you suspected there was a man with me?"

He looked blank, then said, "Give me a clue." When she reminded him of his call the morning after the concert, he started laughing. "Are you talking about the time you told your bird to shut up?"

"How did you know I have a bird?" She was amazed.

"Oh, honey," he said, still laughing. "You've been far more nervous about this job thing than I realized. Look, unless your senator's voice had changed inhumanly since I met him, and unless, also, he was sitting on your shoulder—which, come to think of it, isn't the strangest thing I've ever heard of politicians doing—that screech in my ear was definitely coming from a bird!"

She couldn't help it; she started laughing, too. Before they calmed down, Megan had admitted that if anyone had the ability to sound like a parrot it was probably the senator. By the time they got back to serious topics, she was considerably more relaxed.

"Okay, back to your problems with Carl's order—*and* with me," he said. "Megan, you've just been given a singularly tough initiation by Dinga. Harder than you realize."

"Dinga?"

"Oh, you're acquainted with him. Think about it."

Unfortunately, the answer presented itself just after she took a sip of champagne; she nearly spit it out. "You don't mean—Dinga *Ling?*"

He nodded, drumming his nails on the table before continuing. "George called this afternoon, a few minutes after you left my house. He was in fine form, ranting and raving and claiming you'd stolen lamps after he'd told you he wouldn't extend credit!"

There was a startled intake of breath from Megan. "Why didn't you say something?"

"You know the answer: ask yourself why you didn't confide in me; it's all the same. Anyway, I knew you hadn't stolen anything. But that didn't prove it to George, who said that when we'd had time to get down here, he'd call the hotel for the explanation. When I brought the subject up in the car, though, you just glossed over it."

She didn't say anything; what had happened was perfectly obvious.

"You can probably guess the rest," he said, "but, quickly, I didn't want you to have to overhear my conversation with Ling, so I asked for separate accommodations. I probably would have anyway, though, thinking you'd want a little privacy to get dressed. After that, if I seemed cool, it was because I didn't know how—or when—to bring up a subject we were both trying to avoid." He paused for a moment, evidently to think, and then said, "Both of us have been making the same mistake, Megan; trying to stay off a specific subject for one reason or another. You follow me?"

"I'm not sure," she answered truthfully.

"Well, if a tarantula started walking slowly across this table and we both watched it and kept on talking about something else—just pretending we didn't see it—do you think we'd be more, or less, nervous than if we just admitted we wished it weren't on the table?"

"Actually, Michael," she said teasingly, "my real

opinion is that we'd be wiser to get up and move before we started talking about *anything* else."

"Which is about what we've been trying to do, incidentally. Take the other night when we had that ridiculous misunderstanding about authorizations to adjust Mrs. Klein's unsold merchandise: after you'd swept out the cobwebs in her account—very effectively, I might add—I dreaded telling you about the one spider still wandering around. Considering our personal relationship, I thought it might hurt. But the damned thing just spun another web, naturally, and by the time we got caught in it, we were too tired to escape. That wouldn't have happened if I'd pointed it out immediately."

Megan sighed. "I understand," she said, meaning it. For the first time she knew for sure how selfish her thinking had been: Michael, too, had problems balancing the employer-employee complications.

"Any more secrets we should confess?" he asked, only half-jokingly as he pushed back his chair. Megan hesitated for a moment, but Michael didn't notice. He continued, "Then let's go upstairs. It's getting cold and my suite has a fireplace." While he was holding Megan's chair, he chuckled. "I can't wait to see the look on Dinga Ling's face Monday morning when the billing clerk tells him the facts."

Megan avoided looking at him. She had decided not to tell him she also intended to be present at the event. She wanted to place her letter of resignation personally, and forcefully, in George Ling's hand.

10

He looked at the champagne bottle. "There aren't any fishermen around. Guess we'll have to finish it ourselves."

As Michael walked the few steps to a phone connecting the pool with food service, Megan's slightly anxious thought was: Yes, it appears that *this time* we're finally going to play this scene all the way through.

Upstairs, her shyness was obvious. He took it in stride, as though it were to be expected. While they waited for the waiter to appear with the iced bucket, he encouraged her attempts to cover the awkward period with small talk. She was grateful; given just a little time, enough to ease into the new situation, Megan was positive she would relax. It wasn't as though she hadn't looked forward to this moment—fantasized about it, in fact.

As they chatted about the party, her theory was proven correct: she felt the tension melting. They were seated at either end of the suite's living room sofa. He got up to light the gas logs of the fireplace and Megan said, "We're lucky California nights aren't as warm as the days, Michael. I'm hopelessly addicted to fireplaces. Can anything feel better than a good fire on a chilly night?"

Michael turned toward her; his look suggested he didn't know how to answer. Megan knew immediately what he was thinking. Between two people holding each other at arm's length in the midst of a violent sexual storm, there was no safe, polite response to a question about what feels best on an autumn night. Clank, there went her nerves again. She glanced quickly toward the windows gracing the splendid old room, trying to conceal her embarrassed expression. While she stared wistfully at the glittering sight of Coronado by night, framed by an ocean sparkling with the lanterns of hundreds of bobbing boats, the champagne arrived. When they were alone again, Michael stared down at the sofa, then extended a hand in silent invitation. Megan allowed herself to be pulled, dreamlike, to her feet.

"Honey," he said, "you asked a question."

She nodded, enthralled by the longing in his eyes.

"I want to *show* you what the answer is." He drew her to him, then rocked her very gently. "Oh, Megan, there's so much I want to show you . . . so much I want to tell you . . . so much I want to do with you . . ." He tightened his hold.

She felt the muscles of his thighs contract, then remembered how he had looked that morning, dressed only in skintight briefs. Her own muscles contracted and an explosive little *zirr* of desire shot between her legs. He drew her hand toward his mouth. Very gently, he began to kiss Megan's trembling palm; she could barely feel the pressure of his lips—and yet, she had never felt anything so much in her life. When he started to flicker his tongue against the palm, so softly that the wetness felt no heavier than a feather, Megan felt her nipples harden. Finally, he began to move his tongue in a small circular motion directly in the center of the palm. Megan felt a heaviness descend in the area of her loins. She drew her thighs tightly together, and when she could stand it no longer, she groaned and all her fears and nervousness disappeared.

Michael stopped. His eyes had darkened dramatically; they were two pools of fire. A flush had crept into his cheeks and his breathing had altered. "What I want you to know about that," he said in a voice barely above a whisper, "is that it felt better to me than to you. Giving you that type of pleasure is a way of giving it to myself. That's what lovemaking is, Megan. I'll find out what makes you feel good, honey; that will be part of the pleasure." He drew a deep breath and stared at her. "And you'll find out what makes me feel good. Do you believe me?"

Megan didn't answer. She reached up and twirled a strand of his hair around her index finger. Then she ran her long fingernail across his brow and over his ear, playing teasing games with the earlobe. She saw him shiver.

He asked what she was thinking.

"I'm not thinking," was her reply. "I'm feeling, just feeling."

"And you're going to feel more," he promised. "Lie down, little Meggie—there in front of the fire."

He held his wine to her lips until she had taken a small draught of the cool liquid before he set aside the glass. Then he undressed her carefully, removing even the lace panties hugging her hips. He stripped quickly until he was dressed in only his briefs. Using both hands, he began a careful search of Megan's body. Very slowly and with exquisite tenderness, he touched both her ankles and then moved his hands upward along her long, smooth legs. Megan squirmed. It seemed to her that slow tortuous hours passed before she felt his fluttering touch on her thighs. From her lips a sound escaped: "Aaahhh."

He asked, "Is this good, baby?"

She answered, "Don't stop."

He caressed the inside of her thighs, and her entire body jerked with the sharp bolt of desire. From what seemed like a long distance, she heard him say, "That's it, baby. Enjoy it." She moaned and spread her legs apart.

He moved his hands higher, playing around her hips but avoiding the spot where she most craved his touch. Megan jackknifed her knees, trying to position herself under his roaming hands. But he coaxed her back down with a gentle pressure and said, "Not yet." His fingers felt like a gentle, tantalizing breeze between her thighs. Megan bit the edge of the pillowcase and tried to keep from crying out. He leaned over her and kissed her deeply, her lips meeting his insistent pressure.

She was breathing hard. Her encounter with Michael was building with frightening intensity. Megan sat up and ran her fingers through her hair, which glowed like an amber blaze.

"I wish I could design a lamp as lovely as the way you look in the firelight," he said quietly. She stared down at him and whispered, "I think it's your turn; just lie still."

"But—"

"Shh . . ." she whispered. "You were right. I want to do part of the giving. Come on. Be still and I'll give you a sip of champagne, just like you gave me one. You're beautiful, too," she said after she had replaced the glass. Without shame, her eyes wandered the length of his body and came to rest on the pulsating hardness in his briefs. Very lightly, she placed her palm over him, then she exerted slightly more pressure and said, "These are too tight. I think we should do something about it." Her fingers trembled as she reached for the elastic waistband. By the time she had coaxed the fabric to a strategic point revealing the full visual impact of his desire, both she and Michael had started to shudder violently. For the few moments it took to get the briefs entirely off, Megan's hands seemed unmanageable. She tossed the undergarment onto a chair, slid down on a blanket Michael had brought from the bedroom, then started kissing his thighs, beginning just above the knee. When she got to the V-shaped area at the top of his legs, he gasped and twisted, then reached down for her.

Megan tried to resist. After a short struggle, she gave up and allowed him to drag her full length on top of him. Their lips met and parted, and their tongues engaged in a frantic, almost painful dance of passion. Both Megan and Michael were moaning and gasping and it became impossible to tell where the sound from one ended and the sound from the other began.

Michael fingered one rigid nipple for a moment, then the other. He placed one of the diamond-hard ruby tips between his lips and flickered his tongue purposefully until he heard Megan emit a sound like a just-stifled scream.

Whatever sensations had caused Megan to utter that animal cry of desire, Michael gave evidence through sound and body language that he was experiencing a similar passion. Each time Megan felt the violent twitch of his muscles, each time she heard a gasping breath or a deep-throated moan, her mind and body registered the stimulus as pleasure received rather than given. Somewhere in her frenetic subconscious she recalled that Michael had told her this would happen; giving and receiving would become the same. And she wanted to give even more.

She moved her hand down, finding and softly caressing the bare skin that was the swollen pulsating focal point of Michael's need. His entire body jerked, then tensed. Megan began moving her hand in a slow stroking motion; she could feel blood vessels throbbing against her palm. He let out a loud indistinguishable plea, then slid out from under her and positioned himself on top. For a split second he gazed down at her, then whispered, "Is this what you want?"

Her response was a question: "Is this what it means to make love?"

He nodded. "Yes, Megan. And I love you."

She felt the agonizing relief of his entry and passion became ecstasy. Michael's words were caught in the spiraling tornado of Megan's emotions as she cried out sharply, then began the final ascent to a peak so high that she had never before imagined its existence. After too short a period, Megan's and Michael's voices blended into one audible tangle of total fulfillment.

11

They awakened in the bedroom of the suite. It was nearly noon. A steady gentle rain was sweeping the roof of the old hotel.

"You awake too?" Megan was smiling through a half yawn.

"Welcome to the world, love."

She snuggled closer. "Say that again, please."

"Welcome to the world."

"No, the other part."

"Love." He slipped both arms around her, then repeated it. "Love, love, love. I love you."

"And I love you." Her voice had dropped to a whisper. "Did I tell you that last night?"

"About twenty times, thank God. And you can tell me another twenty million."

"Is it really this easy?"

"What?"

"Falling in love."

He laughed. "I don't know, darling. You and I certainly had no trouble, did we?"

In response, she just sighed, readjusted to get even closer, and let her eyelids droop closed. The soft rhythm of the rain lulled them both back to sleep.

At a quarter of one, conscious again, she slipped from the bed and padded to the living room phone; the desk extended check-out time, and room service cheerfully agreed to deliver orange juice, tea, croissants, and a

Sunday paper. Then Megan used the second bathroom for her shower; considering the amount of sleep Michael had missed during the last few days, she was determined not to disturb him one minute earlier than necessary.

By the time brunch arrived, she smelled deliciously of lilac soap. Her appearance, on the other hand, was slightly comical, for she had gone on a silent forage through Michael's overnight case; the prize was a white bathrobe several sizes too large. Now she stood beside the bed balancing a tray. Michael was asleep on his side, one arm gracefully outflung.

"Ahem."

"Mmmm . . ." He shifted slightly, almost but not quite turning onto his back. Megan had no idea if he was awake.

"Earth to Richardson," she chanted softly.

Once again: "Mmmm . . ." And then: "Hmmm?"

"Base wants a position report. Where are you, Richardson?"

He opened his eyes, blinked a couple of times, then rolled toward her. But instead of answering, he cocked an elbow under his head and stared at Megan. After a protracted moment in which his expression—a mixture of surprise, joy, and tremendous affection—told Megan a great deal, he finally spoke. "Tell base I've reached my destination: I'm in heaven." There was a note of awe in his voice.

She stared back, momentarily overcome with emotion. And then he started grinning wickedly.

"What's so funny?"

"You are. That robe's so big, only your head and the tips of your fingers are peeking out. In fact, considering the hair, you look like a giant white candle!"

"Oh—*you!* Come on back down to earth before I drop your breakfast!"

His next words were seductive and spoken with measured precision: "But I *want* you to drop my breakfast."

In a series of incredibly swift movements, he sat up and swung his legs to the floor, swept the tray from Megan and set it down, then pulled her full-length onto the bed. By the time she recovered, he was smothering her face and shoulders with kisses.

Megan giggled. "And I thought you'd be hungry, think of it!"

"When I have an opportunity to study a real live angel up close?"

They never touched the food, of course. Two hours later, about halfway across the sleek Coronado Bridge, Michael said, "I'm starved! Let's stop at Sea World and grab a hamburger. No—a chili dog would be better. With onions."

"And a big chocolate milk shake?" Megan chimed in. "Michael, you're crazy! Sea World's not a fast-food joint!"

"Who said anything about eating fast? Listen, we've both admitted feeling like kids. Nothing we do has to make sense! Let's end the day with something young and foolish!"

She laughed. "Why not? We've taken a tour of heaven . . . might as well wander on over to the deep blue sea." For Michael Richardson, Megan decided, she would have walked barefoot through Siberia.

As that strange and lovely last day of September advanced toward dusk, Megan said, "We're getting ready to see one of the really spectacular sunsets." Thin streams of burgundy and coral and lemon yellow were beginning to appear on the darkening horizon of the rain-washed sky.

"Let's watch it from the dolphin tank," he said, checking his watch. "The show starts in a couple of minutes."

They sat in the front row, holding hands, and when the dolphins performed a final leap through a trio of hoops, it seemed as though the fat, friendly sea creatures would land in their laps. Somehow they managed to clap without releasing each other's hands. They waited for the crowd to clear out, and when they were alone, Michael pulled Megan to her feet and kissed her long and passionately. He didn't offer a reason; she didn't ask for one.

As though speech might have broken the spell, they kept a meaningful companionable silence during most of the drive home. About five minutes from Westwood, Megan began seeking a bridge back to reality. Sooner or later it was bound to have occurred to her that another workday was approaching; she was anxious that she hadn't yet told Michael about her decision to leave Ling and Son.

Perhaps he needed the transition, too. Unexpectedly, he said, "Did any of those dolphins remind you of Nikki?"

"Nikki? Oh, you mean your warehouse manager! Well . . . he's kinda cute and roly-poly, I'll admit—"

"Not that," he interrupted. "It's the benevolent expression; Nikki always manages to look like he's grateful you asked for his help. And he rooolls everywhere he goes, like the dolphins."

"You have a *very* expressive way of putting things!" she teased. "Nikki's nice, though; very nice."

"He's been with me sixteen years," Michael said.

Megan whistled. "Not many business relationships like that."

He shook his head. "I've been fortunate. It's just sort of an unspoken agreement. Wherever I go, Nikki agrees to follow."

"Is that good?" Megan honestly didn't know.

He nodded, his eyes on the road. "These companies are damned near impossible to run without topflight warehouse managers. Did you know our warehouse covers an entire acre?"

They had turned off the freeway onto an access road and were fast approaching the turnoff to Megan's little house. Her mind wandered involuntarily back to her

pending resignation. The timing was bad; at this point
it would create severe problems for both Michael and
her. She knew she couldn't stay with Ling and Son
though; mention of the warehouse manager had rekin-
dled her resentment. She went over it again: from the
time she had sold Carl on the line to the moment Nikki
had loaded the last lamp into the Toyota, not a single effort had been spared to secure the new account for Ling
and Son: when it had come to George Ling's attention,
not a single effort had been spared to destroy it.

"Penny for your thoughts."

"They aren't worth it," she said, a bit too quickly,
then added, "but here's one that *is*—Michael, this has
been the most wonderful day of my life."

"And mine," he said, swinging into her driveway and
cutting the engine. "It's just the beginning, Megan."

After her overnight case was inside, Megan wandered back to the Porsche with Michael. In the moon-
light, the car gleamed pewter, reflecting their prolonged
embrace with distortions the intertwined couple couldn't
possibly see.

He finally slid behind the wheel and rolled down his
window. "I meant what I said earlier," he told Megan.
"Today was just the beginning. For us, things will just
get better."

Trudging back to the house, Megan felt a slight chill.
Drawing her sweater more securely over her shoulders,
she considered his last words and thought, I hope so. In
truth, she suspected they had at least one more rough
day to face: tomorrow.

As usual after a good night's sleep, Megan's mind
was clearer. If she wasn't looking forward to resigning,
neither did she dread it; it was simply an unpleasant
task, one to put behind her as soon as possible. Anyway,
by the time she returned an unusual number of calls
collected by the answering service, then typed a re-
spectfully worded letter of resignation, there wasn't
much time to worry. Before leaving the house, she tele-

phoned the office and, learning from Adelle that Michael was tied up on an overseas call, requested an appointment; the time was set for three that afternoon.

The remainder of Monday proceeded at the same brisk pace. Most of Megan's customers had started operating on speeded-up schedules. October was traditionally a frantic month in the industry. Retailers were preparing for Christmas, thus pressuring representatives about deliveries and special promotions. At the same time, purchasing agents were revising their final spring-through-summer budgets. The timing was unfortunate and hardly a matter of choice; in just a little more than two weeks, the buyers had to attend the giant National Furniture Show in High Point, North Carolina, where a great portion of the money would be spent. Megan was used to this frantic period; although she herself had never been to High Point, she certainly knew what to expect from her customers during this period: exhaustion and frayed nerves.

Maybe it rubbed off on her. Some time around noon, she started worrying again about the resignation. Although she would give Michael all the time and assistance necessary to find a new rep, this would be a miserable time for him to be faced with it. But when she asked herself what the options were, none came to mind. Megan was no more anxious to start looking for a job again than Michael would be to dig out the file of résumés, but she had been accused of stealing. Stealing! On top of everything else, she continued to be furious at the position in which she found herself.

The only good thing about the unpleasantness looming just ahead was that it would relieve some seemingly unmanageable strains in another area; she *did* look forward to a relationship free of the employer-employee complications.

By five to three, when Megan walked the long corridor to Michael's office, she had the distinct impression something was burning a hole in her briefcase; needless to say, it was the letter of resignation.

At least Michael was running on time; she'd be able to get this over with in a hurry. Adelle alerted him on the intercom, then told Megan to go right on in. Her heart skipped several beats and she took a deep breath, wishing with every fiber that today's mission wasn't about to further complicate life for this man she loved so desperately.

He was halfway across the room, on his way to greet her, when she entered. Megan pulled the door closed, took one step forward—and the phone rang. Michael shrugged and turned back toward his desk; then stood while he talked, propping one foot on the chair.

She took a seat in the same spot she had sat for her so-called interview. It was hard to believe it had occurred just over two weeks earlier. She looked at Michael and wondered, How did I manage to live before I met you?

He was talking long distance, discussing the preparation of samples for High Point. As usual, Megan admired his style. Michael's posture, a slight rigidity of muscular action, betrayed the importance of the subject—in two weeks, a new Ling line would be unveiled—but his voice remained calm, friendly, and reassuring. "Just get the showroom set up," he was saying. "And don't worry about the new shades; they'll get there."

He paused, ostensibly to listen, but he must have pressed a button, for Adelle suddenly materialized. Michael covered the mouthpiece and whispered, "Ask Nikki to come in and bring the mountings for the new lamps headed for High Point." Then he uncovered the mouthpiece, leaned down to jot a note on his desk pad, and spoke again into the phone. "Well, you don't have to worry about that, either. It's only four lamps; if necessary *I'll* bring them. You're aware I'm flying in a day before market starts, aren't you? Which reminds me—

how's the weather in High Point? Leaves started to change yet?" From that point until he said good-bye, Michael was silent. Megan suspected he had switched subjects as a way of implying things were so well under control at his end, there was even time to discuss the weather. It was an excellent management technique. It was also a good example of Michael's executive capabilities, for it was obvious he was *quite* concerned about the status of the High Point samples; while he listened, he made red-flag notations on his desk calendar and organized a memo for the warehouse. Adelle came back in; he ripped the memo from his pad and handed it to her, then looked slightly puzzled when she failed to retreat. As soon as he hung up, he asked if there was a problem.

"I'm afraid so, Mr. Richardson. Um . . ." she paused, glancing in Megan's direction.

"Oh, it's all right," he said. "She's a fully initiated member of the team."

The words came tumbling out. "Mr. Richardson, everyone in the warehouse is talking about it! Nikki went storming out about five minutes ago. He—"

"Nikki?" Michael was incredulous.

Adelle nodded. "No one seems to know what happened. Except that he got a phone call just before he left. And then he . . . well, he just stomped his foot down and walked out."

"Adelle, are you sure? Nikki doesn't stomp his feet or storm out. You know that."

"Yes, sir." Nonetheless, the secretary appeared resolute. "Maybe you'd better go out there and check it. That's exactly what I was told."

Megan's letter forgotten for the moment, all three of them went to the warehouse, where two of the crewmen related the tale. "He looked awful mad, Mr. Richardson," one said, "but he didn't stop to explain. After he slammed down that phone, he was outa here!"

Michael turned to his secretary and suggested she

telephone Nikki's home from the nearby extension. He thought something might be wrong with one of his children.

But there wasn't. In fact, Nikki's wife hadn't heard from him; she was as disbelieving as everyone else. She promised to contact the office as soon as her husband returned.

Michael turned to Megan. "Before we go back to the office, I need to check some new mountings. Did you ever get a chance to look at the new shipment, by the way?"

She shook her head, then followed him to a padlocked door marked OFF LIMITS TO UNAUTHORIZED PERSONNEL. Michael used his key—Nikki had the only other one—and they entered a small room containing tiered display shelves. Three of them were stacked with accessories and lamp bases.

Michael switched on the overhead light. "I think I told you, this shipment's so new it hasn't even been photographed. There—top row: those are the four lamps I'm putting a rush on for High Point. The others can wait."

Megan headed straight for the second lamp on the left. "My God, Michael," she breathed. "This is without a doubt the most outstanding piece of porcelain I've ever seen!"

He made no attempt to conceal his pleasure. "That one was on the drawing board for one hell of a long time. The Japanese artisan did a superb job." She noticed, again, the modesty; Michael always managed to steer clear of any statement that might elicit a direct compliment about his design talent. Indirectly, she intended to praise him anyway.

"That black background," she said reverently. "It's so perfectly smooth it reminds me of . . . of a few very rare examples of Italian onyx." Megan knew that on porcelain, smooth, flawless black was a difficult finish to accomplish. She continued, "And the pattern overlay—it's so *different!* How on earth did you talk the Japanese into doing it?"

"Not easily," he admitted.

She turned to face him. "Well, it was worth it. It makes me think of a flame rising against a perfectly black night sky."

Michael grinned. "Megan, I'm surprised at you; you're mixing metaphors. First the background reminded you of onyx and now it reminds you of the night sky. Which is it?"

She turned back to the lamp, cocking her head to one side. "Onyx," she pronounced at last. "It's a perfect piece of black onyx."

"Then the lamp has a name," he said. "Onyx Flame."

"Pretty good, boss. Congratulations!"

"I didn't say I *like* the name. I can think of one that would be much more descriptive."

She looked puzzled.

"That thing you call a flame," he said, "is exactly the color of your hair. I'd prefer to call the lamp Megan's Crowning Glory. Now, we'd better head back."

Adelle was at her desk, typing, and no further emergencies had occurred in their absence. Thank God, Megan thought; she had arrived at the office nearly forty minutes ago and, as yet, still not had a chance to tell Michael about her decision to resign.

"Any news on Nikki?" Michael asked Adelle.

"No, sir. In fact, it's been quiet for a change. Mr. Ling wants to talk to you when you get a chance; that's about all."

Michael scowled, then paused long enough to allow Megan to precede him into the office. When the door was shut, he said, "I haven't taken up the matter of Carl Jurgen's lamps, Megan. I wasn't sure whether or not you wanted to be here when I talk to George."

She hesitated. "Yes, but not right this minute, please. Before you talk to Mr. Ling, there's something you should know. I—"

The buzzer interrupted. "Mr. Richardson, sorry to bother you again, but Mr. Ling just phoned to say he's on his way in. I guess it was more important than I realized." Michael sighed and switched off the intercom, lifting both arms, palms upraised, in a what-can-I-do gesture.

Then he sank into the chair, propped both elbows on the desk, and formed his fingers into a tepee, waiting. Less than twenty seconds later, George Ling walked in.

Much to Megan's surprise, he was muscular but scholarly looking, probably no older than fifty. He wore an expression of bland benevolence. She wasn't sure what she had expected—a monster, perhaps.

"This is Miss McBride?" he asked. Michael responded with a curt nod.

Ling pivoted, facing Megan. "I'll have to ask you to leave," he said importantly. "This is company business."

Without apparent emotion, Michael reminded the man of where he was. "In here, I'm the only one authorized to throw people out. Are you getting ready to say something she can't hear?"

Megan was acutely uncomfortable. She could only assume there was good reason for directing the scene purposely to humiliate his employer; handling delicate situations with diplomacy was Michael's normal style. *What* reason? she asked herself, squirming.

Whatever it was, Ling had clearly been thrown off stride, too; Megan saw him struggling for composure. Evidently, he wanted foremost to rescue his endangered prestige, for he finally put on an ingratiating little smile and said, "It's for her own sake, Michael. We don't want to embarrass her, now do we?"

Michael came back with: "Generally, people suffer more from words spoken behind their backs. If you're planning to talk about Miss McBride, I want you to do it in her presence. I'll take the responsibility." With impressive nonchalance, he sank back in his chair. Now Megan *knew* he was putting on an act!

"As you wish," Ling rejoined—very smoothly, Megan thought—and then he said the matter only concerned her indirectly, anyway. When he finally got to the point of his visit to Michael's office, the most impressive aspect of his speech was its executive tenor; it was pure boardroom.

"Something inexcusable happened a while ago, and I want you to take care of it, Michael. That man you hired for the warehouse—what's his name, confound it?—anyway, I called down about something and the fool hung up before I was finished with him! Now they tell me he's left without permission, without even punching out! That won't do, you know. In fact, when you were hired I remember thinking maybe it wasn't wise to let you bring string-alongs; they're probably not trained to our standards."

He had evidently fallen in love with the sound of his own voice; if not, Ling must have had some other excuse for failing to notice Megan's and Michael's reactions. Her mouth had fallen open. As for Michael, he came half out of his chair before regaining control. Now he said, "Sit down, George."

Ling waved away the suggestion. "No, no," he said irritably. "There's no reason you can't handle this without further drain on *my* time. Just fire the man. As I told him, *you* certainly wouldn't condone his part as an accessory in Miss McBride's lamp-theft ring." Hardly drawing a breath, Ling leveled an imperious gaze at Megan, then added, "And, young woman, I suppose Mr. Richardson's already dealt with you. Frankly, I'm amazed you had the nerve to show your face in here today—"

Michael had had enough. He repeated, "Sit down, George," and this time the words rang out with decisive menace. When there was no response Michael stood up;

the way he did it caused Ling to take an instinctive step backward.

"One . . . more . . . time . . . George. *Sit down.* Good. Now, I have a few things to say."

Megan had begun to feel like the lone spectator in some weird improvisational playhouse. What followed were twenty of the strangest minutes she had ever experienced; in fact, considering the business backdrop, the scene contained elements of the bizarre. She could only suppose it was because she had missed the first act; to follow this script, one evidently needed to know the history of a volatile character: George Ling.

That he was highly excitable was obvious; at one point, when asked about evidence, he catapulted from the chair and gleefully clapped his hands before revealing that the computer showed no advance payment for the lamps. But Ling might also be seriously neurotic, Megan thought, for Michael was playing *his* role like . . . like Dr. Jekyll trying to find and eradicate Mr. Hyde! One moment he cajoled, allowing his antagonist's worst features to emerge; the next he reasoned, evidently wanting George Ling to draw his own conclusions. At no point was there further display of anger, or even impatience. Whatever Michael's strategy, he was quite practiced at it.

And it worked, that was the amazing part! Right around the time Megan started to think the butler must have done it, reality resurfaced. The little company clerk appeared bearing proof—that handwritten receipt of payment—and Michael's character eased into normal behavior patterns. Instead of taking Ling to task, Michael encouraged him to take credit for having originated the policy whereby customers were never to be inconvenienced by computer deficiencies.

As Megan heard her employer emphasizing that old bromide—mistakes will happen, George—she also witnessed Ling's face undergoing a series of steady changes: from pasty pale, one eyelid twitching involuntarily, to a healthy complexion and confident gaze. Two or three minutes after the clerk's departure, as the company owner was offering to call Nikki and apologize, she found herself thinking that the real George Ling was quite a charming and controlled man. Or was this the character and that *other* personality the fabrication?

The explanation could come only from Michael, of course, and, meanwhile, Megan's mental imagery was adjusting her view of this already fascinating man; he now loomed in her mind as an intellectual giant, a captain of industry, and a five-star general of humanitarianism. She shook her head, commanding a return to reality, then got it when she looked at him.

The scene had taken its toll. Michael Richardson was an exceptional individual, true, but if appearance were any indication, he needed a break. He was tired of problems.

George Ling was on his feet, approaching Megan with outstretched hand. She took it.

"Miss McBride," he said, "you're special. Any other rep would have resigned. Some day I'll repay you for this, um, patience."

She heard herself reassuring him that there were no hard feelings. Megan could hardly believe the words had come from her own mouth!

As soon as they were alone, Michael reached for her. She rested her head on his shoulder. Very gently and probably unconsciously, Michael rocked, back and forth, the way one often does with infants. Megan allowed herself to go with the soothing motion.

"Honey, that was a superb gesture," he said at last.

She kept quiet, not feeling the slightest bit guilty.

"You know," he chuckled, "this thing worried me all day. I was so sure you were going to tell George Ling where he could stick his job. Shows how much *I* know about people."

Now Megan felt guilty! But not enough to straighten

him out! "Listen, Richardson," she said lightly, "I only ask one thing . . ."

"What's that?"

"Would you please—please—tell me what was going on in here?"

12

The subject of George Ling wasn't brought up again that night. Michael gave Megan time to shower and change, then he picked her up and they had an unusually pleasant dinner at his home. It was nice to hear Jeffie's excited update: no problems, thank God, only adventures with Chad, progress with the computer program, the joy of having his father home. Tara had gone out with a new beau; the house seemed unusually quiet, which was also good.

After dinner, Jeffie sat with them in the family room, getting sleepier and sleepier. And each time he yawned, Michael yawned twice. Megan liked the atmosphere, the easygoing and unpretentious feeling of family. And she knew the man she loved was paying her a tremendous compliment, whether or not he knew it, by making no attempt to conceal his exhaustion. Finally Megan herself started yawning—just before ten P.M. she woke up. Michael was asleep beside her, slumped sideways on the sofa; his son was slumbering in a recliner. She got them both up and helped put Jeffie in his wheelchair, after which the teenager insisted he could navigate alone to the makeshift bedroom.

On the way home, she stifled a yawn and said, "I should have insisted on driving over . . . silly for you to do all this."

"No, it isn't," he said. "I don't want you out alone at night."

She was far too relaxed to consider reigniting the old debate.

Inside Megan's front door, she clung to Michael for a long moment after their good-night kiss, suddenly reluctant to release him and face an empty bed. But he needed rest. She gave him a playful little shove and said, "Get out of here, boss. Go get some sleep and tomorrow night, we'll pick up where we left off."

"Since you put it that way I can pull rank," he rejoined. "I *am* the boss, remember?"

Megan found herself pinned tightly against the hard unyielding body. Thirty minutes later, when he finally released her from the unruly and teasing game in which she had become an instantly willing player, Megan begged him not to stop. In response, she got that devilish grin. And then Michael said, "No, I want you to get some sleep—tomorrow night we'll pick up where we left off."

She was left alone with a familiar thought: Michael Richardson simply can't *be* controlled. As she moved toward her bedroom, she smiled dreamily. Well, who wants to control an act like that, anyway?

The next few days passed in a blur of happy activity. Happy for Megan. Sales and contracts for prospective sales progressed at an amazing speed. There were reasons to be grateful she was still with Ling and Son, and they weren't purely financial. The business association had turned into an asset to her relationship with Michael. Megan no longer pretended, even to herself, that she lived for much else than that relationship.

It was ironic, but the period of extreme contentment came from something that might otherwise have made her miserable: Michael was spending eighteen hours a day, sometimes longer, in the office. Nikki had asked for a vacation—"time to think things over," he had said; no one but Michael had sufficient knowledge, then, to oversee and coordinate completion of hundreds of warehouse details critical before the High Point market.

It was the knowledge that both her attitude and her activity were helping him get through the emergency that made her feel good. Business-wise, Southern California was once again becoming profitable; this was a factor no longer worrying Michael. On the home front, Megan quietly made a point of keeping in touch with Jeffie, thus alleviating a portion of the father's guilt; fortunately, Chad was still spending a great deal of time with the boy—they had become fast friends—so she doubted Michael's absence was felt as severely as he feared, anyway. But Megan's most valuable gift was, simply, her understanding; that and her total acceptance—this was one problem that would end the minute Michael stepped on the plane for High Point, she reasoned, so why make it worse by nagging him to slow down?

She had a long expensive talk with her parents in Japan; the transpacific cable probably wasn't necessary to carry the sounds of their boisterous cheers and congratulations when they heard, "Mom, Dad, guess what? I'm in love." Trying to explain why she was happy during a period Michael hardly had time for her, Megan started searching for words. Patricia McBride evidently understood and ended by saying, "Obviously, darling, you two are discovering something really terrific at an early date. And don't forget—when you need his understanding during a rough period, I'm sure he'll give it, just as you are now. Keep it up, Megan; it's worth it."

Megan kept hearing her mother's words. She agreed: Michael would be every bit as protective of her needs—of course he would; their lovemaking had proven as much!—but she scoffed at the very suggestion of "a rough period." Now that the kinks had been smoothed from those first difficult days, Megan could not possibly believe life would ever be anything but perfect.

Lover's fantasies. She didn't have much longer to indulge in this particular one.

Before the blowup, they had one last peaceful conversation. It occurred during one of the nightly phone conversations intended to cover some of their loneliness in that hectic period. Michael always called right around eleven, from the office, of course, and they would chat quietly, usually for no longer than five minutes, then disconnect after getting to the real purpose for the ritual: an expression of love spoken in voices swollen with longing but gentle with mutual sympathy and respect. After that Megan would go to bed and sleep deeply and dreamlessly.

On Friday, she had reason to visit the office unexpectedly. Her news was so good, she literally bounced through the anteroom, waving a kiss to Adelle as she passed, her blue and white striped silk dress flowing with her movements. But Michael had news for her, too, and he insisted on talking first.

"Hey, sit down!" he laughed. "You look like a balloon."

"I can't, Michael! I'm too excited! Tell me what it is, quick, so I can talk!"

He folded his arms, trying to appear bored, then gave an exaggerated yawn and patted his mouth. "Okay," he said dryly, "you're going to High Point."

"That's good," she said in a rush. "Now let me tell you what happened this af—" Megan suddenly stopped. "Did you say I'm going to High Point?"

The problem was that for strictly business reasons, she had always resisted pressures to attend the National Furniture Show. Some reps thought it was an absolute must, but in Megan's opinion, local accounts only fell apart during a prolonged period with no one around to handle delivery problems, rush orders, complaints, minutiae.

While she was organizing an explanation for Michael, she failed to note his increasing disappointment with her frozen reaction. Later she would ask herself if *this* was the point at which everything went wrong; but at the time, she said something that was easy for him to misinterpret.

"I'd like to be with you," Megan mused aloud, still innocently unaware, "but . . . is that a good enough reason to go?"

"Megan!" he snapped. "I wouldn't spend the company's money for personal frivolities! The rea—"

"You mean Ling and Son wants to pay my way?" She didn't understand; in return for supposedly high commission gains, reps were always expected to take care of their own expenses.

"In this case, yes, and if you'll stop interrupting, I'll explain." He went on to say that an important contract agent would be in High Point seeking deals for new hotel rooms, a *national* hotel chain; furthermore, the pricing Michael had just done on some of the pieces scheduled for market introduction would place them low enough for consideration. "You were the one chosen—by George *and* me, Megan—as most capable of selling those contracts." His voice had grown even harder than in the beginning of this confusing episode.

By the time he told her George Ling was the one who had suggested paying her way, she was thoroughly miserable. Michael was making sense, of course—but what had she done to make him so angry?

"Well?" Michael said, "Are you going to High Point or not?"

"Of course," she stammered.

He sighed. "All right, Megan. Then what was it you wanted to tell me?"

She mumbled something about having just made an enormous package sale on their new lamp, Onyx Flame, and that she was on her way to Palm Springs for the signing of the final papers. "Actually," she said, almost apologetically, "I had to talk to you anyway because the chain's buyer wants a two-month exclusive on the lamp. We don't have to deliver until Easter, by the way."

After double-checking her price quote, Michael agreed to the exclusive. *Then he told her she couldn't go to Palm Springs!* His arms were tightly clasped across his chest. Megan thought he was literally standing there waiting for the argument. He got one.

"You can't be serious!" she said.

"By the time you're halfway there, it'll be dark. I don't want you on the road at that hour," he retorted.

"You'd actually have me lose this sale? Their deadline for special Easter purchases is midnight tonight."

If only Michael had been able to drop the brittle tenor from his voice! Perhaps then he might also have put it differently; he could have simply admitted that if something were to be lost, he'd far rather it be the sale than Megan. As it happened, all he said, in those cold demanding tones, was: "I don't want to discuss this. Just *don't go.*"

She got up very slowly, then headed even more slowly for the door. Megan literally prayed Michael would stop her, say something soft and affectionate.

But the door closed behind her and she walked the long maze of corridors in a silence unlike any other she had known in her life.

13

She had planned to spend the night in Palm Springs but when the chief purchasing agent of the enormous chain, China Cove, signed the papers immediately, it seemed unnecessary. If she had ever craved the familiar comforts of home, it was tonight.

Since it was almost twelve o'clock when she got in, she was surprised to hear the phone. She intended to ignore it. It wouldn't be Michael, not at this hour—if ever again, anyway. And she'd forgotten to check with her service before leaving; if customers had called during the afternoon, it was procedure for the operators to try to reach her until twelve o'clock. For once, she was willing to let business details drop; in fact, her clients could have fallen into a black hole for all she cared.

During a portion of the two-and-a-half-hour return drive, she had nursed the hope that Michael would call and explain away the whole mess: some sort of simple misunderstanding, nothing more. It hadn't been a very convincing possibility, though, mainly because the problem obviously wasn't simple. In a way, she blamed herself. On their very first "date"—that historic occasion at the Italian restaurant—there had been pretty clear signals indicating Michael's relentless objections to . . .

To what? she asked herself, trying to remember and piece together the various clues. Well, that was the reason she felt partly responsible; she had *wanted* to overlook anything that might threaten her newfound happiness; in that she had been so successful that now she didn't know the questions, much less the answers. Her recollections were vague . . . Tara had teased her uncle and talked about him "getting over it," or something like that. What was "it," though? There were too many options: from a traumatic experience to the rather frightening prospect that Michael Richardson was one of those men convinced that all women have to be protected "for their own good." She shuddered; surely, if that were the case, she would have suspected it before now.

She had already covered Sinbad; since she had returned, his playful screeches had only gotten on her nerves. Now he started up again; the phone must have been on its tenth ring. She answered it with unconcealed irritation and, as expected, it was the answering service. Megan politely reminded the operator of his instructions to quit after the fifth ring.

"I'm sorry, Miss McBride." The voice indicated it was quite accustomed to aggravated customers. "Your employer said it was urgent, that if we failed to reach you, *we* were to call him back."

Now the operator had her full attention. "Go ahead," she said. "What's the message?"

"From Michael Richardson," the bored voice answered, obviously reading, "Please come by Ling and Son office at nine tomorrow morning. His call came at eight-thirty, Miss McBride, but you weren't—"

"Yes, I know," Megan interrupted. She told the voice it had done the right thing, then refused to take any further messages. The voice said that would be "perfectly acceptable."

"Damn!" Megan said when the receiver had been replaced. There was nothing to be derived from a simple summons to the office; now she'd probably have trouble sleeping, worried about Michael's current mood. Why couldn't he have just said, "Tell Miss McBride I'm sorry she wasn't home for my call and that I love her."

She woke up early, started for her closet, and then just stood there, staring at the neatly arranged row of business suits and dresses. Something was bothering her, but she couldn't think what. Finally she decided it would be better to return to the normal routine: coffee first, then shower, then clothes.

As she poured the second cup, she remembered—today's Saturday, no wonder I was confused; I can't put business clothes on! Megan leaped from her chair and grabbed the telephone. She would call Michael to delay their appointment until later in the afternoon, telling him about her regular tennis game; after keeping her friends waiting a couple of weeks back, she couldn't stand them up now. When she looked at the time—five after six—she decided it was far too early to call and wake up Jeffie and Tara; she'd have to hope he answered his private Ling and Son line before it was time to meet the rest of her foursome.

But he didn't, and because of the location of public phones at the park where her group played, she never made the connection. By ten, when her friends agreed to forego the next set after listening to her dilemma, Megan figured it was a bit late to inform Michael she wouldn't make their meeting on time. She just got in the Toyota and hit the accelerator. When she finally arrived at the office, wearing a brief white tennis outfit with a line of yellow ruffles at hemline and sleeves, she appeared every bit as composed as an airless ball on a bad bounce. In fact, thinking of the clothes, she was actually feeling sorry for herself. Why on earth does this keep happening to me?

Compared to Michael's office, she looked wonderful. There were lamps scattered everywhere; or, in some cases, just shades and mountings and hardware. Megan knew why, of course—he was personally double-checking assembly fittings for the High Point samples—but,

still, it was a shock to see her well-organized employer
seated amid total disarray.

It was too bad the mess had to catch her attention
first. Had she seen Michael's face, instead, she would
have known something supremely important: no man
had ever been happier to see *anyone;* his relief was overwhelming. Whatever the reason for their current misunderstanding, this man loved Megan too deeply to be
contributing to it purposely. By the time she stopped
gawking at the cluttered office, though, Michael had
put on his very temperate employer's mask. It was a demeanor that never failed to inspire respect—and awe,
for this particular executive was strikingly impressive—but it wasn't likely to encourage security, especially not when Megan felt so shabby by comparison.
Unconsciously, she reached up to smooth her dishev-
eled red mane; it seemed to make things worse; the air
contained just enough static electricity to loosen several more strands. Great, Megan thought, trying to act
as though she didn't notice.

Michael looked amused; she wanted to hit him. And
he still hadn't told her why she'd been summoned. Finally she said, "When you called, did you realize you
were asking me to come in on Saturday?"

"Frankly, no," he answered at once. "Would you
have refused to come?"

"I had plans, Michael," she started. Before she could
open her mouth to explain further, he interrupted.

"I see," he said, deadpan.

Megan didn't appreciate that. Nor did she know what
he meant. She had been on the verge of explaining the
delay; and she also would have told Michael she'd
rather be with him than out playing tennis, no matter if
she had to travel to his office or Timbuktu. But she
wasn't going to beg for the privilege of saying it. Megan
had far too much pride for that. In less than two minutes, they had reached a stalemate.

Finally the silence got to her. In a distinctly edgy tone, she said, "Michael, *why* did you call for me?"

"Two reasons. First, I didn't like the way we left things last night; I really wish that hadn't happened. Second, I wanted to make sure you're home safely."

It never occurred to her that the first statement might have been his way of apologizing. All she could think of was that miserable tennis set, when she had tried to concentrate while she worried about his summons, about not being able to reach him. Automatically, incredulously, she asked, "Couldn't we have just talked on the phone?"

He didn't say anything. And in that state of confusion, Megan didn't stop to think of the way she and Michael had spent the preceding days; with total faith in their relationship, a standard had been set: during the hectic pre–High Point period both had made it clear they wanted to spend every free minute together; there had been many calls with messages like "Meet me here at such-and-such a time." If Michael's call to the answering service had been similar—say, just a normal arrangement for Saturday morning breakfast at the coffee shop near the office—it would have made a difference to her.

He still wasn't talking. Now she was completely unnerved. All she wanted to do was get out of the building without making things any worse. So she counted mentally to ten and said, "Look, about yesterday afternoon—you were tired. I can appreciate that."

Michael looked as though her statement was literally the last thing he had expected to hear. Evidently it pleased him, for he relaxed and said, "No, it wasn't just that I was tired. Actually, I really do worry—"

She was afraid they were about to repeat yesterday's scene; before he started giving commands again, she was going to try to slip in at least a few words of her own. It started with: "But, Michael, that wasn't anything to worry about. I've driven to Palm Springs hundreds of times. And you certainly wouldn't have wanted me to forfeit the commission, would you? Well, would you, Michael?"

His relaxed expression fell away; it didn't matter; Megan hadn't noticed it to begin with. Now, in an unyielding tone, he asked if her commission were more important than his peace of mind.

"That's not fair!" she returned angrily. "I'm thirty years old, Michael, not eighteen! Don't treat me as if I were a child."

He shrugged. "Why not? You're acting like one!"

When Megan left his office this time, her exit could hardly be described as slow.

As happy as the previous period had been, now Megan's days passed in a vague fog of depression. Michael's words kept returning to her: "Is the commission more important . . . ," and she was horrified when she started wondering if he might not be justified, after all. First thing each morning, when her mind was clearest, she knew better.

Megan didn't pretend to understand the issues. But she knew none of this had to do with right or wrong, and certainly not with commissions. As she saw it, Michael was determined to alter her personality—forcibly, if he had to—in a basic and fundamentally very important way. This wasn't comprehensible to her, for the woman whose essential character had attracted him in the first place was composed of a little of this, a little of that, and a lot of something else: independence.

She kept remembering an experience in college. She had enrolled in a course called "Sculpting for Pleasure," and her assignment for the semester was a single project. As stated by the professor, a sculptor of considerable success: "Choose something you love and turn it into a statue you love."

Megan's choice had been simple: children. And she had narrowed the field to a single outstanding photograph from *National Geographic*, an Australian toddler looking at his first koala. For the next two weeks, she had pounded and pulled and pummeled and cajoled until the clay was a two-foot-tall mass resembling a chubby human being. Then the hard part had begun, the challenge of detail, of making that mass live and breathe.

Toward the end of the semester, the professor had said, "Just what are you doing, Miss McBride?"

"Trying to make the nose more perfect, sir."

His overgrown eyebrows had risen almost into his hairline. *"Really?* Why would you want to do that?"

"Well . . . it's crooked, sir. Surely no one would buy it this way!"

"But you're not sculpting for sale, Miss McBride. Your assignment was to sculpt something *you* love. Are you infatuated with perfect noses? Have you ever even *seen* a three-year-old with a perfect nose?"

"No, sir."

He had asked her to step back and view her work from a distance. "Of course, the final choices are yours, Miss McBride, but you've achieved something quite rare for an amateur—you've made a face, an imperfect face, full of wonder and joy. Unless you disagree, then I suggest you put away the chisel. Start *adding* to the statue. For instance, put in more movement and muscle tension."

For the next few days, the professor circulated among the students with similar remarks for each one. Then, finally, he moved Megan's statue to the front of the room and said, "Class, I'm going to offer to buy some of your work. Those thinking of a career in art will find that a first sale's a pretty valuable credential. But there are strict conditions attached: I pay only ten dollars per statue and you have to sign an agreement to buy it back in one year at double the price. Are you with me?"

In unison, the entire class had nodded, fascinated.

He turned toward Megan, who had been standing

self-consciously nearby. "Miss McBride, your piece may now be considered *commissioned,* so I'm ordering certain changes more to my liking. The child's hair is a mess; I want it 'combed,' if you will."

Impulsively, she objected. "But, sir—he's standing in an open field, windblown!"

"Nonetheless, that's the way I want it. And a few other things . . ." The professor went on to order a repair in wrinkled clothing, a neatly tied pair of shoelaces, and an "uncrinkling" of the eyes. Then he pulled a contract from a desk drawer. "If you'll sign the revision-and-repurchase agreement . . ."

Megan was embarrassed. "Professor, I'm sorry. I'd rather not. I mean, *you* like the statue one way and I . . . well, I just wouldn't *want* it back!"

The teacher withdrew his contract. "Okay." He faced the class again. "And I sincerely hope the rest of you will react the same way. Don't try to change something that's already got the elements you wanted in the first place. If you do, I guarantee that both you and your client, if you turn professional, will end up disliking the piece." He smiled broadly, then faced Megan again. "Now, Miss McBride, do you want to sell this piece to me just as it is: ten dollars and a buy-back clause?"

She turned him down. She didn't need a professional credential. And she wasn't about to make a foolish business deal. Childhood Discovery resided in her backyard. It wasn't perfect, but she kept it there as a reminder of a valuable lesson: don't try to change the things you love.

Life went on, of course, and Megan learned she and Michael could survive one serious disagreement. Their relationship didn't totally disintegrate because Megan could no longer imagine life without Michael; as maudlin as the question seemed, she honestly wondered if she *could* make it without him. One morning, with eyes still red from crying herself to sleep the night before, she sought solace in Sinbad's company, letting him spend the ritual coffee session perched atop her shoulder. She said, "You know, bird, I would work hard to put back what Michael and I used to have!"

But the day-to-day circumstances of their overdynamic and overstressed lives now conspired to drive the wedge deeper. By the time Megan's desperation drove her beyond the point of histrionics with her parrot—when she finally got up enough courage to make a serious attempt at communication with Michael—it was probably already too late.

At Megan's request, he stopped by her house one evening on his way home for dinner. After an awkward and stilted embrace that bore no resemblance to earlier ecstatic adventures, she started at once into her little prepared speech. The plan was to start off lightly, remembering she was on a subject Michael evidently preferred to avoid: his reason for excessive concern about physical safety. They were sitting in the den-library-bar portion of the house, and a freshly prepared iced pitcher of martinis stood nearby, awaiting the successful completion of their talk. The room was slightly less casual than the connecting office, but he looked comfortable in a big bentwood rocker, so Megan dragged a cushioned ottoman from the sofa setting and perched on top.

"We need to talk," she said.

He nodded.

"Um . . ." she cleared her throat, then plunged ahead. "The fact is, Richardson, there's a tarantula on our table!"

"What?"

She had the feeling he was preoccupied, that she didn't have his full attention—and she'd been so certain he would respond to his own analogy!

"Michael, we can't just keep on ignoring it!"

"Ignoring what?"

Now Megan was positive his mind was elsewhere; he

wasn't even looking at her. Nonetheless, she had gotten this far and she was determined to keep trying.

"Michael," she pleaded, "we're growing farther and farther apart! *You're* the one who told me we can't pretend the tarantulas aren't here, can't just move to another table and assume they—" She stopped, totally confounded. Michael had started grinning. It was that wonderful, teasing, provocative smile she had missed so much lately; but she couldn't help thinking he had picked a hell of a time to rediscover it.

He laughed—really laughed. This was getting ridiculous. It was more than merely rude; it was humiliating.

"Megan," he said finally, "the thing you need to worry about isn't tarantulas. Honey, that bird of yours just hopped up on the bar. He's getting totally soused in that martini pitcher!"

14

What followed was inevitable: gradual slowdown, then a total cessation, of communications, such as they were, between Michael and Megan. She had made no further attempt to draw him out on the personal safety issue. After plucking the half-drowned and thoroughly inebriated parrot from his cocktail, he had said, "Megan, let's not talk about tarantulas tonight; I'm too tired for amateur psychoanalysis." As far as she was concerned, it was an effective indication of indifference; if a ginned-out bird was sufficient excuse for Michael to put off solving the problems threatening their relationship . . .

Actually, she wondered if she had misjudged Michael from the very beginning. Thinking back, Megan clearly recalled her brand-new employer admitting his reluctance to hire female reps; as for his exact words, however, memory of that episode at the Italian restaurant was permanently blurred, presumably because of her nervous efforts to resist the initial attraction. Anyway, Michael was indeed acting like a man who considered women inferior; he might not *ever* intend to explain his reason for ordering Megan around like a child.

After Sinbad's debauchery, on the weekend, she summed up the current situation. So far as she knew, only two positive factors remained in the relationship.

The first and most important was the fact that Megan loved him. That might have been a negative, true;

there was no denying she was heading for a heavy fall. But she listed it with assets because as long as Michael claimed to feel the same way, it signaled some hope, however small. At the same time, she kept losing a constant mental debate: why not fall *out* of love with a man who thinks you're inferior?

Sometimes she was sure it would be possible to bring her emotions more in line with reality *if only* Michael possessed less of the pure animal magnetism, the irresistible physical pull, that caused her knees to go weak in his presence and her empty arms to ache at night, when she was alone. But then, just as she'd convince herself the reaction was completely chemical and would calm down soon enough, something would happen to remind Megan of her phenomenal respect for him. On one recent occasion, the friendly Ling receptionist had told her, "Mr. Richardson saved my baby's life." Michael himself denied this; he insisted the toddler had needed minor surgery, that's all, and that he'd done nothing more than locate and engage a topflight specialist to perform it. Undoubtedly the truth was somewhere in the middle of the two versions, but the point was Megan's increasing awareness—from a lot of people, not just the receptionist—that Michael Richardson never seemed too busy to help solve a problem. Except for ours, she reminded herself.

Secondly, the ritual phone calls continued. This was somewhat surprising, for their quiet dinners around the corner from the office had stopped, partly because attempts at normal conversation were painfully awkward—my God, she thought, the tarantula on the table just sits there, growing fatter and more dangerous!—but also because Megan **had** listened to her friend Sharon's advice.

"Whatever you do, Megan, don't start feeling sorry for yourself! Get out with friends. It wouldn't hurt to see some other men, either, Miss Lonelyheart, and prove to yourself that life goes on." The good doctor and friend had also told her she ought to ask around, find out for herself why Michael overreacted on the subject of physical safety; according to Sharon, he had to have a reason, and if Megan refused to let go of her hopes for the relationship, she nonetheless should learn what, exactly, she was up against. Anyway, Megan had reluctantly backed away from the brief dinners; Michael had been relieved, which had proven disconcerting; he had said she needed more recreation than he'd be able to provide until the High Point pressures subsided. After that, only the nightly telephone exchange kept her going; no way, no matter what her friends had planned, would she miss that eleven o'clock call. As for going out with other men, the advice was absurd! Who on earth could compete with Michael Richardson?

It wasn't until Monday morning she admitted to herself she was experiencing the long and dreaded fall; she'd just had one of those toss-and-turn nights; now she was stiff, inert, and incapable of fooling herself. At five A.M., she tied the belt of her bathrobe, filled a large mug of coffee, and carried it to the little enclosed front courtyard, thinking that early risings had one undeniable advantage: the opportunity to view daybreak. Just as the first shy strands of color appeared, she heard a muted *plop* from the area of the driveway. The *Los Angeles Times* had arrived, probably to remind her the world did, indeed, continue turning on its axis, she thought with a trace of the self-pity Sharon had warned her to avoid.

When the sun completed its miraculous rebirth and the sky was stained pale yellow, she retrieved the paper, then couldn't concentrate on the news.

Last night, Michael hadn't made the all-important telephone call. The facts of real life now rained down like so many rocks, each one striking another bruise on her psyche.

She had no energy. Zip. None. This was a normal symptom of mild depression, or so Sharon had said, and

Megan wasn't to worry about it. She made a mental contract with herself—start a regular exercise program. Normally she settled for one vigorous workout per week—at the Y preceeding her session with the Japanese students—and a few hours of weekend tennis. Perhaps a more structured routine would give her more energy. She got up and went into the house, refilled the coffee mug, pulled her appointment calendar from the briefcase and returned to the patio.

Flipping the pages of the book, her eyes fell on the following notation for September 29: "Carl Jurgen, grand opening party for retl. str., 8 pm, resvtns. at Hotel Del." Megan snapped the book shut. So that had been the date of what her mind had permanently labeled the Coronado Affair? And today's date was—she squinted down at the *Times* resting at her feet—October 5. Short-lived affair, she thought wryly; involuntarily, her mind had returned immediately to the anguish she was trying so hard to control.

When all else had appeared to be failing, that eleven o'clock ritual had been the lifeline of the tenuous relationship. As long as Michael wanted her to know, every night, that he loved her, then another twenty-four hours were secure, if not idyllic. The more dependent she became on hearing those words, the more fearful she was that, one night, the telephone might not ring.

And last night it hadn't. His decision had been made. She took a sip of coffee. Cold. And so was Megan. On an unusually warm fall morning, wearing a long-sleeved velour bathrobe, she was freezing. The realization was a bit much. She finally caved in; burying her face in two chilled palms, she broke down and sobbed.

It made her feel better. While she was brushing the last of the tears from her cheeks, a gentle breeze picked up the top pages of the *Times* and scattered them playfully across the grass. Instinctively, Megan went after them. Within a few seconds, standing in the middle of the yard and remembering another occasion when she had scurried after runaway papers, she was crying again.

It was all so melodramatic, and she knew it. No one would ever be able to understand the nature of such pain, not unless it were someone as much in love as Megan. And who had ever been as much in love as Megan?

That day in her yard . . . She had gone into Michael's arms as though drawn by a magnet. Which, as far as Megan was concerned, was what he was: an overpowering, totally irresistible magnet. And when she touched the magnet, sparks of pleasure ignited into flames of ecstasy. She trembled, suddenly feeling again the fiery touch of his tongue and fingertips; and then Megan began to ache with the intensity of her desire for him—it didn't make sense, but she *needed* to feel the hard explosion of his loins against hers. How could she have made anyone understand that, melodramatic or not, she wasn't certain she had courage enough to endure this fatal attraction, unrequited?

She took several deep breaths in rhythmic succession. Courage. That was the key. She had to shore up her defenses until the passage of time could take care of the rest. The panic began to ebb; finally, she marshaled her thoughts. Forgetting entirely about the scattered newspaper, she trudged back over to her appointment book and saw that there was plenty of time—it was only seven A.M.—for a workout at the Y.

Chad was there, teaching an early swim class. Megan waved, then bypassed the exercise machines and went, instead, to her locker. In a few minutes, clad in a black and white striped racing suit and cap, she was paddling around the shallow end. The water was cool and soothing. It wasn't long before she felt up to swimming laps. She emerged feeling pleasantly exhausted.

"What's the occasion?" Chad asked as she dragged herself over the side.

Megan ripped off the cap, her red hair falling in

waves to her shoulders. "Oh, nothing. Just haven't
been getting enough exercise lately." And then: "Chad,
how can I ever thank you for all you've done to help Jeffie?"

"Mr. Richardson's gift was sufficient, if you please."
There was a dry suggestion of understatement.

"What gift?"

"You mean you don't know?"

"Of course not, silly! If I did, would I ask?"

Chad shook his head. "That man of yours is something else!"

Megan let it ride.

"He donated the remaining funds for our stalled project. We're finally gonna have that special pool for the
handicapped." Chad paused. A slightly worried look
crossed his eyes, then he shrugged and continued. "Actually, since he forbade us to name the pool after him,
maybe I wasn't supposed to mention it to *you*, either.
Too late now. Anyway, about Jeffie—I was trying to repay you, Megan, for all the volunteer hours you've put
into this place. But that doesn't turn out to be easy.
Now we're *really* indebted."

She smiled gently. "No, you're not. You never were."

Chad ignored her. "And on top of that, I've gotten totally hooked on Jeffie."

"Which I can assure you is mutual," she said. Then
her eyebrows furrowed. "Chad—does Jeffie talk freely
to you? About personal matters, I mean?"

"Like what, in particular?"

She hesitated, searching for an answer that would
conceal as much as it told. Finally she said, "It's hard to
explain, but I've got a feeling Michael, um, worries
more than he needs to about accidents. Maybe something happened to cause it."

The Y instructor looked confused. "I dunno, Megan
. . . Jeffie just broke his leg. And he said his mother had
a skiing accident . . ."

Megan shook her head. "It's not that, I promise. Something else, Chad, and it *must* involve cars."

"Well, Jeffie's never brought it up."

"If he ever does, would you let me know? I don't want the subject forced on him but . . . well, I really need to know."

She checked her answering service. Only one urgent message: "Call Adelle at Ling and Son immediately." That surprised Megan. Michael had never before placed his secretary between them. She dialed the office.

Adelle sounded half amused, half frantic. "Thank heaven!" she said. "I don't often see Mr. Richardson in a bad mood, but a few minutes ago he flung open his door and told me he had dialer's cramp from calling your number."

"Sorry. What's the problem?"

"Something about High Point. If you're going to be in L.A. today, the boss needs to meet you for lunch. Early, if possible. Right now he's at a conference in Beverly Hills."

Megan thought a moment. "How about Farmer's Market at, say, eleven-thirty? I'll be wrapping up an appointment just around the corner. Tell him . . . oh, the first Italian place inside the main parking lot entrance."

"I'll get in touch with him," the secretary answered.

Megan knew she could have chosen any of a dozen more convenient—and quieter—luncheon spots. She had been seeking anonymity. If her courage was to be put to a crucial test, and so soon, she didn't want it to happen in a cozy, dimly lit restaurant. She hurried to her locker and changed into the cream-colored linen suit she'd brought from home. She decided the blowdryer wouldn't be necessary—her hair wasn't very damp—so she gave it a quick fingertip fluff. After a light application of lip gloss and mascara, she dashed to the Toyota. Since she hadn't been paying proper atten-

tion to the time, she was going to be late unless she hit
every light perfectly.

It didn't matter. The buyer she had been scheduled to
meet was home, sick. Megan was surprised to realize
she felt relieved. Although she needed normal routine,
she also questioned her capabilities that particular
business day. Perhaps she should steer clear of sales
calls; today she could always analyze her clients' showrooms. With that in mind, she wandered through the
furniture and accessory displays, taking careful notes,
and soon found herself in a connecting clothing department. Designer clothes, no less.

Standing in a corner of the plush boutique was a
faceless mannequin wearing a stunning Stanley
Sherman coatdress—Megan's *soul* was in that dress! It
was sleek and high-fashion yet totally feminine. And it
was coal black. With, say, a conservative scarf at the
neck, it was appropriate for daytime business wear; for
evening, unfastening the top button, it could be
accessorized a hundred different ways. Although the
price was exorbitant, she had to have it. Thinking of the
complicated wardrobe demands for High Point, she told
herself that, anyway, one outfit of this versatility
would save her from having to buy two others.

Megan wasn't fooling herself one little bit. She was
aware whom she hoped to impress in High Point; if anything would tempt Michael Richardson, it would be this
particular dress. She would have bought it at twice the
price. Fortunately, the fit was perfect.

She arrived at Farmer's Market slightly late, flushed
and breathless. Michael stood up and held the chair for
her, polite as always. For Megan, the crush of humanity
in the market faded instantly.

He looked more seductively handsome than ever. His
conference must have been important. He was wearing
an unusually impressive suit; it was severely tailored,
somewhat formal, and very dark: a rich chocolate
brown with barely discernible pinstripes. The subtle

contrast of shades was overwhelming—that brown against the texture of his ash hair and the tan of his complexion. Michael appeared formidable, like a magnificent piece of bronze. Except that bronzes rarely had flashing blue-gray eyes.

He seemed more rested than the last time she had seen him. If anything, he exuded even more confidence and serenity than Megan was accustomed to seeing in this extraordinary man. That must be what comes of making a decision and putting it behind you, she thought unhappily. The crack in her psyche deepened into a fissure.

"Your hair's wet," he said.

The last of her self-confidence drained away. She had misjudged the appearance of her hair. Whoever heard of an experienced businesswoman going on calls with wet hair? Michael's mouth curved into an unfamiliar twist. Was he mocking her?

"I stopped by the Y for a swim," she said, pleased by the composure of the tone. For all Michael knew, she had come directly from the pool, not a Ling and Son appointment. He could wipe that smirk—if that's what it was—from his face.

"Good idea," he said. "Megan, I'm sorry to drag you out of your way but—"

"I told Adelle: no problem."

"—we need to discuss travel dates. As it stands now, we're due to leave exactly one day before market starts."

She nodded.

"This morning I realized I need more time in High Point. The samples will be ready for airfreighting tomorrow. I don't have to stay and supervise, thank God. That means I can get up there earlier, take better care of last-minute showroom details. It's more important than usual: this is the most revolutionary new product line Ling and Son has ever introduced. What I'm getting at is—I'd like for you to come early, too, if you can afford the time."

She nodded again, numb. This would mean they'd have an entire week together in High Point. But she needed to hear him say *why* he wanted her along those extra days. Suddenly Megan felt hopeful, exuberant. She might have been attaching too much significance to one missed telephone call. Michael certainly didn't look—or act—like a man trying to weed a woman from his life.

"Actually," he said, "there's no question of whether or not you can afford the time. In addition to your air fare, I've arranged for you to be generously reimbursed. You see, once we get to High Point, I've got to prevail on you for some pretty heavy assistance. We could fly someone else up but it seems a wasted expense when you're already scheduled."

The fissure reopened and became a great yawning cavern.

"We've got our accommodations—that's right, I told you that a few days ago, but I didn't get a chance to tell you we're staying at the nicest place in town. That should just about wrap up the subject, then, except that I'll pick you up about six tomorrow morning. The flight leaves at seven-thirty."

He reached for the menu, then put it down again. "Oh, Megan—Jeffie would kill me. I promised him that first thing, before I brought up anything else, I'd invite you to the house for dinner tonight."

Under the table, she twisted and untwisted her paper napkin. "Oh, Michael . . . I couldn't. With the change of travel plans, there's so much to do . . ."

"Whatever you say," he said smoothly. "Jeffie'll understand, but he'll be disappointed."

But not you, Megan thought. Aside from needing a hired hand in High Point, you wouldn't notice if I disappeared altogether.

Suddenly Megan felt as though she were suffocating.

It was the intense effort of trying to resist the magnet. She had to get away.

"Michael, would you mind if we skip lunch? My schedule's a mess." She wondered if he could hear the brittle edge to her voice.

"At your service," he said quickly, rising. And then: "Megan, you needn't have asked. After all you did to help *my* schedule . . . and I haven't really thanked you properly, not yet."

"Don't try," she said softly, fighting tears.

Michael came around and pulled back her chair. When Megan was standing, he reached for a strand of her hair. "I like this," he said, fingering a tight damp curl. "The way it springs across your shoulders . . . well, you look very, very young and innocent. Don't you ever look the same way twice in a row, little Meggie?"

Hours later, she would still be asking herself, Why did he do that?

She dropped her business plans, shopped for a couple of hours and then, around four o'clock, went home. By that time, Megan's emotions were running hot to cold to hot and back again. When Sharon called, she said, "If I were a faucet, I'd definitely call a plumber! One minute I don't seem to care much, even wish I'd never *heard* of High Point. Then, suddenly my stupid brain kicks into override—all I can think of is that Michael and I'll be together for an entire week! How's that for consistency?"

"What do you think will happen in High Point?"

"Who knows? But there's no point denying I'm hopeful he'll do a turnaround, that we'll pick up where we left off the night I went to Palm Springs. And you'll never believe how *much* I'm hoping it! Want to hear something bizarre?"

"Shoot."

"Well, I needed to buy a scarf for the new dress I told you about. When I finished shopping, I found I'd purchased a fortune in lingerie—*lingerie,* Sharon! In my whole life I've never done such a thing! Now I've got underwear that'll knock your eyes out!"

Sharon laughed. "Not *my* eyes, dear Megan. Well, there's one good thing about all this. You're finally having fun with some of that money you work so hard to earn. But I hope buying sexy underwear doesn't mean you've decided to start sleeping with Michael again without resolving your problems."

"Who says he wants me to?" she asked gloomily, and then: "Oops, doorbell's ringing. Just what I need—a magazine salesman! Sharon, I'll never get packed!"

"Relax. And I'll take good care of Sinbad while you're gone."

On the way to answer the door, Megan was grumbling to herself. "Relax, relax! I've never been so disorganized in my entire life."

The man at the front door bore no resemblance whatsoever to a magazine salesman. For one thing, he was wearing shorts and running shoes—well, mostly, he's wearing that cocky grin, Megan thought; by now, she knew when she saw it to expect the unexpected.

"Michael! What on earth are you doing?"

He was jogging in place. "Isn't it obvious?" he asked.

"I didn't know you were a jogger."

"There's a lot about me you don't know—"

And she thought, That's certainly true.

"—and, anyway, I just started jogging. This evening. Sure beats cold showers!"

The grin was deepening. Here it comes, Megan thought, holding her breath . . .

And she was right. As he continued to jog in place, Michael's eyes sprouted dozens of captivating little crinkles and a highly suggestive gleam. He said, "Dammit, Megan McBride—I love you!" And, without breaking stride, turned on his heels and jogged away.

15

She didn't even try to figure it out. She was too happy.
The next morning Michael gave her the old cliché
about looking like a million dollars and she knew the
compliment was well-deserved. Why shouldn't she
have looked like a million dollars in her favorite emer-
ald silk dress? She *felt* like a million dollars.

Naturally, *he* looked fantastic. To Megan's secret delight, he had chosen to wear the same chocolate brown
suit she had first seen in Farmer's Market. The only revi-
sion was a slightly more formal shirt plus gold cufflinks.

During the first leg of the flight, Michael described
his friend, Ron Sweeney. He said, "Ron owns a big
showroom in Dallas. We never see each other except at
markets but, for sheer entertainment, he's a good reason to attend; you'll like him. You may not *approve,* but
I guarantee you'll like him."

Megan told Michael he and Ron sounded like the odd
couple.

Michael shrugged. "He calls me the scoutmaster,
claims his wife would never let him go to High Point if
he didn't stay in the same house with me."

"Stay in the same house? What do you mean?"

"For the last seven years we've been sharing the
same rentals—house and car—for both the October and
the April markets. Sleeping space is too valuable for
one person to take an entire two-bedroom house. We've
had a home about, oh, six miles from Market Center."

177

"That explains why you need the car. But isn't it unnecessarily inconvenient? Why not just stay in one of the downtown hotels?"

He looked surprised. "Megan, hasn't anyone ever told you about the eccentricities of High Point, North Carolina, furniture capital of the world?"

"Well," she said thoughtfully. "I know it's smallish and that the trade buildings and twice-annual markets sprang up because so many buyers had to travel that way to see the giants—Thomasville, Drexel-Heritage, among others."

He nodded. "Right. North Carolina's one of the most affluent states in the nation. Textiles, furniture, trucking, and tobacco. Naturally, the leaders in our industry opened their first headquarters near the supply of lumber; and then I assume the plants got so enormous it would have been damned inconvenient to relocate. But think about what happens to High Point between October and April."

"I give up. What happens?"

He laughed. "Not a damned thing, that's what! If there were enough hotel rooms built to house the market overload, they'd stay empty other times. Therefore, the friendly folk of High Point rent out their homes."

"Oh. But *we're* staying at a hotel, aren't we?"

"You'd need reservations at least two years in advance, Megan. Market attendance averages about thirty-eight thousand, versus only thirteen hundred hotel rooms. And it never catches up: for instance, a new Marriott's adding about three hundred rooms but, then, the new Design Center will attract an additional one to five thousand reps, buyers, and manufacturers. In other words, there's just no way."

"So, we're staying in the house with Ron?"

"Nope. I've been saving the details of our accommodations for a surprise, pretty lady. Let me order the drinks, then I'll give you a couple of hints."

She knew it was necessary to iron out the wrinkles in

the relationship before they allowed the issues to become impossibly blurred by their obvious sexual attachment. Suddenly, Megan was worried. She wasn't quite sure why.

He had two martinis to her one glass of Chablis. Between the first and the second, he took her hand. Megan decided there was nothing in life worth worrying *about.* On about the third to last sip of his second drink, she changed her mind. Michael told her he'd pulled off a fantastic coup; he'd arranged to rent a showplace: the home of a famous North Carolina designer.

He leaned across the armrests and whispered in her ear. "At the time he built it, he was in love, Megan. Does that tell you something?"

Yeah, she thought wryly. It tells me Michael's not planning on an immediate problem-solving session.

On the second leg of the trip, after a change of planes in Atlanta, there was even more handholding. Megan began to feel like a young girl on her honeymoon—and, oh, she was so glad to see Michael in this frame of mind! At this point she could admit to herself she had sometimes thought the pressure of preparing for High Point would never end. Now that it finally had, she could well understand the reason for his unusually carefree and celebratory mood. About the other matter . . . well, she couldn't decide whether or not she should have set the record straight.

The FASTEN SEAT BELT sign appeared, and Megan forgot her concern—maybe she *should* have set it straight, but her opportunity had come and gone, at least on this flight it had. Megan leaned over to peer excitedly through the window. Michael laughed and squeezed her hand. "Too much altitude, babe. Wait till the NO SMOKING sign comes on; then you'll be able to see it. In the meantime," he added provocatively, "let's get back to the subject of our house. You have to admit I performed a minor miracle, getting it for us."

"Yes," Megan murmured, "a miracle." She could

have added, but didn't, that if Michael intended to lure
her into a shared bedroom before resolving other issues,
like his oppressive protectiveness, he'd have to perform
a second miracle.

Procrastination wasn't Megan's style. Furthermore,
she'd just had a terrifying new thought—when the timing absolutely forced her to say no to him, what if she
didn't have the self-discipline to do it? And what on
earth had ever made her think it would be so simple,
anyway? She cast a sidelong look at his handsome pro-
file and shook her head ruefully.

When the time came, the ideal approach would be for
Megan to say, "Honey, before this goes any further,
let's just have a quick talk to be sure all that other
stuff's behind us." After a few uninterrupted minutes
or so, they could get on with their lives. For now, she'd
have to hope the plan would work. But a nagging element of doubt made her cringe. Well, she had to do
something, that was for sure. If they were still
disagreeing—and surely they weren't anymore, or why
would Michael be acting so different?—then they were
in trouble.

She stole another glance at Michael, who had turned
to hand his glass to the flight attendant. The way he
looked in that suit didn't exactly enhance Megan's
faith in her ability to resist him. As he reached toward
the attendant's tray, she saw that his hands were beautifully proportioned and groomed. From the visual impact, her senses swung to the tactile: suddenly she
could remember perfectly—no, she could actually *feel*
those hands touching her. In her lower body, she felt a
quick, blossoming need; it was almost painful in its intensity. She sucked in her breath and groaned.

As Michael had predicted, Ron was right there at the
gate. At first sight, Megan thought he resembled an
oversized bouncer at a country-and-western bar. She
suspected that part of Michael's chronic amusement
stemmed from individual physical elements totally dis-

parate from the whole. A man of Ron's sheer muscular
bulk should have had a slow and booming voice; his was
just above alto and permanently programmed for chatter speed. And his head would never conform gracefully
to a ten-gallon hat; it was enormous and beachball-
round under a few scattered strands of prematurely
gray hair. And Megan *did* like him. In addition to a
childlike friendliness, he talked so much she didn't
have time to think; at this particular juncture that was
an enormous relief.

"If you were thinkin' of changing houses, why didn't
you call me first?" he asked Michael. "For God's sake,
why break tradition now?"

Michael turned to Megan, grinned, and winked.

"Me and the gunner are at it again, Michael, and—"

"Hold it!" Michael said, laughing. He explained to
Megan that "the gunner" was Ron's nickname for the
owner of a furniture line he carried. Ron also carried
five other lines in addition to owning a showroom in
Dallas.

Ron added, "Yeah, the gunner always looks like he's
ready to shoot ya down."

Michael interjected dryly, "And this is the man who
started a business that just happens to feed, clothe, and
house your entire family. You make more off Kraftco in
a month than you do off all the others in a year."

Ron shook his head in protest. "The gunner keeps losing reps. He must be doing *something* wrong."

"I've never met the man," Michael said, "but I've
heard he's overworked and overtired—"

"And trying to get all his reps in the same shape!"
Ron said triumphantly.

"Ever hear of compromise? The reps work a little
harder so the boss can live to a ripe old age?"

"Damned manufacturers!" Despite the words, Ron's
grumbling was good-natured. "You just won't try to see
things from our point of view. Well, anyway, I'm gonna
quit this time. For sure."

"Never happen," Michael said. "No one in his right mind would give up a line as hot as Kraftco."

"You're insinuating I'm in my right mind?"

"That's a valid point," Michael joked. "By the way, Ron, you were wrong: the gunner doesn't keep losing reps—they keep losing *him*. You'd do well to keep the distinction in mind."

Megan said, "Excuse me—I'm dying of curiosity. Why are you so upset with the gunner?"

Michael provided the answer. "It's like a soap opera, Megan. Every time I tune back in, the plot's stuck in the same old place. Ron goes bananas when his boss orders him to High Point."

He was watching for her reaction and sure enough—she couldn't help herself—Megan gave him an I-told-you-so look. Michael just rolled his eyes skyward as if to say, "But I *am* the boss and you *are* the rep." At the moment, she didn't welcome the reminder. The subject she'd try to get him to discuss when they were alone was touchy enough without Michael in an authoritarian mood.

They'd been waiting for the carousel to start spitting out baggage. Megan noticed the crowd was light; buyers wouldn't be in for another two days and the only reps in town were those who, like Ron, had premarket sales meetings to attend or showrooms to decorate.

"You've got all the luck, Richardson!" Ron was saying. "With everything else ya got going, ya turn up with the best-looking rep in the industry. Whaddaya think about this place anyway, Megan?"

"So far," Megan reminded him, "I've only seen High Point from the air. It's fantastic from two thousand feet. What do *you* think about it?"

He shook his head. "I've been coming to High Point twice a year for a millenium, and I still don't know. It's like that musical, *Brigadoon,* where the town only appears every once in a while. Weird! Hundreds of thousands of dollars paid out for showroom space, not to mention the millions tied up in display samples, and not a soul sets foot in the marts except for ten days in October and ten days in April. Then the whole town comes to life and pretends it's been alive all along."

Michael had lined up the luggage and located a skycap. He said, "That was poetic, Ron. Now go get the car, will you?"

While they waited, Megan commented, "You know, he's right. I've heard other people return from market with similar statements. Why do you suppose manufacturers and reps haven't pressured to have it relocated to a major city where they already have full-time showrooms?"

"It would be like getting the mountain to go to Mohammed. North Carolina *is* the furniture capital of the world, honey. When we get a chance to drive to the Thomasville factory—the city's named after the *company*, by the way—or if we make it out to Drexel-Heritage, you'll understand. And I could name several other giants, too: Henredon, Century, Hickory . . . Actually, Megan, this works pretty well in a healthy economy, believe it or not. There's Ron."

In the car they veered onto the subject of lamps. Ron complained that his import line wasn't selling because it had the same old tired shapes and patterns from Italy and Japan.

Then he tried to pressure Michael into hiring him for Ling and Son and Megan turned her attention to the drive. For miles they had been winding along a mini-freeway bordered by woodlands festooned in great generous bursts of autumn color. Now Ron turned onto a side street and then maneuvered into a tree-lined residential section.

She tuned back in. Michael was saying, "If you're all that desperate, then why not get away from imports altogether? Get into a really hot domestic line."

Megan had a feeling they were nearing their destination. Ron had made a left turn, then a sharp right, and was now headed deeper into the residential area. The neighborhood was changing; there were fewer homes on larger lots, the twisting road was longer and, if her depth perception was accurate, it was also about to dead end at a wooded cul-de-sac. She began to experience a renewal of the former anxieties.

The car slowed to a stop. Now they could see a surprisingly modern wood and glass structure which gave the appearance of having sprung quite naturally from a small forest. Even Ron was impressed; he stopped chattering.

"Well!" he said finally. "Here you are, Lord and Lady Astor . . . your castle. Wait a minute, Michael—don't get out just yet. One more thing: you're the number one lamp man in the nation. Since I don't *know* of anything really hot, would you look around for me during market, see if you can turn something up?"

"Of course, Ron," he said warmly. "If it's that important, I'll be happy to." He opened his door and slid out, then started around to open Megan's door. Then, he leaned through the open window of the driver's seat and said, "Look, we're going to break another tradition. No first-night dinner. Tonight is exclusively for Megan and me."

"You two have something going?" Ron was obviously astonished and Megan, in turn, was astonished that he was astonished.

Michael laughed heartily. "Ron, have you ever considered how much you might learn if you slow down and shut up long enough to observe what's going on?"

"But, but . . . your secretary said you'd gotten a different house so you could *entertain* more . . ."

Michael laughed again. "That's right, my friend. I'm going to entertain Megan."

Ron scowled. "Boy, are there gonna be broken hearts in this city! I hope it doesn't affect the economic outcome of market! Is this something serious?" He swiveled to look out toward Megan. *"You* tell me, Megan."

Michael answered anyway—which was just as well since she was embarrassed, not to mention overwhelmed, by Michael's sudden unrestrained candor. From behind the car, where he was removing the luggage, he shouted, "It's serious, Ron. Megan's going to be the *permanent* fixture in my life. Start getting used to it."

She stood transfixed. His announcement, if she had understood it correctly, had succeeded in reshaping her entire brain, which was now half questionmark, half exclamation point.

Ron whistled and got out of the car. Then he said— and it was the first time she'd heard him speak in slow, evenly spaced tones—"Congratulations, Miss McBride. You have just become the most hated woman in North Carolina. But don't worry. Southern women don't bear grudges too long!" He winked at her, hopped back in the car, gunned the engine, and sped off down the road, loudly crooning "Play Me Lonely Hearts and Flowers."

Megan decided that potential unpopularity with the women of High Point might be the least of her problems. The hour of reckoning was fast approaching, and she couldn't quite keep track of all the points to be reckoned with. Maybe she could procrastinate at least until after dinner.

The house was a delight, just as the accommodations coordinator had promised Michael. Even more contemporary inside than out, the house had an entry level that contained kitchen-dining-living areas, and the main feature of the living room was an incredibly large circular firepit, surrounded by custom-built conversation sofas. Megan loved the soft, loose, oversized throw pillows scattered everywhere; each was a different color accent of the outside scenario. And what a view it was! Floor to ceiling glass, unhampered by drapery, drew the beauty of North Carolina right into the room. The air sparkled with tiny sunbeams illumining the spectacular autumn collage.

She sighed. All in all, the setting was spectacularly romantic. During all this musing, of course, she had forgotten that Michael would be placing their luggage in the master bedroom. Her memory was jarred when he called down in unmistakably provocative tones, "Hey, ba-by . . . everything I need is up here. Everything but you. Come and see."

She jumped. "Michael, I can't do that," she called back, trying to sound casual and to stall for time to think of a way to begin their problem-solving conversation. "The only thing on my mind is a long hot bath."

"Well, there's a perfectly adequate tub up here—and I'll scrub your back."

She trudged upstairs, not seeing any way around it. And her first sight of the owner's suite took her breath away. It was the entire top level. Between connecting sleeping and sitting areas, double French doors swung out onto a veranda which in turn led to a handsome pool-spa. Michael had thrown open the doors; now he leaned lazily between them, arms casually folded, one foot crossed over an ankle. A slight breeze ruffled his hair. For a moment she stood staring; the look she gave him was reflected in the look he gave her.

16

He straightened and started toward her. Megan searched for words that might sound playful.

"Oh no you don't!" she exclaimed. "I'm determined to have that bath!" Her eyes scanned the room and she ducked behind the first door; fortunately it was the bathroom and not the closet. Trying not to think about what she was missing, she turned the tub water on full force.

When she finished bathing, Megan realized all her clean clothes were in the bedroom. Peeking through a tiny crack in the door, she saw that the coast was clear. Michael had placed her cosmetic case on the floor just beside the bathroom door, her suitcase was lying on a luggage stand across the room, and, presumably, the garment bag was in the closet. She smiled at the thoughtfulness, fastened the giant towel more tightly around her, and tiptoed over to the bag. As she surveyed the contents, she was amused by the irony of both her thoughts and her behavior. Off and on since arriving at the rented house, she had been forced to remind herself that, yes, there really *is* a good reason for wanting to delay our lovemaking. But now she was sneaking around as though she might get caught in an illegal act! On top of all that, she was trying to get Michael to slow down on something she probably wanted more than he did! It was confusing, to say the least.

While she told herself that all the troublesome issues

could be brought out in the open and cleared away during dinner, she rummaged through the suitcase; the sight of delicate lace bras and panties and camisoles, plus a long white satin nightgown, elicited a sheepish grin. She located the spacious walk-in closet containing her garmet bag, unzipped it, and scanned the contents; about a third of the way in, she came across the new black dress. After looking at it for a moment, she shook her head: it was something to be saved for market.

Instead, she chose a loose two-piece ultrasuede her parents had mailed during a recent trip to Hong Kong. It was tan; an oversized decorative zipper running the full length of the overblouse categorized the outfit as definitely casual. She padded back to the suitcase to decide what color underwear was compatible with tan.

Michael had evidently accepted the alterations of his plan. Megan made her way to the main level and found him working in a clever nook containing a built-in desk between walls galleried with framed newspaper and magazine photos. Good, she thought; when Michael pulled papers from his briefcase, only a bona fide emergency could divert his attention. Walking carefully on the thick carpet, she went into the kitchen and checked the time. Six-thirty. That was also good; they could go out for dinner plus a short but serious conversation; afterward, they'd still be relatively fresh. Walking normally, she approached Michael's work area.

"Ahem."

"So there you are—finally!" he said, rotating the swivel chair and putting aside the pencil he'd been using to make notations on a computer printout. "If I get up, very slowly, and walk toward you, very slowly, will you disappear behind the nearest door again?" His eyes sparkled.

"Stay right where you are," she answered lightly. "That's good. Now close your eyes and don't open them till I give the signal. I'm going to do something that'll *really* mystify you."

His eyes fell shut. Megan pressed her lips gently against his forehead. She was leaning over, supporting herself with both hands gripping the arms of the leather chair. Without opening his eyes, Michael reached up and pulled her onto his lap.

"This is the kind of magic I enjoy," he said softly, nuzzling her neck. "Mmmm . . . you smell good. What *is* that perfume you wear?"

"Opium."

"Apropos," he said. Then he planted dozens of soft tiny kisses on her hair, on her neck, on her ear. A bolt of frantic desire shot through her.

"Are you in a different mood?" he asked.

"Different from what?" she asked, then wished she had just let the question go.

He grinned. "I don't know. Just how would you describe the mood you were in?"

She relaxed; Megan felt she could handle the light-hearted bantering. She said, "I'd describe it, sir, as the mood of a woman who wanted to get cleaned up after a day of traveling."

He put a finger on her lips. Instinctively, Megan drew the finger into her mouth and started a gentle caressing with her tongue. Underneath her, Michael shifted abruptly; then she felt a tightening and a brief shuddering of his thigh muscles. In response, Megan's buttocks tightened; a perceptible trembling started in her own thighs. Without realizing it, she had pulled Michael's finger deeper into her mouth; her arms had gone around his neck and she was running a tapered fingernail around his earlobe.

His legs stiffened and parted. "Ahhh . . . Megan. My God! These past two weeks . . . Never again! I'll never go so long without you. Do you want me? Oh God, Megan—stop for a minute! I can't take that much longer."

He removed the finger from her mouth and placed it under her chin, tilting her head. Her eyes were glazed, pupils slightly dilated. Michael ran the finger from her

chin to her neck, tracing a slow but purposeful pattern;
it led to her zipper; very, very slowly, he slid it down.
And then he placed a fingertip on her breast. When an
almost agonized moan escaped Megan's lips, he put
forefinger and thumb directly on the rigid, supersensi-
tized pink flesh, pinching gently, then pulling. Her
senses went totally haywire. Sight, smell, touch, taste,
sound: all converged in one physical area to create a
bomb. It was exploding; at the same time, it was gathering strength for the ultimate explosion.

"Honey . . . baby . . ." he moaned. He had removed
his hand from beneath her blouse. In the area he'd been
touching, Megan ached; she grabbed his hand and tried
to guide it back.

"Megan, love—don't! Stop now." He lightly kissed
her forehead, coaxed her from his lap, and then, when
she tottered on her feet, stood to steady her. The assistance was offered at arm's length, however, and when
Megan moved to step back within his embrace, he said,
"Baby, let's go to dinner now. If we keep going the way
we are, the night will be too short. Think of it, angel . . .
we've got an entire night to make love. But slow down."

Like a robot, she moved her head up and down, not totally comprehending.

"Honey," he said softly. "I'm going to let you go now;
can you stand by yourself? I've got to call a cab."

Again: that slow mesmerized nod. Michael melted
away toward the kitchen. By the time the taxi pulled up
in front, the full impact of the experience had hit her.
Finally she understood—

She had no power to control desire of this intensity.
Not in this house. Not alone with the object of the desire. And she no longer cared, either. If Michael wanted
her to forfeit her independence, then the forfeit would
be less painful than losing him. *Anything* would be less
painful than losing him.

He opened the front door for her. They were halfway
down the sidewalk when he suddenly stopped. "Damn!"

"What's wrong?"

"I forgot . . . While you were taking a bath, I called home. Chad was at the house with Jeffie and he asked to talk to you."

"Is it important?" she asked, puzzled.

Michael shrugged. "He said you had asked for some information, which he now has. That's all I know."

My God! Megan thought. What she had requested was anything that might shed light on the mystery behind Michael's reactions! To say the very least, it was important, maybe now more than ever. Michael told her he'd left Chad's apartment number on the desk. "Go on inside and get it over with," he suggested, "while I tell the driver to wait."

She dialed impatiently. After the connection had been made, Michael wandered in to stand beside her. He didn't hear much because Megan contributed very little to the conversation, just an occasional "yes," "no," or "I see." At the end, she said, "Well, Chad, your timing couldn't be better. A lot of things make sense now." Her tone was decidedly upbeat and the mood was even more evident after she hung up. Michael said that, whatever the news, it must have been good. When she failed to comment, he didn't press.

The cabdriver was told to deliver them to a restaurant called Market Square, and then Michael settled into the backseat and took Megan's hand. She was thoroughly relaxed, thinking to herself that the answer to the mystery had been surprising, yes, and a bit more complicated than she could have anticipated, but it was nothing they couldn't discuss, and certainly nothing that need threaten the relationship.

Market Square was located on the ground floor of what had once been a furniture manufacturing plant. The enormous building was a brick box in direct contrast with its plush, almost elegant interior. They entered a combination cocktail-waiting area; it was an attractive assortment of sofas that were rapidly filling up. Several people, both male and female, jumped up to greet Michael. He returned the attention in his normal easygoing manner, and each person received an uncomplicated introduction to Megan. Keeping a proprietary arm around her he said, simply, "I want you to meet the most wonderful woman in the world."

Before long, she realized she had started feeling that way. Michael's friends and colleagues were reacting with a mixture of awe and admiration. Their comments ranged from "Good grief—so there *is* someone special enough for you!" to "Congratulations, Miss McBride. We should have known that when he finally did it, he'd prove his good taste once and for all."

And then there were the invitations. Dozens of them, or so it seemed to Megan. In fact, she had the impression of a big party waiting for the guest of honor to arrive. Much more than Megan could previously have grasped, Michael was a VIP in his industry. And an exceptionally respected VIP at that. When they finally sat down, she felt dazed.

"Wine?"

She nodded.

"I enjoyed that," Michael commented. "And I hope you noticed . . . everyone's duly impressed. What'd I do to deserve you?" His eye caught on something behind her left shoulder. "Look at that, little Meggie!"

Twisting to follow the direction of his gaze, she saw a decorative grouping: lamp, silk floral arrangement, and several leather-bound books. The lamp was an obvious Richardson design; in fact, it was still included in the Ling catalog.

"I always get a kick out of that," he admitted. "I suppose it would be the same as if, say, an author saw someone reading his book." When he started grinning, Megan thought he was embarrassed to be talking so freely on a subject which normally elicited such modesty. God, she loved him!

They joked and chatted and exchanged greetings

with new arrivals. It seemed that at one time or another, everyone had worked either for or with Michael. "Remember me?" one man asked. "You gave me my first job in this crazy business." Michael did indeed remember; he also remembered the names of the man's wife and mother.

"What another drink?" he asked. "Or are you getting hungry?"

She started to opt for the wine, then realized she was slightly tipsy. They headed for the dining room, where Michael did the ordering: shrimp scampi and rice pilaf.

Over salad, he said, "We're certainly getting our share of attention."

"Surely you're accustomed to that!" she teased.

"I said *we*, Megan. Look around; people are staring." He leaned far forward, taking both her hands in both of his. The words that followed were spoken in deep and husky tones: "I can just imagine what's going through all those minds. Later tonight we'll be the subject of dozens of fantasies."

Before she could respond, the waitress came to take their salad plates. As soon as she left, Michael said, "I feel a little sorry for all these people."

"I can't imagine why."

"I guess, little Meggie, that I feel sorry for anyone who isn't *us*. Our lives will be even better than their fantasies. Together we'll give new meaning to the word *reality*."

The waitress returned with the entree. Megan took a bite, then laid aside her fork. This was as good an opportunity as any. Michael had just expressed a terrific thought and she couldn't think of any further excuse to procrastinate. If she and Michael wanted to give new meaning to the word *reality*, they might as well deal now with the old meaning. If they couldn't change it they could sure whittle it into a more acceptable shape, get rid of the sharp corners and rough edges.

She said, "You know—I believe you're right. With you I honestly believe reality can be . . ."

While she searched for the right word, Michael supplied the entire ending. He said, "It can be like a fairy tale. I'll take you to my castle and keep you there forever. I'll protect you from fire-breathing dragons."

It was such a perfect example of his mood that Megan couldn't help laughing. "Honey, this is the twentieth century!" Her eyes danced; not even to herself could Megan deny that images of strong handsome men—and Michael certainly qualified as a knight-in-shining-armor type—appealed to her feminine instincts. But she was more than merely feminine; she was a human being, and it wasn't fairy tales they needed to talk about.

She leaned toward him and, trying to keep it light, said, "Confidentially, Richardson, I don't want you to protect me. That would be a waste of valuable time. I mean, I can think of other things"—seductive emphasis on the word *other* left no doubt what Megan meant —"I'd rather have you do for me."

"Then I shall awaken the guards, pull up the draw-bridge, lock the castle door—and *do* them."

"Oh, you!" she teased. "You're impossible. Why don't you *fire* the guards, plant *daisies* on the drawbridge, and throw *open* the door? Then we can go out and make love in the daisies." She took a bite of shrimp.

In mock chagrin, he said, "What? And leave my kingdom unprotected?"

"Listen to me, Richardson: I . . . don't . . . want . . . to be . . . protected."

He stopped buttering a roll. "All right, Megan; game's over. I'll admit I've been trying to avoid it but we *are* talking about that silly argument we had before you went to Palm Springs, aren't we?"

She nodded.

"Exactly what, then, do you want to discuss?"

Megan couldn't tell much from his tone, and his face

seemed perfectly calm and reasonable. Nonetheless, she reminded herself to go slow; this man could look cool while everything around him burned to cinders. She chose her words very carefully. "How about telling me if everything's okay now."

"Sure. It's over. Behind us. Finis."

"*Is* it over, Michael?" Megan certainly wanted to believe that. "The next time I have to go on the road, for instance—"

"We'll cross that bridge when we come to it."

"That sounds ominous. If I'm not mistaken, it's the drawbridge again—you don't want to cross it; you want to pull it up."

He sighed. "Poor little Meggie . . . This is important to you, isn't it?"

"I don't deny that," she said slowly. "But, Michael, it's important to *us.*"

"Well, I just can't get into it. I need at least one day off from . . . from all the damned crises."

She sighed, reminded herself that she'd known it wouldn't be easy. "Honey, if anyone's earned a day off, it's you," she said gently. "But this isn't a crisis."

His eyebrows furrowed. "Frankly, Megan, I'm afraid it'll turn into one. And I have an excellent reason for feeling this way, even if you don't know what it is." She reached across the table and placed both hands over one of his. Waiting until she was certain his eyes were locked onto hers, that he could read the sympathy, Megan said, "Michael, I do; someone told me. But it's just not—"

When he interrupted, his tone was harsh. "Dammit, Megan! If you know so much, why are you trying to change the facts of life? It *isn't* safe on the roads! I'm not about to give in and send you out to be slaughtered. Furthermore, I'm still not in any mood to be psychoanalyzed."

Instinctively, Megan shrank back in her chair. It had never occurred to her that Michael was capable of speaking that way. Now, within a split second, he covered the rage with his well-practiced look of bland acceptance; for Megan, it wasn't quick *enough.* She barely heard his next words: "I'd never forgive myself if the same thing happened to you."

Later that night, alone in the lovely master bedroom of the High Point home, she had plenty of time to think. There had been no further angry words; by mutual assent, both she and Michael had been willing—Megan had even been anxious—to return to safer topics of conversation. The effort had been excruciating. Home again, they had simply melted in opposite directions. Michael had insisted she take the owner's suite.

What Chad had told her was simple: Michael had been on the scene of an accident. Later he had been the prosecution's chief witness in a long and painful criminal trial that sounded to Megan like a travesty of justice.

Her briefing didn't entitle her to all the facts, of course, not as quickly as Chad had given them. But she knew that several years ago Michael had been waiting out a red light at the corner of Wilshire and Oakhurst, near the serene and dignified Beverly Wilshire Hotel. Since it was fairly late in the evening, traffic was light. And there were only two pedestrians in the crosswalk. Evidently Michael was just watching the teenage girls—both of them nicely dressed and groomed youngsters—as they crossed the street, chatting, when he heard a horrendous noise to his immediate right. Within seconds, one person was dead, another person was paralyzed for life, and a third was wandering around in a daze. It was this third party, a man who suffered no injuries, who had caused the tragedy. Traveling Wilshire Boulevard in excess of fifty miles an hour, he had rear-ended the car in the lane directly to Michael's right, sending it into the pedestrian walk, where it hit both teenagers.

Amid the godawful carnage it soon became obvious

why the uninjured driver appeared dazed. He kept yelling, "Hadn't anybuddy gotta drinkie?"

Michael sold his business, Light Years, and then gave a year of his life to the trial—and to the families of the two girls—after the district attorney informed him that the responsible driver had been arrested twice previously for driving while intoxicated. Although the drunkard waited out the trial in comfort—he was released on five thousand dollars bail—there didn't appear any question he would eventually be convicted of murder. But that didn't happen; he was found guilty, yes, but only of involuntary manslaughter. His punishment was a two-year sentence—suspended. The father of the dead girl didn't get off so lightly; he went insane. The parents of the other teenager were still hopeful that a specialist could be found to restore their daughter's useless legs.

Michael's concern was understandable. Chad had said that, according to Jeffie, he was an encyclopedia of horrifying statistics on the combination of drinking and driving; at any given hour, he could say exactly how many drunk drivers were likely to be on the streets; at night, the figures were astoundingly high.

There wasn't a single thing Megan could do. She knew—but Michael didn't—that keeping her out of cars and taxis in the middle of the night wasn't protection against the insanity of drunk drivers and judicial processes working for the benefit of the criminal.

So the question was: now what? She also knew how incredibly much in love she was with Michael Richardson.

17

Over morning coffee, Michael behaved as though nothing untoward had happened the night before. Megan didn't know whether to attribute the relaxed atmosphere to his business obligations or his common sense. Whichever, she was grateful. Neither of them needed to dwell on past history.

Having managed to conceal the dark circles under her eyes, she had then put on a simple paisley shirtwaist. Her long hair was pulled back from her face and secured, bandeau-style, with a matching paisley scarf. This caused another comment from Michael that she never looked the same way twice.

She said, "My purpose is comfort. I forgot to ask what you want me to do today, but I suspect it has something to do with the samples. Weren't they due in yesterday?"

"Right. United airfreight. By now they'll be in the showroom, which will have to be totally reorganized; those displays have to look perfect." He said he wanted her to check all the price tags against the new computer formula, then added that Henry Hill, the showroom manager, would be busy with other details.

When Ron picked them up in the rental car he told them he had been summoned by the gunner to an early morning sales meeting. Megan was surprised she felt as good as she did. The morning air was crisp and clear and smelled invigoratingly of the wooded North Carolina hills. Although she knew her problems were more serious than she'd ever before suspected, a business day was no time to worry about them; anyway, that wouldn't help Michael. For the time being, Megan had no particular plan and no hope for immediate improvement; it was a situation she was determined to accept. Temporarily. It *would* eventually improve; Megan would find a way to *make* it improve.

Naturally, Ron griped all the way to Market Hall about his boss; he and Michael continued to disagree about whether or not he had the nerve to quit—Michael insisted he couldn't afford to, that he'd go bankrupt— and Megan lost track of the banter, watching the scenery, until she heard her name mentioned.

"She does incredibly well with just one line," Michael was telling Ron. "I can't really describe Megan's sales technique, but in her first week she'd made more of a commission than the former rep in his entire last month." He went on to describe her sale of Onyx Flame to China Cove; Megan was enormously encouraged by the compliment.

"So what's your next step, Michael?" Ron jibed. "You plannin' to cut her commission scale because she's making too much money?"

Michael shook his head. "I know what you're saying. In this industry, that kind of thing happens way too often."

Ron opened his mouth but Megan, sitting in the backseat, leaned forward and tapped his shoulder. "Please, Ron," she begged. "Let me say it . . . just this once!"

The Texan nodded.

"Damned manufacturers!"

The car pulled alongside the curb directly in front of the market building where they lingered long enough to arrange an afternoon meeting point.

While the men spoke, Megan studied the twelve-story structure that was the international marketplace of the world furniture and accessories industry.

Ling and Son was located on the fourth floor of one of

the original wings of the main building. The company
had a prime corner location near the elevators, and
Megan was delighted at first glance to see the product
line so well displayed. Clean, sparkling showcase windows announced LING AND SON in simply designed gold
letters. To a buyer approaching the space, the visual
impact could best be summarized in one word: *classy*.
Three thousand square feet were devoted to custom-
built display cases of varying sizes; some of the cases
were lined in neutral velvets, others in subdued suedes
or satins, and each contained the lamp and/or accessories most appropriate to the mood. Small accessories—
ashtrays, bud vases, finger statues—had been skillfully
juxtaposed with the more imposing pieces, and fresh
flowers and potted plants were scattered charmingly
throughout, mainly to punctuate the well-planned traffic areas. Even the work desks were discreetly arranged.

Megan was thrilled. For reps, selling was a complicated enough task without the burdensome problems
posed by ill-arranged showrooms. She looked for the
manager, anxious to congratulate him, and saw Michael already in deep conversation with a short wiry
man familiar from description. As she approached, she
saw that the discussion was an extremely troubled one.

"Michael, I *can't* display merchandise I don't have!"
the showroom manager was saying.

"Yes, of course," the president replied soothingly,
"but—oh, Megan, this is Henry Hill, the gentleman I've
been bragging about. Megan's our new Southern California rep."

Hill's eyes lit up. "My goodness! You'll certainly be a
complement to our showroom!"

"Thank you," Megan replied, "but it's you who deserve praise. This is a magnificent display."

"I appreciate that, I really do, but on the other hand,
Michael says—"

"Oh, relax, Henry," Michael said, patting him on the

back. "All I said is that you should have called me
about this last night. That's the reason I had Adelle
give you the phone number at the rental house."

"But what could you have *done?*" Henry asked, literally wringing his hands. "I called all the airlines when
the shipment didn't show up on the United flight number you gave me. And the California office was closed
down by then."

Michael smiled. "I don't know what I could have
done, Henry, but it really wasn't necessary for you to do
all this worrying alone. I might have taken some of that
off your shoulders, don't you think?"

"Oh! I see!" the manager said. "Very kind of you."

Megan agreed. She knew that most men in Michael's
predicament would have been furious with the employee who failed to report a crucial missing shipment.
As usual, her employer, not at all like "most men," had
chosen to calm his manager so they could return to solving the problem.

"Why don't you try calling the airlines again, Henry?
And then check the receiving dock downstairs; maybe
our shipment just got waylaid in the confusion—you
can imagine the amount of merchandise that must be
arriving down there."

He was trying to sound casual about the sample shipment. But Megan had a feeling of impending doom. She
wondered about Hill's emotions; surely he wasn't that
easily fooled. Megan knew that half of the new items
had been due in yesterday; those twenty lamps and accessories comprised the most outstanding products of
the new Ling and Son line. In other words, it was precisely those lamps and accessories the buyers were expected to find most attractive. She made her way
through the showroom until she found an L-shaped
area that served as both dining facility and communications center. Michael was just replacing the receiver of
a wall phone.

"Struck out," he said. "I thought maybe I could catch

an early warehouseman; but it's just five o'clock in California. Nikki's the only one who ever got in that early."

"You'll call George Ling at home, won't you?"

"I suppose there's no choice."

"Michael?"

"Hmmm?"

"I'm sorry this is happening. Is there something I can do while you get it cleared up? Something that might help?"

He stared at her for a long moment and then, very softly, said, "Megan, you could stand right here. I like that . . . just knowing you're nearby."

She hadn't known it, but something tough and abrasive had been lodged deep within her. With his words, it dissolved; in its place was a curious serenity. For Megan, it was the first realization of the importance she attached to Michael's emotional well-being. Everyone viewed him as a man of iron, of unbendable poise and confidence, of endless capabilities; no one was like that. And at moments such as these, Megan had the reassurance she had something valuable to offer. The intangible can be quite tangible, she thought, and then she was struck by an irony: her mind had been forming words like *his needs* when it was actually hers that were the point. Megan needed to be needed. His words came back to her: "Giving becomes receiving." He had spoken them just before teaching her the meaning of lovemaking . . .

Her heart skipped a beat. She wanted to enfold him in her arms and . . . and what? she asked herself. She had never loved him more than at that moment. And she wasn't at all sure how she felt about herself, Megan McBride. Standing beside the telephone, Michael Richardson appeared to her as not only the most strikingly handsome man alive but also, at that moment, one of the loneliest. And she was thinking of her importance to him when, in truth, she was incapable of helping him in *any* respect. He had spent last night alone and he would spend tonight alone. For the hundredth time she asked herself if her precious independence were worth all this torture. Considering *why* Michael felt as he did, couldn't she just accept it?

Snap out of it, Megan! She jumped just as though the command had been spoken aloud rather than mentally. How long had she been in that stupor? Michael was still gazing at her; had it been a split second or thirty seconds or a minute? Had everything she felt shown through in her eyes—and what was Michael thinking now?

She took an instinctive step toward him, then stopped dead in her tracks. The silent voice was issuing warnings. This is a business situation, Megan, and that man is your boss; right now, the way he needs your help is with *business.*

Megan cleared her throat. "Michael? Shall I get George Ling's number for you?" Before he could respond, she had turned to a nearby table and opened his briefcase. Henry Hill walked in just as she was handing Michael his business directory; there was no news from either the airlines or the receiving dock. Henry started chewing distractedly on his thumbnail. She tried soothing the showroom manager with an offer of hot coffee. Michael looked at her with an expression of amused gratitude; he was riffling through his briefcase, evidently searching for information he wanted on hand during the call to George Ling.

Henry was recovering. He said, "Michael, I'm *so* sorry about this. For what it's worth I want you to know you can count on *me.* I intend pushing what's here as hard as it's humanly possible to push it; after all, we do have *some* of the new intros in. And as for the rest . . . well, the old line *is* good, you know; some of your *finest* designs are in it."

Poor Henry! He was making things worse by implying that the samples would *never* arrive. Megan shuddered at the thought.

Henry had turned directly toward Megan. *"My goodness!* You should be glad you weren't associated with this firm before Michael came along. Why, our things were staler than last month's *bread.* But now . . . well, just *everyone* in the know pays attention to us. Not that it's surprising, of course. From the minute all of us found out *Michael Richardson* would be aboard our floundering little ship, we just knew things would be better. In fact"—he looked quickly around, as though checking to make sure the room was free of spies—"no one understands how the Lings managed to snare one of the top lamp men in the country." In the showroom, a little bell tinkled. Coffee forgotten, Henry Hill jumped up and scampered out.

Michael had dialed; he was obviously waiting for an answer at the other end. With the phone cocked precariously between ear and shoulder, he used both hands for locating and organizing material in front of him. Before much time had passed, he went through the predictable phases, from telling Ling he was sorry to have awakened him to explaining about the missing samples.

"So I'm going to have to ask you to get dressed and go on down to the office, George. At this point, the best course is to check the warehouse shipping—"

Whatever the nature of the interruption at the other end, for the next sixty seconds, it claimed Michael's full attention. And during that time, also, his face turned ashen. It wasn't long before the reason became clear.

"Are you trying to tell me that you decided canceling the air shipment to High Point was a viable way to *economize?"*

Once again, he listened. "George, the samples would've been ready for normal trucking if the problem with Nikki hadn't occurred. The success of the entire fiscal year . . ."

Megan lost track for a few moments. Henry Hill had

crept up beside her to say he had to get right back to the showroom, but in the meantime it had occurred to him to tell Michael, just in case he wanted to ask Mr. Ling about it, that the catalog photographs hadn't arrived, either. She nodded, then scribbled a quick note and shoved it in front of him. When he read it, he looked up, incredulous.

"Wait just a minute, George," he said. "Something else has come to my attention. Last week, we requested an emergency photography job so we could get the catalog photo supplements here in time to give them to the reps coming in for market. The photographer was going to stay up all night developing, then mail the photos here the next day. But nothing's arrived. You know anything about that, by any chance?"

The next words out of Michael's mouth were: "You *what?* George, can't you see that doesn't make any sense? The cost was in the photography itself, not in the prints and the mailing! Besides, reps can't sell on the road without catalog photos; what kind of economizing is that?" He took a deep breath and then continued, so calmly the voice was actually ominous. "Why don't we just cut this short, George? Suppose you tell me two things. Number one: is there anything I can do to change your mind about airfreighting the samples? Number two: if not, how do you suggest we sell when we have neither the pieces nor the photos?" At the end, Michael simply said, "I see. Then there's no point in further discussion, is there? Please give your father my regards."

Megan had started signaling to him. He covered the mouthpiece and asked what she wanted.

She said, "If there would be no transport cost to the company, only normal merchandise transit insurance, would Mr. Ling release the samples for shipment today?"

Although Michael clearly considered the question strange, he asked it. After he hung up, he turned to

Megan. "What on earth was that all about? George said
yes, naturally." Before she could answer, he grinned
and said, "Let me guess—you're acquainted with someone who has a magic carpet!"

Mysteriously, she said, "Might be, boss. Just might
be . . ." Then she became very serious. "Michael, can
you tell me exactly how many pieces are missing? Then
figure the approximate size and weight?" Within a few
minutes, working with the long printouts in front of
them and a pocket machine for the calculations, they
had run the statistics on nine lamps—including all the
shades and various other paraphernalia—plus three
pieces of statuary, two large planters, and several boxes
of small accessories. Michael had explained there was
no way, short of talking to the Ling warehouse, to hone
in anywhere near the exact weight; they plundered
Henry Hill's neat files to find bills of lading on shipments approximating the size of this one.

When they finished, Michael said, "Now, Megan, I'm
sorry to act like an employer on you, but I think you
should tell me what this is all about."

She didn't even hear the statement. Her answer was,
"Michael, are all the samples packed?"

"Some employer-employee relationship *we* have!" he
griped good-naturedly. And then: "Yes, they're packed.
Now are you going to tell me what's going on? To tell
the truth, I don't believe in magic carpets."

"No?" She looked up. "Then can I interest you in
fairy godfathers?"

He just raised those tantalizing blond eyebrows.

"Actually, Michael," she said more seriously, "we
might be just wasting time. Until I know if this'll work,
I'd rather not tell you any more. Can you leave your
telephone credit card with me and just sort of disappear
for a few minutes?" He got up and walked toward the
showroom, shaking his head.

When she located him again, he and Henry were com-
paring price labels with the computer sheets. Megan

handed a small slip of paper to Michael. "Mr. Richardson, sir," she said humbly, "would it be too much trouble for you to telephone Mr. Ling and ask him to give instructions to the warehouse? In two hours, they're to deliver the samples to this hangar at LAX. Then they're to release them to the individual whose name is on the paper. He'll also need Mr. Ling to call the company agent and arrange for an insurance rider."

Michael's mouth fell open. Henry Hill kept looking from one to the other and back again, trying to decide if they were playing some sort of game.

"Oh!" Megan added suddenly. "Do you think it would be a good idea for someone to pick up the catalog photos? They might as well travel on the same flight."

He said, "I'll ask Adelle to do it." The voice was dulled by shock.

Finally Megan couldn't stand it any longer. She burst out laughing. "For someone who never loses his cool, Mr. Richardson, I think the look on your face is priceless! And yours, too, Henry!" She wiped her eyes and said, "I didn't perform a miracle, you know! I mean, the Red Sea didn't part, it didn't snow on the Sahara. All I did was call the father of one of my Japanese students. He's an airline pilot, and I remembered his telling me last week he was fulfilling the FAA requirements for his captain's license. He has to get a certain number of jet hours with an instructor and he said they were using a Lear jet. I just thought it was a shame to have no passengers and nowhere in particular to go with such an enormous plane. Well, now he has a destination. And our samples might not be very good company, but at least he's carrying *something*."

In unison, Michael and Henry Hill shook their heads.

"Maybe I'd better take you two out to breakfast," Megan said at last.

But Henry stayed on to cope, alone, with the computer pricing. And since there was no way to rearrange the showroom until the samples arrived—they weren't

due until early evening—Michael took Megan on a social tour of the High Point marketplace. He had evidently sensed her disorientation, for he said, "After
breakfast I'll see to it that this town's as familiar to you
as your own kitchen."

They ate at the Top of the Mart and Michael used the
window as a map. No wonder she had been confused!
Spread below them around the Market Hall was an
area of several square blocks containing individual
manufacturer's showrooms.

Michael took a sip of orange juice before he explained, "High Point's actually just a figurehead because of the Market Hall location. The network runs
one hundred and fifty miles east to west, from
Burlington, North Carolina, to Lenoir. To see the whole
market, Megan, you have to travel that entire hundred
and fifty miles, known as Furniture Highway. But only
the buyers do that. Meanwhile, we're stuck here in the
middle with a perception problem. What we're missing
are some literally legendary places and factories and
showrooms. Some of them are large, some small; some
are famous, some not yet and never will be, some are
successful, some failing; some are gaudy, and some are
tasteful. But the whole is fascinating by virtue of sheer
scope, if nothing else."

When they walked outside, they headed for one of the
showrooms. Michael had suggested that the Shepard
place was a natural starting point. During the walk,
she marveled at the variety of showrooms they were
passing; if anything, Michael's overview had been un-
derstated. If one showroom obviously housed a manufacturer with limited funds, the next might be
ostentatious in its decorative outlay. As they neared a
complex Michael said was fairly new and extremely desirable, Hamilton-Wren, Megan noted the beginning of
uniformity; here, all the showrooms were rich and
classy. Just before they entered the building marked
SHEPARD IMPORTS, Michael put a hand on her shoulder,

then gently spun her to face the market building now about three blocks distant.

"Wow!" she said and then grinned, turning to face him. "Michael, I haven't said wow since I was in high school! But I see what you mean. Once you get a look at catwalks connecting wings that run over city streets, then you know the place is bigger than it seems on the inside."

Andrew Shepard interrupted a conversation with one of his reps to extend one of the warmest greetings Megan had ever received from a new acquaintance. He was a robust smiling man who wore a short but impressive beard that couldn't conceal a permanently rounded mouth. She was charmed, and even more so when his wife, Lisa, appeared. Lisa Shepard had an olive complexion and hair that was almost a duplicate shade of her husband's; they were two different sizes of the tanned, dark-haired midwestern American prototype. When Michael announced he wanted to introduce them to "his girl," they both expressed sincere delight.

"So—what have you been doing these days, Michael? Besides falling in love, that is?"

Lisa spoke up. "When you're doing that, what else can you possibly have *time* to do?"

"She is right, of course," Andrew said, his black eyes dancing. "That is the reason I haven't had time for anything in all these years. Every day Lisa makes me fall in love with her all over again."

Megan believed that. There was something very special about these people and their relationship. From what Michael had told her, she knew they had a grown daughter; somehow the years and events had not diminished their respect for each other. Here was a couple who had made their own reality, to use Michael's phrase. She stole a glance at him, wondering if he were thinking along the same lines—wondering if the two of them would ever find their way *back* to reality so they could begin to structure the future he envisioned.

Michael must have explained the reason for their stroll. Andrew was saying, "You mustn't think you are the only one confused, Megan. Market reminds me of the old joke about the elephant and the three blind men. The man at the trunk said the elephant was a snake, the man at the side said it was a wall, and the man at the tail said it was a rope!"

When they stopped laughing, Lisa Shepard said, "Megan, please let Andrew and me know if there's anything we can do to make you feel more at home."

They had already done it. As they left the showroom, Megan was more determined than ever to find the key that would unlock the solution to Michael's and her problems.

They had just reentered Market Hall when a total stranger crashed head-on into Megan. Her purse flew up and over her head, then landed inside the revolving door from which she had just emerged, which so shocked the present occupant, he just kept right on revolving back out onto the street, dragging the purse in his wake. When he finally got around again and stepped into the building, the purse stayed on, continuing its circle dance. The stranger who had run into Megan scrambled after it. He succeeded only in grabbing the handle before someone entered one of the little revolving cubicles and gave it a shove that sent him sprawling; now he had the handbag but the spilled contents pirouetted from outside-to-in, inside-to-out, like little horses gone wild on some crazy carousel. Megan would have done something about it if she'd been able to stop laughing. By the time she recovered enough to see clearly, the stranger was on hands and knees: every time the door completed a full revolution, he reached in to pluck another fistful: two pencils and a lipstick tube, one compact and a checkbook. She couldn't tell much about him from that angle, seeing only the top of a balding head.

Michael was leaning against a column, obviously enjoying the scene.

He said, "Congratulations, Megan—somebody finally did it! I didn't think any woman could bring Bob Betts to his knees, but you've got him literally groveling."

Betts got up, dumped the contents of Megan's purse on a nearby chair, and then grabbed her hand, pumping it. In a staccato voice, he said, "Glad to meetcha. I'm from Chicago and you're the new girl everyone's talking about. It's time for me to go to a sales meeting or I'd stay and chat about all this, but you know how the damned manufacturers are." He released her hand and turned; then he was gone.

"What an incredible performance!" Megan said.

From Michael: "You have to admire a guy who can make jokes at the end of a long workday, late to a sales meeting, and after spending five minutes chasing lipstick tubes. I like that about this industry: it sure doesn't take itself too seriously."

A couple of minutes later, when they reached the elevator, Megan was on the verge of asking Michael for an explanation about George Ling's behavior when the big doors rolled open and Henry Hill stepped out.

"Oh, good, I found you," he said, beaming. "I've got *wonderful* news—the samples just arrived. Your friend the pilot said to tell you he was sorry he couldn't hang around, Megan; his airplane had to be returned to California."

That conversation had taken place in the late afternoon; Michael and Megan would not find time for another personal conversation until the morning market opened.

From a friendly competitor, Henry Hill had arranged to hire one truck and one strong warehouseman; Megan and Michael collected the rental car from Ron's parking space and followed them to the airport. When they got their first actual glimpse of the sample boxes, evidence of relief was ample; in fact, it grew a bit too abundant for Michael's taste. Megan heard him say, "Slow down, Henry! That's the third time you've hugged me!"

By two A.M., none of them appeared particularly anxious to do any hugging. Pride alone was keeping Megan on her feet; since midnight her desire for sleep had become as real as her aching blisters. But at least—and at last—all the lamps were assembled. Despite all Michael's care during the last few days at the office, nothing could have warned him that the warehouse would pack the components in such a jumble that only a jigsaw puzzle champ could have set them straight. Finally, all that remained to be done was to unpack every accessory box and fit the statues with the correct mountings, get all the price labels and . . .

She covered her mouth and yawned again. Just after dawn, Michael poured her into a taxi. Megan barely remembered stumbling into the house. She slept, awakened about five that afternoon, then dressed and called Ling and Son. When there was no answer, she got another cab and, in due time, arrived at a beautifully decorated showroom displaying new introductions even more exciting than she'd previously realized. In the back room, Michael and Henry were asleep in chairs, their heads propped over folded arms on the luncheon table. This time the taxi-loading was reversed: *she* poured *him* in; but she also accompanied him home and guided him to his room. Then she threw off her clothes, went skinny dipping in the cold pool, and, finally, gave up and turned in early. It didn't matter; her schedule was so fouled up, she figured it couldn't possibly get worse. Naturally she was up before daybreak. That was okay; it felt good to be awake and alert in the quiet early morning. She read the paper which was delivered at the front door. One headline announced "Market Opens Today: 70,000 Samples and 3800 Trucks Clear Loading Docks"—and she brewed a pot of coffee and fried enough bacon to feed an army. When a hint of light began teasing the North Carolina horizon, she went upstairs and drew a bath. She emerged feeling excited and fresh and ready to sell a million dollars' worth of Ling and Son merchandise; one of the reasons for her high spirits—just one—was the dress she had chosen. Megan was wearing the new Stanley Sherman; she looked terrific in it.

Michael was dressed and seated at the kitchen table, reading the paper and munching absentmindedly on a piece of crisp bacon. Before looking up, he said, "Is that you, love? You—"

One look was all it had taken. "I haven't the vaguest idea what I was about to say," he admitted. "Megan, I don't believe I've ever seen anyone look quite that . . . that . . ." He finally stopped, then laughed at himself. "I guess the word I'm looking for is *beautiful,* but in this case it doesn't seem quite adequate."

"Thank you," she said, blushing slightly under the glare of his frank appraisal. Then she couldn't think of anything else to say. They were just staring at each other. If the last few days had progressed a bit more normally, it occurred to her, then they would have felt free to *act* on these feelings rather than having to rely on endless clues, like the generous compliments passing back and forth. Wouldn't the relationship ever get back on track? Remembering all those laps in cool water last night, she realized quite well that her physical memory tapes still held perfect recall of how exquisite that relationship was—is?

The little voice in her head cut in: Megan, you started out wishing for something normal, like a good-morning kiss, and you ended up in the bedroom *again.* She sighed and thought, Every time you look at him you start wanting to be back in his arms, just the way you were that night at the Hotel Del Coronado.

She smiled. Funny, but she couldn't tell whether the spirit in her brain was praising or chiding. The latter, probably. After all, she had promised herself to stay away from sexual involvement until other aspects of the relationship were secure. Her first sight of Michael always made that seem impossible and today was no exception; he was wearing a light gray suit with tiny interwoven silver threads; a patterned blue, gray, and silver silk tie; and an expensive silver blue dress shirt with silver cuff links. Sleep had erased last night's pallor; his skin still glowed with the remnants of his summer tan. And always, always, there were the tantalizing eyes and the provocative lips; together, in a certain mood they gave the impression of suppressed violence—sheer energy, she supposed, for Michael was far from a violent man. Yet, in their lovemaking . . .

He was asking a question: "What shall I tell the first buyer who asks if you're for sale?"

"Hmmm?"

"Never mind, little Meggie. I know what to say—sorry, she's taken: *mine.*"

She noticed he didn't sound very apologetic. In fact, if his tone—and a sudden bright flash of warning in the eyes—were any indication, then Michael's statement had been intended to convey something else entirely. To Megan, not some imaginary buyer, he had been saying, "It's time you learn to deal with the fact." She put it out of her mind; probably the product of an overactive imagination.

Ron was dressed to the nines. Correction: overdressed to the nines. Later, Michael put it into words: "He looks like a displaced Manhattanite trying to look like a cowboy trying to look like a western Al Capone." He added that it was part of Ron's image. "He knows people talk about it; in fact, he considers it a harmless bit of free publicity." She shook her head—the things people would do to lure buyers into the showroom! Ron would have told her, "Honey, you ain't seen *nuthin'* yet!"

When they caught sight of Market Hall, from the distance traffic would allow, she made the only comment that was appropriate: "My God!"

It was a circus with forty rings and hundreds of ringmasters. Cheerleaders from the local high schools were twirling batons and turning handsprings; children of all ages ran in zany crisscross paths trying to hand out mountains of free literature.

Now the market had a personality. Of course, Megan thought—no one judges a circus when the tent is empty!

The scene inside was no calmer; in fact, until more progress had been made with the entrance lines, it couldn't even be described as organized chaos. National markets were about as easy to get into as White House cocktail parties. Ron said, "There it is again: masses for passes." Megan now understood why Michael had double-checked his briefcase for their entry cards. As they fought their way through, Michael paused occasionally for hurried introductions.

"They really do come from all over!" she said, amazed.

He laughed. "Honey, this is just the beginning. Right over there"—he pointed to a spot beyond her vision—"is an entire desk of linguists, just standing by. Before this is over you'll have talked with people from every free industrial nation on earth. Remember—furniture is a worldwide commodity."

Megan started to say something, then stopped when a reporter's flashbulb went off, momentarily blinding her. When she got her bearings again, Michael had melted into a group stepping lightly in front of them. Since he was approaching the pass gate that would finally spill them into the showroom area, she sighed and started elbowing her way; this was no time to get lost.

18

By the time Megan and Michael escaped, it was seven
o'clock; a couple of stragglers lounged on the showroom
sofa, sipping wine, but the serious buying was over for
the day. Henry Hill had disappeared and Michael's
Washington reps had volunteered to remain until the
departure of the last guest.

Downstairs in the lobby, Megan surveyed the scene
and giggled. "Michael, look! Remember how lively
everyone was stepping this morning? Half the people
down here now are carrying their shoes! And the other
half are limping."

"Welcome to the National Furniture Show, Megan!
How're *your* feet?"

"They've felt better," she admitted. "But strangely
enough, I feel marvelous. Today was so, um—"

"Exhilarating? It should have been. You outsold
everyone in the showroom."

"Oh! You don't know that! I heard you say you
weren't going to start the daily tallies until noon tomorrow."

"I don't need a calculator for everything, you know.
In fact, the other reps were talking about you. They
said the only reason you were selling more is the way
you look in that dress."

Megan did a quick double-take, then felt silly. The
reps wouldn't have said that; and if they had, Michael
wouldn't have told her. It occurred to her for the first

time, though, that he had been complimenting her
dress all day; to say the very least, she was pleased.

They stepped outside; in the gentle darkness the
place bore no resemblance whatsoever to the morning
madhouse. Even the cars seemed to be moving along at
a subdued pace. Ron was supposed to pick them up; Michael had warned her there was little chance he'd be on
time.

"Cold?" he asked.

She shook her head. "It feels good, actually. With the
spotlights, not to mention all our lamps burning, the
showroom's an oven."

"Be grateful," he said. "It wasn't just the lights,
honey; it was the number of buyers. The building management keeps the thermostats turned way down during markets, trying to compensate for crowds and
display lights; on a slow day you'll be shivering like an
Alaskan duck hunter staring into an empty sky. Speaking of skies, look up; we've got a full moon."

Megan told him it was lovely but, in truth, it wasn't
the first time she'd noticed it. The moment they'd left
the building, the big pewter ball had been playing exotic games with Michael's appearance; sun-streaked
strips of blond shimmered silver in contrast to skin
seeming even more deeply tanned. She had almost commented on it, almost paid him a compliment; then she'd
hesitated for fear the words might lead in a direction
she wasn't yet prepared to handle. Anyway, Michael
was probably weary of adulation focused on his looks;
Lord knew he'd received enough of it that day!
Women—and some men, she conceded—meeting him
for the first time went through a predictable and understandable series of reactions, from shock to awe and
back to composure; as for those already acquainted
with him, Megan strongly suspected some of their reasons for visiting the showroom. Michael himself, of
course, invariably ignored—or didn't notice—these re-

actions, without breaking pace with his normal easygoing brand of dignity.

She heard a now-familiar cough and sputter; the rental car had asthma. Ron spun the wheel toward the curb. About halfway home, after a brief exchange of sales reports, Megan began to suspect Ron's day hadn't gone as well as he would have them believe. There was tension that had not existed in the big man's voice before. He never cracked a joke and never mentioned the gunner. Michael didn't seem to notice; he kept staring out the window, obviously involved in some deep private thought. Megan wished she knew what it was.

The front door of their house was standing open and a late-model Plymouth was parked in the circular driveway. Henry Hill leaned against the side of the car, then straightened and walked forward when he saw them approach.

Michael was obviously surprised. He rolled down the window. "How come you're still here, Henry?"

Still here? Megan was lost.

"Well, I put the boxes inside—"

Michael said, "Just a minute. Sorry, but we'd better let Ron go." He opened the door and climbed out, then held out a hand for Megan. There was a minute's exchange about whether or not Ron wanted to go out for dinner; he said he planned to sit home and do some "heavy drinking." Michael said nothing, but his face darkened and he was obviously on the verge of commenting when the Texan gunned the engine and sped away. Megan had no trouble understanding his concern—on the airplane, he had told her Ron was a teetotaler.

"Okay, Henry," he said finally. "Come on inside." And then: "It was nice of you to deliver this; damned nice."

The showroom manager beamed. Obviously the reference had been to two large containers now standing in the entry hall; they were Ling and Son sample boxes, identical to those unpacked before market. Megan couldn't imagine why Michael would need them at the house; but, then, it wasn't any of her business.

Henry Hill said, "I forgot where you told me to leave your keys. Wouldn't want you locked out of your own house!" He looked around. "Boy, this is some place!" There was a decorative partition directly in front of the big entry doors, but it made no attempt to block from view the spectacular living room to their right. Following Henry's gaze, Megan saw that the room was softly lit despite the fact that no lamps had been switched on; the moon was a giant silver light bulb.

Michael took the keys and spent a few more moments thanking his manager; then he asked if Henry wanted to stay for a drink. Megan noticed that he didn't offer to explain, or to tell her the contents of the boxes, so she didn't ask.

At first, it seemed that Henry Hill would decline. Clearly he wanted the drink; just as clearly he was afraid he might be intruding on a very private affair. In Megan's mind, all sorts of alarms sounded; for the first time since their arrival in High Point, she experienced real panic. She and Michael would be alone until they went out to dinner, *if* they went out to dinner; both timing and recent behavior patterns indicated it would be ridiculous—childish—to claim she had a headache, she was exhausted, she needed a long hot bath, etcetera.

But, in fact, she did need a long hot bath; it would give her a few minutes to think. Having formatted at least that much of her plan, her head cleared. She heard herself saying, "Henry, you've had a pretty exhausting few days; please stay for cocktails."

The showroom manager looked enormously flattered; he accepted immediately. And Michael appeared grateful, as though he knew Megan was being gracious in consideration of his need to reward a loyal employee. By the time she went to the bar to mix Michael's martini and Henry's wine spritzer, she felt like a grade-A heel.

She only sat with the men for two minutes. Then she asked to be excused. "If I don't start primping now," she lied, "Michael'll end up having to wait when we go to dinner. You two go on with the cocktail hour; I'll be back by the time you're ready for a second round." As she walked toward the master suite, she smiled. When she didn't return at refill time, they would undoubtedly entertain each other with complaints about the endless hours women spent on their makeup.

Since the Jacuzzi couldn't be seen from the living room, she put on a sapphire bikini and headed there instead of the tub. The little round pool gurgled and bubbled when she threw the switch; while it warmed, she waited on the side; it was as good a spot as any to start her thinking.

As she saw it, the problem had changed in character. If at this point she failed to confront Michael with the fact of how determined she actually was on the subject of personal freedom, then she left him open to feelings that might be worse than the confrontation. She imagined herself in his place. Presumably he was expecting more of the night than it actually promised. When the expectations were dashed, Megan knew how she herself would react to vague excuses: she'd simply feel rejected, period. Nothing promised more pain than that; she remembered it from the period following that single missed telephone call. No way was she going to put Michael through the same thing; she loved him far too much. She sighed and threw off her robe, then slid into the Jacuzzi. Her decision had been made. She hadn't a clue how to minimize Michael's reaction when he was once again guided to the topic he was determined not to discuss.

She was just heading back to the room, retying the robe at her waist, when the French doors opened and Michael stepped out. He walked toward her and said,

"You needed a few minutes' peace and quiet, didn't you? Market can have that effect. Feel better?"

She smiled gratefully. "My feet don't hurt quite so much. You should try it."

"In a while," he said. "Maybe after dinner. Speaking of which, will you do me a favor?"

"If I can."

"Put on the black dress again."

She was surprised; most men would be loath to admit such fondness for a piece of clothing. An irony popped into her head. This is certainly a switch from what I've been worrying about: Michael's asking me to put clothes *on.* Aloud, she said she'd be happy to. He excused himself to return to the living room. Megan had a feeling something strange was going on down there. And then she remembered their visitor; undoubtedly Michael had only wanted to get back to Henry.

But Henry wasn't in the living room. What Megan saw when she entered struck her as slightly modified from the previous picture; at first she couldn't identify the change; Michael had cleared away the cocktail glasses and plumped all the throw pillows. But there was something else . . .

Onyx Flame—the porcelain lamp she so admired—it was sitting on an end table, gracefully lit by a low-wattage bulb! But why? Michael was seated nearby; when she entered the room, he stood.

"Come over here, Megan," he said softly; his words were less command than embrace. She hesitated, digging long fingernails into her palms. I'm not ready, was her desperate thought; for the first time, Megan realized she had no resources whatsoever for handling such a situation. She couldn't claim lack of interest, not when the thing she most desired in life was Michael Richardson. My God, she admitted silently, I can almost feel his arms, his lips, the way his thighs tense when he holds me . . . Her lower body was filling with the warm fluid rush of her terrible need.

Slowly, she moved toward the sofa. If only he'd give
five minutes to talking, she thought, but her mind immediately supplied a definitive fact: clearly, Michael
had planned this interlude, right down to the mysterious detail of the lamp. If Megan hadn't been able to
draw him into discussion at other times, there was no
way now, not tonight—one does not direct Michael
Richardson, she thought. Unless she retreated from her
self-avowed determination to get him to agree on policies regarding her personal independence—unless
Megan gave in entirely—they were about to reach the
absolute dead end; if the unwelcome issue were dragged
forth at this point, Michael would be frustrated, and
possibly downright infuriated.

When she was within a few feet, he told her to stop. "I
forgot something," he said, then crossed the room to a
complicated-looking stereo system. There was a small
sack on the console; he removed the contents, a cassette
tape cartridge, and slipped it into a slot; punching a
control button filled the room immediately with music.
When Michael saw Megan's astonished reaction, he
smiled; the voice she heard was Barry Manilow's; not
only that, the song was "I Can't Smile Without You."

He said nothing, just walked toward her. In Megan's
mind's eye, Michael was gliding; she herself felt suspended in air, floating. When he took her hand, pulled
her forward, it was real enough: she recognized the familiar fire ignited by his touch. Moving together, they
reached the center of the living room. Now she was in
his arms; they were swaying, not really dancing, to the
haunting melody. Just before Megan's eyelids closed,
she saw that outside, beyond the big glass windows, the
trees of North Carolina were also swaying; keeping
time to the rhythm of a gentle breeze. Her arms went
up and around his neck. She felt his breath at her ear.
She trembled violently. Michael tightened his grasp.
Megan tightened hers.

He spoke in a whisper, almost a gasp. *"This* is our

song, babe. I'll never even try to smile without you. Megan . . . little Meggie . . . I love you."

She pressed closer. For some reason a tear trickled from the corner of one eye. When it dropped onto Michael's silver blue shirt sleeve, he didn't notice. And by that time, she felt the pressure raging in his loins. Megan's buttocks tensed, her hips seeking closer contact. From somewhere deep in her throat, a moan escaped. Then she said, "God help me, I love you too." When there was a pause in the music, Megan hardly noticed. Michael grew still and she lifted her head, seeking his lips. But he was saying something: "Baby, I have a present for you." He dropped one arm, then used the other to coax her toward the sofa. When they got there, she saw a small, elegantly wrapped package on the end table where Onyx Flame glowed in silent approval. He placed the little box in her hand and told her to open it. Inside, Megan found a jeweled pendant on a delicate gold chain. She didn't know what to say. The design, apparently executed in black onyx and hundreds of minuscule rubies, was identical to the design of the lamp; when the light touched the sparkling gems, the flame became a living torch on a velvet background; she could hear it roaring against the night sky. And she could hear the rush of her own pulse.

"The minute I saw you standing near the lamp," Michael said, "I knew you had to wear jewelry the color of that fiery hair." He put his palm on the back of her neck, stroking gently; then he lifted the thick hair and said, "Megan, put it on." She took the pendant, slipped the chain expertly into place, and fastened the clasp. Michael put his hands on her shoulders, turning her to face him. He nodded. "It's what I imagined. Like your hair. In some lights, it's a torch; in others, it's just a hint. Stand up and walk away, where I can see it from a distance."

When she had retreated about five feet, still unable

to think of appropriate words, Michael shook his head.
He said, "The black dress is perfect, but not the scarf."

After he had asked her to put on the same outfit,
Megan had accessorized exactly the same as earlier
that day, for the showroom. She had considered
dispensing with the businesslike scarf concealing her
neckline, yes, but had quickly discarded the idea; after
all, seduction had been something to avoid, at least until they'd talked out the other matter. Vaguely, she now
perceived how helpless she had been to alter this scenario. Sometime there would be hell to pay, but right
now, soaring to the heights, she just didn't care. And
when she felt his fingertips brushing her neck, loos-
ening the scarf, the thought was lost altogether. Megan
didn't even look down when the strip of black and white
silk floated to the carpet.

Without restraint of fabric, the pendant rested in the
cleavage of her breasts, just below the top button. Michael's fingers manipulated the closure, trying to un-
fasten it; when she felt his touch against her skin—he
was trembling with the effort to remain gentle—there
was a sudden sharp intake of breath. Then, seemingly
all at once, several things happened: the top of the dress
conceded, falling open; Michael stepped back, looked at
her for only a moment, hungrily, and then scooped her
into his arms and started up the stairs.

He placed her gently on the bed, then lowered himself
to lie nearby, yet not close enough to touch her. With
one arm folded beneath his head, one leg jackknifed on
the bedspread, he was facing the ceiling; his breath
came in short sporadic gasps. Megan rolled toward him,
needing relief from her own exquisite agony, but he
said, "No, not now," in a voice tortured with passion.
"Let me calm down." After what seemed forever, Michael groaned, "Oh, little Meggie—it's been too long.
Maybe we should . . ."

His words trailed into the tense air and her brain suddenly overrode her supercharged emotions. Remem-

bering the night at the Hotel Del Coronado, recalling every detail of lovemaking when it's taken at an unhurried pace, she knew part of this was up to her. "Honey," she said hoarsely. "I'm going downstairs. To get us some wine."

Michael just nodded. When she came back, the bed was empty; Megan heard the gurgling of the Jacuzzi and knew where to find him. She carried the slender crystal wineglasses outside and, approaching the little whirlpool, saw Michael stretched almost full-length in the warm water. His head was tilted back, resting on one tiled edge, and his eyes were closed. There was a pile of clothes sitting on a chair and, through the pulsing, vibrating activity of the clear blue liquid, Megan just barely made out the fact that he wore only underwear; as before, it was dark blue and very, very brief. She stopped, took a deep breath, and then closed the distance between them. Before the grassy area ended, she kicked off her shoes in order to avoid making noise. This way, without disturbing him, she was able to kneel and place the cool edge of the wine goblet at his lips; he took one deep swallow before ever opening his eyes.

When she saw the way he looked at her, Megan immediately followed his silent command. Now it appeared there had been good reason for her intemperate shopping binge. The dress fell at her feet, revealing a one-piece satin and lace confection, jet black, cut high against her thighs and low against her bust; she made no attempt to remove the flame pendant. Without shyness, Megan slipped quietly into the pool beside Michael, then reached behind her for the wineglasses, handing one to him. After only a couple of sips, Michael took her glass and put it back on the edge. He pulled himself to a sitting position and Megan into his arms.

Their kiss was slow at first, and gentle, as though both were hesitant to release the restraints. Gradually, however, the tension swelled, then burst beyond their abilities to contain it. Michael's tongue explored the inside of her mouth; when Megan's answering movements became too frantic, he moved on, kissing her ear, then flickering along the inner edge until she cried out.

Both his arms had been around her; when her passionate call rang into the cool night air, he dropped them to his side; he also adjusted his position, coaxing Megan to do the same; instead of sitting on the shelf of the pool, now they were kneeling in the main body of water. This time, when Michael reached forward, his hands found her buttocks; with a demanding pull, he forced their bodies together. Again Megan cried out—his urgent moan was the rejoinder—when she learned that flimsy nylon briefs did nothing to conceal his urgent need; nor could her own satin garment protect her from the contact shock of that hard throbbing demand between his slender legs.

Michael's hands began moving over her. When they brushed the lace just above her breasts, Megan reached instinctively for the tiny straps holding the garment in place. After she stripped them away, then pulled the satin down to her waist, she searched for the elastic band of his briefs and, finding it, ran her hands slowly underneath; exploring. The tempo of his breathing increased. She heard him take a deep breath, then she felt him shudder; after that, at last, she felt the touch of his fingertips on her nipple. From that time on, it seemed that Megan's reactions raced with the whirling, exploding waters around her.

Her hands were near the point they sought, beneath his underwear, when he broke the mood. "Stop," he moaned. "This isn't right. I want it to be better for you."

As he removed her hand, she tried to tell him there was no way it could be better. But, as usual, Michael Richardson would make the decision. He backed up slightly, looking at her and breathing hard. The black garment was floating free at her waist, revealing everything above. "God, you're gorgeous," he said, "and, baby, I'm determined this is going to be the best night of your life."

Megan knew what he was doing. Still, though, she was far too excited to welcome the enforced interruption. Her body was a network of taut nerve endings, each one screaming for relief. Even the bubbles breaking against her tight, swollen nipples served to further increase the torture. Evidently Michael could tell what she was thinking. A slow, amused half smile played across his mouth; it seemed to be saying, "I know . . . but the longer you feel this way, the more you'll feel later." Aloud, all he said was, "Remember, we're learning about lovemaking, not sex."

They sat by the side of the Jacuzzi, dangling their feet in the water and sipping the wine. Michael kept one arm lightly draped over her shoulders; in an unconcealed attempt to bring his physical needs under control, he told her a shaggy dog story; gradually she felt her body loosen, knowing that as long as they were together, it would continue making demands only Michael could fulfill. About ten minutes passed. He said it was time to go inside, extending his hand; after Megan took it, he wrapped one arm tightly around her until they were out of the night air.

When he mentioned food, Megan was surprised to realize she was hungry. Michael stood beside her in the kitchen, helping arrange a platter of fruit while two bowls of chili heated in the microwave. Then he disappeared into the living room after patting her on the rear end and telling her how "cute" she looked. Since her total attire consisted of the now-dry black undergarment and a frilly little white apron she'd located in one of the drawers, it was probably true. As for Michael, wandering around in tight blue briefs that accented every detail of his firm physique, Megan didn't have the words—or the nerve—to describe her opinion of his appearance.

When she carried the tray into the main room, he had a big fire going in the circular firepit; and Barry Manilow's album was playing in the background. Outside, the wind had picked up; there was a strong suggestion of rain. It was a time to be relaxed, and happy, and incredibly in love. If Megan had been asked if anything could ever go wrong between her and Michael, she would have laughed at the question. After the chili bowls had been emptied, their song started. Michael pulled her to her feet and, this time, they really danced; he moved expertly and with confidence; it wasn't until Manilow's last bittersweet phrases that the tempo of their movements slowed and the lovemaking began again in earnest. Once again, he carried her upstairs; there would be no further interruptions until early the next morning.

For the rest of Megan's life, she would cherish the memory of that long and beautiful night. With rain pelting the ceiling of the big house, and a wind threatening to tear it down, Michael proceeded to demonstrate that all she had learned, all she had felt at the Hotel Del Coronado, had been but a primer.

He urged her senses to unimagined experiences; at one point, when he pressed his fingers through the smooth satin, then moved them lightly between her legs in a gentle rotation that grew increasingly faster, she actually grew dizzy; her knees jackknifed and her hips rose in the air. And then he withdrew, waiting to see what she had in store for him. He allowed her to tease and explore, to use her mouth and lips as she had never before dreamed, and then he retreated again, gasping and telling her it was her turn.

His voice, his words, were unpredictable. One moment, she heard him say, "Hurry, babe. Yes, oh yes!" and then, gently, Michael said, "Let me kiss you, Megan. I love you." And when they kissed, it was with tenderness, as if to reaffirm that *this* was what it was all about.

The rain was pounding furiously on the roof at the precise moment both the lovers reached the end of human endurance. Michael looked down, desperately, and whispered, "Now, baby? I don't think I can wait any longer," and she wrapped her legs around him with a purpose greater than the storm raging outside. A few moments later, his cry—followed by hers—was muted by a ferocious clap of thunder. When the lightning followed, it illuminated two totally satisfied people, one lying on top of the other, with his fingers still intertwined in her hair.

19

Their throats were dry. For some reason, probably the rainy night, Megan thought of hot chocolate. When she told Michael, he ruffled her hair and teased, "You mean just like Mama used to make? Sure, come on; while you're stirring, I'll stoke up the fire—it'll be fun."

For a long time afterward Megan would wonder . . . If she hadn't wanted hot chocolate, would things have turned out differently?

The barely glowing embers gave off just enough light to spark life into the new pendant. She had never taken it off and now, finally, she tried to thank him. Throughout the soft, halting words of her appreciation, Michael sat perfectly still, staring into the fire. When Megan finished, he remained that way for a long moment. And then, slowly, he got up and walked over to the little nook containing the desk. His briefcase was on top; Megan watched him unlock it, reach inside, then put something in the pocket of his robe. When he turned around, Megan saw that, for the first time in her experience, he looked, oh, a bit shy; not uncertain of himself— not Michael!—but, rather, as though he were dealing with a matter of unusual sentimental importance; to say she was puzzled would have been putting it far too mildly.

When at last he spoke, now sitting again, she noticed a note of awe; his voice was soft, low. "I have something else for you." From the pocket, he withdrew another gift box. Megan ripped away the paper and saw a case obviously from the same jeweler who had crafted her pendant, only this one was smaller.

She was about to lift the little hinged lid when she paused to ask a sincere but slightly self-conscious question: "Honey, what did I do to deserve all this?" He told her to open it; then she'd see.

But even when Megan was confronted with her first sight of the most outstanding ring she had ever laid eyes on—a large square-cut diamond surrounded by dozens of tiny twinkling rubies—*still* she didn't understand. Not until Michael removed the ring from the case, slipped it onto the third finger of her left hand, and said, "I want you to be my wife."

It should have been the most beautiful single moment of her life. She wanted to marry Michael. She loved him. *Mrs. Michael Richardson . . . Megan Mc-Bride Richardson . . .* It even sounded good. But there was no way she could accept the proposal.

If it had *ever* occurred to her that this might happen, she would indeed have forced the problem-solving discussion, even if it meant a grade-A, knockdown, screaming, kicking battle. Mr. and Mrs. McBride's daughter was head over heels in love, true, and she was also confused. Among friends and business associates alike, she was known as a no-nonsense, get-it-over-with problem-solver. Unlike many other people, she also knew the difference between problems and temporary annoyances; of course, in order to make such a determination, she had to know the facts. In the case of her relationship with Michael Richardson, one crucial bit of knowledge had entirely escaped her attention: he wanted Megan to spend the rest of her life with him.

She knew why she hadn't foreseen it—it would have seemed too good to be true. Always before, thoughts of their future together had contained no specific time span, for she could hardly have dared hope his feelings were as strong as hers. Therefore, their disagreement, upsetting though it certainly was, had never been regarded as an issue to be dealt with *contractually*. Marriage was a binding agreement, the most important two people would make in their lifetimes. They were to accept—forever—all that was known about each other: individual requirements, strengths, and weaknesses. Megan knew that the woman Michael was now asking to share his life would turn into a nagging malcontent, a shrew, if she tried to forfeit the independence so precious to her, so much an integral part of her. But Michael was no more aware of the facts than she had been. Both parties to the proposed new contract needed to clarify the terms, which could only be accomplished with a more realistic discussion than had so far been attempted. At this point, knowing how crucial was the answer Michael awaited, she desperately wondered how she could make him understand they had merely to *delay* the agreement, to adjust one vital clause. She wanted words that would prove there was no way she could ever reject him; to do so would have been the same as rejecting her own reason for living.

As the seconds ticked by, Megan tried to imagine what her friend Sharon would advise. For a fractional moment, no longer, she received a mental answer saying that this wasn't a time for words at all . . . that marriage contracts were emotional, not business . . . that she could just put her arms around Michael and get a little sleep, do the talking later. But the comforting temptation was erased by images of the next day, when Michael's friends and colleagues would no doubt congratulate her for something she alone would know was not yet a confirmed reality. And then what? It wasn't likely—but it was always possible—that he would categorically refuse to back off regarding the personal independence issue; if he wanted his way more than he wanted Megan . . . No, she couldn't duck this; it had to be squarely confronted in the best manner she could find.

Which didn't turn out to be good enough. Later she'd be able to see that Michael had stopped listening halfway through her first sentence. What, exactly, had she said? Something like: "Darling, I didn't know, honestly I didn't, or I'd have made more of an effort to avoid something like this, but . . ."

Sharon might have said, "For God's sake, Megan! He probably thought you would have wanted to, oh, *set things straight*, to let him know from the beginning that you weren't looking for a long-term commitment! You know how people are nowadays; undoubtedly, he thought the thing you wanted to *avoid* was his proposal. And haven't you ever heard of *provisional* contracts? The kind that say, 'I'd like more than anything to work with you and we can iron out the wrinkles when it's convenient'?"

Once Megan returned to Los Angeles, her best friend's outward reaction, no matter what she might actually have been thinking, was a good deal more sympathetic. However, the doctor did admit it would have been better for Megan to follow Michael after he got up from the sofa, shaking his head. "After all," she said without intending any blame whatsoever, "whenever we realize someone we love is hurt, there's one sure way to soothe the pain—say nothing, just put your arms around him." Days afterward, of course, the excellent advice was meaningless. For the fact was, Michael had said something vague—Megan recalled it as: "You really don't owe me an explanation, you know; I just made a mistake; it's not the end of the world!"—and then he had gotten up from the sofa and cheerfully announced it was time to get some sleep. He did *not* walk up the stairs to the master bedroom. Megan didn't pursue him—she had been too horrified to move—and the next morning, as he was prone to do, he acted as though nothing had ever happened.

Since the National Furniture Show observed no holidays, Saturday was business as usual. Emotionally,

Megan was feeling so dreadfully battered that the professional demands came as a much-needed temporary salve; she wouldn't have time to sit around licking her wounds, that much was certain.

Michael was also short on time that morning; long before Ron's appointed arrival with the rental car, he called for a cab. This was to enable him to make an early meeting, or so he said, for Megan's overwrought condition created the suspicion that he merely wanted to avoid riding with *her*. Before he left, during an awkward period at the kitchen table, they passed the normal polite greetings, then silently shared the newspaper; in truth, Megan couldn't have claimed to have read a single word.

When, at eight-twenty, her ride hadn't materialized, she grew worried. By a quarter of nine she gave up and followed her employer's example: she called a taxi. She had dialed the showroom to get Ron's telephone number from Michael and then had learned from Henry Hill that her employer really *was* in a meeting. While she listened to the explanation that Michael was in conference with a group of Japanese artisans gathered at Shepard Imports, she also sighed. This information counteracting her earlier suspicion made Megan feel like an utter fool. Thus preoccupied, she almost disconnected before poor Henry finished talking.

"The boss'll *kill* me if you hang up! He's been calling here every five minutes, wanting to know if you've come in yet."

"How come?" Despite the casual words, her heart had skipped several beats. If Michael was in a meeting, yet continually trying to reach her, was it possible he felt equally bad about last night? Or—more important— had it dawned on him that a brief time expenditure now, just a few minutes devoted to candid conversation, could open the door to a lifetime of nights like the one they'd just spent?

Henry Hill was explaining that Michael's and An-

drew Shepard's meeting had bogged down when the interpreter from the translating pool had called to say he
was running three hours late. If help didn't arrive soon,
two of the Japanese gentlemen would miss homeward-
bound flights. "I said to Michael," Henry rambled, "I
said, what can Megan do about it, but—"

"Sorry," she cut in. "My cab's here. I'll go directly to
Andrew Shepard's. Just let Michael know I'm on the
way." Without bothering to wait for an answer, Megan
slammed the phone down, grabbed her purse, and ran
outside. She could just imagine what was going on at
that stalled meeting; considering the extraordinary politeness of the Japanese, everyone was on his fiftieth
bow, and by now there would be some painfully sore jaw
muscles from nonstop smiling. Maybe Lisa had thought
to open up the famous Shepard daiquiri bar a bit earlier
in the day; it wasn't sake, but it was a damned sight
better than nothing.

There were five Oriental gentlemen in the Shepards'
conference room with Michael and Andrew. Judging
from their self-conscious, rather strained expressions,
the group had been drinking coffee, not daiquiris. Before
Megan entered the room, Lisa warned her: "Watch
out—the silence in there is so loud it'll shatter your eardrums!" Megan was also briefed on the purpose of the
gathering: since many of the Ling and Son products
were made by the same artisans who supplied Shepard
Imports, Michael and Andrew had requested a joint
meeting to discuss the possibility of placing even more
orders with these particular men; first, though, they
had to convince them to try some revolutionary new
shapes and patterns. Before Megan opened the door she
whistled. That wouldn't be easy. Her years in Japan
had taught her that the Orientals considered American
taste a bit odd, to put it mildly; since the artisans' real
profits came from from reorders, they always flatly refused to produce an object they considered displeasing
—for sure, it wouldn't sell, they reasoned, so why

bother?—and, in fact, the Japanese were only pleased by their own art forms.

When she walked in, five men jumped to their feet; by the time the two Americans, Michael and Andrew caught up, their Eastern colleagues had doubled into the ritual bow of greeting. They really *do* need help! Megan thought with amusement; as she placed her palms on her thighs, bending deferentially from the waist, she hid a half smile; the whole scene reminded her of a long-ago visit to a friend's church; try as she might, Megan had found herself kneeling while the rest of the congregation stood, or rising just as they went back on their knees.

She looked at Michael, waiting for him to order her into action; to proceed earlier would cause him to lose face with the artisans. It was all she could do to keep from cracking up when he put on an ingratiating smile and said, in a tone that would have fooled anyone not familiar with English, "What the hell do we do next? I've never been stuck without an interpreter before."

Speaking with exquisite respect, Megan said, "Introduce me—in English. All I need is their names. And when you've finished, sit down; if you don't, they'll keep standing."

In a voice that sounded like an apology, and with her eyes facing the floor, Megan said, *"Hajimemashite?"*— How do you do?—five different times. The names became "Shoten-*san*," "Ishikawa-*san*," "Takeda-*san*," "Kameda-*san*," and "Inoguchi-*san.*" With each introduction, the bowing started all over. Then, when the last of the foreign gentlemen was seated, Megan made one final bow, this time to the gentleman sitting next to the only empty chair. *"Makotoni moshiwake gozaimasen,"* she began, followed by a seemingly endless string of words evidently resulting in permission to sit. Finally she was settled and telling the Americans their meeting could begin, but Andrew couldn't resist a brief tease. "Wait, Megan!" he said. "For Michael's sake I

must know if you made a date with Mr. Kameda! That
was a very long conversation." When she explained
that all she'd said was "Sorry, I'd like to sit here," Andrew's mouth fell open in amazement.

By the time the lengthy session ended, Megan
thought both American men had probably learned to
recognize the Japanese words for "I'm sorry." They'd
certainly heard them enough! Each time Michael took a
design from his portfolio, one or the other of the visiting
artisans would apologize, then ask Megan to explain
that the unusual shape would be too expensive to model
and mold, or the colors couldn't be accurately repro-
duced. Too bad, she thought; since Michael's ideas
really were new and exciting—and highly salable—all
parties to this excruciatingly polite cultural battle were
losing the war.

Finally, Andrew Shepard said, "Unless Megan has a
suggestion, we should call a halt, I'm afraid."

She had been drawing little connecting circles on a
scratch pad. It surprised her when Michael said, "I'm
game. What would *you* do next, Megan?"

As she opened her mouth to tell him Andrew had the
right idea—just call a halt—a scene flashed into her
mind. It was from her early teens, before her family
moved back to the States. Gavin McBride had taken his
daughter on an overnight trip into Tokyo and they'd
stopped first at a big factory. For the new building he
was about to start, Gavin explained his need for a revolutionary new bolt, plus the automatic riveting machinery to drive it. Megan recalled that the owner of the
manufacturing plant had continually turned the funny-
looking bolt over and over in his hand, then said
"Sorry, no can do." But Megan's father had nonetheless
constructed his building with *that* bolt, made by *that*
factory.

She turned to the artisans and, with typically humble
tone and smile, started into something that, judging
from the looks on their faces, sounded to Michael and

Andrew like a string of phonetic gobbledygook. When
she finished, she dropped her eyes to the table, as expected, but stole sideways glances. If, after ten or so seconds, the foreign businessmen had said nothing, it was
still better than the monotonous "I'm sorry." At last,
they started talking among themselves, and the discussion became increasingly animated. When, finally,
Megan translated their request to reexamine Michael's
lamp design, she would have given anything for a snap-
shot of his expression!

The rest of the meeting didn't go perfectly, only better. Neither of the Americans let on, of course, that they
hadn't the vaguest idea what had caused the improvement; Michael simply continued, seemingly unruffled,
in his normally patient way. When the Japanese were
enthusiastic about learning the color formulas, he gave
them; when they balked at too-radical designs, he
backed off graciously. Andrew Shepard's luck was
about the same.

In one crucial area, neither man made headway,
which was a terrific disappointment to Megan. She
kept repeating the bastardized words *kokyu na ceram-
ics* for "exclusive"—the Americans asked her more
than once, "Are you sure they understand?"—and then
she'd ask for *hosho zumi,* a guarantee. To no avail. The
artisans had no earthly idea, nor could they provide
any clues, about the way original designs were being
knocked off before ever reaching the companies that
held the meaningless copyrights.

At the very end, her mind started wandering—she
was hatching a dangerous, but nonetheless *very* appealing plan that just might help solve the problems with
Michael—and she had to request various repetitions of
simple sentences. By that time, all the other parties
were so exhausted, no one really cared. And the Americans, including Megan, were about to be hit with an
overwhelming number of telephone messages.

Andrew Shepard's efficient but thoroughly swamped

receptionist handed the entire stack of call slips to
Megan. As she separated hers from Michael's, she saw
that Adelle had phoned with the news that both of the
George Lings—junior *and* senior—were flying into
High Point that evening. She was surprised; he had
never mentioned they would be attending; when she
saw his reaction to the message it became clear he
hadn't *known* it.

Megan didn't have time to ponder the matter; twice
within the last hour, Henry Hill had tried to reach her:
once about a hotel contract agent planning to stop by
the showroom before noon, and again to say the China
Cove purchasing agent needed her—"urgent," the note
claimed. This was the buyer who had been so pleased
with the Onyx Flame package deal, particularly the arrangement for a temporary exclusive on the lamp; all
Megan could imagine was that the chain had suddenly
decided the lamp was needed before Easter. Whatever,
it was time to get back to Market Hall. First, she had to
retrieve her briefcase from the conference room.

Michael was waiting at the front door, chatting with
Lisa and Andrew. When Megan tried to make a hasty
departure, it was Shepard who stopped her. "Now,
now"—as usual, there was that ever-present smile in
the voice—"surely you are not too rushed to clear up the
little mystery we've been discussing. How did you get
our Japanese friends to consider the new shapes and
colors?"

Megan said, "Um . . . can I explain it later?"

From her employer: "It can't be all that complicated!"

"Well, no," she said, stalling. "But I—"

Lisa Shepard interrupted. "Gentlemen, you're wasting your time. If ever I've seen a woman with a secret,
it's now." She winked at Megan.

For a moment, Michael looked as though he thought
he'd misunderstood. Finally, he just asked, "Is there
something to hide?"

"Not at all," Megan said pleasantly, "but if you don't mind, I'd rather not go into it right away." Michael Richardson minded *very much,* that was perfectly obvious. And it was also just fine, she thought—unless he wanted the information in the worst possible way, her plan couldn't succeed; now, all Megan had to do was keep her nerve.

They walked together in relative silence to Market Hall. She diverted his attention by inquiring the reason for the Lings' arrival. "Search me," Michael said. And that was all; but he put both hands in his pockets and marched the remainder of the distance in preoccupied silence.

For Megan, a sudden new thought was sparked . . . One of the reasons they weren't communicating well was, simply, lack of time. For more than two weeks, she had been intensely curious about George Ling's unpredictable behavior, and Michael's unconventional but clearly knowledgeable way of handling it; nonetheless, daytime hours never offered a spare moment to request the explanation. Although time would undoubtedly stretch farther when market ended, still it bothered her to be trying to involve Michael in a serious personal conversation during this particular period; in fact, knowing he was far busier than she was, it seemed downright obnoxious. But it isn't, Megan reminded herself; not if we're ever again planning to discuss spending our lives together. After another experience with Andrew and Lisa Shepard, her determination to solve the problems had increased. Wryly, she tried to imagine the good-humored Andrew ordering his wife not to drive alone; no way! With that, she commanded her mind away from the subject. As they entered the elevator leading to the showroom, she was back on the Ling issue. Megan had a strange feeling, the way things were going, that no one's job with this firm was very secure; if Michael got fed up and resigned, then George Ling, Jr., would very likely toss out the whole lot hired during his tenure. It wasn't a very pleasant thought and, on the other hand, she hardly wanted the man she loved to have to keep juggling personalities and priorities. There *must* be some good reason he'd put up with it this long, she knew, but for the life of her she couldn't imagine what it might be.

20

With his normal magpie chatter, Henry Hill met them at the door. Fortunately, the majority of his excitement stemmed from an unusually brisk sales morning. Right in the middle of one particularly enthusiastic sentence, however, he interrupted himself. "Oh, Michael! Your secretary gave me some messages I didn't think belonged in the one I called over to Shepard Imports. I'm supposed to let you know two things: Mr. Ling, the old man, is catching a plane right after his ship docks; he might not make it on schedule. And Mr. George Ling, Jr.'s not feeling good. That's exactly what Adelle said."

"I can well imagine" was Michael's dark comment. Surprised, Megan looked at him sharply, and as soon as Henry scurried off to wait on a customer, he said, "George sometimes convinces himself I was hired exclusively to protect him from his father," then strode off to make some phone calls. She would have followed and asked for an *immediate* explanation if the China Cove purchasing agent hadn't chosen just that moment to stride through the showroom door.

Megan liked the China Cove chief purchasing agent. He was an enthusiastic, highly excitable individual who had given literal rave reviews to Onyx Flame. Not only had he predicted it would become one of the best-selling lamps of all time but, in this case, he had also put his company's money where his mouth was. She had very much looked forward to introducing him to

Michael. Therefore, when he started loudly accusing Megan of fraud and thievery, she was so shocked, she grabbed the back of a chair to steady herself.

Henry Hill came running. The minute he saw Megan's chalky complexion, he grabbed her and started barking orders at the momentarily silenced purchasing agent: "For God's sake, pull the damned chair around!" Megan knew quite well she had been nowhere near fainting; nonetheless, she sank into the chair, grateful for Henry's timely assistance. Much to her surprise, the showroom manager was quite capable of handling the situation; the glare he now leveled at the man from China Cove was a dare if ever she had seen one.

"I . . . well, maybe I came on too strong," the buyer was stammering, "but the fact is, this woman sold me on a product she said was designed exclusively for your firm. We paid an advance installment for a quantity lamp order—*and* we paid an extra premium for the rights to advertise it temporarily as our exclusive—but I found out this morning that another lamp company has it in stock. The exact same lamp! Wouldn't *you* call that fraud, young man?"

"Actually, sir," Henry said with imposing dignity, "before I started terrorizing people, *I* would call the designer who holds the copyright. And as soon as you clear out of my showroom, that's exactly what I intend doing. His name is Michael Richardson, he's the president of Ling and Son, and he should be back in just a few minutes." As Megan watched, it seemed that Henry Hill was growing taller.

But the China Cove agent shrank. He said, *"Michael Richardson?* Miss McBride should have told me! Look, I don't want any trouble with Richardson. If . . . if he says he designed the lamp, well, that's good enough for—" A trickle of perspiration was running down one cheek; the buyer suddenly pulled a business card from his wallet and offered it to Henry. "Just tell Mr. Richardson, will you, that we have, um . . . a slight problem with the exclusive. I'd sort of, um, appreciate a call from him. When he gets a chance, that is." Without apologizing to Megan, he slithered away.

At the end of the spectacle, she made no move to get up. Henry asked if she were all right. She nodded, told him how much she admired his reaction, and then admitted she was very tired. It was true. In addition to the speeded-up work pace, there was jet lag, one night of nonstop activity setting up the showroom—she tried not to think of the *other* night, of the reason, then, for not sleeping, but a tear sprang instantly to her lashes—and, now, this absurd scene. While Henry Hill hovered above, looking increasingly concerned, she thought, So much wasted emotion . . .

"You need a nap," he proclaimed. "It's lunchtime and the contract buyer won't make it back till midafternoon. Here, I'll go call you a cab." She didn't object. Within half an hour, in the big lonely bed of the master suite, she was sound asleep. The alarm was set to go off in exactly sixty minutes.

It wasn't the sound of the clock that brought her around. It was the gentlest, freshest breeze Megan had ever felt; although she couldn't remember opening the French doors, she was certainly glad she had.

Bless Henry Hill for sending her home! She was totally revitalized. This was very likely not entirely attributable to sleep, for she had dreamed of Michael, a soft gauzy collage of all the positive elements of their relationship, including fragments of tender-wild lovemaking. Her emotions remained wrapped in fantasy; indeed it seemed unfair, this need to open her eyes and return to reality. To prolong the moment, she yawned and stretched, like a sleepy kitten. Even the nylon of her underwear—matching bikini and camisole of almost the exact pale pink as the outfit she'd thrown over a chair—felt cool and smooth against her skin.

"Are you awake?" The sound was barely a whisper but she sat bolt upright. By the time her brain had registered the voice as Michael's, she was looking simultaneously *at* him and *for* a wool afghan that had apparently fallen to the floor. He was walking toward her; for some reason, all she could think of was her lack of clothes. With things the way they were between them . . .

He sat on the bed. Instinctively she crisscrossed her arms over her breasts and drew slightly away, then felt silly. He looked momentarily surprised, then shook his head; sadly, she thought. "Come here, baby." Michael didn't bother waiting for blind obedience, he scooted forward, folding her up like a child. *"I'm* not going to hurt you, little Meggie." As he stroked her long hair, rocking her as he had on one other occasion, she understood that the sympathetic pose was genuine; but for the life of her she couldn't figure any reason for it.

Once she got over the reflexive inhibitions after being caught without clothes, she stopped caring why he was here like this in the middle of a business day. It was enough just to relax into his arms, to let the now-familiar feelings flow over her, then ignite. Also, it had occurred to her that Michael might have finally realized he and Megan were semipermanently trapped in a misunderstanding not entirely of her creation; maybe, without need for the inconvenient plan she had devised, he would now offer to talk candidly on the personal independence issue.

Michael was saying something. "When Henry told me about your condition, I was seriously tempted to go after that maniac from China Cove; but, first, I had to make certain you're all right. No more fainting spells?"

She was astounded. "I don't have fainting spells!" It was obvious that Henry Hill had exaggerated her "condition" and that, furthermore, Michael was thinking of the one and only time she ever *had* fainted; naturally, she thought, it had to happen while she was at his house. At this point, when Megan so desperately needed him to recognize her as someone fully capable of looking after herself, it wouldn't do to become categorized as a female swooner. Before he could comment, she added, "That stupid scene with the buyer was nothing more than an extremely rude surprise, Michael. I guarantee I don't go around passing out when business deals fall apart."

"You don't want me to let you go, do you?" he asked. There was a strong hint of amusement in his tone; Megan was fairly certain she wasn't being taken seriously.

Her unusually firm reply was: "No. I just don't want you holding me for the wrong reason."

He dropped his arms and stepped off the bed, looking down at her. "For God's sake, Megan! Is it against your religion to let someone worry about you? Your reactions are totally neurotic! And frankly, my dear, it's getting boring." Clearly, Michael was no longer amused; he was furious.

Megan knew when to keep quiet. Of the two of them, she suspected she was the more angry. Neurotic indeed! In the stare-off that followed, she was definitely up to the challenge.

He wasn't intimidated, that was obvious. Considering the increasingly furrowed forehead and those ice-cube eyes, he was simply becoming more exasperated with each passing second. When he finally spoke, the only thing that surprised her was the sheer depth of the hostility.

"Miss McBride, I don't honestly know why I keep fooling with you. For my relatively peaceful tastes, you're the type who enjoys mixing it up just a bit too much."

If he had been aiming with fists rather than words, Megan would have been doubled up and gasping for air. For no one on earth did she want a peaceful existence more than for Michael. Furthermore, she was learning the hardest way possible that the man's view of her was totally different than she had imagined; although he had consistently introduced her as "the most wonderful woman in the world," his real opinion was brutally low. At that precise moment, she came far closer to fainting than she had earlier, in the showroom.

Pain overwhelmed anger. Megan needed so desperately to be relieved of her agony that she sought it in an unprecedented manner; in a frail, uncertain voice, she begged for a retraction: "Surely you don't mean that."

It wasn't an easy signal to catch, not coming, as it did, from a woman with Megan's pride. If there had been the slightest hint of hysteria in the statement . . . But her effort to contain the rising emotion had kept the tone down; she had sounded almost calm.

He sighed. "Don't start telling me what I think." And then: "Look, after last night I should have known better than to come out here with open arms; you don't need me. Let's just forget this whole miserable episode. I've got to get back to work. Before I do, though, I have to know what you said to change the minds of those Japanese artisans." He waited longer than she would have expected before snapping, "Well, are you going to tell me?"

She was trying to pull herself together, to decide whether there was enough worth salvaging to merit the inevitable hassle. Since her mind would *not* clear, she stuck to the plan out of nothing more than panic. About the relationship, all Megan understood was that she loved Michael. Now, for the third time, he was demanding information about her translation.

"No." The word was little more than a whimper.

In a flash, he reached over and grabbed her by the wrist, using the handhold to pull her from the bed. "If nothing else, Megan, you're going to be a dutiful employee. I won't take a chance that empty promises were made on behalf of Ling and Son. Tell me what made those men change their tune."

She shook her head.

His voice changed. It was low, deliberate, and far more menacing. "Do you have an excuse for this?"

After a hesitation that didn't help matters, Megan whispered, "I want to make a deal with you."

He dropped her wrist and folded his arms across his chest, then crossed one ankle over the other. "What kind of deal?"

"Just to talk, Michael." Her voice grew stronger. "There are some subjects we don't seem to be communicating very well, and—"

He laughed; there was nothing funny about the sound. "What an incredible understatement!" Michael looked at his watch and said, "This is a waste of time. You're not even making sense. If I ask you something— very politely—would you please pay attention, then give me a reasonable answer?"

"Of course, but first let me explain—"

If he heard, he gave no indication; his next words sliced right into hers. "Andrew Shepard's done nothing to deserve this, whatever it is. And he needs the same information I do. Would you please let *him* know what you said?"

Dazed, she nodded. She certainly didn't want Andrew caught up in the intrigue.

"Then I'm leaving. And I expect you back in the showroom within half an hour. Your trip was paid so you could sell the hotel contracts."

Without another word, he disappeared.

Like the veil of night, a total void replaced his presence. Megan had had no previous experience of this particular nature—Michael was terribly mistaken, for Megan was every bit as peaceful as he—therefore, she took the strange feeling as a type of calm acceptance. Had she been able to see the way she walked over to pick up her clothes, like a zombie, or the strikingly blank expression in her eyes, she would have immediately recognized textbook symptoms of shock; temporarily at least, her mind was going to assist her through the grief of unbearable loss.

Henry Hill continually asked if she were all right. The hotel contract agent simply appeared intimidated with her emotionless negotiating style; fortunately for Ling and Son, all he cared about was the appearance of the lamps and their cost to him. At the end of the meeting, he shook her hand and said she was definitely in the running for the deal. Ironically, in the brief remaining portion of the afternoon, she made a couple of sales to West Coast buyers whose demands normally would have required much greater effort. Their reactions indicated they wanted only to see the products, close the deal, and get the hell out of this lady's way. As soon as the last one had signed a purchase order, Megan looked at her watch; seeing six o'clock straight up and down, she got her purse and briefcase, then walked out without remembering to say good night; later, when Henry Hill tried to give her a message from Michael, he couldn't find her.

She went directly to Shepard Imports. At this time of evening, while other showrooms were emptying, Andrew traditionally drew a crowd with his wine bar. Megan walked around and through the various little cliques, recognizing no one and giving a false impression of indifference. When she saw that Andrew was surrounded, she found a seat, clasping folded hands in her lap. Quite a while later, when she still hadn't been noticed and it became obvious the party was growing larger, she found her way to the little conference room, thinking to kill the wait with paperwork. She hadn't expected the room to be occupied but Lisa Shepard was there, operating an old-fashioned adding machine in what had been Takeda-*san*'s chair.

"Trying to escape the noise?" Lisa asked warmly. "This is a good place to do it."

Woodenly, she said she had a message for Andrew. Lisa asked if she could take it, save further waiting.

Megan nodded. But when she went into the explanation, she started sobbing; the combination of shock wearing off and the company of a sympathetic woman had been too much.

21

Although Megan was both embarrassed and humiliated, it was just as well that something—anything—had detained her. While Lisa Shepard was trying to persuade her to confide the problem, Michael was walking through the front door of Shepard Imports. When he had left messages for both Megan and Ron, then had been unable to locate either, his mood had not improved. Now, oblivious to the goings-on in the conference room, he stood at the bar with Andrew, drinking wine and cooling off.

In effect, poor Lisa was forced into a guessing game. Megan McBride simply wasn't comfortable bothering someone with personal problems. So the first question had been the most obvious: "Has something gone wrong between you and Michael?" Megan didn't lie; she said nothing at all. From there, as she dried her eyes and tried in vain to reassure Lisa, the overall impression received by the other woman was slightly inaccurate. On the surface, it must have appeared that an argument had developed over the handling of the Japanese translation; after Lisa was asked *not* to reveal to anyone but Andrew Megan's exact words to the Japanese artisans, she seemed baffled. What she told Megan was: "Andrew told me you handled the situation this morning brilliantly. But look, if you and Michael are having a tough time juggling business complications, you should be able to sit down and talk it over. Megan,

251

I've never *seen* anyone more in love than Michael Richardson! Don't give up now. Remember, if there's only one thing wrong, there must be an awful lot that's right."

It was the last few sentences that helped, especially Lisa's opinion that Michael was definitely in love. When the two women walked out to the showroom together, they appeared amazingly composed. Megan had replaced her smeared lipstick, and the slightly reddened eyes might have been products of fatigue. She faltered only once, and then briefly—when her eyes saw Michael, still at the bar—and then she allowed herself to be coaxed forward by Lisa Shepard's gentle hand on her back. For ten minutes after that, she managed to chat, almost as though nothing were wrong, with the boisterous assembly at the bar; at one point she caught Michael looking questioningly at her, as if to ask if she'd followed his orders; she nodded, then turned immediately toward the man on her left.

Lisa walked them to the door. She asked if they wanted to join Andrew and her for dinner. When Michael explained that, within the hour, he was going to be hearing from both the arriving Lings and didn't have the vaguest idea how things would proceed after that, Lisa asked if he'd forgotten Megan's familiarity with Oriental culture. "Why don't all of you go over to the Chinese restaurant together? The evening can sort of take care of itself." Megan reacted too late; before she knew it, Michael had said, "Good idea! That's exactly what we'll do." Poor Lisa! She was trying to mix oil and water.

Since Adelle had told the Lings to contact Michael at the rental house, their next destination was predetermined. Megan was glad. In the taxi, she took the very first opportunity to say that she didn't intend going out again; as she put it, wild horses couldn't drag her to a Chinese restaurant with a feuding father-and-son team.

Michael didn't seem to care. All he said was: "As you wish. And, by the way, George and his father *aren't* feuding." In a voice heavy with fatigue, he explained that George, Jr., had two problems, neither of which his father was aware of. "First, he's the number one son of a wealthy Chinese family."

"Which means he was expected to take over the business," Megan filled in.

Michael nodded. "And what he really wanted to be was a high school baseball coach. When he hired me, he confided that he feels so incompetent at business, he's terrified every morning of his life. He's certain people are always laughing behind his back."

"How tragic!" Megan was sincere. She tried to imagine how her life would be if her father had insisted she become an architectural engineer. Anyway, she had seen complications of this nature during her years in Japan, where customs were identical: fathers did not tolerate sons who expressed career preferences; nor did they tolerate sons incapable of following in big footsteps.

"His second problem is that the senior Mr. Ling was one of the outstanding businessmen of his time. Since he also happens to be George's only living relative—and all too typically Chinese—his son's terrified of losing his love and respect. When George hired me, he admitted that he goes haywire, mentally, every time his dad is due home from one of his long sight-seeing trips. And that's where Mr. Ling's coming from: right off a cruise ship. As usual, George has spent the last few weeks worrying about losing face. He imagines every godawful error the old man might catch him in, like letting the warehouse crew get away with grand theft, or spending too much on samples and catalog photos. In that state of mind, he starts making the errors. As you've seen."

"That's tragic, too," Megan said, finally understanding Michael's tactics the day he'd confronted George on the spurious theft issue; it seemed a tremendous burden—only Michael would have enough patience to bear it. "What are you supposed to do about all this, Michael?"

He shrugged. "I once promised George Ling, Jr., that I'd try to save him from himself. During the last few weeks it just hasn't been possible. Until recently, with all the added pressures of preparing for market, I didn't realize what bad shape he's in. Anyway, the rest of the time, he's one of the nicest, most sensible people you'd ever hope to meet. Incompetent, yes, but nice as hell. He'd have made a terrific baseball coach; three years in a row he lettered on the UCLA Varsity."

She asked if the senior Mr. Ling were such a terror. Michael said, "Judge for yourself." And then he added, "Never mind, I forgot you won't be going with us." Once again she noticed the voice; he couldn't have cared less whether or not she joined their group for dinner. As exhausted as Megan was with problems, she'd have gladly taken on the Lings, if only to hear that Michael Richardson still needed her, still cared about her company.

Without warning, he changed the subject. "Megan, I can't understand why the hell we're having to take this cab! It doesn't do much good to rent a car if Ron doesn't show up with it. This morning, when he picked you up, did he say anything?"

"Oh, God," she groaned. Off and on during the entire miserable day, she had reminded herself to mention it had started with Ron not arriving for the morning pickup. It was one of those things; whenever she'd thought of it, Michael hadn't been around. Now she explained.

His irritation vanished. "Look," he said quickly, "that's bad . . . not at all like Ron. And I just remembered what he said last night, about going home and getting drunk. If you're willing to handle the phone calls from the Lings, I'll get the cabby to take me over to our old house."

Megan just sighed, wondering if she could hear the phone from the Jacuzzi. Dutifully, however, she told her employer she'd be glad to take the calls from Ling and Son. At least the constant demands were keeping them from any further arguments; they didn't have time for them.

She was out by the pool, searching for a phone plug-in, when she heard the unmistakable sound of a very loud doorbell. She assumed it would be Ron, therefore ending the unwelcome intrigue, and hurried to answer it. But the person standing on the stoop was about nine hundred years old; furthermore, if Santa Claus had been Chinese, Megan was positive this was the way he would look.

His stance made it clear he expected to be recognized. She thought, Well, who else can it be but—

"Mr. Ling? Come right in, sir. I'm Megan McBride, your new Southern California rep."

"And a good one, too, from what my son's written," he said as they passed into the living room. "Has George arrived yet, by the way?"

She answered no, then hurriedly told him Michael hadn't yet come in, hoping the remark would stand without question; obviously, signals had gotten crossed somewhere. Surprisingly, Megan found she didn't really mind. In a short time span, the old man had come across as one of the most thoroughly charming gentlemen she'd ever met. Not only was there absolutely no evidence of senility in this eighty-seven-year-old, but he was one of those rare individuals who gave off inverted waves; like magic, they sucked people in. For the next fifteen minutes, after she had served cheese and wine, she sat, mesmerized, while Ling told her of growing up in pre-Communist China; the millions of wrinkles on the old face disappeared; she might have been talking to a young boy wandering the fields and cities of his

homeland. By the time he answered her questions
about bringing his family to the States and starting the
business, she had correctly inferred one major fact, and
guessed at another: George Ling, Sr., was equally in
love with the Orient and with his adopted country. That
his American-born son, whom he obviously adored,
might wish to pursue a career outside the business that
had provided such comfort and security was a concept
he wasn't even capable of grasping. Generation gap
plus culture gap; in today's modern times, it existed
even in the Orient.

At one point he commented that she seemed to "know
our ways." When Megan briefly detailed her unconventional upbringing, it seemed, by comparison, ridiculously mundane. But the Chinese-American said, "Ah,
so," and then, with a twinkle in his old eyes, added,
"Then Ling and Son is indeed fortunate. I have long
thought we need more people of your qualifications."

At that exact moment, Michael walked in. He had
Ron in tow, and the Dallas man looked as though he
had spent the past twenty-four hours trying to hold the
world up. Alone.

Needless to say, Megan's employer concealed his surprise. Without breaking stride, he introduced Ron as a
Texas showroom owner; then he welcomed the firm's
founder and politely inquired about his High Point accommodations. With amusement, Ling said he would
probably never become accustomed to sleeping in the
home of a total stranger but that, nonetheless, it was a
welcome improvement over his berth on a constantly
rolling ship. When the ancient gentleman said, "During this last trip, I began to suspect I am tottering on
the verge of middle age," Michael laughed with genuine amusement. What a welcome sound, Megan
thought!

George Ling, Jr., called; she invited him over, reported the development, then excused herself to refill
empty glasses and prepare more hors d'oeuvres. Mi-

chael, too, got up; he told Mr. Ling he wanted to help carry the trays.

The minute they were alone in the kitchen, both started talking at once. He said, "Okay. You go first."

"What's wrong with Ron?"

"Yesterday, the gunner fired him. In addition to feeling like a fool, he now admits knowing why I kept saying he'd never quit. According to Ron, this'll force him into bankruptcy."

Megan just shook her head; life wasn't easy.

"Now," he said, "tell me about Mr. Ling. Did he say why he's in High Point?"

"Yes. It's nothing wrong. George has been writing him about your success getting new designs from the Japanese and he wants to see for himself, that's all. Apparently he's convinced that this miracle, as he called it, can restore the company's leadership in the industry."

"Well, he's right about that," Michael said dryly, "but he's in for a letdown. There's going to have to be a lot more progress before this deserves to be called a miracle."

"You made some of it at this morning's meeting," she said, wishing immediately that she'd bitten her tongue off instead of reminding him of the highly volatile subject. Megan turned immediately toward the refrigerator; before she could walk away, however, Michael had caught her arm.

"Don't do it," he warned. "Surely you must realize I have to know, especially now, what happened."

She stood her ground. Under the prevailing circumstances, he could hardly afford to have a raging fit. "Mr. Richardson, I tried to state my terms; you didn't listen. If you really want to know what I said to your artisans, it's up to you."

Unexpectedly, he dropped her arm and said, "I was too hard on you this afternoon, Megan; if I said anything that hurt, I hope you'll give me a chance to make it up."

The doorbell rang. When he went to answer it, her overcluttered mind kept echoing his last words. There was no doubt he had sounded sincere—perhaps there had even been a note of anguish in his voice—but she had no way of judging whether or not this might be merely a ploy, something to soften her resistance to providing the information he wanted. Megan tried not to dwell on it as she rearranged the tray. Nonetheless, new hope caused her enough preoccupation that she had to remind herself continually to be more careful with the cheese knife. By the time she returned to the living room, having no idea this night was about to become the single most important of her life, she had nicked herself three different times.

Although Mr. Ling remained central, the group seating had been rearranged. George, Jr., now occupied Megan's former place. He wasn't exactly sitting; the posture could more accurately be described as a miserable huddle. That wasn't so surprising, Megan thought. No, what interested her was that *Ron* had moved; he was sitting on a couple of pillows stacked near the old man's feet, listening with rapt and unmistakably cheerful attention. Whatever Mr. Ling had said to bring about such a dramatic change, he was evidently in the process of concluding.

"And so, young man, there's no need at all for you to consider bankruptcy. Just do the same thing I did: take on a partner and get some help with the overhead. When everything's healthy you can buy him out. And if he doesn't want to sell, you can just let him have it and start another showroom; that was *my* solution. But get *all* the lines you now have in perfect shape before you advertise for the partner, mind you, or you won't have a clear negotiating field."

"That's amazing," Ron said. "It'll work! There's a lot of people looking to get showroom space who can't afford to start from scratch. I could use someone to help me run the operation, anyway. Why didn't I think of it?"

Ling said, "You young people, here in this country, you don't know the difference between a big problem and a little one. When I was a boy in China, I'd have given quite a bit to have something so minor on my mind."

George Ling, Jr., winced. Then he spoke for the first time. "You never told me you once had a partner, Dad." It sounded petulant, like a reprimand, but there was more to the tone than that. Megan could tell that, like the others, George found everything about the elderly gentleman fascinating; but she also discerned the vast difference created by filial respect. George worshiped his father; if any son had ever been a prime candidate for ulcers, she now understood why it was this one.

"It was long before you were born," he explained. "When you were very young, I used to talk about it. And it's no coincidence, my bringing up the subject now. In a way, it's because of that old partnership that I'm here tonight. The man's been on my mind quite a bit. With that first firm, he went on to build an empire. And now his son's in contact. I got the letter during the cruise." He turned to George and said, "I need to discuss this with both you and Mr. Richardson. The fact is, son, we've got a serious purchase proposal for Ling and Son; if you wouldn't mind giving it up, I think there's a whopping big profit to be made. *If* we play our negotiating cards right."

22

If a Rolls-Royce had driven into the living room, it could have passed right on through via George Ling, Jr.'s mouth. Megan, too, looked dumbfounded. In fact, of those gathered around the old man, Michael was the only one who appeared less than astounded; he seemed to find the development amusing. She thought she might know his reason: nothing else about the day had been expected, therefore why should it end on a normal note?

Mr. Ling explained that their trump card was the new "design power" Michael was establishing with Japan. Since they were the *only* firm getting exciting import accessories, Ling and Son could justifiably demand an outrageous price. "First, though," he said, "I've got to be firm with my facts. Just how far along are we, Mr. Richardson?"

The company president shot Megan one of those looks-that-could-kill, then answered, vaguely, that there had been "recent progress." It didn't work; Mr. Ling wanted to know how recent and all other specifics. Michael tried to avoid the inevitable with an abrupt ending of his tale of the morning meeting at Andrew Shepard's. Once again, no go. The old man said, "To get them to agree, we must have made some major concession. Did you have to hike the artisans' fees?"

Once again Michael looked at her. When she just rolled her eyes skyward, he gave up and said, "Mr.

Ling, I don't have the slightest idea. Ask Megan. She was the translator."

"You, Miss McBride? You didn't tell me you speak Japanese. But of course! I guess you would, after all those years." She had obviously gained tremendous face, not an easy accomplishment for a mere woman.

Before Mr. Ling could ask the next—and the obvious—question, Megan had made her decision. If she were going to play this game, she'd continue playing for keeps. With Michael, it was clearly such a win-or-lose proposition, anyway, that she thought, If this particular gambit fails, at least I'll know what went wrong. As it was, with him refusing to discuss other issues, she had no real idea what was destroying the relationship.

Speaking boldly, she asked the founder of Ling and Son if she could have a few moments alone with him. He nodded. For some reason, Megan absolutely loved it when he looked expectantly at the men, waiting for *them* to clear out. By the time they were summoned back, Ling was chuckling and his young female companion was just sitting by, looking innocent.

He said, "Mr. Richardson, you and my son make a good team."

For the first time that evening, George Ling, Jr., smiled. In fact, he beamed.

"This is some sharp lady you hired. I don't usually go along with practical jokes, but this will be an exception. If she wants to tell you herself what went on in that meeting, she's earned the right. I'll tell you one thing, though: she makes a better Oriental than I do. Without giving away a damned thing, she made all the right moves."

Now Michael looked astounded. Mr. Ling, on the other hand, had returned to a more serious countenance. He was looking at his son; Megan thought the gaze was immeasurably sad.

"George," he said at last, "You've done so well with the company. The amount we can make from this sale can take care of three more generations. But maybe you'd rather not give it up, son . . ."

His voice faded. Something made Megan look over at Michael. For a bittersweet interlude, they were once again of the same mind. When he returned her look, she could tell that he, too, had guessed who was making the sacrifice. They would probably never know what had caused it, but the old man had evidently decided he wanted a happy son more than a prosperous business. As Megan reflected on the extraordinary meaning of the word *family*—letting her mind wander to Jeffie, to Tara, to Mrs. Simmons, to the thought of being with Michael morning, noon, and night—she grew melancholy. It took a great deal of concentration to bring the group back into focus. And when she did, the old man was still talking, but on a different subject.

"So you'll leave immediately?" he asked, apparently speaking to Michael.

The answer was: "Yes, sir. It'll only take about one day in Los Angeles to get ready. What about you, Megan?"

She admitted her mind had been wandering.

"Mr. Ling wants us to leave High Point and pack for Japan. While I firm up the deals on the new designs, he says you're the only one he trusts to do the translation."

For the second time in less than an hour, her mouth dropped open. She pulled herself together in a hurry. Thinking of the opportunity to see her parents, of going with the man she loved to one of the most romantic lands on the face of the earth, she wasted no time telling Mr. Ling she'd be ready whenever Michael was.

To herself, she thought, My darling, I'll always be ready when you are. Maybe this will give us the chance we need.

But she couldn't tell what he was thinking. His face was an appropriate business mask, nothing more.

For the period immediately following the departure

of their guests, Megan's employer—for that was the moment's interpretation based on his serious expression—remained unreadable. Under the circumstances, it wasn't upsetting. She, too, had dozens of priorities competing for mental attention; preparing for a short-notice trip to Japan would be challenge as well as pleasure. In unison and without wasting time with polite conversation, they worked quickly and efficiently; Michael got the glasses into the kitchen while she took care of the snack plates and trays. When he sat on the sofa, making notes on papers from the briefcase open on his lap, she tidied up around him, brushing away crumbs and straightening throw pillows. At some point, she considered the word *family* again: this relaxed and unpressured atmosphere, now so obviously temporary, could become the constant balancing factor against their daily business demands. She remembered the night Michael and Jeffie had fallen asleep in the Richardson family room; this addition—the youngster whose company so delighted her—completed her fantasy portrait. Once again she thought of the accusation that she enjoyed "mixing it up"; there just wasn't anything Megan treasured more than peace. If she couldn't offer it at the cost of her independence, it was because she was incapable of separating the two—to her, the freedom to react and be accepted as an individual was a factor that ensured tranquillity.

She was almost finished when he spoke. Immediately, she noticed his voice had lost its business tenor. "I think we should talk," he said. "Just for a few minutes. Do you mind?"

Without answering, she took a seat, wary of another argument. Since he'd given no indication of the topic of discussion, there was no way to know whether or not she minded. Megan warned herself not to react so negatively. In truth, she could hardly deny welcoming *any* reason to prolong their time together. Trying to jog her sense of humor back into action, she thought, What excuse could I use for throwing myself into his arms?

The two pillows Ron had stacked at Mr. Ling's feet were still on the floor. Now Michael snapped his briefcase shut and used the pillow-chair to get into a position facing her; he stretched both long legs straight out, then braced his palms on the thick carpet and leaned back; it was the first time that day she had seen him look totally comfortable.

He stifled a relaxed yawn. And then: "Interesting the way things turn out. This must be when we're expected to dust off the old cliché—all's well that ends well."

She could only assume he referred to the two Lings. Wanting to close this day with the casual give-and-take they'd failed to establish earlier, Megan said yes, and that with George Ling freed of business obligations driving him crazy, Michael's life after the sale was likely to undergo a drastic change for the better.

"Probably. Right now, that's hardly important, though. I'm talking about you and me."

Megan sucked in her breath. A crushing, relentless attack of anxiety took hold.

"Before we go any further," he said, "I want you to know I'm grateful for the way you handled the evening. That hors d'oeuvre tray was such a work of art, the guests couldn't possibly have realized they hadn't been invited. When you decide to be gracious, not to mention resourceful, I'm amazed how effectively you pull it off."

When you decide to be . . . Was it double-edged? She was so frightened, she couldn't clearly have stated her own name, and there was certainly no available response to the compliment.

There was a long pause. At last, in a gentle tone, he said, "Megan, you keep saying you want to talk to me. It's . . . how can I put this? . . . it's difficult. Whenever we finally have time, you don't seem to have anything to say."

Unfortunately, his point was justified, she thought.

So often, for instance when he had telephoned, she took far too long trying to figure out how she was expected to react; then she'd realize Michael was hanging on the other end, just waiting. Now she felt silly.

He sighed, then combed his fingers through his hair, no longer appearing relaxed.

"Okay," he said calmly, "let's skip the in-between and get to the one thing we absolutely *have* to decide. How do you feel about the trip? It's important to the Lings; on the other hand, you shouldn't feel forced to go."

Without further encouragement she found her voice. "But, Michael, I want to!"

The emphatic response obviously surprised him. He asked her about it.

"Well . . ." Megan faltered again, uncertain how much was safe to divulge right now. In this ill-defined conversation, she felt emotionally naked. Finally, she told him how much she looked forward to seeing her parents.

His rejoinder was: "I see."

If Megan had learned anything, it was that when Michael made that statement, he definitely did *not* see. But what was it he wanted to see? She was doing it again, she knew: keeping quiet when she wasn't sure how to please him; it wasn't helping.

She suddenly saw the truth that had existed ever since he had asked to talk: that night, her resources weren't up to a discussion of personal issues. Even if he came right out and announced his intention to deal with the independence factor, *she* couldn't have done it, not then. Something beyond the mere fact bothered her, but she didn't know what . . . like trying to think of a name, and almost, but not quite, grasping hold before it escaped again.

She looked at Michael and understood that between them, there would always be times one or the other needed something besides words. Now, she wanted only to take his hand, walk out to the Jacuzzi, unbutton his top button . . . In short, she'd have given anything for a repeat of last night.

In a peculiar voice, he was saying, "Megan, we seem to have reached the point when we have to make an agreement."

Once again, the terrible anxiety slapped her sense-less.

"Are you listening? We'll need to take this trip like almost total strangers, two people thrown into a tempo-rary business arrangement."

From its former hiding place deep within, she now felt the anguish spread across her face. In its wake, the question she asked was a plaintive whisper: "Why?"

"It surprises me you'd have to ask." He sounded sin-cere. "Did you imagine you could have things both ways?"

Lost, she asked what he meant.

"Look," he said, repeating the unconscious hair-combing gesture, only more impatiently, "this whole thing is frankly beyond me." Megan heard a clipped and distinctly nervous laugh, then he continued. "I know we've reached the age of the playgirl. But I'm not equipped, Megan. Saying I love you seemed to me like more than a game."

"Michael, I—"

He raised one palm. "There's no need for apology. But we *must* make the agreement about the trip. For the Lings' sake, we have to do the job with our senses intact. These little plots of intrigue can't start all over again. If you feel tempted to let it happen, Mr. Ling will simply have to get another interpreter."

She couldn't imagine how he had managed to say it in such a soft voice. And it turned out to be all she could take. Megan buried her face in both hands, trying to banish the nightmare.

Within a split second, Michael was holding one of her wrists.

"Megan, *please* don't do that. This is no time for a sympathy play." He pulled her to her feet and into his arms.

The kiss she had craved seemed brutal now, a punishment heaped on someone he neither liked nor respected. When she didn't respond, he released her and left the room while her eyes remained locked shut. Once she reopened them, she had a peculiar feeling of freedom. Something was gone.

It was her desire to repair the relationship. Obviously, that couldn't be done. In Japan, there would be absolutely no problem keeping things on an impersonal level. Without emotion, Megan reminded herself to give Michael her agreement tomorrow. Then she walked upstairs, to spend her last night in High Point. She was glad she would be sleeping alone.

At seven the next morning, when she made it down to the kitchen, Michael was already gone. There was an unsigned note on the table; it looked like a timetable: "Ron will be by at eight. Meet me at the Light Loft at eleven—sharp. We have to get back to the house and pack for a three o'clock flight." There was no signature.

For a few minutes, drinking coffee, she was tempted not to show up at the appointed time, not to bother putting in an appearance at the market, not to do any of it simply *because* Michael was the one giving the orders. Fortunately, Megan retained a modicum of common sense; she'd never behave so childishly. With irritation, however, she thought he might at least have supplied the location of the Light Loft. Time was tight enough without having to search the entire vast building for a lamp showroom.

Yesterday, Michael had been able to do no wrong; today was quite a different matter.

Ron was still excited about Mr. Ling's advice. Although Megan didn't say much—as usual, the Texan supplied all the words—she, too, was pleased. She genuinely liked Michael's friend.

Her mind kicked in the memory of the flight from California, when Michael had expressed such pleasure at the prospect of introducing her. Inwardly, she felt a twinge of satisfaction—if she were such a playgirl, Michael would have been able to see it long before that plane trip; people just don't change overnight. Her employer wasn't such a genius after all. Although Megan no longer gave a fig about Michael's opinion, she very much resented last night's insinuation. And the physical abuse. Never again. She would earn her trip to Japan, and the translator's fee Mr. Ling had quoted; then it would be her pleasure to steer clear of Michael Richardson.

When they pulled up in front of Market Hall, she cleared her mind of the negative thoughts, then gave Ron a warm good-bye kiss on the cheek. He made a few shy remarks about "wishing the two of you every happiness." During a sentimental spiel about how there wasn't a finer person alive than Michael it was all Megan could do to keep her mouth shut.

In truth, she wasn't particularly proud of her attitude. Walking through the market lobby, she forced a lighter pace into her step and a cheerful tune into her head. It *wasn't* one of Manilow's.

Henry Hill knew all about the Japan trip; the Lings had stopped in early. He hugged her at least a dozen times and in spite of herself, Megan started laughing. "Henry," she said, "I think I love you. If only there were some way to bottle that enthusiasm!"

She went with him to the back room, where they spent the next forty-five minutes going over her sales sheets, clearing up questions, and making corrections necessary for the final market tally Henry would prepare on closing day. Then she dialed the number supplied by the hotel contract buyer; when she didn't reach him, as was predictable, she started composing a letter with information that might be required while she was out of the country.

Henry came back in, looking worried. He said someone had just come in looking for Michael. "I think he said he was an attorney—and, boy, does he look like he means business! I don't know what to do, Megan; he plans to wait, just to stand around my showroom floor!" She agreed to go out and try to persuade the intruder to leave.

He didn't appear the slightest bit intimidating, Megan decided. Perhaps Henry was one of those people who automatically cringe at the sound of the word *attorney*. Anyway, the man whose hand Megan shook was quite pleasant-looking.

He said, "So *you're* the one! Now I can see what all the fuss was about!" Beneath a well-groomed short beard, he flashed a broad smile, then slipped a piece of paper into Megan's palm before continuing. "I'm Jack Graham. Sorry to be late with the information you wanted. It took forever to dig it up."

She didn't think there was any way to bluff her way out of this. "I think I owe you an apology," she admitted. "For the life of me, I can't think what you're talking about!"

He was an unusually poised individual. Instead of appearing ruffled, Graham just laughed. "Market does that to people: think nothing of it. I'm referring to this morning's scene between Michael and your friend from China Cove."

Naturally, she continued to look blank. This time Jack Graham was surprised. "Megan," he said uneasily, "didn't Michael tell you he was going after that idiot who called you a thief?"

She shook her head. Yesterday's unpleasant incident regarding Onyx Flame seemed a million years past. She asked when Michael planned to "go after the idiot."

"It's done," Graham answered soberly. "This morning at seven, we found his house. When he answered the door, Michael grabbed him by the collar and spent the next five minutes describing how long he was going to keep him in court for defamation of character. I was asked along to witness that there was no attempt at bodily injury. Anyway, I guess your boyfriend plans to follow through. He asked me to supply the name of a good attorney."

"My God," Megan breathed. "Did Michael tell you *why* he did such a thing?"

Graham seemed to consider the question peculiar. He shook his head. "No, not in so many words. On the other hand, the man was lucky he didn't get killed, the way Michael talked about not letting people terrorize the woman he loved. The reason seemed pretty clear!"

"This morning?" she asked, positive she was dreaming.

Graham nodded. "At seven. Michael was determined to catch him before he left his house." Suddenly he stopped to ask the time, then said, "Listen, I've got to run. I hope I haven't said anything to upset you." Megan was quick to offer reassurance; later she would realize she had forgotten to say thank you.

The next thing she knew she was outside the building, breathing in fresh air and walking with no particular destination. A few things had started taking shape in her mind and before she made the rendezvous with Michael she wanted to give them a chance to jell.

Last night, there had been some vital point, like a link in a broken chain, flirting elusively in her head. Now it stood out with crystal clarity: if she could be too tired, too pressured, too confused—whatever, as long as it was real—and therefore *totally incapable of communicating,* then Michael most certainly had a right to similar incapacity. Furthermore, if a normally fair and intelligent individual were ever to bog down, it would happen under a terrible crush of priorities, such as those confronting the Ling and Son president after Nikki's departure.

Between them, what had really been going on? she asked herself.

They were in love; newly in love, at that—how often had she and Sharon marveled at friends' mistakes during such periods? Michael wanted to protect her from something he perceived, accurately, as a real threat. She was resistant, and then he started giving angry orders, treating her like a brainless child. But was that what he had *intended?* The point was important. Wasn't it possible the original episode—that painful scene in his office the day she went to Palm Springs—had blown out of proportion during a situation too highly detonated with other pressures?

Megan didn't doubt Michael would be better off erasing that godawful accident he had witnessed from his mind. But such things were permanently impressed. It would be with him day in, day out. He would continue to be fighting mad with nowhere to vent the frustration. From what little Megan knew of life, she knew something about overwhelming frustration; her mind called up a scene following the aircraft accident in which she had lost her husband, when her father-in-law kept screaming at the chaplain who delivered the news. "What the hell do you *mean,* he was killed by a faulty wing stabilizer?"

If she couldn't suggest a way to dig down below the slush fund of rage and frustration—and she kept asking herself, Can't I?—then she had to decide whether its effect on Michael was great enough to pose the threat she had been assuming. Her real fears had started, and built, from the point she had detected an unwillingness to discuss the issue. She had even, at times, suspected he was guilty of a sort of cruel vanity, a cheap male power play dependent for fulfillment on blind obedience. All of this Megan had derived from his consistent, and indignant, refusal to be drawn out on the subject.

But how easy was it, even under the best of circumstances, for Michael to talk to her? Although she wished it weren't true, last night's discussion had left no doubts that her stop-and-start conversational technique, the little quirks she'd developed after falling for someone whose opinion meant the world, was throwing him off stride. And no wonder! How would she feel, she asked herself, if he hit her constantly with meaningless silences? On the issues, then—and trying to prompt a discussion under the worst possible conditions—it seemed entirely possible that he knew, precisely as he had told her, there was no way they could discuss it.

She had shut him out from the rest of her life—a convenient device, speaking of protection—because his words were painful. But now she was replaying those words. And hers as well. The sequence of the conversations, her failure to risk coming right out with "Honey, all I know is how much I love you . . ." If anyone were to blame, mightn't it be she? She expected him to be so forthright while she constantly held back. In their lovemaking, did Michael act like the type of man who would withhold affection, or words? Megan knew better.

Finally, she cleared her mind of all but last night's experience, occurring as it had when they were both exhausted, not to mention besieged with considerations left over from a singularly frantic day. If she hadn't allowed nerves to erase the spaces between the lines, she would have understood—Michael's entire message, probably conveyed through concealed pain, was that he thought the rejected proposal meant she viewed the relationship as temporary. In other words, he might as well have said, "I'm already hurt enough that your feelings aren't as strong as mine."

But Megan had turned him away, then proceeded to blame him bitterly—for not loving *her*. And this morning he had gotten up early to square accounts with a man he thought had caused her pain. She shook her head. Michael Richardson wasn't hurting Megan McBride; in that particular department, she was doing quite well all by herself.

She had made a full circle of the building, and the time had come to find their meeting place. As she entered the revolving doors, she put on the first genuine smile of the day. There was one last thing she would have to concede—the information about yesterday's translation—and she couldn't wait to see the look on his face when he learned there wasn't much to it!

The unfamiliar showroom turned out to be easily located. When she found her employer in the coffee lounge, she was relieved, but not very surprised, to see him appearing quite composed—incredibly handsome, as usual—despite the early morning run-in. Megan managed correctly impersonal greetings, both to Michael and the owner of the Light Loft, a tall, sympathetic-looking man named Cain. They were at the tail end of a stalemated negotiation. Michael wanted Cain to place his domestic lamp line in Ron's Dallas showroom; in turn, the other man insisted on signing Michael to produce exclusive designs on a royalty basis. It was an interesting proposal, at least to Megan, although she knew he had no time to pursue such a sideline. As they started into the wrap-up—poor Ron wasn't going to get this line—she was struck again by how faithfully Michael Richardson stuck to his bargains. He had promised to help a friend and, by damn, he was going to try, no matter what his other pressures.

The men were getting up. Howard Cain turned toward Megan and said, "We've sort of ignored you. I didn't want to, believe me. Lisa Shepard told me the most fascinating story last night, when I was at their place for wine."

Megan made a quick decision. Knowing the answer, she asked, "About the Japanese translation?" Cain nodded; she saw a sense of humor in the eyes and thought, Good! Then she looked directly at Michael and said, "You know, it just occurred to me, you haven't yet heard everything that happened in that meeting."

Michael's blond brows shot up. He said nothing.

Never letting her eyes stray from his, she went right on. "You'll recall that the artisans kept saying sorry, no can do?"

"How could I forget?"

"Well, I told them you understood perfectly why they couldn't do it—such tasteless designs! I waited a few seconds, while all that nodding was going on. Then I said, 'But Richardson-*san* wonders . . . if there were several *hundred* orders for these ugly products, *then* might there be a way to do it?'"

23

Singapore Airlines Flight Eleven departed Los Angeles
International Airport precisely on schedule at one-
fifteen P.M. After sweeping through the international
dateline, the jumbo jet would touch down at Narita International Airport, Tokyo, at four-thirty on the afternoon of the same calendar day. Among its weary
deplaning passengers were one Michael M. Richardson
and one Megan A. McBride.

They had flown the distance in the nonsmoking section of the business class; like many others, they had di-
vided their time between working, sleeping, eating,
and talking. Neither of them had ever noticed the looks
of admiration from men and women of various national-
ities who were struck by the sight of an unusually
handsome man and a stunningly beautiful woman.
Megan was wearing a jet black dress with a strikingly
lovely pendant the color of her gleaming long red hair;
Michael was dressed in the chocolate brown suit she
had once told him was her favorite. People had tried to
figure out, but couldn't, if they might be honeymooners.
Their conversation, and the looks they so often gave
each other, were deeply serious. But there was no way
of knowing if they discussed love or foreign currency
fluctuations.

Three people met them at the airport: one Japanese-
born, one Irish-born, the last obviously American. The
first was Mr. Yasuda, Michael's agent; the other two

were Gavin and Patricia McBride. From the monstrous
industrial seaport of Tokyo, all parties would board a
bullet train bound inland for the historic imperial capital of Kyoto. Before returning to their apartment in a
Tokyo suburb, Megan's parents would stay overnight
at the Miyako, their daughter's hotel. The agent would
deliver the group, supervise their check-in, and double-
check the comfort of their rooms; then he would make a
discreetly polite retreat to his home a few blocks distant.

As expected, Megan's parents gave their approval of
Michael within the first fifteen minutes. When they
were boarding the cab for the train station, Gavin
slipped his daughter a meaningful wink. Patricia Mc-
Bride, meanwhile, was absorbed with Michael's answers to questions regarding the current American
business scene; she kept nodding agreement in a way
Megan knew to be her silent compliment to the man
talking.

She herself was pleased to be getting along well with
Mr. Yasuda, a man firmly in control of the Japanese
porcelain industry whom Michael had confided to
Megan was his favorite overseas agent as well; in many
ways, there were similarities between Mr. Yasuda and
Mr. Ling. Although he was Japanese, younger, and had
brown hair, she thought he, too, must be cousin to
Santa Claus; at the same time, he was the epitome of
the perfect Oriental gentleman. Beautifully enunciated
Japanese syllables and grammar, plus a fine conversational grasp of English, indicated a superior education,
an observation that would later fascinate Michael.

After the flight, then the zoom of the bullet train,
time and events finally halted at their destination. Although the Miyako catered to East and West alike, it
was simply not conducive to thoughts of an overacceler-
ated modern world. For one thing, the hotel, nestled
amid sixteen landscaped acres on a wooded hillside, af-
forded a clear view of the ages-old Imperial Palace across

and high above the city. If there were no samurai
lounging around the lobby, no shoguns holding court in
the penthouses, one nonetheless sensed the indelible
imprint of their footsteps. As the group waited for Mr.
Yasuda to complete the registration procedure, Michael spoke quietly of the history. Gavin McBride's
comment was a quote from a Greek mystic who had
made Japan his home: " 'Remember that here all is
enchantment—that you have fallen under the spell of
the dead—that the lights and the colors and the voices
must fade away at last into emptiness and silence.' "

Part of the complex was Western and the remainder
was *ryokan,* traditional Japanese-style inn. For this
single night alone with her parents, Megan had requested a Western room connecting with theirs; Michael would be staying in the *ryokan.* And it appeared
the travelers would soon be able to settle down for the
night; two bellboys had started sorting and loading baggage onto separate carts. Although it was still early—
Megan wasn't sure, for she hadn't yet reset her watch,
but she estimated it was just about nine—the McBrides
showed normal parental concern that their globetrot-
ting daughter get a good night's sleep; Michael said
if ever there were a time for room service and lights out,
this was it.

Mr. Yasuda had made his graceful departure after
turning down the proffered dinner invitation. Michael
was telling the McBrides he would see them bright and
early for breakfast when Gavin cut in with, "Just a
bloomin' second, if you please! Not so fast, lad. We've a
bottle of sake in our case and a yen to get acquainted
with the man who's captured our lass. You'll come
along with us now, and we won't be keepin' you long!"

Megan giggled, then exchanged affectionate glances
with her mother. Both knew quite well that Gavin was
capable of nearly unaccented American speech; when
he wanted to conceal sentimental dialogue, however, he
reverted to the brogue. Michael Richardson didn't

stand a chance—whether or not he wanted to, he *was* sharing the trip's first cup of sake with her father. With consistent poise, he tipped his bellboy to take the bags on alone; overall, his reaction would have led one to believe that the Irish summons was his entire purpose for the transpacific voyage.

She couldn't help wondering what he was really thinking. As they entered the spacious elevator, following the uniformed young man with their luggage, she reviewed the events of the last three days; it didn't take long, for not a lot had happened since their hasty departure from High Point.

They had talked, of course, but no real attempt had been made to broach subjects of critical concern; Megan's first observation had been that Michael finally appeared to realize they needed to explore the routes that had led so painfully to their current sidetrack.

It had started in the cab on their way from Market Hall. He had turned to her and asked, "Little Meggie . . . what did it mean? Why did you suddenly change your mind and tell me what happened with the artisans?"

Before answering she warned herself not to expect miracles. She knew little of what was going on in his head, but it certainly wasn't likely he had experienced insights similar to the ones that had hit her. Very simply, she said, "Because I love you. And I want to marry you."

She saw the cabdriver look sharply into his rearview mirror, then return his eyes to the road when he saw he'd been caught at it. From Michael, there was no reaction for a long few moments. Tears were stinging Megan's eyelids.

Finally he said, "I think too much has happened. If we ever had anything, we let it slip away."

Digging her fingernails into her palms, Megan fought for control and reminded herself that, less than an hour before, a total stranger had told her a story that proved Michael loved her.

"Isn't it possible," she said in a quivering voice, looking down at her lap, "that our whole problem was being too busy to find out what it was, exactly, that we had?"

"I'm not sure I know what you mean."

Remember, she told herself, his situation hasn't changed. Now he's got all the old priorities plus a new one: Japan. And, despite that seeming calm, he had to be thoroughly exhausted. When he admitted he found her words confusing she had to take it at face value unless the entire stupid mistake were to repeat itself.

"Well, I still love you," she made herself say. Then she thought, The trip will change things, the trip will change things . . .

None of this did her parents know. With a mere thirty-six hours in Los Angeles before taking the flight Adelle had scheduled, there had hardly been time to repack appropriate clothes, call Sharon—she could hear Sinbad screeching "Door! Door!" when her friend answered the phone; apparently all was well with him— and type business correspondence. During her brief long-distance conversation with her parents, she had explained only Mr. Ling's request to translate for Michael.

She hadn't talked at all to her employer. The silent telephone loomed like a constant unwelcome reminder. And when she had wanted to call Jeffie, it had seemed, under the prevailing circumstances, an act that might be interpreted as pushy. To control the ensuing pain from all these details, Megan forced her concentration to considerations necessary for getting off to Japan, period.

Aboard Singapore Airlines, the passengers who had imagined Megan and Michael to be honeymooners would have been disappointed, for their conversation was indeed strictly business. As for those who felt certain that, no matter what their formal relationship, the

man was *definitely* staring at the lady with longing,
Megan would have agreed. From time to time, unless
she was very much mistaken, Michael's expression did
not match his impersonal words.

They were in the McBrides' room—it looked like any
to be found in the States, perhaps a bit nicer—and Gavin had poured the sake, starting with Michael's cup.
The polite banter was becoming increasingly relaxed,
so much so that Megan's father evidently felt comfortable enough to broach personal matters. But he would
start, naturally, with something on the light side. It
turned out to be her pendant.

"Megan, me lass. I know you don't buy jewels for
yourself. But that one you're wearin' around your neck
is a beauty. It wouldn't have come from your friend
here, now would it?"

"Yes, Dad," she answered, determined not to let embarrassment ruin this one evening with her folks.

"Never seen anything like it," Gavin ventured, leaning forward and squinting at Onyx Flame, the necklace. Megan was on the verge of attempting to divert
the awkward situation with a description of the lamp
Michael had designed when she heard her forthright father say, "Such gifts aren't given lightly, not when
they're of such a value. I'm a-thinkin': can this be a
modern new custom for gettin' engaged?"

The too-quick looks that passed between Michael and
Megan said it all. Patricia McBride stepped in immediately to tell her overly enthusiastic husband that en-
gagements were announced, not forced to the surface.
Then she changed the subject quite smoothly, and it
wasn't brought up again until parents and daughter
were alone. Then it was the mother who, wasting no
time about it, turned and asked what on earth was
going on. As tired as Megan was, she was so happy to
have them to confide in that she told the story without
omitting a single detail. At the end, Patricia put her
arms around her daughter. Gavin just continued sitting

as he had been; but he had a familiar look on his face. Megan knew the Irish cupid wasn't about to stop interfering.

For Megan and Michael, the following day had been planned as a necessary break to provide rest and reorientation following all the travel. At breakfast in the main coffee shop, it soon became apparent that the senior McBrides couldn't be talked into staying over for the day. Gavin had a meeting in Tokyo; he explained he had already tried, and failed, to reschedule it. Their bags were already in the lobby, so they were off after a final cup of coffee. Patricia kissed her daughter and told her not to worry, they'd all get together during everyone's next free day; since Megan had no idea how long Michael would require to complete his business with the artisans—and since, also, she had never needed her mother and father more than now—her good-byes were tinged with an amount of reluctance neither parent could fail to discern.

She closed the door of their cab, then stood watching after them. When she turned toward the hotel, she wished the moment were more private. Michael was waiting politely nearby, and Megan was fairly certain that anyone in his position could easily read the little-girl-lost look she was trying so unsuccessfully to conceal.

As they reentered the lobby, he said something that surprised her—"Let's spend the morning in Nara." She had been so certain he would want to go immediately to Mr. Yasuda's office, day off or not! Megan literally glided to her room to peel away the business clothes; it had occurred to her that the last—the *only*—totally undemanding day they had spent together had been that long-ago occasion in San Diego. She put on dark blue jeans and a T-shirt of almost the identical shade, decided not to take off the single gold chain around her neck, and then fluffed her already combed hair before starting out; just as she opened the door to the hall, she realized how excited she really was: still barefoot! Shaking her head in amazement, she went back in and dug tennis shoes from her still-packed suitcase.

Michael was wearing jeans, too. Megan was astonished, having never seen him in anything but business clothes. Well, she thought, feeling slightly naughty, I've seen him wear *less*. It was too bad the errant thought had popped into her head; for the rest of the day, she wouldn't be able to get it out. His jeans did nothing to help, for they contoured perfectly to the lean and muscled legs; then too, wearing a soft gray sweatshirt, he looked more masculine than ever— *rugged* would have been the right word—in comparison to his usual dignified elegance. Once they were aboard the tour bus, she stole another look and decided that, no, nothing could alter Michael's elegance, not even casual clothes; but still she was thrilled to see him this way—for once, he didn't seem to have a single business care.

The ancient city of Nara, only a short bus trip from Kyoto, was a thousand-year step back in time. If other towns contained their historic spots and shrines, it was fair to describe the entirety of Nara as a monument to the incredibly rich and lovely Japanese past.

After the previous day's confinement to planes, trains, and taxis, Michael and Megan shared a desire to walk. For this purpose, they couldn't have chosen a lovelier season; October is traditionally the island's favored month, a blend of summer vitality and freshness with certain bittersweet elements forecasting change: the delicate woodland forests showed, now, just a hint of color among the multimillion green leaves. Naturally, they started with a Buddhist monument—as a youngster, Megan had dreaded the very thought of seeing yet another religious shrine—and, as Michael had predicted on the bus, it turned out to be well worth seeing. Once inside Todaiji Temple, she found herself staring up, overwhelmed, at the *Daibutsu,* or Great Buddha, the world's largest bronze statue.

"My God," she breathed, craning her neck. "Is that as big as I think it is?"

"It certainly makes *you* look like a midget, little Meggie," Michael replied. She held her breath, noticing the affectionate nickname. Every once in a while, but not often enough, Michael forgot his stiff intentions of treating her like a total stranger thrown temporarily into an unusual business situation. Turning to look at him, trying not to be obvious, she was disappointed. His face was relaxed, yes, and it was also lit by the humor he so often found in Megan's reactions; but that was all. Sighing, she looked again at the statue while he read from the tour book. No wonder she felt so tiny—not only did the *Daibutsu* weigh four hundred and fifty pounds, but each of its *thumbs* was sixty-three inches long!

Another couple had approached to stand gawking at the statue. Michael tapped Megan on the shoulder and when she asked what he wanted, he leaned close to her ear and whispered, "I think that's the size man it would take to handle you!"

She didn't have the vaguest idea whether he was joking or expressing an actual complaint. But she did know the statement wasn't one he would have made to a stranger. Furthermore, he had just given her the first opening since their arrival to express emotion. Megan had determined, after all the lost opportunities, all the time when she might have spoken but had let nerves get in the way, that nothing of the nature would occur during this trip; if this was her last chance with Michael, he would know how she felt, win, lose or draw. Pride was no longer a factor. Very slowly and deliberately, she swiveled, then locked eyes with Michael's. And in an appropriately low tone she said something with only one possible meaning: "There's one interpretation of your sentence I perfectly agree with. In this very place is the only man on earth big enough to hold my interest."

His eyes blazed and, instantly, the rhythm of his breathing altered; unfortunately Megan didn't know what to make of the changes. Before she might have figured it out, he had resumed the impersonal mask and was telling her it was time to go.

"Ready for something besides temples?" he asked.

When she only nodded, he consulted their map and led the way to an area marked with a simple sign: DEER PARK. Almost at once, the reason for the name became abundantly clear; they stepped into this tranquil cedar and oak environment and found themselves immediately surrounded. Evidently the graceful woodland creatures had become dependent on human handouts. Megan couldn't resist; she reached out, slowly and smoothly, to touch one of the little animals between two furry baby antlers. When the deer responded by turning his head to nuzzle her outstretched arm, she dropped to her knees and put both arms around his neck.

In babytalk, she was communicating with the deer, who appeared frankly puzzled by the whole affair: "You're beautiful. Know that?"

Michael lowered himself to the ground, propped on one knee; the other was jackknifed in an inverted V, where he now rested his forearm. When she looked over, intending to ask if he wanted to get closer to the deer, she caught him looking not at the animal, but at her. He made no attempt to withdraw his gaze and she grew very still. In her arms, the small creature now seemed restless.

"I think he wants to be released," Michael said softly, keeping his eyes pinned on hers.

"What if I don't want to let go?" she asked playfully. Michael scooted closer to her, then leaned forward and gently pried her loose. The deer scampered away. "There," he said. "Did that hurt?"

She nodded. "He felt so good in my arms."

He had taken off the mask. Now he stared at Megan with a haunted, almost painful expression. Finally he

spoke. "Do you need something in your arms so much,
little Meggie?"

"No," she whispered, dropping her eyes to the
ground. "Just you. You alone. I love you, Michael."

Without another word, he got to his feet and pulled
her after him. They had been kneeling close to an ancient cedar tree, and Michael backed Megan to its
trunk, then imprisoned her by placing both hands on
the tree, one on either side of her. For a long memorable
moment they looked deeply, hungrily, at each other;
then, finally, he slackened the tension in the rigid arms
and, with a small moan of submission, allowed his body
to fall against hers.

It was a kiss unlike any other they had exchanged.
They were aware of others passing by, therefore of the
need for restraint. But Megan felt his legs trembling
with the effort and she knew her own control was no
better; never in her life had she felt a need so urgent. If
Michael had decided to lie down on the spot, drawing
her on top, she would have been powerless to resist.
And now, although she knew the embrace would soon
have to be broken, her tongue flickered against his with
a greater passion than during that final beautiful lovemaking in North Carolina. With the most extraordinary discipline, she kept her lower body from moving to
meet the hard contact point swelling beneath the zipper
of his jeans.

Michael drew away, breathing hard; it was abrupt, as
of course it had to be. He pivoted and slumped against
the tree trunk. When at last he was able to talk, he said,
"Well, now you know how to *get* me into your arms."

He took several deep breaths. Her own breathing was
smoothing out, and she was about to whisper a message
of purest love and gratitude when the world fell apart.
He said, "And now *I* know the type of temptation that
has to be resisted."

24

Right after dawn the next morning, Mr. Yasuda arrived at the Miyako to reverse his earlier procedure at the desk. Megan heard him tell the hotel manager that the Americans would be returning in exactly two days and that he expected accommodations precisely as before; she wanted to interrupt and explain her desire to stay in the Japanese section but was afraid the request would create undue delay. They were facing a one-hundred-and-twenty-mile drive in and out of the myriad tunnels cutting east through the Japanese hills to Seto, the center of the vast porcelain industry. In her excitement she soon forgot the disappointment about the room, for she was about to see something very few of her countrymen would ever be allowed to witness.

Mr. Yasuda and Michael called the porcelain artisans *makers,* a term she would have to get used to. There were many makers—only a few as accomplished as the ones she had met in the Shepard conference room, however—and almost all had learned their craft from ancestors who, in turn, had passed it down the family for centuries. Megan's first surprise was the size of their plants, for they weren't so much factories at all, but rather homes annexed to fit the particular needs of their specialty. And clients of Michael's stature were invariably treated with the cordiality one would expect when visiting another man's home.

Always it began with food. The maker's wife—or if he

was unfortunate enough not to have one, his mother or grandmother—entered the room bowing and carrying a tray of pastry and fruit juice, coffee and tea; during this traditional welcome period, commercial matters would not be discussed. But when the businessmen retired to the conference room, thus began a flurry of activity Megan had trouble keeping up with. Michael carried his portfolio, Mr. Yasuda made copious notes, and both his Seto office assistant and the maker's flew constantly around the room fetching color samples or taking and labeling instant snapshots of greenware: undecorated porcelain pieces on which Michael would sketch quick expert design details with a special black pen. Every color had to be precisely ordered, every border and outline discussed—is this to be fired gold or should we make it a slightly darker green than the inner panel? If a lamp base would require something special, say a particular bronze handle, it was Mr. Yasuda's task to coordinate receipt from the handlemaker specified by Michael. And always, always, there was the consideration of whether or not the maker would produce a different shape, an untried and untested pattern or color. Then, at the end, Megan could step out while Michael's agent consummated necessary negotiations regarding price. On the way to the next maker, the two men would calculate the retail market value—after the addition of lampshade, hardware, and mounting—while she slumped in the backseat, trying to catch her breath before it started all over again.

During the two days in Seto, Megan's keenest interest was sparked at those times it became necessary for Michael to determine when specific designs would lend themselves to specific techniques. The ancient names bandied between him and his agent were legendary: Kutani, Satsuma, Imari . . . When she saw the big kilns, and the workers who would load them, then her mind conjured images of the artisans' ancestors. Things had changed all over the world, even in this old island country, and Kutani was no longer made exclusively in that village, where the special clay necessary for its production had been discovered. Nor was the elaborately colored, under- and over-glazed Imari an art confined to the famous shipping port of its origin. Even Satsumaware had spread beyond its namesake kingdom. Nonetheless, Megan still heard the clash of mighty armies outside these places where art would reign forever with the strength endowed only by the serene and dignified Oriental belief in beauty.

She was awed by her employer's patience, persistence, and, most of all, talent. And Megan wasn't the only one. Although he continued to appear totally unimpressed with the stunning beauty and innovation of his designs, every Japanese who bowed to Michael Richardson did so with more than a merely polite flourish; if ever she had witnessed genuine respect, it was now. It even came from Mr. Yasuda, himself obviously a powerful figure in the industry, for he let it be known that this was "one of the top designers in the United States." To the makers and their employees the combination was potent; Megan often wondered if her part of the trip had actually been necessary. Although she continued to meet with resistance to revolutionary drawings and production requests, at which time the technique borrowed from her father's long-ago experience went into effective action, it was hard to imagine that a man of Michael's magnetism and capability *could* need her.

The attitude had crept into her thinking about personal matters as well. In her lonely single bed at the Nagoya Kanko Hotel, she despaired of ever again being one with this giant she loved. He had proven quite well that he could, in fact, resist her. And why shouldn't he? There were women more fascinating than she, more brilliant, more beautiful; Michael attracted superlatives. Once again, she was giving up.

He certainly said nothing to create this growing despondency. If anything, both he and his agent were quite willing to credit Megan entirely with the success of the trip. Mr. Yasuda had changed from simply an outgoing personality to a buoyant and admittedly excited individual; one could hardly doubt he was genuinely encouraged by the progress. But when he and Michael started discussing her poise, her trick of immediately converting to Japanese-style thought and behavior patterns, she tuned out, thinking they were trying too hard to give her a sense of belonging in this exclusively male world she had entered.

Despite a fast-growing trend toward modern nonsexist thought and behavior, Japanese men by and large still held to the customs and beliefs of their fathers. Outside the large cities, a woman was expected to walk discreetly behind the superior male, to prepare his evening meals creatively, and to raise his children perfectly. Since she had grown up in Japan, Megan was accustomed to it; women's liberation was a long way off.

Despite the fact that Michael's makers were far too educated in the ways of the world to treat their wives unkindly, there had been ample evidence of the old philosophy. It was visible from the very first, as a matter of fact; waiting for the bullet train in Tokyo, they had seen wives carrying mountains of luggage and struggling to maintain holds on small children as they walked behind empty-handed husbands. And it never failed to embarrass Michael. On that first night in Seto, after Mr. Yasuda had retired to his room, leaving his companions to sip the last of their green tea, he brought the touchy subject into the open, asking Megan how she felt about it.

She shrugged. "Judgment isn't up to me, thank God. I wouldn't want to live with it. But then I don't have to."

He shook his head. "Every time I see it, I feel guilty."

Megan didn't think there was any reason for that, and she told him so. Then, trying to insert a light note, she said, "How do we know these women aren't perfectly content? The last I read, the Japanese divorce rate was one in twenty-five. That's a fair comparison with ours, I'd say."

Michael seemed to be studying her. "You don't believe what you just said. These women can't be happy."

Megan sighed. "You're right—I don't believe it. The way I feel about personal freedom . . ." All of a sudden she brightened again. "You seem to like my father. Listen to this: he sure wasn't going to let *his* little girl learn to bow and scrape and sit home alone."

"I can well imagine," Michael inserted. "But raising you here, that must have been a challenge."

"Indeed!" Megan said with laughter in her voice. "When I was about seven years old, I got the one and only spanking Gavin McBride ever personally gave his little angel. My crime was getting caught carrying my grade school idol's books and following, head down, in his footsteps. Years later, Dad admitted he'd been waiting across from the schoolyard off and on for a solid year, hoping never to find me doing such a thing, but prepared to handle it if he did."

His laugh was genuine. "Now I like him even more. Did you learn your lesson?" He raised one palm. "Never mind! If I don't know the answer by now, I never will."

If Megan had been in any other mood, she would have seen a tailor-made opening and seized it. As it happened, the dynamics ceased at that precise point. She noticed the late hour instead of the thoughtful look on Michael's face, then she told him she was ready to turn in. He had been about to say something, which she never suspected, and her weary statement caused him to close his mouth and push back his chair.

During the next day's final session with a maker, Megan had yet another chance to speak on the previous evening's topic, this time purely by accident. Michael and Mr. Yasuda were gathering materials from the cluttered conference area when she emerged from the powder room to find an elderly kimono-clad woman gliding on slippered feet in her direction. She recognized her as a relative of the maker—*which* relative, she couldn't quite recall—who had floated in and out of the meeting with endless overladen trays of fresh fruit, soft drinks, and tea. As soon as she saw Megan in the hallway, the old woman stopped, bowed, and clasped her hands correctly in front, waiting for the guest to pass. But then, when Megan started to slip by, as she was clearly expected to do, the older lady stopped her, saying, "Please, it is so seldom I meet an American girl with Japanese. Would it be impolite for me to ask about your women's liberation?"

Megan explained candidly, watching closely for signs of the listener's reaction. It soon became apparent—only by the look on her face, for she would never have been so impolite as to make a negative remark—that the maker's relative considered the whole thing silly and possibly even suspected such American women of being slightly insane. Although she didn't let on, this predictable response amused Megan. It seemed the two held only one common opinion. When the old lady, obviously embarrassed about the question, inquired whether the women's movement had spurred promiscuity, as Japanese men so vehemently insisted, Megan pursed her lips and said, "I don't know what's caused it, but it exists like an out-of-control plague. And I don't mind telling you it's hard to be an unmarried woman when everyone takes personal favors for granted. But take my word on the fact that we haven't all gone mad. I, for one, still believe some things are sacred."

From around a bend in the corridor Megan and her Japanese companion heard a discreet cough. Then Michael materialized and informed her the car was loaded for the drive back to Kyoto. She didn't ask if he'd understood the conversation.

They would have to return to Seto, for their business was unfinished. But tomorrow marked the beginning of important Kyoto festivities in which Mr. Yasuda, whose great-grandfather had been a powerful samurai, would play a key role. The agent was clearly looking forward to the prestigious annual event—one marking his first invitation to participate—and, as he started describing the warrior's costume and the grand parade that would convert the streets of the imperial city to a bygone era, her eyelids drooped and she finally gave up and stretched across the backseat of the luxurious Toyota coupé.

She was dreaming. The scene was one that couldn't have existed, for it revealed a street surrounded by Japanese hills but containing no lights, no traffic, not even concrete. There were only four characters: Megan, wearing a white kimono; Michael in a samurai's smock with the obligatory weapons, standing with feet apart and an obvious intent to unsheathe the sword; the maker's old relative, looking identical to how she had looked today, only sitting cross-legged on a grassy knoll; and the China Cove buyer, also ready to fight, wearing warrior's garb similar to Michael's.

Megan was frightened. Terrified. The argument was about her, but, in the strange way that dreams unravel, there was no background; it didn't seem to matter. The point was, Michael's samurai opponent had grown to monstrous proportions—well over seven feet tall and with the weight of a sumo wrestler—and she knew the man she loved wasn't likely to survive the battle. As the swords were released and the giant bore down on Michael, the old woman said, "Good, such women don't deserve their men!"—and Megan screamed.

When she was fully alert, she found herself in Michael's arms, sobbing. Mr. Yasuda had stopped the car;

the front passenger door gaped open and the kindly
agent peered anxiously toward the backseat.

"Honey . . ." He was stroking her hair. "Baby . . .
it's all right, only a dream." In that now-familiar manner, he rocked her until the tears stopped. At one point
she heard him telling Mr. Yasuda she was exhausted,
that he'd worked her far too long and hard since she'd
taken "the damned job."

"I'm okay now," she said at last. "Embarrassed as all
get-out, but okay. You can go back up front."

He shook his head, then told his agent it was okay to
drive on but he'd sit in back. They had another fifty
miles to go and she suddenly wished it were a thousand.

If she had required positive proof of Michael's physical need, that magical trip to Kyoto would certainly
have provided it. Nothing was said. Not one word. But
the nonverbal communication turned Megan back on to
all of life's lovely possibilities.

Not that it was easy. Michael's casual arm over her
shoulders was already playing havoc with her senses
when he slipped a hand under one loose sleeve and
started running his forefinger lightly, lazily, up and
down her arm. By the time he started the motion *underneath,* near the point where her breast pressed against
her forearm, Megan's entire body was a torch preparing
to ignite into a raging inferno.

She wanted to touch him but dared not. And then the
instinct became overpowering; trembling, she slipped a
hand into the one lying free on his lap. Now, in addition
to the other torture, he started gently fingering her sensitive palm as well. Megan struggled to keep her
breathing normal; it didn't help that she could hear the
harsh staccato rhythm of his.

The fingers of one hand started circling against the
frail fabric of her bra, roaming closer and closer to her
nipple, but not close enough. When she became afraid
of making some involuntary noise that would be heard
by the driver—when she knew their illicit play would

either have to stop or go forward—she tried to signal Michael by squeezing the hand in his lap. But that was when the real challenge actually began, for, in that supercharged moment, she felt the hard throbbing pressure between his legs. At her unexpected touch, Michael's thigh muscles tensed violently; from their lovemaking Megan could clearly visualize the shuddering contraction of firm buttocks. He turned her hand over and pressed it hard against him. Then he moved the still-wandering fingers above to her nipple. Megan buried her face in his shoulder and caught his shirt sleeve between her teeth; she honestly wondered if she would survive.

As soon as the lights of Kyoto came into view over the fast-approaching horizon, Michael gently maneuvered to untangle them. When he moved to the opposite side of the seat, rolling his window all the way down, she decided the plan had definite merit and followed suit. Surely Mr. Yasuda must wonder why, all of a sudden, we need so much fresh air! she thought. But if the agent had any notion of something amiss, he never let on. If he had, Megan wasn't sure she would have cared; being in love with Michael Richardson was a matter of pride, not shame.

More important—a thing of incredible, almost heartbreaking joy—he had rediscovered his own tenuous faith in their love. The fact had been displayed through actions rather than words, true, for the restrictions in Mr. Yasuda's backseat prevented a bold exclamation of those three words, I love you. Now Megan literally craved the reaffirmation. Very soon she would feel the caressing sound of the all-important three words. When they were alone.

Over and over, like a refrain running faster with each repetition, a single phrase played in her head: When we're alone, finally alone . . .

Michael was talking to his agent: good night, thanks, see you at the festival tomorrow. He was closing the car door. He was taking her hand, squeezing it once, briefly. He was leading toward the entrance; the doorman was bowing them in. He was reregistering. He was putting one arm around her, reaching with the other for the elevator call button. Soon now . . . they would be *alone.*

"Miss McBride!"

She recognized the voice behind her; it was the assistant manager, a friend of Mr. Yasuda's who, before, simply hadn't been able to do enough for them. Megan turned and smiled, rehearsing her reply: "No tea tonight, thank you. No fruit. Nothing but privacy."

The man spoke in rapid Japanese. "The doorman told me you'd arrived. I have a message, very good news. Your parents are here"—he pivoted, pointing to a spot on the far side of the lobby—"waiting in the sushi bar. Of course, I gave them the connecting room again."

It was all so quick, the change she had to make from dazed lover to welcoming daughter. Michael helped; once the development was explained in English and the assistant manager was beyond earshot, he gave her a sympathetic pat on the shoulder before dropping his arm.

"Come on," he said. "It's impossible to be disappointed about seeing those two."

Well, yes, she agreed without saying so, but her reservations were clearly readable.

"Now, now," he teased, then shrugged. "Anyway, perhaps we're being dense. After all, some things just aren't meant to be."

Whether he was expressing disappointment or some deeper, darker emotion, she couldn't tell. And there wouldn't be time to ask. He had taken her hand again, this time to lead in the direction of the Miyako sushi bar.

Her parents hadn't been eating, it turned out, as much as killing time. They studied her closely; with Patricia's hug, Megan felt her mother's unusual concern.

That silent distress signal of a few days back, just before her folks had pulled away from the hotel, must have come through loud and clear.

During the greeting period, no one moved to sit down. Instead, Gavin kept piling yen onto a little tray beside two half-empty cocktail glasses; Patricia, meanwhile, announced her husband's decision to stay out of his office for the remainder of the week.

Her dad stuffed his wallet into a hip pocket; then he surprised Megan, who had thought she was no longer capable of being thrown off guard by this unpredictable Irishman. With hearty enthusiasm he grasped Michael's upper left arm and said, "Me boy, you and I are going out to do the town!" After that, with characteristic determination and no further explanation, he propelled his prey from the bar. Remembering Gavin's serious expression during their long talk a few nights back, Megan knew he planned to follow through with . . .

What? Since she had no idea, another question was added to the disquieting list: Dear God, why me and why now? Following her unsuspecting mother to their rooms, Megan knew she had just asked the *only* one who might have known whether or not these new cogs in the wheel would foul up the delicate machinery—permanently.

In spite of it all, she slept well and long. By the time she awakened, her parents had finished their breakfast. With obvious amusement, Gavin told his daughter not to expect Michael any time soon. He said, "We were out a wee bit late, lass, and your fellow isn't quite the expert drinker I am!"

Great, she thought—Michael's first chance to get to bed early in all the time she had known him!

The new day was an Oriental gem sparkling with clear bright sunlight, freshened by air containing the first nip of autumn. It was appropriate, for the festival of *Jidai Matsuri* was the most revered of the island's fall celebrations. It was also the grandest: the procession would begin at the gates of the Imperial Palace and unfold for two and a half miles. By the time it had stretched the entire route, citizens from all points of the nation would have witnessed history in the form of ghosts from the period of Emperor Kammu, twelve hundred years past. Only when the ghosts slept again would the Japanese be content to view the inexorable change of seasons: the maples could then complete their spectacular red transition into the long snowy winter. With the Festival of Eras, a new one could begin.

She needn't have worried about Michael. When he stepped off the elevator, meeting the group for a leisurely walk to their reserved seats near the palace, he looked sensational. He was dressed in a light gray dress shirt, no coat or tie, with darker gray slacks and every ash hair in place, appearing rested despite Gavin's warning to the contrary, and Megan was once again struck by the fact that the man was physically perfect. No, she thought, he's no male mannequin; it was more that his imperfections were so potently irresistible.

As she crossed toward him she searched for signs remaining from their interlude in Mr. Yasuda's car. A smile, a wink . . . anything would suffice. Incredibly, Michael was wearing the dreaded mask; if he even knew Megan existed, it was only as an acquaintance, a fleeting association. With pain verging dangerously close to panic, she moved instinctively to her father's side, then slipped between both parents and kept walking, head pointed forward, feet moving one after the other.

In keeping with the historic spirit, Megan had donned the one and only kimono she still owned, a jade green blended cotton with an intricately embroidered red dragon whipping its long tail across her breasts. Now she found herself nervously fingering the neckline. The others were obviously enjoying the stroll while each slight traffic noise, even the excited chatter of costumed children, added to her discomfort.

Michael must have assumed the neckline was too tight. At a crosswalk, he stopped. With a thoroughly gracious smile, he said, "That can be fixed, you know. I'd hate to have you choke to death on all this authenticity!" When he unfastened the top braid without so much as asking "if you please," Megan wanted to strike him. And that was her entire problem. She wanted to vent frustration; in her opinion, this stop-and-start attitude of his could no longer be excused. It was a total mystery that a man as thoughtful of others as Michael Richardson failed to realize how very much easier the situation might be if he'd summon the decency, or the nerve, to say, "Hey, it's over between us. Not interested anymore. Sorry." Maybe he *had* no nerves, she thought bitterly. Nothing ever seemed to rattle him.

Patricia had requested a detour to the intersection of Shijo-dori and Kawaramachi-dori, the streets renowned as an international shopping paradise. When the men groaned, she quickly added, "Don't get your male plumes all ruffled; I just want to window-shop. Anyway, it'll be fun—think of all the weird get-ups we'll see!"

When they crossed the famous Kamo-gawa bridge, her mother's point became abundantly clear: spread along the banks of the river below was a remarkable melange of spirited teeming humanity. The air crackled with excitement. And if there were a single historic costume remaining in all of Japan, Megan would have been surprised. She was staring at thousands of samurai and a fair smattering of arrogant shoguns. One group even carried an emperor on his lofty portable throne. Since the gathering was for an early picnic lunch before the noon start of the procession, paper umbrellas bloomed like instant poufs of color. Michael shook his head and said he'd never seen anything like it. This was something on which they could certainly agree; despite having grown up near Tokyo, she hadn't either.

As they neared the shopping section, the crowd grew denser. Had the Japanese been a less politely inclined people, false steps might have led to mayhem. Megan had all she could do to steer a safe path, never mind a clear one, for there was no such thing on this festival day.

She stopped, as always on such occasions, to speak English with a group of schoolchildren escorted by a harried young teacher. Very frequently when she was recognized as an American, the friendly Oriental youngsters took charming delight in showing off their newly acquired language. Megan always enjoyed it, and now it was particularly refreshing since it ended up providing a much-needed laugh. Evidently this group was learning French and English simultaneously. Their leader stepped up to her and soberly announced, "Good bonmorning! I am enchantee to see vous in our country!" Although his astonished teacher would no doubt correct him later, Megan wasn't about to have the boy lose face with his comrades. Without skipping a beat, she replied, "And moi too, mon friend. Bon festival!" When she turned away she heard a dozen giggles and one overriding voice—"Now, class!" Some things were dependable the world over.

Nothing else about the day seemed to be working her way; it shouldn't have bothered her to find that Michael and her parents had disappeared. But it did. In a crowd this enormous, reconnection could easily take hours. Getting "unlost," as Gavin had called it during her childhood, was a difficult job indeed on the overpopulated main streets of Japan. She sighed, realizing her best bet was to remain in a contained area and let *them* get unlost. Slowly she turned left on Kawaramachidori. The very first thing that caught her eye, sitting front and center in a department store window, was Onyx Flame. Except for brass in place of the wood mounting offered by Ling and Son, plus an atrocious lampshade that Michael Richardson couldn't possibly have ordered, the lamp was exactly, in every detail, like the one that had been released from security at the factory less than two weeks ago.

She stood pacing in front of the store, back and forth, back and forth. The issue of industrial theft, a seeming misnomer when one thought in terms of artistic design, was one that often had plagued Megan and all her colleagues. Nor had she been able to learn a single fact beyond the nothing discovered at that meeting in Andrew Shepard's showroom. And it was so critical! The firm that finally succeeded in protecting copyrights would have an incredible competitive edge. Imagine being able to safely maintain a hold on a best-selling exclusive! she thought.

How on earth had Michael's lamp base traveled all the way from the States back to the Orient in such a short time? The theft simply *had* to have occurred before Ling and Son ever received it. Right here, or rather in Seto, someone must be operating a ring to sell original designs to local manufacturers. But who? Megan was positive the makers weren't lying to her; they really didn't know; furthermore, they were miserably embarrassed whenever the subject came up—it simply wasn't polite to steal a copyrighted work of art! It wasn't *Japanese*.

From the background she heard Michael's voice sorting itself from the rest of the crowd noises. When she finally saw him, she motioned excitedly. When he saw Onyx Flame, his mouth dropped open.

"How in hell?" he exclaimed. "If it were an older design, then I could understand. But with something we've just received?" He shook his head. "There goes our theory about the culprits being American."

Gavin McBride sauntered up. "Nice lamp," he said when he noticed the object of their attention.

"Yes," Megan agreed dryly, "It certainly is, but . . ." She explained the mystery.

"Simple, me lad and lassie," her father said casually. "You're making far too big a deal of it. If you look at the obvious, you'll see right away what the problem is. And it isn't theft."

Michael just stared. Megan thought the older man had probably gone mad; this wasn't something to figure out in a jiffy after first hearing of it.

"Give up?" Gavin asked.

"A long time ago" was the reply from Michael.

"My boy, if you never specifically instructed your makers not to sell their extra samples here in Japan, then they're unloading them just like all the other warehouse excess. I guarantee that if you go inside and take a look at that lamp, you'll find an imperfection, something that places it in a distress category."

"My God," Michael said. "You might be right!" He bounded into the store and examined the merchandise from the side not visible through the window. When he came out he said, "There's a glaze stain on it. The maker would never have sent it to us like that."

Gavin said, "Now take a look around you. Hundreds of American tourists on the street today. All of them innocent-looking. Practically every one with a camera. How much you want to bet that not every heart here is so pure?"

"They take a photo, then have the piece redrawn. It's sold to some highly reputable but unsuspecting American lamp manufacturer who's going to be pretty ticked off when he learns his expensive original design's been stolen by Ling and Son. Dammit all!" All this from Michael.

Gavin shrugged. "Well, now you know. I'd suggest you tell your makers to destroy their samples."

"At the very least," Michael grumbled.

Megan asked her father if she could have a few moments alone. "With my boss" was how she put it; after they promised to stay put, Gavin wandered off in another direction.

She started hesitantly. "Michael, I want to say something I'm afraid might sound . . . oh, presumptuous. May I do it, anyway?"

"Of course." Her question seemed to amuse him.

"Well . . . you had a super offer back there in High Point. When that man asked you to design on royalties. If you enjoy designing as much as I *think* you do . . ."

"Go on."

She took a deep breath. "Ling and Son's going to be sold. Maybe you don't want the hassle of new ownership; it's usually not much fun. Anyway, what if you just stuck to designing? With what you know now, it might be possible to protect your copyrights. And a totally exclusive Richardson design would be worth a bundle of royalties."

He was silent for a long moment; Megan was relieved to see a genuinely thoughtful expression. Finally he said, "I'd have to think about it. But on the surface it's certainly appealing. No more executive responsibilities . . ."

She nodded, then started to tell him that was all she had to say. But he spoke again. "Little Meggie . . . you really care about my welfare." He didn't seem to expect her to respond, so she didn't. Why bother when the answer was so obvious? She turned toward the sound of her father's warning to hurry up or they'd miss the beginning of the procession.

The drums were deafening. And the color literally hurt her eyes. Megan adored it! The ghosts were rolling from the Imperial Palace, as though the emperor's house were spilling centuries of collected personalities grown too numerous to be contained. She sat forward in her seat, squinting, trying to pick Mr. Yasuda from the samurai cavalry charging forth on horses smaller than those to be found in the States, but enormous in scale to Oriental bodies.

Michael leaned across and shouted, "I don't recognize him, do you?"

She yelled back. "It's a professional makeup job. Hollywood couldn't do it better!" Before falling asleep in the car the previous night, she had heard the agent say each samurai would spend about two hours in the physical transformation. It worked: this was *real.* Even the horses were from the era of the warlords. Never had Megan imagined such decoration! According to the individual shogun's personal colors, the steeds stepped proudly under tens of pounds of bright, extremely ornate finery; massive amounts of sterling silver gleamed from their backs and sides. Each samurai color group followed behind the lord of sworn allegiance.

The procession went backward in time, beginning with an army troupe of the relatively recent Meiji Restoration. In something over two hours, when the last historic apparition disappeared from their line of vision, Megan, her parents, and Michael would have viewed the citizens and customs of over a thousand turbulent years. For her, the next thirty minutes went by in nothing flat.

But evidently not for Michael. On the first occasion she looked over, he was shifting uncomfortably on the wooden seat; the next time, only a few minutes later, he was down-and-out squirming, no doubt about it. Megan looked quickly forward again, hiding a pleased smirk. She remembered his highfalutin gesture that morning, when he hadn't even bothered asking if she wanted the top of her kimono unfastened. And now it occurred to her to wonder: if the seat's not to his liking, I wonder how he'd feel if I suddenly ripped it out from under him? Oh, dear me, she thought . . . catty, catty! Perhaps it was true that hell had no fury like a woman scorned.

"Megan!" he wailed. "Before the next two hundred years pass, I'll be at least a thousand! Let's get up and take a walk."

"I don't want to miss anything," she returned.

"Come on. I want to talk to you!"

She thought, Oh, he does, does he? Well, Michael wrote the book about keeping people waiting to talk! With a funny little smile, she mouthed her answer: "Not now."

"But it's important!" he screamed.

Again she shook her head.

So he stood up and shouted, "Okay, I guess I'll have to do it this way." Michael took a deep breath and then yelled at the top of his voice: "Megan McBride, I love you. Will you marry me?" Then he leaped to her side and gave her a very long kiss; the crowd's applause was for them and not the passing ghosts.

25

The next festival in Megan's life would occur exactly ten days after *Jidai Matsuri*. And Mr. Yasuda had insisted the wedding take place in the breathtaking traditional gardens of his Kyoto home.

Mrs. Yasuda and Patricia McBride fluttered around a guestroom, now temporarily converted into a dressing chamber, arranging the exquisite but extraordinarily complicated bridal kimono purchased after two full days of nonstop shopping. The bride herself was still and quiet, which didn't seem to bother her dressers. They continued turning her here and there, tying this and fastening that, all the while understanding a young woman's need for final moments of uninterrupted reflection.

Megan would approach the minister amid a gathering of friends from both her countries, Japan and the United States. She didn't know how her mother had done it, but the right overseas calls had somehow been accomplished between all the other hectic preparation activities. Sharon had asked another doctor to cover her practice; she would be maid of honor. Michael had been similarly blessed; his oldest friend Terry Costa had flown in to act as best man. On the same flight, the good-natured Terry had also escorted Michael's widowed mother, now living with an elderly sister in Arizona; the tall, handsome Mrs. Richardson had stood looking at her son's fiancée for a long thoughtful mo-

ment before breaking into a grin that might have been
Michael's and throwing open her arms. There were
others, too, who had come from the States. By far the
most important was Megan's soon-to-be son, Jeffie; a
few tears of joy had rolled down his elfin cheeks when
he crutched toward her at the airport; typically, ten
minutes later he was proudly announcing that he'd received a publisher's letter of interest in the computer
program.

Gavin McBride was pacing outside in the corridor.
Throughout the days since the Festival of Eras, he had
been wise enough to realize that Michael, too, needed
assistance. Since that time, Patricia and Megan had
seen him only when they specifically called for him;
this they did infrequently, for giving his little girl up
had made him as nervous as an Irishman caught in a
whiskey raid. But, as he had said, if he were to give her
to anyone, it would certainly be Michael. The dressers
found yet another piece of fabric to wrap around her
and Megan sucked in her breath dutifully, then smiled.
Bless Gavin McBride's heart! Had it not been for his in-
terference, the bride and groom might still be stuck in
lovers' limbo.

After the unorthodox proposal, Michael had taken
Megan to an elegant and very intimate restaurant
overlooking all of Kyoto. Just after dark, when the fire
ceremony climaxed the earlier procession, they had a
ringside seat. By that time, the gorgeous diamond and
ruby ring was on her finger for good. And she had heard
her fiancé's apologetic admission about not really understanding; the issues bothering Megan were not clear
to him before the coincidental events of the prior days.
In addition to a great deal of timely looks at Japanese
men and their imprisoned women, he had seen the extent of Megan's loyalty and love; it seemed incredible,
he said, that anyone could have been so tired, overworked, and confused as he had been in High Point. To
cap it off, he told her, Gavin had arranged to have him

invited to serve on a congressional committee designed to study suggestions for the national drunk driving problem; at the moment he realized that there was indeed a productive outlet to his enormous rage, the accumulated weight of years of it had drained away.

It seemed they had everything, she and Michael. Families that adored them, loyal friends—and a new professional adventure. Michael had spent many concentrated hours with Mr. Yasuda on the subject of designing for royalties. It was the agent's firm opinion that American manufacturers were spread far too thin in the area of design. Taking only a few clients, and with both Michael and his agent drafting contracts and policies to protect copyrights, they could resolve a great many headaches for an industry that had suffered too long from its own lack of resources. Michael was extremely enthusiastic about giving up managerial responsibilities for a quieter, more leisurely pace. And Megan was frankly relieved; the man she had fallen in love with would now have more time for his family.

Gavin was barking out the time at five-minute intervals. Megan pulled herself in line with the full-length mirror, leaned down to kiss her mother, then waited, not so patiently now, for the securing of the elaborate Japanese headpiece that would nearly cover her uplifted red hair. When she saw by the mirror that a few wisps had fallen in waves around her face, it pleased her; Michael had always liked it that way.

The guests were in the garden. She heard the music, a sentimental Oriental symphony piece she and Michael had chosen together, but she saw nothing. To conceal the bride until the very last moment, the *shoji* screen had been tightly drawn. Mr. Yasuda stood by, waiting to signal for the processional march—this part of the wedding would be American—and when he saw Megan, he smiled as her father might have done. Gavin himself soon appeared from around a corner; his daughter reached for his properly folded elbow. Before they started out, Megan found a way, in spite of the elaborate headpiece, to put her arms around her father.

The groom was in a gray morning coat with gray and white striped trousers. Behind him the now-blazing maples were reflected in a little Japanese pond; and a bit of light struck Michael's ash hair. She walked slowly forward, thinking, Oh, God, how I love him. From the expression in his pale blue eyes, his thought was nearly the same. When all was said and done and the couple said, "I do," no one present doubted their sincerity.

They stayed two hours at the garden reception. Although Megan and Michael were aware of very little but each other, they would later talk about what fun it had been. If nothing else it was a lively hodgepodge of East and West. Just before they folded their hands to slice a tiered white wedding cake, they participated in the traditional *sansankudo:* both bride and bridegroom were required to cement their troth with three sips each from three shallow cups of sake. When Megan changed clothes for the limousine that would deliver them to the site of their first night as husband and wife, the Miyako Hotel, she was sad about only one thing: no rice would rain on her head; in the Orient, the waste of rice is a criminal offense. To compensate for the missing American tradition, there was a great deal of bowing accompanied by boisterous shouts of *"Banzai! Banzai! Banzai!"*

Michael had checked out of his Japanese-style room. For the first time, and together, they would see the *ryokan* honeymoon suite. A bellboy led them through the autumn landscape and over exquisite natural pool formations until, at last, they stopped at a house connected to the main hotel only by a stone pathway. They slipped into the little footlets waiting just inside the sliding rice-paper doors. When the uniformed boy retreated, they turned toward each other, each offering their arms.

He kissed her with exquisite care and tenderness, as

though the new Mrs. Richardson was a creature too fragile for man's rough hands. Megan tried to return the sentimental gesture; but, before too many minutes had passed, she felt the urgency of time and a need grown too great for containment. Her parents had kept them apart before the wedding, and now the senses interrupted but far from vanquished since that night in Mr. Yasuda's car flared into magnificent fury.

Michael felt the tensing of her body. He moved his lips from hers and kissed her very softly on the back of the neck.

"I love you."

"Show me," she breathed. "Michael, I want you."

"Go slowly, little one. Remember?"

She started to speak, to beg. Then she paused. This was the man who had taught her the beauty of lovemaking. And they were in the world's most romantic country, a land she knew as well as she knew the United States. Perhaps she could contribute something to their first night as husband and wife. Megan drew her head back and gazed up into his eyes. She said, "Darling, there's a bottle of sake on that little table over there. See it?" She made a small gesture with her head.

Michael nodded. "Then, if you will, I'd like you to pour us both a cup. I'm going to the bath to start running your water."

He knew it was some sort of game, she could tell by that wonderful grin creeping onto his face. And he would play along. But he asked her to give it a name.

Her answer was lovely but vague. "My precious husband," she said seriously. "You gave it a name the first night we ever spent together: lovemaking."

He would soon learn that she intended to treat him in the manner she imagined to be typical for Japanese husbands, but with a twist that he could provide, if he felt like it. And he did.

It started when the enormous oak tub was filled with

very hot water and the little room was clouded with steam. Megan and Michael had been sitting properly on the floor—at her insistence, on opposite sides of the low table—sipping sake and trading sincere affirmations of love. She wondered how he felt; looking at her new husband without feeling the freedom to touch him had provoked the excitement of an illicit adventure. In a central part of her body she felt an ever-increasing demand, a warm and moist insistence that—this time—she knew would be fulfilled.

She got up, bowed, and said, "If you're ready, my lord and master, your bath is waiting."

Without a word, he led and allowed Megan to follow behind. When they entered the private bathing pavilion, Michael turned instinctively, then reached for her.

"Oh no, lord!" She pretended to be shocked. "This is *your* time. Let me help you off with those clothes." With a wicked smile, Megan stepped close and placed both hands on the closure of his belt; she proceeded as steadily as trembling fingers would allow; and always, when he tried to participate, behave any way but passively, she would simply step back and fold her arms. Megan's only concession was to the steam; she was finally forced to peel away her two-piece beige suit. She stood before him with only frilly bra and bikini, causing Michael's breath to quicken instantly, and her desire swelled dangerously. Could he tell, she asked herself, that the charade was just as much torture for her as for him? It was a very long time before the last of Michael's clothes fell away. And then, when Megan saw the slender body temporarily changed and hardened by emotions gone wild, she had to fall back against the wall and take several deep breaths before continuing.

In the traditional manner, the Japanese do not bathe in their tubs; this process, the soaping and scrubbing, is accomplished outside the big oak fixtures. Generally, a stool is provided for comfort; nearby, the bather will find soap and cloth; a shower directly above will rinse away the suds and drain directly from the floor. Megan suggested that her husband might prefer to sit. "While I bathe you," she added slyly.

"Megan, you can't be serious!" he exclaimed, already too excited to talk with total clarity. "Baby, I could never stand it!"

"Couldn't you *try?*"

He sat down. And then, what Megan did could hardly be described as scrubbing. Using her hands alone, no cloth, she slid the soap along his body in highly creative patterns starting with his feet. When she reached the inside of his thighs, her motions became more delicate, almost feathery. And her husband moaned, then placed one arm against the nearby wall, bracing himself. Megan's own thigh muscles were continually contracting now; and her breathing was shallow and ragged. At one point the soap slipped from her hands but she didn't seem to notice; with fingers made light only by extraordinary effort, she simply kept caressing him in small, brushing circles . . . higher and higher.

"Touch me," he whispered, and she obeyed.

And then her husband said, "No, Megan. No!" With a jerky, strained movement, he got to his feet and pulled her from the kneeling position. The water rained down on them both while he forced her into his arms, then locked her desperate frame so tightly against his that there could be no hope of escape, nor did Megan want to escape. She was twisting, bending forward against him, moving her hands everywhere she could feel his need. Their lips met; their tongues sought satisfaction but only increased the agony. And the thin soaked fabric of her undergarments seemed to Megan an exquisite barrier. Michael finally stripped them away. At almost the same time, he cut the water and grabbed for the big towels. Within a few moments, he had his still moaning young wife cradled in his arms.

"Love," he said, stopping to brush her forehead with a kiss. "I'm going to carry you out to the bed now. And

then I'm going to lie down. *Beside* you. We'll find out—
together—whether it's East or West, male or female
that's best. And this first time, maybe it'll be too quick.
But, little Meggie, we've got the rest of the night, too.
And then we've got the rest of our lives."